Lin[c]

discover libraries

This book should be returned on or before the due date.

11.16

DSK

1 3 DEC 2016	15. MAR 18	1 7 JUL 2019
1 6 FEB 2017	1 5 JUN 2018	
2 0 MAR 2017		1 9 SEP 2019
2 3 MAY 2017	1 3 JUL 2018	2 5 OCT 2019
1 1 JUL 2017	2 8 SEP 2018	
9 AUG 2017	2 6 NOV 2018	3 0 DEC 2019
6 NOV 2017	2 2 JAN 2019	2 5 FEB
0 8 DEC 2017		
08 JAN 18	20. FEB 19.	13/9
6 FEB 2018	2 9 APR 2019	
15. MAR 18	1 9 JUN 2019	
1 2 APR 2018	1 9 JUN 2019	

To renew or order library books please telephone 01522 782010
or visit https://lincolnshire.spydus.co.uk

You will require a Personal Identification Number.
Ask any member of staff for this.

The above does not apply to Reader's Group Collection Stock.

05121877

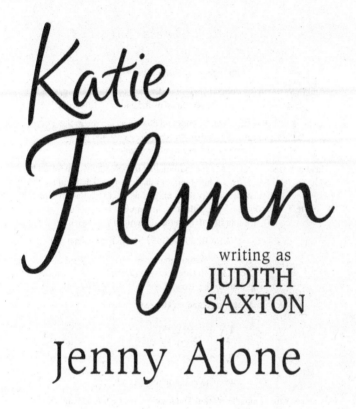

Katie Flynn

writing as
JUDITH
SAXTON

Jenny Alone

arrow books

Published by Arrow Books, 2014

6 8 10 9 7

First published in Great Britain in 1987 by Michael Joseph Ltd

Arrow Books
The Random House Group Limited
20 Vauxhall Bridge Road, London, SW1V 2SA

A Penguin Random House Company

www.randomhousebooks.co.uk

Addresses for companies within The Random House Group Limited can be found at: www.randomhouse.co.uk/offices.htm

The Random House Group Limited Reg. No. 954009

A CIP catalogue record for this book is available from the British Library

ISBN 9780099564683

Printed and bound in Great Britain by Clays Ltd, St Ives plc

For
Diane Bryan,
Sue Roberts and *Sue Cartwright,*
who showed me the funny side
of sadness.

ACKNOWLEDGEMENTS

I should like to thank Mrs Marjorie Howe of Rhyl for all her help and for reading the MS in its original, tatty, state; I am also indebted to Stret Stretson and Ann Toye of Chester, who told me what goes on behind the shutters in a Private Shop!

CHAPTER ONE

The board nearest the door which led on to the communal landing creaked. We've been here five days, Jenny thought, as she and Posy let themselves out early on their first Monday morning, but already that board irritates. I wonder what you can do about a creaking board? If Dirk were here . . .

She banished the stupid, irrational thought, because if Dirk were here the first thing he would do would be to leave the place, creaking board and all; it was not his scene. Instead, she considered the morning ahead of her as she and her daughter descended the dark, narrow stairs.

'Got everything, pet? Your new pencil case? Dinner money?'

Posy, in her too-large blazer and rigidly-pleated skirt, nodded and clutched Jenny's hand tightly as they crossed the dim, anonymous hall and let themselves out of the big front door with its stained-glass panels and its heavy much-used doorknob. They both knew that nothing had been forgotten, for had they not spent the entire previous evening checking? It had comforted Posy to see and touch her new possessions and it had comforted Jenny to be doing and not thinking.

There was nothing to do in the flat; Mrs Grant, the landlady, had cleared out all traces of the summer visitors when she advertised it as a winter let. Jenny had got out the elderly carpet-sweeper and pushed it dutifully across the thin, dust-coloured carpet, and she had fished out the broom, whose soft, useless bristles had all been pushed in one direction like trees on the high moors, and had tried her best to brush the mud-coloured linoleum around the hand basin. Faint and gnat-like dust did arise but the dustpan was so distressingly curved that when you swept most of the dirt went underneath it; redistribution rather than annihilation. She had thought about cleaning the windows – which needed it – but there were no suitable dusters and no Windolene, and the furniture was cheap, scratched and unbelievably ugly, not

1

the sort of furniture which could be improved by polishing. Besides, Mrs Grant did not supply polish.

Money was of course short. Consumed with guilt, Jenny had cashed in all her available family allowance tokens to equip Posy for her new school, thinking defensively that desperation could make thieves of the best of us. Mark was seventeen and still at school so she also received an allowance for him, but in fact he was Dirk's responsibility now, not hers. Still, she told herself, it was only a very minor theft and beggars cannot be choosers, besides which Dirk knew Posy was starting school today but had offered no help, so surely he could scarcely blame her for using whatever money was available?

But at least the rent of the flat was paid. Dirk was paying it a month in advance and had said he would continue to do so. He had mentioned an allowance but so far she had had neither the time nor opportunity to visit Mr Croft, his solicitor, as Dirk had told her she should. Today being Monday she could walk up to his office, but guessed that she would put it off. It was bad enough living through this nightmare of rejection and lonely strangeness without going to the solicitor and finding that Dirk meant it, that this was for always, that he was paying just so that he would never have to see her again . . . she was not yet strong enough to contemplate the sinking of heart and stomach which would follow such a revelation. Not even the prospect of money to buy food and bits and pieces for her small daughter could compensate for being entirely cut off from Dirk.

'Mummy, do you think that girl goes to my new school?'

Jenny switched her attention to the child; Posy must be hating this every bit as much as Jenny did, after all. She was four years old, too young to understand the sudden change in her circumstances, too young to be left with Dirk at the farm no matter how hard a life with Jenny alone might be. A tiny, match-thin child, quiet and introspective, Posy had always seemed scared of her handsome, confident father and her noisy, cheerful brothers. It had been taken totally for granted by both Jenny and Dirk that, no matter what happened, Posy would go with her mother. The boys, both away from home, would not yet know that the break had come. Mark was at boarding school studying for A levels, and Philip, the eldest, was at university hoping to become a vet. Neither, Jenny thought, would worry unduly over their mother's departure or their father's new infatuation. They had their own lives to lead and when at home they led them with all the energy – and sensitivity – of young bulls put to a heifer for the first time.

Shocked at her own choice of simile, Jenny wondered when her motherly love for the boys had turned into a rather resigned sort of affection. She thought it had begun when they went away to boarding school because on their return it was clear that they took almost no interest in their mother, whilst being totally fascinated by their father and his various pursuits. They were casually affectionate towards her, laughed at her rather than with her, brought girls home rather as a young dog brings in rabbits, and kept their feelings and thoughts very much to themselves. She was surprised at their success with women since they never tried to hide the fact that in their opinion the entire female race was not even second- but fourth-rate. She had concluded that some women must enjoy being treated casually as possessions. It was not until Dirk's infatuation for a teenager began to be obvious even to her that she realised she too came a poor fourth to her sons, the farm, the string of fast cars that Dirk had possessed and now to a sly, mean-mouthed, big-breasted blonde who was not quite a year older than Jenny's eldest son.

'Mummy? Do you think she's at my school?'

Guiltily, Jenny stared ahead to where another small figure trotted along, swinging a satchel in the early September sunshine.

'Sorry, darling, I was thinking. That little girl, do you mean, with the navy blue satchel? Yes, I expect she goes to your school, she's wearing a blazer like yours. Shall we catch her up and ask her?'

'No!' Posy's small fingers clutched her hand convulsively. 'No, Mummy, please not!'

'All right, it was only a thought; she isn't a new girl, like you, she's probably in the next class up,' Jenny said diplomatically. 'Let's step out a bit though darling, don't hang back, or we'll be late.'

'All right,' Posy said. Now that the danger of an unwanted

3

introduction was over she relaxed her grip and began to skip along quite light-heartedly. 'Look, isn't that a nice little white dog? I wish Belle was here.'

'Never mind; we'll send her a postcard, shall we?' Dirk's sheepdog Belle was semi-retired but she was a marvel with a flock of sheep and had a way with children too. A crafty, skinny, wall-eyed border bitch, she had insinuated herself into the house as other dogs took over most of her work, and she and Posy were often to be found curled up together beneath the big old kitchen table, Posy chattering away to Belle and even pausing for answers, oblivious to the outside world.

'Belle can't read,' Posy said shortly. 'Mummy . . . why couldn't Belle come with us?'

The question had been raised already; Posy had not once asked why they had left the farm nor why her father had not accompanied them, nor whether he was well. She asked after Belle's health at least five times each day.

'Belle's a working dog, she'd be unhappy in a flat with no sheep to round up,' Jenny said patiently. 'Besides, Mrs Grant might not like a dog in her flat.'

'Someone's had a dog there,' Posy pointed out. She was jumping the pavement cracks and narrowly avoided landing on one; she swung on Jenny's hand, then took an exaggerated leap forward. 'Golly, it nearly got me that time, did you see? Someone's had a dog, there are hairs on the sofa and there's a brown bowl with *Dog* written on it under the sink in the kitchen.'

'Darling, how do you know? You can't read!'

'I can read that,' Posy insisted. '*Dog*, it says. It's a bit like Belle's dish at home, though not so nice of course. *Dog*, it says.'

'Does it? I hadn't noticed. This is the school; shall I come in and find your classroom with you?'

No words were necessary; a convulsive tightening of the fingers in her own and the flush that mounted to Posy's forehead made the answer clear, yet the question had to be asked because Posy was an odd little creature. It would have surprised but not astonished Jenny had Posy insisted on going into school alone; Posy was independent in unexpected ways. Her first visit to the dentist had been conducted in solitary splendour, with Posy taking one look at the chair, the fountain and the pink drink and then waving her mother outside. Jenny, remembering how it had taken the combined efforts of herself and her sister-in-law to get Philip through the door on his first visit, had told Dirk about Posy quite proudly, only to be firmly cut down to size.

'Women don't have sufficient imagination to be afraid,' Dirk had asserted. 'They don't feel pain like men do, either. Well-known fact.'

But now the two inferior, insensitive females, holding hands, were approaching the school together. The school was new to them both; for Posy had never been inside any school, though Jenny had been a regular visitor to the village school when the boys had been small. If things had been ordinary, Jenny reminded herself, Posy would have known most of the other children here and several of the teachers too. But at this school, Ysgol Maesydre, she would be a complete stranger.

'I think we go in that entrance, over there,' Jenny said as they climbed the concrete steps which led up onto the playground. It was a large, low, modern building at the top of a sloping green with young trees dotted here and there, and it was hedged on three sides and chain-linked on the fourth. 'Can you remember the name of your teacher, pet?'

'Umm . . . no.' Posy decided. 'That door?'

'Yes, I think so. All the smaller children seem to be going through it, anyway.'

She walked towards the door, conscious of a ridiculously thumping heart and more guilt-feelings. She should have registered Posy the moment Dirk had broken it to her that he had found her a winter let, but she had kept hoping, expecting, that he would change his mind, send Bronwen packing, so apart from a telephone call the previous Friday she had had absolutely no communication with the school or the teaching staff. A crisp, middle-aged voice had told her that term started today and to bring Posy in, and that had been that. No questions then as to why she had not previously registered, no explanation as to the whereabouts of the school. The voice had just accepted that she had moved into a flat and needed a school for her daughter. But once they got her, would that content them? Or would they want to know why she was thirty miles from home, apparently husbandless, feckless, moneyless?

Inside they paused, uncertain. A passing child, looking a brisk ten-if-she's-a-day, stopped and smiled at them.

'Can I help you? Do you want the headmaster, or Miss Lloyd? Or has she forgotten which room she's in?' she asked, addressing herself to Jenny.

'We're new,' Jenny said apologetically, knowing at once that she should not have said 'we'. 'Was it . . . do you have a Miss Freda Jones? I seem to remember the name.'

'Yes that's right. And Miss Ursula Jones. They're both admission class, so we call them Miss Freda and Miss Ursula. Come on, I'll show you.'

She led them past chattering lines of children, all bouncing about and calling to each other, to a door which led into a wide and pleasant room, mostly of glass so that it was very light, with pictures on the walls and tables scattered about. There were small children everywhere making a lot of noise, but above it all rose the dolorous wails of a fat, sandy-haired child with a woman kneeling beside her. The woman looked up as the door opened and got to her feet.

'Ah, here's another new girl, Sandra, do you see, you aren't the only one!' The woman smiled at Jenny and held out a hand to Posy. 'I'm Miss Freda Jones and you must be Posy Sayer, since I haven't met you and all the rest of the class came in for a day last week, just so that they could get used to school. You and Sandra were the only ones not able to come, so you may feel a little strange.' She put a gentle hand on the shoulder of the sandy-haired weeper. 'This is Sandra; she's never left her Mummy before and . . .'

She stopped. Posy had released Jenny's hand, stepped forward and was trying to pat Sandra's beefy shoulder, which was a good deal higher than her own. 'Well, Sandra dear, Posy wants to be friends and she's new, like you, so why don't you take her over to the sand-table and show her how to make a castle? Or there are bricks . . . coloured pencils . . . if you like you could . . .'

She let her voice fade to a murmur as the two small girls

eyed one another cautiously. Sandra had stopped crying but now she put both palms against her eyes, wiped them briskly, smearing her face with dirt and tears, and addressed Posy. Jenny would not have been surprised had she said, 'Dr Livingstone, I presume', but Sandra's words were much more to the point.

'Are you my friend?'

Posy thought, frowned, then answered seriously.

'Yes, I'm your friend. Are you my friend?'

'Yes.' The answer was out almost before the question was completed. 'That's our table, the one with the blue and yellow bricks. Miss said I could have the blue and yellow bricks.'

Miss Freda Jones gave Jenny a small, conspiratorial grin as the two children moved away from them.

'Aren't children amazing? Now Mrs Sayer, I don't want you to feel I'm pushing you out, but if you'd like to go off now and see the office staff . . '

Jenny was halfway to the door when someone jerked at her skirt. She looked down, her heart sinking. It had been too good to be true, of course. Posy's small face was anxious.

'Mummy, where do I live? Sandra lives at 14 Conway Street.'

'We live at . . er . . . Flat 3, 24 Beechcroft Road, Rhyl.'

'Flat 3, 24 Beechcroft Road, Rhyl. Are we on the phone? Sandra is; she knows her number.'

There was a hint of desperation in the words; poor Posy! Once her address and telephone number had been all but engraved on her heart, it had been a matter of pride to be able to chant them at the slightest provocation. And now all she really knew to be safe and unchanging was her name.

'We are on the phone, but I don't know the number. Tell you what, darling, we'll learn it together, tonight. How's that?'

'All right. Mummy . . ?'

'What darling?'

'Is that our address for ever?'

What could she say? She had no more idea than Posy how long they would be in Beechcroft Road. Except that the flat was a winter let, so they could not possibly stay there all summer long.

'No, not for ever. We'll go somewhere nicer, or perhaps . . .'

But Posy did not wait for the rambling sentence to finish;

perhaps she divined that there was no answer to her question, not yet. Instead she turned back to her new friend just as Miss Freda Jones reached them.

'Oh, by the way Mrs Sayer, I forgot to ask you to be a little early this afternoon, please, when you call for Posy. If you could be at the infants' entrance at five to three? Only don't come through the doorway please, because it upsets the children to see mums hovering. If you could wait outside and arrive just that bit early . . .'

'I'll be there,' Jenny said stiffly. She spoke stiffly because desolation had attacked her. What reason had she to be late? She had nothing to do, nowhere to go and no one to care how she spent the next few hours. She could go outside the school now, sit down outside the gate, and probably she would remain undisturbed until mums began to call for their young later in the afternoon.

The thought was so silly that she smiled despite herself and Miss Freda Jones, relieved, smiled too. Moments before, her young freckled face had clouded a little; she thought she had given offence somehow, Jenny realized, but it was impossible to explain.

'Until three o'clock, then,' Jenny said as cheerfully as she could. 'It will seem strange to have five whole hours to myself!'

Miss Jones' expression, still a little anxious, cleared completely. You could almost see the penny – albeit the wrong coin of the realm – drop.

'You'll miss her, of course. Never mind, think what fun weekends will be!' She flashed a bright smile and then moved back to her small flock, leaving Jenny to let herself out of the room and walk up the corridor with its smell of chalk and gym shoes. Glancing sideways at the internal windows she thought ruefully that, no matter how friendly, school would always be to her a benevolent prison, the teachers warders, the headmaster the governor. Further up the corridor the impression was heightened by the smell of a school dinner cooking; cabbage, fatty lamb and cornflour gravy were the items Jenny diagnosed, followed by sponge pudding and custard. Posy was a fuss-pot; what would she make of the food?

Jenny pushed open the swing doors leading into the play-ground and there was the September morning again, still early, still smelling faintly of bonfires and roasting chestnuts. Despite herself, Jenny felt a bounce come into her step as she ran down the sloping green and towards the school gate. It was a lovely day if one could contrive to forget one's wormlike personality, which Dirk had so grown to dislike over the years that in the end he had been forced to spurn it, to cast her aside.

The recollection dimmed the sunshine a little, because no one likes to know they are tedious and unlovable, but Jenny braced her shoulders and pushed the thought out of her mind. There was a group of mothers talking round the gates but a cursory glance showed her that they were all terribly young, barely out of their teens. Certainly not in their mid-thirties. She turned right, away from them, though she knew it was not her way home, but she dreaded curious glances, perhaps even questions. Who was she, what was she doing here, why was a woman so old – and plain, that went without saying – bringing a child of four to school?

She found that she was shaking, which was ridiculous. The women had probably not even noticed her, let alone her various inadequacies. Nevertheless she reached a turning and took it briskly, wanting to look as though she were too busy to stand about gossiping, as though she had friends waiting at home. Or a husband.

She found herself walking along a cinderpath which ran between the school and the back gardens of adjoining houses. It was rather nice, with the school's thick autumn-tinted hedge down one side and runner beans, raspberry canes and the backs of rabbit hutches on the other. A rich slice of suburban life, those gardens were, as different from her previous existence as one could imagine.

For the first time in ages, Jenny felt an easing of the tension which gripped her so cruelly that she was perpetually stretched on a rack of strained nerves and muscles, a physical stretching as well as a mental one. It had first started weeks ago, when she had found out about Bronwen; was it really possible that one day she would wake without ex-cruciating aches all over, that she would be able to turn her head without agony stabbing at the nape of her neck and into her shoulders, that life might be, if not pleasant, at least less painful?

She had barely covered twenty yards, however, when she heard voices from the other side of the hedge. She peered and saw a class of children assembled on a round daisy-studded patch of turf. They were obviously about to play a game or hear a story; idly, knowing herself to be rootless, time-wasting, she stopped to listen.

'Make a circle, children. That's right, a nice, big circle. Now we all take hands and space out a bit . . . Frank, if you don't like holding hands with girls then why are you standing between Susan and Rebecca?' A quick squeak from Frank in reply made the other children laugh, though Jenny was unable to distinguish his words. 'Ah, I see; then change places with Sarah, would you?' A pause for scuffling. Jenny was sharply and rather pleasantly reminded of Joyce Grenfell's rendering of 'The Nursery School Teacher'; she almost expected to hear the immortal words, *Sidney, don't do that*, for there were overtones in the young teacher's voice of the immortal Ms Grenfell, but instead, instructions for the game about to start continued.

'We're going to play "Poor Jenny" first; who wants to be Jenny? No, Paul, not you, we have a girl for Poor Jenny, don't we, children? Haven't you played it before, Fay? Never mind, it's ever so easy, you'll soon pick it up.' More squeaks. 'Yes, that's right, it's rather like "Poor Mary is A-weeping", but this is a prettier tune. Come on now, you can be our first Jenny, Sarah, you know how to play. Now see, Fay, Sarah stands in the middle and puts her hands over her eyes, the rest of you move slowly round and round and sing the song, then Sarah will choose a partner. Come on, I'll start the singing.'

The voices rose into the balmy air whilst Jenny stood listening.

> Jenny's alone in the ring,
> Who will come dance with her?
> Who will come dance with her?
> Jenny's alone in the ring.

It was a lament in a minor key and the aptness of the words punctured Jenny's mild sense of dreaming and brought reality, like cold water, deluging in. Jenny *was* alone; who would come dance with her, now that Dirk had cast her off?

It was absurd that a children's song should have caught her off guard, but a sob fought to rise up in her throat and tears blurred her vision. She had not cried since they moved into the flat; perhaps her bewilderment and unhappiness had been too deep for tears, but now it seemed she could not stop. Tears coursed down her cheeks, sobs tore at her throat, her chest heaved and her shoulders shook whilst her mouth pulled itself into odd shapes and she abandoned herself to grief. Behind the hedge an altercation broke out, shrill voices implored 'Miss' to hear them, but Jenny, oblivious, wept on. She could not even walk away, all she could do was to let the tears fall whilst her loneliness, her despair, grew and grew until even the sun no longer seemed to shine.

She might have remained there until she turned into a pillar of salty tears, she thought afterwards, except that, out of the corner of her eye, she saw movement. The group of women was breaking up and one of them was approaching her along the cinder path.

It brought her to her senses. She swung round, scrubbed her eyes fiercely with the backs of her hands, and set off in the opposite direction from the pursuing female figure. A quick glimpse had been sufficient to determine that she was a mum; jeans, sandals, casual jacket. The last person Jenny wanted to see her like this was another parent, and one, furthermore, who might want to talk. Jenny began to hurry, feeling the tears dry on her cheeks with the wind of her going. If only she could escape before the wretched woman saw her! She knew that if someone were to ask what was the matter she might say something to give the game away, and that was the last thing she must do.

Illogically, she felt that so long as she did not admit her plight then it did not really exist; she had not told Posy that Daddy had made her leave, she had turned it into a sort of holiday adventure. Mummy was tired and needed some time at the seaside, Posy had come along for company, Daddy would take care of them, come and see them sometimes . . .

11

She had no idea how much Posy believed and it did not much matter; what mattered, to Jenny, was that the situation should remain fluid. The fewer the people who knew, the fewer the explanations that would have to be offered when everything was all right again.

By the time she emerged from the cinderpath into a small bungalow estate, Jenny felt she would pass casual inspection and slowed her frantic pace to a more normal walk. But even so, she walked purposefully. If you pretend you've got something definite to do before you know it, it is true. Micawber-like, she trusted that something would Turn Up.

And it did. Presently she came out on to a main road and drew level with a large board proclaiming that this was the Botanical Gardens. Jenny slowed and peered over the brick wall which separated the gardens from the road. She loved gardens and gardening and had worked hard at making the farm garden a thing of beauty, for it relaxed her in a way that housework never had and, like most farmers, Dirk had no time for flowers, lawns or rockeries. They paid for no sports cars. If I had time, Jenny found herself thinking, I'd love to go round these gardens properly.

She turned in at the gates on the thought; one thing she did have now was time.

It was pleasant in the gardens. On her left as she entered was a sunken bowling green, beautifully cared for with two sprinklers sprinkling away, each with its own private rainbow. Then came more flower beds, and palm trees, strikingly poised against the pale blue of the sky, and a brilliant display of dahlias and some of those plants called yuccas, yellow-flowered and, Jenny thought, smelling rather nasty.

Overlooking the bowling green was a wooden building with large windows and a colourful, clean appearance. It had the word *Cafe* written in cream-coloured letters on its green fascia board.

A cup of coffee would be good, but of course it was far too early yet, the place would not be open. However, the paths, lightly gravelled and hedged with box, were pleasant to stroll along and there were greenhouses in the distance and a display of the tiny, hardy cyclamen which had Jenny round-eyed with envy. Marvellous little flowers, perched like brilliant butterflies amongst their fat, luscious foliage, they were a breath of the Mediterranean she had never visited, that Greece she had known only through books.

The gardens were still almost deserted, though one or two gardener-like figures lurked in odd corners, tying up or pegging down, spraying or pruning, and the greenhouses beckoned. As she walked along the empty, early-morning paths, Jenny felt a quiet peacefulness begin to flow over her, soothing her sharp-edged, painful thoughts. She remembered occasions in her youth when, unjustly punished, she had been sent to bed to cry until there were no tears left. After the tears had all been wept, first there came emptiness, then a kind of lethargic peace and finally, if you were lucky, a sense of proportion. Jenny remembered a terrible row over her teddy bear. It had been on her first visit to her mother, just after her mother's second marriage had brought a stepfather and stepbrother into her life. She had been staying with them for two weeks and Nigel, five years her senior, had tried to disembowel her teddy with his penknife. Having fought him and lost she had tried, rather ineffectually, to stab him in the leg with that same knife, which he had cast down in order to trounce her more effectively. Her stepfather, deaf to any but Nigel, had lammed into her until he was breathless, thrown her into her bedroom and locked the door on her. She could remember the river of tears she had shed, the way she had clung to her poor, wounded teddy, and then the gradual easing of the misery, as though she had literally bled away some of the hurt with the tears. At length, by the time her mother had come up and talked to her, she had even begun to understand why it had happened, how very much worse it had been for her to attack Nigel with a knife than for him to attack her teddy, for a teddy can be sewn up at home, but a stepbrother would have had to go to hospital, and would have suffered in a way a teddy could not.

She had a wry mental picture of herself, a skinny eight-year-old with lank, mousy-fair plaits, being led downstairs, to say she was sorry to Nigel and to accept her stepfather's abject, stammered apology with at least an attempt at good grace.

So now, with the peaceful feeling that follows tears

painfully shed, she examined the greenhouses through the misty glass, for they were still firmly locked against the cool air. After that, she wandered over to survey the children's playground and decided to bring Posy here, after school. The peacefulness was also mercifully numbing; Jenny stalked a fat blackbird and it let her come right up to it before taking off with a warning squawk sufficiently loud to put every other bird for miles on the qui vive. Strolling back, she smiled at two men putting kaffir lilies out. The lilies were in pots and the pots were being buried, reminding Jenny of *Alice in Wonderland*; later visitors would exclaim at the lilies' brilliance, never knowing that they had been greenhouse reared.

The sun was growing warmer and Jenny's desire for a cup of coffee grew overwhelmingly, so she decided to make for the cafe once more. She had overslept that morning in the infuriating way that happens when sleep will not be courted, so that one lies awake from midnight to six a.m. Black thoughts had circled like vultures in her mind preventing rest, and then when they began to quieten she dared not sleep for fear of oversleeping. Naturally she had dropped into an exhausted slumber around seven o'clock and had been woken, bleary and dazed, by Posy at eight. No time then for tea, bacon or even bread and butter. She had dressed, all thumbs, anxiety making her stupid, had boiled Posy an egg and made her a row of bread-and-butter soldier boys and a glass of milk, and had then scuttled about getting ready, so that all she herself had managed to devour before leaving had been two bites of the crust off the loaf and half a cup of tea. Now the need for a cup of coffee, to drink at leisure, became imperative. She almost ran the last few yards.

She tried the door and it gave way under her hand. She stepped inside. A man was wiping down the long counter with a cloth that smelled clean and fresh. Jenny went over to the counter. The man straightened and grinned at her. He was tall and heavily built with reddish clumpy hair, the sort of hair that would curl were it not kept so short. He also had a broken nose and that air of slight bewilderment which seems endemic in men doing women's tasks. Jenny smiled back. Henpecked? Homosexual? But no, that last seemed unlikely;

he looked too tough and ugly, more like an ex-boxer running slightly to seed than a gay with a metaphorical flower behind the ear. Cauliflower ear, she thought, and smiled again, then spoke quickly because sometimes thoughts travel further than they are meant to.

'I don't suppose you're ready for customers yet, but I'd love a coffee when you finish cleaning up. Would it be all right if I sat down until then? I've been on my feet for what feels like a lifetime, though it's only a couple of hours really.'

She was tired, now that she came to think about it. She would be glad to sit down. Unhappiness and tension suck the energy as the sun was sucking the dew off the grass out in the gardens.

'Sure, help yourself.' He flapped the cloth towards the dozens of identical little blue-topped tables. 'Plenty of choice, you see. Make yourself comfortable and I'll bring your coffee in a couple of ticks. Want something to eat? We do a nice line in cakes.'

Jenny glanced at the glass case with its four empty shelves and then back at the proprietor. He followed her eyes, then clapped a hand to his head.

'Damn, I've not put today's delivery out. Hang on a moment.'

He disappeared into the back to reappear almost at once with an open cardboard box containing a variety of shop cakes. He set them out in the display case, then stood the empty box down and fished under the counter, producing a large white loaf and a packet of butter.

'Sorry, you're a bit early or I'd be more organized. We do various sandwiches and barm cakes, or I can toast you a teacake under the grill,' he jerked a thumb at an ancient cooker behind the counter. 'Not much to look at, but it makes good toast.'

'I'd love some buttered toast,' Jenny said longingly. At home everyone had a proper cooked breakfast with lots of hot coffee and cereal and toast to start the day off well. 'Do you make buttered toast?'

'Naturally.' He looked at her penetratingly while reaching for the bread knife. 'What, no breakfast?' He cut a thick slice, hesitated, then cut another. 'Me neither, so I'll have some too, keep the wolf from the door for a few hours.' He looked ruefully down at his shirt front. 'The trouble with this place is that a mouthful is easier than not, if you understand me, and exercise mainly consists of washing up.' He slid the bread under the grill and produced two very large white cups.

It seemed silly to go over to one of the tables now that they had exchanged a few words, so Jenny stayed where she was, leaning on the counter and sniffing the delicious smell of toasting bread. Presently, a few, deft ministrations to the coffee machine by the proprietor brought it to life, and it rewarded him by whooshing black coffee into one large cup. When it was half full he shut the tap off and moved the cup under another tap, which whooshed steaming milk into it and then frothed the two together in a manner which brought the saliva rushing to Jenny's mouth.

'There you are; cup big enough for you? We keep these big ones for navvies, farmworkers and thirsty housewives.' He produced a bowl of sugar from beneath the counter and slid it across to Jenny. 'Help yourself; I won't watch.'

'I don't take it as a rule,' Jenny said, tipping a delicate half-teaspoonful into her cup. 'But today I need cheering up, so I'll treat myself.'

'Good for you; but I'm a three-spoon man myself,' the proprietor said cheerfully. He had made himself a cup of coffee as well, and now he ladled sugar into it with a prodigal hand, stirred it, sipped, then stood the cup down, exhaling ecstatically. 'Aah, we make a good cup of coffee, me and the old Tardis there; not a bad way to start the day, except that my day started four hours or so ago.'

Jenny was about to reply in kind when he gave a shout; thin blue smoke was hazing up from the grill. He snatched the toast out, then slapped butter on it so freely that Jenny felt it would have been churlish to complain about the charcoal.

'There you are.' He pushed the plate towards her. 'Sorry about the more-than-even tan; shall I knock tuppence off for nearly cindering it?'

Jenny bit, chewed and swallowed. Then she smiled and shook her head.

'No, I'll pay up. It's delicious.'

He named an absurdly small sum and Jenny was fishing pennies out of her purse when the door behind her burst open and four old men came in, mackintoshed and flat-capped despite the sunshine. They hailed the proprietor cheerfully; plainly, they were regular customers.

'Mornin', Bill! Ah tole the park super', you can move them sprays soon's you like, ah tole' him. How can four ole' fellers play a gamer bowls when them tinklers is atinklin' right in the miggle of the green, ah says. So super', he says they'll be out of our road by ten-thirty. Now lads, who's for tea and who's for coffee?'

The speaker, a brisk little man in a white cap and loud checked jacket as well as the afore-mentioned mackintosh, strutted up to the counter with his three friends in close attendance. Retired, surmised Jenny, and enjoying every minute.

'I see th'art busy this marning!' An ancient in a green tweed cap, with a face so seamed and wrinkled that it was only possible to guess at his expression, indicated Jenny and chuckled squeakily at his own joke. 'Eh, lad, quite a rush, innit? 'Oo sez the season's over, eh?'

'Not I,' Bill said. Jenny thought he looked like a Bill, with a sturdy dependability about him and something of the sea too. Sailors were often called Bill. 'I started here a year ago last Easter, you know, and I was dead worried at first when no one came in. There's a crowd in over the Easter weekend, see, then a quiet patch until the May Day weekend, then another until Spring Bank Holiday, and after that it goes quiet again until the schools break up. Then it's all go until September, but even now, if last year was anything to go by, I'll be rushed off my feet, weekends.'

'Aye; then one weekend it'll rain and there won't be a soul on t'beach,' the third member of the party pointed out. 'Followin' weekend there's the sun again and it's that warm you don't know how to keep your coat on, yet not a soul appears. It's as if there's some secret signal, though I've been here nine year' last June and I've not discovered what it is yet.'

'Ah, well,' Bill said philosophically, 'the sun hasn't forsaken us yet. Four teas as usual, is it? And what about a bite, gentlemen? I've got fresh teacakes, some rather good scones, and the cakes have just been delivered.'

'Aye, well, put a couple o' teacakes under the grill, one for Fred an' one for me,' White Cap remarked. 'Them others 'll poison their insides wi' cakes, I don't doubt.' Laden, the four of them tottered to the nearest table and collapsed into chairs with much creaking of joints and joviality. White Cap sipped his tea noisily and then addressed the proprietor again. 'Now what'll you do when winter comes, young feller-me-lad? None of 'em stay here all through the winter, you know. When are you off? Med your pile, yet? Done okay, have you?'

'I've made ends meet, though paying for help during August was a bit of a blow,' Bill said serenely, with his back to the room as he kept an eagle eye on the teacakes under the grill. 'With a bit of help from the nippers at weekends I can manage now, though. I'll stay here, but I'm going to try hot lunches, like the pubs do, see if that'll bring the winter takings up. Last year was pretty poor and I did close for a week or so, but I shouldn't have to now I'm getting a bit more established.'

Old heads shook doubtfully; some went on shaking rather longer than seemed necessary. Jenny, watching anxiously, concluded that the combined ages of the four at the other table would be a startling sum.

' 'Ot lunches? Oh, you mean dinners, I dessay. Well, there's them factory workers mekking pye-jammers, they might come over. A sight quicker to come 'ere than going into town.'

'And there's teachers, from t'high school,' the quietest of the four volunteered. 'They like to get away from t' kids come dinner time, so I've heard. This 'ud be nearest for 'em.'

'There's a few offices round here, when you come to think,' Green Tweed Cap said, munching on a cake topped with such virulent looking marzipan and so scarlet and glistening a cherry that Jenny had already marked it down as highly toxic. 'Aye, tha's not such a bad idea. You might do wuss, lad.'

'Aye, so he might.' White Cap sipped noisily at the dregs of his tea. 'And so might us, for you mek a good brew for a young 'un.'

More octogenarian laughter, with a few wheezes thrown in for luck. Were they really going to play bowls, Jenny wondered, sipping her coffee as slowly as she dared. They made nodding and drinking tea seem pretty athletic pastimes; whatever would happen when they had to bend down to throw the woods?

Bill came round the counter for a second round of teas just as the door opened and two more customers entered. It was the men who had been bedding out the lilies, with chunks of garden earth falling off their boots onto the clean and shining tiles. Jenny sighed for Bill, but he did not appear to notice.

'Morning Bill, morning all,' the elder of the two said. 'Two teas and two cheese and pickle butties on the slate.' Bill acknowledged the order with a nod, handed round the tray of tea to the old men, and then returned to his own side of the counter. He had not, Jenny now realized been idle whilst exchanging backchat with his customers. He had spread out a couple of loaves of bread, in slices, along the back counter and now he was buttering them and putting various fillings on to the pieces. Grated cheese was sprinkled from one container, shredded chicken from another, pink plastic ham from a third. Having decided on a second coffee Jenny felt entitled to carry her cup and plate over to the counter and to stand watching as Bill swiftly made the two cheese and pickle sandwiches ordered by the gardeners. He handed them over, took her dirty crockery, and then with the speed born of long practice he made two more sandwiches just as the machine brought itself to frothing point, cut them into triangles and encased them in cling film. Finishing off her coffee, he handed it to her with a friendly nod and returned to his sandwich-making.

What had sounded like an argument at the octogenarians' table turned out to be, once she started listening with all her attention again, a discussion on the relative merits of double digging, mulching and debudding chrysanthemums. At the next table the two gardeners listened, nodded, shook their heads and munched. Behind the counter, no doubt, Bill continued to make sandwiches. Jenny sat there sipping the good hot coffee and wondering about Bill. Was he a retired sailor? They were supposed to be handy at various feminine

19

tasks. Or he could be a soldier. Air Force? Yes, now that she thought about it, he could have been a boxing champion of one of the forces in his time and now he was down on his luck, trying to make his pension keep a family . . .

She eyed his back, which was broad but tired-looking. As he moved he thought she could see a tattoo through the thin material of his shirt; or was he just one of those incredibly hairy men? But that seemed unlikely, because red-haired men were usually fair-skinned and freckled, they didn't run to dark, hairy backs and chests. If it was a tattoo then she would come down for the navy. It did seem likeliest; sailors were practical, quick and neat. No wonder he made sandwiches at twice the speed she could if he had spent most of his life packing oakum or stitching sails together on the high seas.

She was surprised and a little dismayed when the four old men creaked to their feet. Surely she had not been sitting there that long? But she had, of course, and as she made her own way to the door she reflected that it was not a bad thing. The time had passed quite quickly despite her conviction that today would be at least a century long.

Walking slowly back into town, she thought a lot about the cafe. It was so nice and clean, the food was cheap but delicious, it was a good place to be. She would like to spend an hour or so there every morning, sipping coffee, eating toast, passing the time. When she passed the pub on the corner and glimpsed from its clock that it was noon she was immensely cheered. Marvellous! Without any effort on her part a whole morning had passed, and pleasantly too. Then of course she felt miserable, because to think like that was to admit she was wishing her life away; would she spend the next goodness-knows-how-many-years watching the clock inexorably ticking away the hours, days, months? Glad at every passing minute simply because it was passing, bringing her a minute nearer the grave? But now she was being absurd as well as morbid because if Dirk were to stop supporting her, which she supposed must be his eventual aim, then she would very soon have to work for her living and that would put an end to meaningless time-wasting.

If Dirk meant it, if he were never to want her back, then what would she do to earn her living? That cafe was nice, she would not mind working in a place like that, but of course Bill did not need any help, he could run it alone except in August, he had said as much. However, there must be other cafes. She knew she was unsuited to most jobs because she lacked experience. She had left school at seventeen in order to marry Dirk, and having been a farmer's wife for eighteen years was no recommendation to a would-be employer, she was sure. She could not even drive a car; Dirk did not approve of women drivers. She could type, but only with two fingers and book-keeping was – ho ho – a closed book to her. In fact the list of things she could not do was so long that it would be easier to compose a list of things she could manage. It would be a pretty short list at that.

I can cook, but only for a family; I can rear sons, bear a daughter, lose a husband . . . she snatched her mind off a subject which was only going to bring back the black depression. She could tell that though it had lifted it had not gone; it hovered, waiting to pounce like the blood-sucking vulture it was. Treat it like an illness best avoided and don't even think about it, she advised herself. That way you may keep it at bay until it loses its power, until the depression becomes a paler and paler grey, fading in the end to a shade so fragile that it can easily be conquered.

After all, I've only been here a few days and I'm learning to cope, she told herself as she reached Beechcroft Road. It was true; she had found this morning that taking an interest in other people kept her mind off her own troubles, that enjoying the beauty of a garden in the sunshine did the same, and that brisk walking, for she had walked briskly ever since passing the pub clock, not only speeded up circulation and caused a certain breathlessness but also stopped the mind from darkly brooding, because to brood really well one needs a hunched-up pose or a sheet over the head in bed, or even merely an open mouth and unseeing eye, a total disregard for what is happening around.

She reached No. 24 and stood for a moment contemplating it. A tall thin house built of red brick, with a tiny walled garden ten feet by five and a quarry-tiled path leading to the front porch. The porch was glassed in on three sides, with sand and dead leaves piled up in all the corners and rings all over the tiles from the bottoms of milk bottles. Had it ever been a real home, or had it been built for a boarding house? It had certainly never been designed for flats, but that was now its lot. Mrs Grant had told her on Friday, when Jenny was moving in, that she had once taken summer lodgers. 'Flats is easier,' she had said succinctly, handing Jenny her keys. 'We keep ourselves to ourselves, like.'

Jenny had hoped it was true, because in her misery the thought of having to be sociable was simply unbearable. But now, staring up at the house, she thought about the other inhabitants, almost wondered about them. There were half-a-dozen or so flats reached by her staircase and the same amount, she supposed, in the other half, for No. 24 had once been semi-detached until the Grants had bought both halves and joined them by the simple expedient of bashing a couple of holes in the party-wall. She knew nothing whatsoever about her fellow-sufferers and little enough about the Grants.

Mrs Grant had revealed that 'we' lived in the basement, but just who was covered by that 'we' had not been made clear. She had mentioned a son, Martin, who had proved to be a small, dark boy with a large head and a thin body; he reminded Jenny of a mushroom, though that may have been largely due to the fact that mushrooms were said to flourish in dark basements. Mrs Grant, when she mentioned him, had allowed her voice to sink reverently; so reverently that Jenny had very nearly made the mistake of assuming him either dead or not long for this world. Instead, Mrs Grant inferred that he was a genius; certainly he was distinctly unchildlike. During the three days that she and Posy had been in the flat there had been no evidence that a boy of fourteen lived in the building also. No feet thundered up or down the stairs, no groups appeared in the backyard, no loud and tuneless pop music reverberated through the Victorian solidity of the house. Martin existed – Jenny knew that because she had seen him wheeling his bicycle around the side of the house when she came back from a quick visit to the shops on the Saturday morning. He had not spoken to either of them nor even acknowledged their existence; he had given them a quick, under-the-lids glance – a glance typical of a mushroom not over-fond of the light – and had pushed his bike a bit harder so that he might disappear a bit quicker.

As for Mr Grant, she had no idea whether he was dead, alive, or a convenient figment to make Martin the mushroom respectable. Mrs Grant had not mentioned him, and when a man had squeezed past them in the hall and made for the basement stairs Mrs Grant had not even spared him a glance, far less an explanatory word or two.

The front door was rarely locked but Jenny got out her latchkey just in case. She glanced at the garden as she went up the path. Dear me! To the right, she saw crazy paving, a brick wall and some half-hearted ferns, to the left, more crazy paving, a very small round flower-bed piled with dead leaves, and a standard rose tree devoid of blooms. Crazy paving could be a challenge; why had the Grants not tried to seed the paving cracks with some of the pretty, easy plants that flourish in such places? Wild thyme not only looked pretty, it smelled attractive too, and then there was aubretia, and rock roses . . . even stonecrop looked good in crazy paving.

She reached the porch and turned the handle, half expecting resistance, but it opened easily. Inside, she was met by the dark, slightly sinister smell of the house, which made her stomach lurch. It would be the first time she had been alone in the flat since they had arrived. It was a cheerless place even on a sunny morning; Jenny could imagine all too clearly what her flat would be like when the weather got colder, how inadequate the tiny electric fire would prove. It was all so impersonal, geared for a two-week stay at the most, and though crowded it still managed to seem empty, presumably because there was no reassuring clutter. You could open a drawer and there would be the four ancient, slightly rusting knives, the bent forks and tarnished spoons. There was also one serving spoon, a blunt carving knife and one of those tin-openers which rely upon brute force and ignorance to make them work properly. Two inadequate saucepans and a cheap tin frying pan, one cake tin and a plastic measuring jug completed what Mrs Grant had complacently described as 'a complete set of kitchen tools and utensils'.

All these implements were crammed into a tall, rather wobbly cupboard which stood to the right of the hand basin, but there were also two reasonably comfortable though shabby armchairs, the type that have chintz cushions and wooden arms, two unnecessarily commodious wardrobes, in the smaller of which lurked such things as the carpet-sweeper and the brush and dustpan, and of course two beds, a creaky wooden double for Jenny and a smaller edition for Posy.

A gas ring, the electric fire and a chest of drawers completed the furnishings. They had the use of a bathroom and kitchen, and a good thing too since Jenny distrusted the gas ring and only ever boiled a kettle on it and, this morning, Posy's breakfast egg. Since the flat was officially for four persons there was also another tiny room with two beds next door. Even in September, however, this room was both cold and damp; Jenny and Posy, without more than a glance exchanged, had shut the door after their first inspection, locked it and intended to forget that it existed. A foray to steal the blankets when the weather got colder might possibly be necessary, but otherwise they would not bother with the second bedroom.

Jenny, crossing the hall, thought fleetingly of home; at the farm there were cupboards so full that even opening them was dangerous. Balls of wool, writing paper, a bridle which needed mending, photograph albums and tangled webs of string rubbed shoulders with tennis racquets, old unpaired gym shoes and a once-magnificent kite. But here? She and Posy had not had time to collect things; upstairs she knew that, apart from Mrs Grant's 'equipment', cupboards and drawers would be bare and empty and would smell faintly of dust, mice and stale cheese.

The difference, stupidly, brought tears to her eyes and she was hurrying up the stairs, intending to hide away in her room until it was time to fetch Posy, when her way was blocked by a pair of feet. They were attached to a girl coming down the stairs who had stopped in mid-flight so that Jenny had to stop as well for the stairs were narrow and the girl was wide.

'Hello! Are you No. 3?'

'Oh, yes, I . . .' Jenny's voice sounded creaky with disuse and unshed tears but the other appeared not to notice.

'I guessed you must be.' She held out a hand, smiling as she did so. 'I'm Sue Oliver, I'm in No. 4 opposite you, the one the old hen describes as having a sea view.' She did not lower her voice and Jenny cringed; she did not want to have Mrs Grant down on her as well. As well as what? But it was a pointless question to ask herself when she knew the answer was so painfully comprehensive.

'Oh . . . hello. I'm Jenny Sayer.' She felt she ought to elaborate but could not think how, so contented herself with smiling whilst examining the other girl. She really was extraordinarily beautiful, with a smiling face which made Jenny think of dolphins, so gentle the expression, so upturned the mouth. She had very pale skin and full, dark hair which fell in waves down on to her shoulders and she was wearing a smock dress in a dramatic shade of deep red, a colour which made her astonishing pallor even more striking. She had lovely eyebrows too, thin, winged, black as night, and her long slim hands had finely shaped nails enamelled to the exact shade of her dress. She was wearing high heels and she was so tall anyway that she positively towered over Jenny. She was also very pregnant.

'Nice to meet you, Jenny. I'd ask you in for a cup of coffee and a chat but I've an appointment with a fellow who prods my lump and tells me whether Tiny Tim's moved up, down or sideways. See you.' She squeezed past Jenny, both hands holding her huge stomach as though she could physically remove it from its customary position for the mutual convenience of being able to pass on the stairs, and clattered away down the rest of the flight.

Jenny continued up the stairs rather more slowly. What a fascinating person, and how brave, not to say reckless! Mrs Grant had made it pretty plain that her lodgers came or went at her will; how dared Sue talk about her in such unflattering terms without so much as lowering her voice! The old hen, indeed! Jenny, letting herself into her own room, found she was smiling. There was something very hen-like in her landlady's beady eyes, beaky nose, and huge, low-slung bosom.

Downstairs, the front door slammed. Loudly. Insouciantly. That Sue! I'm glad I've met her, Jenny mused, filling her small tin kettle at the hand basin and carrying it over to the gas ring. She fetched a packet of tea and some dried milk from her store cupboard, then put them back and turned off the gas. Why on earth should she lurk up here like

25

a spider in its web, when the day was sunny and bright and the town waited to be explored? There would be plenty of days when the flat would be a refuge, from the cold, from boredom perhaps, but now it felt more like a prison; at least it was a prison to which she herself held the key, where she could come and go as she pleased.

There was the beach, as well. She had always loved the beach and the sea, so why should she not go into town, buy herself a sandwich and a can of coke, and sit on the sand and have a little picnic? Money was certainly short but tomorrow was Tuesday, family allowance day, and Posy would be getting a hot school meal at lunchtime.

Another day I'll go and see Mr Croft and find out about the allowance Dirk mentioned, she promised herself, hurrying down the stairs. But she knew she would not; it was too soon, too final. Mr Croft would have to wait until she had come to terms with simply being turned out of Dirk's life.

She crossed the hall quickly and opened the door; the sunshine met her and the salty, invigorating smell of the sea. Previously, she had not even noticed it; now she breathed deeply, then choked on a laugh, remembering her gran when the family decanted from the car on some long-ago outing and the way Gran would cry, 'Breathe deeply children, take that ozone right into your lungs!' Useless to tell Gran that sea air was not ozone; Gran *knew*. She had not been a despot and an autocrat for nothing!

Walking down Beechcroft Road, it occurred to Jenny that most probably all these tall thin red houses contained quantities of people taking winter lets. How odd! – others, like herself, like Sue Oliver, like the man on the top floor who kept pigeons and mumbled a greeting when you passed him. Yet the houses did not look large or generous enough for such a crew; they were Tardises, every one, with narrow exteriors concealing huge interiors.

Someone had said something about a Tardis recently. Who, and in what context? But she could not remember and suddenly she was on the promenade and there was the sea, impossibly blue, incredibly clean and fresh, and the sand stretched out, white-gold and empty; and there would be shells, and little pools, and perhaps seaweed.

Jenny hurried forward, her heart lifting, happy for the first time for many weeks. The seaside! All her memories of the seaside were early ones, or happy days when she had taken the boys on bus trips down to the coast. She and Dirk had never visited the seaside because Dirk did not care for it. Perhaps she had found the one place where his shade could not haunt her. She took off her sandals and stepped luxuriously down on to the warm sand.

CHAPTER TWO

'That's all thank you, Mrs Oliver. Baby's certainly a lively one! Doctor will see you again in a week.'

Sue resisted an ignoble impulse to reply in kind – as to a five-year-old – and made for the door. Odd how the mere donning of a uniform and association with children as yet unborn could turn a woman into a babbling idiot. On her last visit to the clinic she had actually heard the nurse saying to a hugely inflated prospective mum, 'Now remember what doctor said, dear; we must have plenty to drink, we don't want our waterworks to start giving trouble, do we?'

She had not been in the town long, only two weeks, because at first it had been easy to hide her pregnancy, so she had stayed in London, in the flat that she and Hugo had bought between them and made into the sort of home they both wanted. But she had known she would have to go, it would not have been fair to stay once her condition became obvious.

Because Hugo had never made any secret of the fact that he did not want children. It was not that he disliked them, she had always thought that, had things been different, he would have made a very good father. It was the state of the world and what it had already done to him.

Hugo had escaped from East Germany with his mother after his father had been first imprisoned and then executed. He had been a child of no more than seven or eight at the time, but man's inhumanity to man had been impressed on a sensitive mind at what was obviously a sensitive time in his life. When Sue met Hugo he was kind, charming and highly intelligent, but all his friendships were light, all his affairs fleeting. She had first realized he loved her when she had woken in the night to hear him stifling sobs; she had thrown her arms round him and held him very tightly and he had hugged her back, and amongst the incoherent mutterings which had gradually calmed she had managed to gather the fact that he did not want to love, had fought againt loving, but had been caught unawares. When you loved, he explained, you put yourself and the loved one at risk in some dreadful but apparently indefinable way. Because she was his, she would be a hostage to fortune. Suppose war came, suppose the house caught fire? Suppose . . .

She had marvelled at his ability to turn something as beautiful as their love into fear and dread, but she had not let it damp her own warm and vigorous feelings and in the end she had made him see that it would be better to suffer whatever the fates flung at them together rather than apart. She had built up his confidence with tenderness, affection and humour, until the day came when he had insisted on marriage, had been proud of her, had been heard to boast about his wife's way of doing things.

But he did not want children and Sue had not intended to spoil things by getting pregnant. Indeed, she still did not know quite how it had come about, for she was fairly sure she had taken her pills and behaved just as she ought. At first she had told her body indignantly that it really ought to behave itself and stop trying to worry her; all this sickness in the mornings, this thickening of the waistline, must be a trick. But at last she had acknowledged the truth and faced what she must do.

Hugo was an artist and a mountaineer. Climbing was his passion and one she could scarcely share since she was terrified of heights. Even watching him scale a sheer rock-face brought her out in a cold sweat, yet she would never have acknowledged the fact to him. Why make him unhappy? So she was not surprised when his chance came to join an expedition to climb in the Caucasus and to paint as well. Sue had cheered him on because she knew it was what he wanted. It would also, most conveniently, take him away during those last crucial months when she would be least able to hide her condition.

She was not ashamed of her pregnancy, then, but she wanted to keep it a secret from Hugo. So she decided to leave her lovely job and their delightful flat and go somewhere quiet where she was not known to have her baby. Once it was born she would of course put it out for adoption, and then return to the flat, smiling and slim, to await the arrival of her man. In the old days, it might not have been so simple to see that the baby got the sort of home she wanted for him, but now it would be a piece of cake. People were clamouring for babies, she had been assured; hers would be taken by a couple not only compatible in colouring and general looks but also in thoughts, feelings and income. She would be doing the baby a good turn, she told herself defiantly when she woke in the night, alone, and then felt the unseen company of him as he turned and kicked within her. A London flat was no place for a baby, a fashion and features editor on a glossy magazine no mother for a baby and a man who climbed mountains no father for one. This way he would have a home-loving mother, a rich and successful father and a home by the sea in the country. There would be dogs and chickens and pigs . . .

She had lied shamelessly when talking to the adoption people, of course, painting a very different picture from the reality of her life with Hugo. She had denied her marriage, had made herself out to be less glossy and had even worn – and that had hurt – a pair of round-lensed, eye-shrinking specs, which had caused her to walk into furniture and address women as 'sir'.

All for you, Tiny Tim, she told him in the long watches of the night when she missed Hugo and had vague, painful longings which would not come out into the open so that she could dismiss them with scorn. All for you, curled up in the warm down there. One day you'll thank me, except that you won't ever know anything about it. One day. And in the meantime she wrote articles for her magazine purporting to come from the south of France, where she was supposed to be studying fashion and writing a series of features on living in a foreign country. Fortunately she knew France quite well and had in any case an inventive mind. The fashion side she frankly cribbed, with help from a French friend who toured the shops and boulevards for a small commission.

Yet as she swayed out of the clinic and down the road in the general direction of the flat, she was not thinking solely of Hugo and of her lost life, she was also thinking about that girl from No. 3 – Jenny, wasn't it? Part of her mind assessed her shrewdly: good expensive clothing, good shoes, a marvellous complexion and lovely hair, though it was doubtful she appreciated it since Sue had yet to meet the woman who liked that very soft, very fine, mouse-coloured hair. It had to be cut extremely well to look good and perms were fatal; it simply frizzed. No make up, which was unusual she supposed vaguely. Nice eyes, very large and set wide apart. Grey eyes, or were they hazel? Hugo would have noticed. Not beautiful, not even pretty, but something more. A face with character, Hugo would say. An unhappy face.

Startled, Sue thought again about the girl on the stairs. She had looked unhappy, but that might have been just a transient mood. On the other hand, people alone in winter lets might easily be unhappy; she was not, but then she knew that her life would be on the up-beat again when spring came. Others might not be so fortunate.

Thinking of spring could put a dance even into her present heavy step. Spring meant Hugo and Hugo meant, quite simply, happiness. Sue smiled at the whole world as she made her way along the pavement towards Beechcroft Road.

Jenny was halfway up the flight of stairs to her room, having left Posy at school for the third day, when she heard the altercation. It was coming from the shared kitchen. Mrs Grant's claim that the flats were self-contained was really a figment of her imagination since everyone, from the Twiggs in the attic to the mystery man in the basement, did their cooking in that kitchen as well as all their washing up. Only a very unfussy midget could have coped with greasy pans in the small hand basin in their rooms and the gas rings were all equally inadequate, Jenny presumed. At any rate, she had speedily realized that the kitchen was quite a community centre for the various flat-dwellers residing – temporarily – at No. 24.

It was not much of a kitchen either, if you were honest. It was on the half-landing above Jenny's flat and had once been a bedroom. It overlooked someone else's miserably small backyard and even that meagre view was obstructed at the moment by the drooping leaves on a lean and cadaverous lime tree which had somehow managed to reach second-floor height, and the window was filthy without and only marginally cleaner within, since officially it was Mrs Grant's task to keep the room tidy.

In fact the tenants were pretty good on the whole and did their best to keep the room respectable, but it was not easy because everything was either chipped or blackened or both, and there was no way you could blame Mrs Grant. If there was no chip-pan it was because the tenant before you had taken it, if the tea-towels were threadbare it was because the new ones had been stolen – or burnt, or thrown away – the week before you arrived. Mrs Grant knew she could get away with murder in the kitchen and acted accordingly.

Jenny had been slow to realize the possible advantages a shared kitchen held for a landlady and so had lost a good saucepan, three thick tea-towels and a half pound of butter before Sue warned her.

'My love, don't say you left them in the kizzie?' Infuriatingly, Sue could scarcely get two sentences out without shortening or otherwise bastardizing a word or two. 'That was madness! The old hen will be clucking over them this very minute, tucked away in her basement.'

'Oh, but Mrs Grant said . . .' Jenny had fallen silent, remembering just what Mrs Grant had said. She sighed. 'I see. I thought it might be the mystery man on the ground floor – does he use the kiz . . . kitchen?'

'At dead of night, probably. Don't worry, we'll catch him at the weekend, probably, trying to get in first with his meat and two veg,' Sue assured her. 'But the old hen comes up regular as clockwork; if you catch her she says she's cleaning, which is a laugh. What she's really doing is nicking anything decent left around, so the rest of us ignore those tempting cupboards and even the fridge and lock everything up in our own rooms, even butter.'

'But she's got a key to all the rooms, surely? She could get in, I bet.'

'Yes, you dope, but who could she blame for the resultant losses except herself? She's no fool, the old hen.'

Now, mounting the stairs, Jenny was tempted to go up to the kitchen just to see who was shouting and why. She had only met Sue two or three times but she liked her and wanted to know her better. However, she had intended to go straight back to the flat, drink a cup of tea and have a slice of toast, and then take herself off to see Mr Croft. Despite the most stringent economies she was becoming desperate for money, she really should be sensible and go and discuss Dirk's allowance with the solicitor. Yet if she just nipped up to the kitchen for a minute it wouldn't stop her going to see Mr Croft later – if she was still in the mood.

Accordingly she climbed the stairs but by-passed her own flat and went straight to the kitchen. The door was open and she could see Sue perched on the draining board, and another girl sitting on the square table, only she was blonde and small and, at half past nine in the morning, still clad in a fluffy mohair dressing-gown and pink mules. Could it be No. 5, perhaps?

'Morning,' Jenny said, stepping into the room. 'I thought I heard your voice, Sue, and I wanted to see you for a moment.'

'Well, don't hover, Jenny-wren, come right inside,' Sue said briskly. She was buttering a thick round of toast which she waved at Jenny. 'Want some? The work of a moment to shove another slice under the grill.'

'Please; only use my loaf, it's beside the sink,' Jenny said. 'Any tea going? Er . . . is this No. 5?'

Sue clapped a hand to her brow and closed her eyes dramatically. She had long creamy eyelids tinged with lavender – by nature, not artifice.

'Darlings, my head is a sieve. Brenda, this is Jenny Sayer, No. 4. Jenny, meet Brenda Crisp, who is indeed No. 5.' The two girls murmured at each other, exchanging smiles and a quick all-over glance. 'Did you hear the fuss, you nosy thing you, and come up to see who was being killed? Brenda here wants someone to stand in for her at work so she can get out for an hour, lunch-times, but when I said I would she was disgusted.' Sue sniffed. 'She's old-fashioned and square and a fuddy duddy, I told her.'

'Unlike you, who are far from square,' Brenda said, gazing pointedly at Sue's jutting stomach. 'Honestly, Sue, what would people think? Anyway, it's only a small shop, you probably wouldn't fit behind the counter and suppose one of the oddballs came in? I mean if they chase me, at least I can run. You'd be a cinch.'

'Anyone chasing me at the moment would be an oddball indeed,' Sue said rather gloomily. 'It's so long since I had any cuddling that I'd probably quite welcome an oddball.' She giggled. 'What a spiffing expression, oddball – does one take it literally? *Do* your customers have . . .'

'Honestly, Sue, if you don't shut up . . .' Brenda began. She had the fair skin of a natural blonde and right now it was tomato-coloured. 'Just remember not everyone knows where I work; Jenny probably thinks I'm the madam of a brothel or something.'

'Call her madam,' murmured Sue. 'For all I know Jenny might be your most regular customer! For all I know . . . hey, hang on a mo'! – Didn't you say you wanted a job, Mrs Sayer?'

'Don't I just,' Jenny said fervently. This really would kill two birds with one stone; if she had a job she would earn money, and if she was earning money she would not need Mr Croft or Dirk's allowance.

'Well, actually, I want someone for a week as well,' Brenda said, turning rather doubtfully towards her. 'Could you manage a whole week? It pays well, you'd get around eighty quid.'

'Eighty quid! But could I do it? What sort of shop is it? I've got a little girl in school, I have to pick her up at three-thirty, I don't know whether that would interfere with it.'

'A little girl!' Brenda rounded on Sue. 'You are too bad; what would Mr Sayer think if he found out she'd been working in the Private Shop?'

'He's probably your most regular customer,' Sue said, unrepentant. 'Would he mind, Jenny? I've not met him, yet.'

'He wouldn't know; we . . . we're separated,' Jenny admitted.

The two girls stared at her for a moment, then Sue turned to the cupboard and began to fish out the cracked and ancient cups that were kept within. Brenda, as if triggered by the same recollection which had started Sue hunting for cups, grabbed the grill and rescued the toast. Sue spoke with her back to the pair of them, her voice still slightly muffled by the cupboard.

'Yes, of course; why else would you be in a winter let? We've all got our reasons, I daresay; mine sticks out a mile.'

'I'm here because I'm experienced in Privates,' Brenda said rather huffily, earning a rich gurgle of mirth from within the cupboard. 'Well, it's true, they always put me into a new shop for a few months, just until people get used to it.'

'I suppose some people move in because they're having houses built, or they're only in Britain for a short space of time,' Jenny suggested. 'Though why the Twiggs are here . . .'

'I think they're permanent,' Sue said, emerging almost as red in the face as Brenda had been. 'You've not been up to the attics, but I don't think even the most indigent holidaymaker would take those rooms, and with Bernard being in work and having his pigeons in the old loft above the garage, I daresay the old hen thought she couldn't do better.'

Jenny made noncommittal noises; she rather liked Mrs Twigg, who took in light dressmaking, or so she had told Posy, and Bernard seemed pleasant enough, though so bashful that whenever he saw her he went scarlet and dived into the nearest doorway to hide until she had passed.

'Well, all right, so now we've cleared all our mysteries up,' Sue said now, spooning tea into the pot. 'I'm here because of Tiny Tim . . . have him and then return to the land of the living, sort of thing . . . Brenda's here because her firm sent her, Jenny's on the run from her ex-husband.'

'No. I'm not on the run, I – I expect he'll ask me to go back,' Jenny stammered. 'We're separated, not d-divorced, it's very new, I don't think . . .' Her voice trailed into silence.

'Then if you want to go back, why did you leave?' Brenda said at last, when it was obvious that Jenny had run out of steam. 'It doesn't make sense. Men leave you if they're fed up, women leave men when the circumstances are reversed.'

'Not farmers. Dirk's a farmer, his family have lived there for hundreds of years. He got the flat for me and . . . and moved me into it.' Confession suddenly seemed the easiest way out. 'He's got a girl living with him. A young girl.'

'Oh. Well, you'll be here for a bit, then,' Sue said. 'Going to take Bren's job?'

'You know I'd love it, but . . . what's a Private Shop?'

'It's what they call a sex shop,' Brenda said, sounding defensive. 'You must have heard of sex shops; think of all the fuss here when it was first opened! The boss said all the letters in the papers and the women's institute threatening to chop vital parts off the customers were a marvellous free advert. You can't have missed it!'

'It was probably before I came, I've only been here a week tomorrow,' Jenny explained. 'And there wasn't a sex shop in the village, nor in the nearest town, or at least I don't think there was. What do you sell?'

'Nothing terrible. Dirty magazines, naughty underwear, various contrivances . . . some blue films, a few rather explicit photographs, that sort of thing.'

'I keep meaning to pop in and have a look at your stock,' Sue said, crunching toast whilst pouring tea into a cup from rather too great a height. Some splashed her and she swore. 'Damn! Yes, I'd like to see what you've got in at the moment, but it's a bit like coals to Newcastle, or do I mean shutting the door after the horse has fled? Well, whatever. Do you think Jenny could work for you?'

'I wish she could,' Brenda said, giving Jenny a sudden impish grin which lit up her rather sulky full-lipped face and made her seem much more likeable. 'The boss will send someone down from Wrexham if I can't find a replacement for my week off but I've got things going which I don't much want anyone I don't know poking around in.'

'I would if I could,' Jenny said wistfully. Her mouth watered at the thought of what she and Posy could eat with eighty pounds at their disposal. 'The trouble is, I can't ask anyone else to fetch Posy because I don't know anyone else, and . . . well, what time do you close at night? Perhaps I could pay someone to bring her down to the shop for me.'

'How old's Posy? Four? No, I don't think it would be a very good idea.' Brenda's skin had darkened again. 'We don't close until eight-thirty and then all the planks come in you know; perverts, too. I wouldn't risk a child of that age.'

'Planks?'

'Oh, Jen, Brenda comes from the wilds of Chester, they speak a diffy language from us,' Sue said. 'Planks are what you and I know as thickoes, yokels, hicks, dum-dums.'

'I see. Then I suppose it's out,' Jenny sighed, with visions of steak and kidney pie, bacon and chops vanishing over the horizon. A diet of cheap fruit and vegetables, brown bread and watered milk was beginning to lose any attraction it had ever had, and baked beans were becoming a four-letter word. 'Oh well, I'll go and pester the job centre again.' Mr Croft's name had been all but on her lips when honesty had made her think again. She could not bring herself to go and see him, so she would have to try for work, though the job centre had held out little hope yesterday when she had called in.

'You mean you've *never* had a job?' the girl behind the counter had said with rude incredulity. 'I don't mean since you got married, I mean before, when you left school.'

'Here, have some toast,' Sue said. 'Bren, do you know it's nearly ten?'

Brenda gave a shrill cry and vanished through the door, scattering toast crumbs. Sue got up, shut the door behind her and returned to her former perch. Over her cup she looked very kindly at Jenny.

'Look love, far be it from me to interfere but why do you want a job so badly? Your fellow ought to be supporting you and the kid, you know.'

'He's paying the rent. I think there's an allowance . . . he told me to go to a solicitor, only . . .' Without warning, the black tipping feeling threatened to come over her and she closed her eyes, catching hold of the table edge. That was the trouble, if she thought or talked about what was happening to her she remembered that Dirk, the one person in the world she thought she could trust totally, had let her down, and that meant that the whole world might suddenly decide to play her false, the earth might tip, the sky might darken, nothing was what it seemed.

'Jenny? You all right? You've gone awfully pale.'

'I'm all right.' Jenny opened her eyes and sighed as the world steadied once more. 'It's just that when you've known someone for ages, been married to them for eighteen years, and something happens to prove that you don't really know him at all it shakes you.' She tried to make it sound light and casual but somehow her seriousness showed through, shaming her.

'Yes, I know what you mean; I daresay most women do. What you're trying to say is that a man let you down. Well, love, that happens to a good many of us.'

'To you? Oh, surely not. The father . . . didn't he . . . wouldn't he . . .'

'He's married,' Sue said with commendable brevity. 'But I'm all right, no one's let me down. I'm doing just what I want to do if the truth were told. I am very much all right Jack, so don't waste any pity on me. But unless I'm much mistaken, you and Posy are having it hard.'

'Yes.' Jenny longed to confide, yet hesitated. Could she tell Sue about Mr Croft? But then Sue would insist that she, Jenny, visit him; she could not possibly understand all the baffling fears, the sudden stupid superstitions, which had sprung up in Jenny's life. If I touch the window of the greengrocer's shop before that red Fiat goes past then Dirk will take me back. If I can go all day without anything other than cups of tea then there will be a letter for me in the morning. That sort of superstition. Every time the telephone rang she wondered, with a sinking heart, whether it was Dirk ringing up with an ultimatum. But what ultimatum could he hand her, now? He had sent her away, she was no longer his, no longer even a welcome visitor at the house she had called home for eighteen years. He could do no more than that to her – could he?

'Then you really should get in touch with your husband.' Sue was stroking her bump absent-mindedly, as though the infant already lay there needing the comfort of her touch. She's going to make a marvellous mother, mad ways and all, Jenny found herself thinking. She'll adore that baby . . . but she won't spoil it, that isn't Sue. She'll bring it up so beautifully, with teasing and affection and with heaps of kindness, because Sue's kind . . .

'Well? Don't say you've never even mentioned maintenance?'

'Maintenance?'

'Now, Jenny, you must know about maintenance. Look, if you want to suffer no one can stop you, but must Posy? She's his daughter, after all.'

Jenny fetched a huge sigh and picked up her cooling cup of tea. She sipped, then spoke.

'Right, I'll come clean and tell you that Dirk gave me his solicitor's name and address and told me to call in there to

38

receive some sort of allowance. But if I went, and there was money, and I took it, it would make the whole thing so final, as if he was even paying me money to have me stay away.'

'That isn't why they pay . . or perhaps it is, but even so! You go and see the chap, love, and take the money, otherwise he could claim you were self-supporting or some such thing. Incidentally, how have you and Posy managed, this past week?'

'Family allowance,' Jenny said briefly. 'I've felt horribly guilty because one of my sons, Mark, is still on the book and that makes me a thief because he's a charge on Dirk, not on me. He's at boarding school, you see. Since Monday I've not even bought a cup of coffee, let alone a bun, for fear I'd find some other expense I hadn't bargained for.'

That had been a greater deprivation than perhaps Sue could guess; wandering round the town, perambulating up and down the paths of the Botanical Gardens, unable to visit the cafe because she could not even afford a packet of crisps.

'Then you're mad, unless you're punishing yourself, and if he slung you out and installed a teenage mistress he's the one who wants his bum kicked.'

'I don't have to punish myself,' Jenny said in a low voice. 'He's done all the punishing. Just sending me away . . .'

Her voice sank; the pain of that rejection was like a knife in her bowels. For years and years he had wanted her, either used or loved her, she could not now decide which. If it had been love, then surely he could never have simply cast her off? If she had been just a body in his bed, then why had he sometimes been tender, always turned to her? And in either event, why had she been supplanted by the detestable Bronwen – unless he had never loved her and had discovered love with Bronwen for the first time. Which seemed unlikely since he was forty-seven, no longer even a young man. Or did the young not love truly? But I did, mourned Jenny, I did.

'Yes, I'm sorry, of course that's how you feel, now. Later, perhaps . . . look, would it help if I came with you? To see that solicitor?'

Jenny had not known how she longed for someone to say those particular words. To have Sue's company in the lion's den would make it almost a pleasure trip. She felt the smile begin and spread until it stretched from wall to wall.

'Would you? You wouldn't mind? It would be marvellous.'

'Of course I don't mind, I'm intrigued, actually. It'll be interesting. What's the chap's name?'

'Mr Croft. His office is on King's Avenue, off Wellington Road. I walked past it once but I've never been in.'

'Right. We'll go at once, before your resolution cools.' Sue slid off the draining board, thumping heavily on to the brown lino, and walked across to the door. She was wearing a blue pleated maternity dress with a white collar and a scarlet string tie. It looked incongruously smart with her faded, down-at-heel mules. 'Call for me in ten minutes; I'll have a pee as we pass the loo. One of the odd things about being preggers is the number of times you widdle; I mentioned it at the clinic and everyone's the same, it appears. One woman said it's your bladder being squeezed up by the baby, which I can well believe. Do you know I weighed myself in Boots yesterday and I swear the scales cried for mercy? I wonder if he's twins?'

The two of them strolled through the sunny streets, taking their time. Wellington road was always busy and today the pavements were thronged with shoppers and even the cafes were filling up.

'I'll treat us both to a coffee and cream cake if I get some money,' Jenny said recklessly. 'It'll be good to live dangerously again.'

They both laughed. It was the sort of day when laughing came easy, especially to Jenny, with Sue in charge and Sue plainly bent on being amusing, furthermore. She pointed out every bargain in the shops, lamented that her shape made most of the garments impossible, shrieked over a joke-shop window crammed with plastic dog-turds, fried eggs and ink blots, and cooed over a pink-clad, rosy-cheeked baby sitting up in her pram outside the main post office and burbling happily to herself. By the time they reached King's Avenue Jenny was feeling young, relaxed and almost attractive, but when she saw the name on the brass door plate all her old fears rushed back. Despite Sue's presence, she still dreaded the finality of being paid off.

But, when she tried to hang back, Sue would have none of it.

'In we go,' she said gaily, pushing open the half-glassed front door with the words *Croft & Mallow, Solicitors, Commissioners for Oaths* engraved on it. 'Which door, I wonder?' She threw open the nearest door and entered with confidence, only to back out at once, almost trampling Jenny underfoot as she did so.

'Help, it's the gents' loo! I bet that chap feels a fool though, far worse than I do. I'd like to know why they don't have a sign on the door . . . ah, this one says *Enquiries*, let's try here.'

'It'll be a broom cupboard,' prophesied Jenny, but she was wrong, as she saw when Sue bounced inside. It was a large office with several people in occupation: a spotty girl sat at a typewriter, a middle-aged woman wrote intently on a pad of paper with a telephone to her ear, and a young man crossed the room with an armful of files. The girl was nearest the door and looked up as they entered, though she did not immediately stop clattering on her machine.

'Yes? Can I help you?'

'We're looking for Mr Croft,' Sue said, since Jenny seemed to have lost her tongue. 'Is he in? Can we see him?'

'D'you have an appointment?' The girl stopped typing and leaned forward, probing her hair with a pencil; it was greasy and needed a good hard brushing. 'What name shall I say?'

'My name's Jenny Sayer,' Jenny said feebly. She hoped that the girl would send her away but she merely nodded and pressed a key on a black telephone by her side. After a moment a man's voice said, 'Yes?'

'Oh, Mr Croft, there's a Jennifer Sayer here to see you.' The girl's eyes slid incuriously across them. 'And a friend.'

'Oh, right. Give me five minutes, Miss Jones.'

The girl let the key spring back again, then addressed them as though Mr Croft's words had reached her ears alone.

'He'll see you presently. Will you take a seat?'

There was only one chair. Neither Sue nor Jenny would take it, and by the time the young man had put down his files and fetched a second chair the bell was ringing on the spotty girl's intercom. She pressed the key down once more.

'Yes, sir?'

'Send Mrs Sayer up, please.'

The girl led the way out of the room along a short corridor, and up a flight of brass-edged linoleum-covered stairs. Dust was thick on the barley-sugar struts which supported the bannister and there was an air of neglect about the stairwell, but Mr Croft's room, when they reached it, was neat and well cared for. It had a brown carpet with thick pile, a tan and gold rug, a gas fire in the grate and a rubber plant on the window-sill, which partly shielded from view a tiny backyard and the crammed brick-and-tile backs of countless boarding houses. In its shade some black and white photographs lurked in silver frames: a small, stout wife and two ordinary-looking children; a dog which had incautiously moved and so appeared twice on the print, once solid, once ghost-like, an elderly lady with a mouth like a rat-trap and an even older man who appeared to be all beard and glinting pince-nez. No wonder he keeps them on the window-sill rather than on his desk, Jenny found herself thinking; he doesn't actually have to look at them there!

Mr Croft stood up when they entered, then leaned forward, his knuckles resting on his huge mahogany desk, and looked enquiringly from one to the other. He was tall and thin, but somehow not healthily so. He reminded Jenny of a weed which has outgrown its strength, or a straw which, sucked too often, has become soggy and drooping. Yet the wedge-shaped face was handsome enough, the dark eyes bright and hard and the patent-leather hair thick and gleaming.

'Good morning; Mrs Sayer?'

He was looking at Sue; men would always look at Sue if they could, Jenny thought; her friend had a magnetism which not even her obvious pregnancy could dissipate. Sue smiled coolly at him.

'I'm the friend. This is Mrs Sayer.'

He held out a thin well-manicured hand. Jenny, shaking it, noticed that he was a strong gripper. Someone must have told him about fishy handshakes, she decided unkindly; she was sure such firmness of touch did not come naturally to him, or could that be prejudice? For she had already decided she did not care for Mr Croft.

Delighted, Mrs Oliver.' He had got round to Sue at last, having shaken Jenny's hand for a couple of seconds longer than she felt was strictly necessary. 'Now do sit down, both of you.'

He bustled about arranging chairs, then sank down behind the desk and rummaged in a drawer, producing a long legal-looking brown envelope.

'Ah, here we are! Your husband instructed me to give you this weekly, so if you'd care to come into the office next Monday morning, you shall have the next instalment.'

He held it out and Jenny, taking it, tried to ignore the sickly sinking of her stomach which accompanied the feel of the stiff brown paper between her fingers.

'Well, Mrs Sayer? Aren't you going to open it?'

Jenny gazed at the envelope lying in her lap. Money. This smarmy telegraph pole was paying her off.

'Is it obligatory? I suppose I could . . just hand it back. Couldn't I?'

He smiled reasonably. Now he looked like a shark cynically amused by the antics of the swimmer he was about to devour.

'Of course, Mrs Sayer, but then your husband would be able to say you had turned down his offered maintainance and that might well create a precedent.'

Jenny, disliking him more every second, now saw that Sue was smiling, leaning forward and looking confident and even more amused than Mr Croft.

'And if she accepts the money, Mr Croft? Does that mean her maintainance will be set at whatever Mr Sayer has seen fit to put in the envelope? Presumably it works both ways.'

A little of the confidence left Mr Croft's face and his eyes cooled perceptibly.

'As to that . . . Mr Sayer has been, in my opinion, generous.'

Jenny slit the envelope open. No message, not a word, just a number of bank notes. She spread them out and counted. It seemed a small fortune, and every week she could collect a similar amount. But . . . Dirk had not even written her name on the envelope, he had simply stuffed notes into it, dropped it off on Mr Croft and gone home. And that meant that he had been to Rhyl at least once since she had left the farm and he

43

had not even bothered to come round to make sure Posy was all right and the flat satisfactory.

'Well, Mrs Sayer? Is that sufficient or, as I said, generous?'

She was about to say that it was when she saw a tiny movement from her right; Sue was warning her. She put the money back into the envelope and spoke slowly, thoughtfully.

'I really couldn't say, Mr Croft. This is the first time I've lived alone but presumably I'll need clothing, bus fares, all sorts of things, once I grow accustomed to my . . . my change of status. At the moment I'm still too new to being a one-parent family to see just what my needs – and Posy's – will be.'

Again she saw the flicker of movement; this time it was a nod.

'Very well, Mrs Sayer. I'll tell your husband you've accepted the money but will apply to him through myself for an increase should you need one. Will that do?'

Jenny was about to say that it would do very well when Sue intervened. She leaned forward and spoke directly to the solicitor.

'But surely, Mr Croft, this will all be done legally? Through the courts? I imagine Mr Sayer wants either divorce or legal separation and then it will be up to the courts to decide how much should be paid to Mrs Sayer. I believe it's usually a third of the husband's income.'

For the first time Mr Croft looked definitely wary and his words sounded decidedly defensive.

'Ah, but we must not move too precipitately; this is not, as yet, a legal matter and may never be so. Mrs Sayer has moved out but neither party has shown any desire for a legal separation, far less a divorce. I cannot believe . . .', here he smiled with shark-like ingratiation at Jenny, ' . . .that this will be a permanent rift.'

Sue gave a snort; it could not be disguised by a fancier name.

'Mrs Sayer moved out because her husband brought a woman to live with him . . . no, let's be truthful, her husband turned her out! He even got her a flat, doesn't that seem fairly permanent to you?'

44

Jenny longed to deny it, to shout at Sue to be quiet, but Sue was obviously making a point which Mr Croft did not at all wish to hear, for his lips thinned and his eyes grew angry. He stared at Sue with something akin to hatred.

'It's only a winter let, Mrs . . . er Oliver, and anyway that is very much a matter for the people concerned. I wish you good morning.'

Sue got gracefully to her feet but Jenny bounced upright, so annoyed over Mr Croft's words that all her humbleness and self-distrust vanished.

'I wish you good morning too, Mr Croft, and if you see my husband when he next comes in you might inform him that, if he thinks I've been put in a winter let so that he can have a six month affair on the cheap, he's in for a big surprise.'

'Mrs Sayer, the last thing I want . . .'

He was on his feet trying to get between them and the door, but he was too late. Sue grabbed the handle and held the door open and Jenny escaped through it to hurry down the stairs, until Mr Croft's desperate voice over the bannisters caused her to pause for a moment.

'Mrs Sayer, please . . . I feel for you in your unfortunate situation but I'm sure things can be resolved . . . I want you to trust me, to know that I'm working for your interests as well as those of Mr Dirk . . . I believe you have the *same* interests, Mrs Sayer. If I was a little harsh it's possibly because I expected to see you alone, to be able to advise, discuss . . .' Over the bannisters he gave her a rueful smile which accorded ill with his calculating eyes. 'Forgive me, my dear, and let me assure you that I didn't mean . . . the words were badly phrased . . . next week, when you come in . . .'

'*If* I come in,' Jenny said tightly. 'I don't see why the money can't be posted to me.'

'That's the whole point of my taking the money from Mr Dirk; he wants me to see you each week, to be able to reassure him that you're managing.' He had followed them down the stairs and now he hurried ahead of them and held the front door open, his head a little tilted, his smile wider and more shark-like than ever. 'After all, eighteen years is a long time; he can forget them no more than you.'

Jenny, through the doorway and moving down the

45

pavement with Sue at her side, merely smiled and nodded an acknowledgement as they escaped into the cheerful bustle of Wellington Road, but once they had rounded the corner she let out her breath in a long, quiet whistle.

'Phe-eew! Now that's a man I didn't take to! Oh, look, a cafe with an empty window table, let's nip in and take the weight off our feet. I can buy us coffee and cakes now, I could even afford lunch if you felt like it.'

'Don't chuck your money about,' Sue advised as they took their seats at a glass-topped table and ordered coffee and toasted teacakes from a weary-looking waitress with dark circles under her eyes. 'I don't like all this business about not asking for a legal separation. Does he think he can just drop you and pick you up again whenever he feels like it?'

'He knows he can,' Jenny said frankly, taking the envelope out of her handbag and transferring some of the contents to her purse. 'He's not wicked, Sue, just foolish and misled. It started, I'm sure, because he wanted to see if he could still attract a young girl and then before he knew it he'd bitten off more than he could chew.'

'Oh, yeah? Then why didn't he spit her out? Why bust up a good marriage? I'm not denying it was a middle-aged infatuation to start with, but these things tend to leave permanent scars if nothing else. Would you really creep back to him if he called?'

Jenny thought about it whilst the weary waitress stood the two cups of coffee and the teacakes down on the glass table-top. She wondered why the glass did not crack under the heat, then picked up her cup and took a sip. It was good, and suddenly she felt ravenously hungry. She put her cup down and bit into the teacake, which was smothered in butter and deliciously hot . . . steak and kidney pudding for tea she thought exultantly, feeling the money in her purse warm her mind and almost warm her stomach, too. What was more, if Mr Croft had been speaking the truth, then Dirk was not paying her off, he did care still, he was still looking after her, keeping an eye on her . . . he would want her back when the winter was done!

'Well? Would you go back?'

'Oh, yes! I know it's shaming to admit I've so little pride, but he's all I've got, apart from the boys. I was only seventeen when we got married; it was immediately after I left school, actually, and he was so marvellous to me, so exciting and handsome and kind . . . he taught me everything about the farm that I needed to know, he protected me from his family, because they thought I was too young, silly, brainless. He protected me from my own family too in a way, because my father expected me to go home and help him run the hotel, and Dirk saw I'd be nothing but a skivvy so he made excuses until my father got tired of asking me back. And then Phil was born, and Mark only a year later, so I wasn't much help socially, but he never complained. Life was so good . . . oh, yes, I'd go back like a shot.'

'Boys?' Sue stared over the rim of her cup. 'Did you say boys? I knew you'd got one, but . . .'

'That's right. Phil's at college, he's going to be a vet if he passes the exams, and Mark's still at school.'

'At *college*? Good God, woman, how old were you when Dirk married you? Five?'

Jenny giggled. 'Seventeen; I told you just now. And Phil's eighteen so I'm getting on for thirty-six.'

'Never!' Sue's disbelief was flattering and Jenny felt the colour rise hot in her cheeks. 'Well, who'd have thought it? I thought you were about my age.'

'And how old are you, pray? Having wormed my age out of me . . .'

'Twenty-seven. That means there's a hell of an age-gap between Mark and Posy. Why was that?'

'Dirk wanted a couple of sons, farmers do tend to like lads, and he thought two children were plenty. But I found I was having Posy and I wanted her, so he let me go ahead.'

'*Let* you? Croopus, Jenny, that's the most male chauvinist thing to think, let alone say! And what have the boys said about Dirk turning you out and having a teeny bopper in your place?'

'Nothing. Well, they don't know. Mark spent the last fortnight of the holidays staying with friends and went straight back to school from there, and Phil had a job in France, helping with the wine harvest or the cheese harvest or something. I couldn't bring myself to tell them on the phone or in a letter and besides . . . I kept hoping it wouldn't happen, that Dirk would get sick of her and we could cover it all up.'

'Hmm. To fester in darkness?'

'It won't, because he should have got her out of his system; or at least, that's my theory. In the meantime, I have to live with the fact that he's got someone else. Which is horribly hard.'

'What about getting someone else yourself? That would shake him rigid, I bet!' Sue chuckled and chewed teacake. 'Go on, give him a taste of his own medicine.'

'I don't know anyone, and anyway I couldn't. I'm not made for casual affairs, I don't think. And if he heard he might decide to keep Bronwen just to . . .'

'To spite you?' Sue's lovely brows arched. 'How charming you make him sound! No, don't ruffle up, tell me about his mistress.' She shook her head chidingly, 'And don't wince over the word, love, it's not such a terrible thing to tell the truth.'

'No, I know, it's just that I still can't believe . . . Well, Bronwen's a farm secretary. She came to help out with the books and so on, and then when the summer came and she was having to stay later and later Dirk moved her into the spare room. The boys were away and there was plenty of room so it seemed quite sensible. I rather liked her, you know, thought she was sweet.' Jenny sloshed the tiny amount of coffee left in her cup from right to left, from left to right, watching it surge against the thick china. 'I must be very dim, I never even suspected what was going on but I think everyone else knew, and in the end it was his changing attitude to me that gave him away.'

'How did it change? Was he an attentive husband before?'

'No, I don't think so. But he began to . . . to shy away when I went near him, especially if she was there, he wouldn't let our hands touch . . . he'd pull back sharply if it looked like happening. And then in bed . . . well, he came up later and later, and he didn't want . . . he never even woke me if I was asleep, and when I began to lie awake and wait for him he behaved as if . . . as if I might contaminate him in some way. It was a nightmare, it was almost a relief to wake up, to realize that he was carrying on with Bronwen.'

'How did you find out?' Sue asked gently. 'Unless you'd rather not tell, of course.'

48

'Oh, the usual way. I walked into the office to ask if they wanted coffee and . . . well, they were . . . you know.'

'I do indeed. Poor Jenny-wren. Do you hate talking about it? Is it still too raw?'

'I've told you more than I've told anyone else,' Jenny said, pushing her coffee cup away from her. 'I hate even thinking about it, actually. If I wake in the night and happen to remember a particularly nasty moment I shake and the black feeling comes back and I want to stick a knife into them both for what they've done to my life. She spat in my face by having an affair with Dirk right under my nose, and he spat in my face by letting her.'

'Letting her? Oh, love!'

'All right, his guilt is as great as hers. Greater, probably. But I feel she was the thief, not he, and it's she who robbed me. Perhaps she only brought into the open a discontent and a disgust of me which was in Dirk all the time, I don't know, but it's such . . . such a waste! She hasn't worked for years, given birth to children, managed a great rambling farmhouse, yet it's all been handed to her on a plate. She slid into my place as neatly as though I'd been doing it all just for her, as though I'd never existed, and Dirk has pushed me out of sight and out of mind because he's got her to . . . to . . . because he's got her.'

'And you still think his infatuation will end just like that? Is he a proud man?'

'As Lucifer. Why?'

'Because it'll take humility to admit he's made a mistake and to ask you to come back, and because some men need change the way women need permanency. Don't bank on anything, behave as if this was for ever, learn to live alone, and if you're wrong, then you've all the more reason to rejoice.'

Jenny pushed back her chair and stood up, then she heaved a deep sigh.

'I know you're right and it's what I try to tell myself. Now let's not talk about it, let's just think how nice it will be to have some money! Have you got to get back to the flats, or could we take a look at the shops? I want some meat to do a steak and kidney pudding for Posy's tea, and I'd like to buy some coffee and some drinking chocolate instead of making do with tea all the time.'

'Yes, that would be fun,' Sue observed as they left the cafe. 'Tell you what, I'm still earning my usual salary and I've got another cheque due at the end of the week, so how about having lunch and going Dutch? I know I want a holiday when all this is over, but I've been doing all right so far, I can afford to eat and to save.'

'What exactly do you do?' Jenny asked, as they made for the nearest butcher's shop. 'I've never asked difficult questions about your bump, but though I know the father's a married man, wouldn't he help you to support yourselves, you and the baby? You were determined that Dirk should pay for his daughter, after all!'

'I'm a fashion journalist. And as for the bump's father, he won't be asked to support either me or the little'un, because the bump's going to be one of the lucky ones – he'll be chosen by his parents, not just landed with 'em.'

'You mean . . . you're putting him out for adoption? Oh, Sue.'

'Don't *Oh, Sue* me,' Sue said a little sharply. 'What would I do with a baby? It would cramp my style, to say the least.'

'Yes, I suppose . . . but these days . . . you could get it a nanny, you could . . .'

'Oh, yes, sure I could, if I was just thinking of myself. But I'm not, I'm thinking of the bump as well. He'll be far better off with a couple of adoring parents who truly want him than living hand to mouth with me. Right?'

'I'm sorry. Yes, I'm sure you're right. Where shall we have lunch? You know the town much better than I do.'

'Much better? My dear girl, I arrived exactly a fortnight before you did, and I'm not sure anyone will provide what I crave for, which is kippers. They niff, you see, or I'd have had them in the flat, but in a cafe I could enjoy them without qualms. D'you think we could get kippers anywhere?'

Jenny made comforting we'll-find-you-kippers noises and led the way down the busy High Street towards the promenade, which seemed a likelier source of kippers than the more conventional types of cafe. But she had seen Sue's beautiful, curved mouth droop when she mentioned having her baby adopted and prattled innocuously but constantly until her friend seemed her usual carefree self. Then they turned into a large restaurant and though kippers were not on the menu Sue pronounced herself satisfied with roast lamb, mint sauce and crispy baked potatoes. Over their meal they talked of other things and kept well clear of emotional subjects.

It should teach me a lesson Jenny thought, as they ate sponge pudding and custard, it should teach me that it isn't only deserted wives who have sore places in their minds.

The day had begun well, and after lunch it simply got nicer and nicer, though in a quiet, unemphatic sort of way. The two of them went to the job centre and shared the commiserations of a fat and friendly clerk, who told them that there would be very few jobs going now until the Christmas rush started.

'We're seasonal, you see,' she explained, 'and once the season's over we've got a good few unemployed of our own. But come early December you'll maybe get something.'

When Jenny, having plumbed the depths of the indoor market, scoured Marks & Spencer from the ladies' lingerie to the food section and followed this up with a nostalgic wander round Woolworths, caught sight of the time, her squeak of dismay was not echoed by Sue.

'Ten past three? So what? If we walk at quite a normal speed we can be outside the school by half past. Yes, I did say "we", I need exercise and it will do me good to see some kids. I've not exchanged a word with Posy since you moved in; suppose you wanted me to babysit sometime, or suppose you got a job and needed Posy to get used to being met by someone else?'

'You're a pal,' Jenny said sincerely. 'You've no idea how much better I feel after today.'

'Haven't I? Possibly as much as I do. Don't forget, Jenny-wren, that you weren't the only stranger in this town!'

'Did *you* feel a stranger? But you're so glamorous and self confident, and anyway you knew Brenda and Mrs Twigg and . . . don't laugh, you did, didn't you?'

'Stoopid! I met Brenda a week before you did and Mrs

Twigg at about the same time. Look, I've got one advantage over you; I'm pregnant, so I meet lots of women in the same boat . . . sorry, in the same situation. And you've one over me – you've got Posy, so you'll meet lots of mums. Other than that we're two of a kind.'

'You mean we've both been let down by men? But you said . . .'

'Oh *Jen*, how you leap to the wrong conclusion! No, we're temporarily without men, I'm Sue alone, you're Jenny alone; but only alone from the point of view of a lover. We've made a good friend each today, haven't we? I've found a shoulder to cry on and so have you.' She laughed. 'God, what a couple of wet weeks I make us sound! But you get my drift. And talking of friends, how's Posy making out? It must be a helluva change for her.'

'Yes, it was a change all right, but actually . . .' she paused. How to explain the lure of a one-room flat to Sue? How explain it to anyone who had known the farm, the woods, pastures, stables, animals? Yet she could understand it, in part at least. Posy loved being in one room, with her mother just a few feet away during the night so that the dark held no terrors. She enjoyed eating a meal with the television on in front of their noses, having Jenny's undivided love and attention in a way that would never had been possible at the farm.

'Does she miss it horribly? The farm, the animals?'

'Well, no,' Jenny said, still sounding rather apologetic. 'She's only four and Dirk never did have much time for little girls. He hadn't wanted a daughter and made no secret of it so he didn't encourage her to hang around the farm. Not that she showed the slightest urge to do so, I might add! At home she spent a great deal of time under the kitchen table, with her story books or her paints and paper, or just with Belle. Now she misses Belle horribly, especially when we go on the beach, but she's accepted that she won't see her for a bit.'

'Under the kitchen table? Who the hell was Belle?'

'She's Dirk's sheepdog. She was semi-retired and spent a lot of time under the table, and Posy used to crawl under there with her and fall asleep all mixed up with Belle. They adored each other; poor Posy never mentions her father or

brothers but she asks after Belle two or three times a day. You
know what children are when they're small, they identify far
more easily with animals than they do with other human
beings.'

'I didn't know that,' Sue said thoughtfully after a long
pause. 'Kids are even rummer than I thought they were; good
thing the bump doesn't know how hopeless I am or he might
refuse to come out at all. What does Posy do now then, with
no Belle and no kitchen table either?'

'You'd be surprised. We haven't been here long but she's
coming out of her shell a lot. She's got a friend called Sandra,
sometimes I take the two of them on the beach together, they
both adore that, and she's learning to do her letters, so she
spends quite a lot of time making a's, b's and c's. She helps
me to cook, which she never did at home – only toast, or
pouring the cornflakes into the dishes, but that's cooking
when you're four years old. She's settling in remarkably
well.'

'And you? Have you joined the PTA, or Gingerbread, or
tried to go to one of those singles clubs or whatever they're
called? If you like acting you could join the Little Theatre
group; anything so you don't just stagnate whilst waiting for
Dirk to whistle.'

'You don't think he will whistle though, do you?' Jenny
said quietly, as they arrived at the school gates and joined the
other mothers waiting just inside the playground. They took
up their position against the chain-link fence which divided
the infants from the juniors, far enough away from everyone
else to be able to continue their conversation in private.'You
think I ought to be preparing myself for years of . . . of this.'
Her gesture meant not just years of chattering mums but
years of waiting, alone, for Posy. 'I know I'm not young or
pretty, but once, Dirk thought . . .'

She was quickly and rudely interrupted.

'Crap! For Christ's sake don't go getting a chip on your
shoulder just because one worthless fellow has got tired of
seeing the same face on his pillow morning after morning!
You don't look any older than me, you're lively, intelligent,
and if you weren't so unhappy you'd find men would take a
great deal of interest in you. As it is, you radiate so much fear

and uncertainty that people think you want to be left alone. I did, only . . . well, I've been radiating similar feelings myself just lately, so I had a fellow feeling.'

'You? Radiate fear and uncertainty? Who are you trying to fool, Sue? You're so calm, so sure of yourself, so . . .'

'Not really. Inside, I'm all of a twitter. I've never given birth before and doing it alone, for someone else, isn't my idea of a rest-cure. However, I breathe deeply and try to relax and try, as well, to make the best of what I've got. Go thou, Jenny-wren, and do likewise.'

'Oh, but it's so hard,' Jenny moaned, staring towards the door through which the infants would presently emerge. 'I've been so dependent on Dirk, for so long, that I feel like half a person without him.'

'All the more reason to try harder, then. Look at those conifers over there – see them? They're so close together that you can't see light between them. Now, if you look hard you'll see that the branches on the outside are strong and thick, because they've got space and light to grow strong and thick, but the branches on the inside are thin and weedy. If you rooted one up, do you think that the one that was left would stay lop-sided, with thin branches on one side and thick on the other? Or do you think it would simply die? It wouldn't, it would grow bigger still, and stronger, and in a year or two the branches would be equal, the way they were meant to be. You're just a little conifer, poppet; you've been close to Dirk but now he's moved back a bit you must grow strong without him.'

'Charming, I'm noticeably lop-sided! No wonder people avoid me!'

'Don't muck about, you know very well what I mean. If you want to, you can be independent and even enjoy life.'

'I do see what you mean, actually. But I don't really want to be independent, I like being a wife and a natural leaner.'

'Ah, you say that now, but . . .' The doors opened, a teacher visible between them holding back the flood, then she stood aside and the children flowed out into the playground. They all seemed to be shouting, laughing and talking as they headed for their mums, eager to tell all about their day.

Posy rushed up to them, beaming, then hung grimly on Jenny's arm, swinging on it.

'Hello, darling; Mrs Oliver's come to meet you as well, you see. Did you have a good day?'

'Call me Auntie Sue,' Sue said firmly. 'Who's your friend, Posy?'

'Oh, it's Sandra. Mummy, Miss Freda Jones said could Sandra walk home with us today, because her Mam's taken her brother Nick to the hospital to see a speshaler about his earache. She said to say that Sandra's Mam would be ever so grateful and would we give a knock, fourish, at their house, 'cos they'll be back by then. She said she wouldn't have asked, only it's Nan's whist afternoon.'

'Yes, of course she can come home with us. In fact, we'll stop off at the Gardens for twenty minutes and get ices and you can have a go on the swings, then we'll be back at round about the right time for Sandra's Mam.'

'Golly, ices!' Jenny's heart smote her as pleasure was replaced on Posy's face by a worried frown. 'Can we afford ices, Mummy?'

'Today we can. Go on, run ahead, and Sue and I will come along behind!'

'What a phenomenal memory!' Sue remarked as the two small girls trotted ahead and then slowed to a walk. Heads bent, they appeared to be absorbed in deep discussion. She giggled. 'Look at them, two little old ladies setting the world to rights! Does your Posy always talk like a tape recorder?'

Jenny considered, laughed, and admitted that Posy did tend to repeat conversations verbatim.

'And not only conversations; when I read to her, if I miss a bit she's on me at once. She knows just about all the big *Rupert Annual* by heart and all the Beatrix Potter's. I'll have to get her some more books though, we only brought nine or ten.'

'There, you see, I told you Dirk's allowance wasn't a fortune,' Sue said, reverting to an earlier conversation. 'Isn't she like you, though!'

Jenny frowned. Posy was small, fragile-boned, with soft, light, baby hair which curled on to the tender nape of her neck and big, clear, baby eyes which still shone with an innocent friendliness, which the years would soon dim. *Were* they alike? Posy's nose was just a smudge, her mouth, scarlet-lipped, was just a child's mouth, her teeth were tiny, first pearls.

'Is she? I think she's too young, too unformed, to tell. But she's not a bit like the boys were; they were the image of Dirk from the day they could toddle – earlier!'

They had been beautiful babies, handsome little boys, wildly attractive young men. Dark, with a high colour, straight backs, broad shoulders. Open faces, big smiles, white teeth. Arrogant though, she thought suddenly, and willing to shoulder anyone aside to get their own way. Posy might not be striking or vivid, but she had a lot of sweetness in her character and perhaps that was more important than good looks in the end.

'Well, she may only be superficially like you now, but I bet she'll be the spitting image of you when she's got a year or two more in her dish. Now, where do we go for those ice-creams?'

The little girls were already in the gardens, heading at an increasingly quick trot for the cafe. Jenny and Sue followed suit.

CHAPTER THREE

Slowly, undramatically, almost cosily, the September days passed and began to form a pattern. Jenny bought an alarm clock, which woke her at seven-thirty on weekdays and did not sound at all at weekends. She made Posy breakfast but contented herself with tea and sometimes bread and butter, for her lively appetite had lessened with her greater in-activity.

Walking Posy to school and returning to the flat took up an hour, sometimes longer if she went around the Gardens or took a look at the shops. Cleaning the room was a somewhat perfunctory business, but she usually had a good go at the bathroom twice a week, and the toilet as well. Mrs Grant caught her scrubbing the blue lino in the bathroom one wet morning, and made Jenny jump by demanding, in acid tones, whether the floor was not clean enough to satisfy her tenants. Jenny, who had bitten her tongue when she jumped, had answered too hastily for tact.

'It's clean enough *now*,' she had said. 'We could do with some more Harpic for the lavatory, though.'

It caused Mrs Grant to give a juicy, contemptuous sniff, but despite Mrs Twigg nervously exclaiming that she only hoped Clara wouldn't go and take one of her dislikes to the Sayers as a consequence, it seemed to have done no harm. Indeed, the following day a new Harpic appeared and the day after that some bath cleaner. And Jenny, scrubbing up and down the hills and valleys of blue lino in the bathroom and pink in the toilet, decided to suggest carbolic soap next.

Lunch-time was a welcome break, now that she and Sue invariably shared it. They did not eat much but whatever they ate, they ate together, in the kitchen if it was wet, on the beach if it was fine; and Sue, on her clinic day – Wednesday – , treated Jenny to what she described as a slap-up nosh, in a hotel at the far end of the promenade. In return for being fed, Jenny accompanied Sue to the clinic, reading the magazines whilst Sue and her lump were prodded and examined, chatting to her during the interminable waits.

Tuesdays were Mr Croft days. Usually she returned to the flat after leaving Posy, did her housework, peeled some potatoes for the evening meal and then fetched Sue. The two of them walked into town and up to the office, though Jenny usually climbed the stairs to Mr Croft's den alone. She never sat down now, or chatted, explaining that her friend was waiting in the hall, so that she could take her money and go. After that, the two of them had lunch – this time on Jenny – and then shopped, ferreting out bargains with great enthusiasm.

Thursdays were early closing and on Thursday you could buy cheap vegetables in the market and cheap cakes in Marks. Thursday tea was always nicer than other days, because of the cheap cakes and the bruised fruit which Jenny made into either pies or crumbles. Mondays were rather grim because it was the day before pay-day and Jenny's purse was usually empty; Dirk's allowance had turned out to be meagre rather than generous, when you took into account buying Posy a winter coat and the cost of things like washing powder.

'Didn't you buy washing powder before, when you were at the farm?' Anna Matheson asked. The two girls were in the kitchen, Jenny doing her washing, Anna lounging against the draining board watching her. Anna had the flat opposite Brenda's and was not popular with the other tenants because, as Mrs Twigg put it, she 'brought men in,' but despite her reputation Jenny rather liked her. Anna was brash and bawdy and not very clean but she was as honest as the day was long and quite unrepentant about her weakness for men, even admitting to Jenny that she could not have managed on the money paid her by the social had she not had 'friends'.

'Yes, I bought it, but I didn't pay for it,' Jenny explained. 'We had an account, I used to ring up or walk into the village when we ran out of something, and when we did our big shop, about once a fortnight, Dirk paid by cheque. I just used to choose what I wanted.'

Anna's eyes rounded. She had very large pale-blue eyes and bleached straw-like hair. When she was surprised her resemblance to a doll that Jenny had once owned was striking.

'Gawd, no wonder you think things are an 'orrible price! What a lovely way to live though.' She put on her posh voice. 'I'll hev six of them, James . . . no, make it eight!'

'It had its advantages,' Jenny admitted. 'Though you'd be surprised how much I enjoy making a meal out of nothing – there's days when I look at Posy tucking in and I think the whole meal, pudding and all, cost me less than a school dinner, and I'm really thrilled with myself.'

'Yeah, well, I s'pose there's that. Wish I could cook; but there's always fish an' chips.'

Fish and chips were expensive, a luxury which Jenny and Posy had had only once since they moved in. Jenny had taken Posy and Sandra to the local cinema on an unexpected half-holiday, and afterwards they had bought the fish and chips, carried them back to the flat and eaten them straight from the newspaper. They had tasted far more delicious than they had done at the farm, eaten off warmed willow pattern and accompanied by lots of generously buttered bread and various condiments.

'I'll teach you how to do an apple pie one day,' Jenny said to Anna now, half threateningly. 'You love it and it's dead simple to make, so why not?'

'One day. When I meet a guy who's worth a bit of trouble, I'll keep you to that. Bye, love.'

And Anna had tottered off on her scarlet high heels to do her nails, put her hair in rollers, paint her face . . . and all without bothering to have a good strip-down wash, far less a bath.

Left alone in the kitchen Jenny had continued to wash Posy's white socks with what was left of her washing powder, whilst she wondered about Anna. Was the girl what Dirk used to call a tart, or was she just a friendly, fairly unfussy creature who allowed men to sleep with her and occasionally accepted presents? Impossible to tell from Anna's conversation, but possibly Sue or Brenda would know. Mrs Twigg thought they were all rather wicked, it was no use asking her. Besides, Mrs Twigg did not like Anna; she obviously suspected Bernard of having an interest there, and resented it. Jenny was sure that the only birds which Bernard noticed were pigeons but she could scarcely say so. Privately, she and Sue had admitted to one another that Bernard seemed more likely to take a fancy to the mystery man on the ground floor than to Anna, but Mrs Twigg, for all her nods, winks and pursed lips, was far too innocent for such a thought to cross her mind. Bernard had to be Saved from that Wicked Woman, and to that end Mrs Twigg scarcely ever spoke to Anna, would leave the kitchen hastily when Anna entered, and had tried, surreptitiously but definitely, to persuade Mrs Grant to move Anna on.

Her thoughts comfortably active, her hands enjoying the warm water and the simple task, Jenny considered Mrs Twigg. She was a dear and she did love Posy! On rainy Sundays Posy and Mrs Twigg sat up in her room, one on each side of the electric fire, and made shell ornaments whilst Mrs Twigg either discoursed on Bernard's difficult childhood or instructed Posy in her art.

Once, Mrs Twigg told Jenny proudly, she had done a lot of shellwork, individual designs too, and had made quite a nice little bit of money. But now all they seemed to want was crinoline ladies, owls and large dogs, and since she needed to sell whatever she made, she had, perforce, to make what would sell. Yet even though she affected to despise her products, Jenny had seen the care which went into the placing of each shell, the way Mrs Twigg would ransack her collection for a perfect match, and knew that, stereotyped though her art might have become, it was still an art in which Mrs Twigg was proud to excel.

Posy loved the shell people and took great pride in adding to Mrs Twigg's shell collection. At weekends she and Jenny haunted the beach at low tide, carrying their finds carefully home in Mrs Twigg's large linen collecting bags. Mrs Twigg, afflicted with arthritis in her hands and rheumatism in her knees, admitted that collecting the shells was not the pleasure it had once been, but to Posy it was a joy second to none. The excitement of the search and the thrill of discovery were not even much dampened by rain, though occasionally, carried away by the quantity of material cast up during windy weather, Jenny and Posy had returned home wet as any drowned rats.

And Mrs Twigg appreciated their labours, furthermore.

With her thin grey hair in its corrugated perm ('Where does she find someone, in this day and age, willing to make her hair look quite so ghastly?' Sue had once asked) and her little, short-sighted eyes screwing and unscrewing behind her unflattering glasses, Mrs Twigg positively radiated delight over every single shell they collected.

'I see him . . . as the petal of a flower!' she would exclaim, staring very hard at a tiny pink shell no larger than a baby's fingernail. 'My goodness, you two are hard workers – so *many*, and all so perfect!'

Bernard did not spend very much time up in the attic rooms and when he was at home he was usually in his bedroom. Muffled sounds, every one of which Mrs Twigg knew by heart, would come through the thin partition wall, to be laconically – but proudly – explained.

'That's his shoulder exercise,' she would exclaim at the sound of effort coming through the wall. 'Hear that – he's adding more weights!' as a clattering made itself heard. Posy came back full of stories of how Bernard must be the strongest man in Britain.

'He has a bench in his room so he can do bench presses,' she told her mother. 'When he does squats there's awful groans, but Mrs Twigg says he knows when to stop.'

'I'm sure,' Jenny said cautiously. 'Er . . . are you sure she said he . . . er . . . does squats?'

It sounded so rude she was sure Posy must be mistaken but the following day, when returning a thimble to Mrs Twigg, she heard the expression for herself. First, however, there came a sound halfway between a bellow and a roar, which nearly caused her heart to stop. She gasped loudly and clutched Mrs Twigg's arm.

'Good God, what on earth . . .?'

'It's all right, dear, it's only Bernard, doing his squats. Ever so hard, they are, he gets his bell-bar across his shoulders and then goes down into a sort of crouch and then comes up. Ooh, ever so hard, only the very best men do 'em.' She patted her own skinny, rheumatic knees. 'Strengthens you there, you see? My Bernard doesn't just want muscular arms, he wants to be strong all over!'

Bernard did not look particularly strong though, despite all the effort he put into it. He was large, seemingly overweight, and he shambled, rarely looking anyone straight in the eye. Thick toffee-brown hair overhung his eyes and bunched over his ears, but in his favour he had a remarkably sweet and piercing whistle, which Jenny occasionally heard when she had the kitchen window open and Bernard, outside, was cleaning out his pigeon loft.

Rinsing the socks now, and considering her morning, Jenny remembered that it was Friday and her heart, which had been high, sank a tiny bit. Fridays were dull because every Friday Sue worked non-stop at her rattly old type-writer, getting what she called her piece sorted out. She usually worked all over the weekend, saying that it suited her better to have four lovely lazy days and three hellishly busy ones, but Jenny missed her sorely on a Friday. And in the nature of things, Friday was the last day before the weekend, and though it was pleasant to have a lie-in undisturbed by having to make breakfast or start housework, though it was lovely to have Posy's constant companionship, weekends were . . . flat? Sundays in particular always seemed strange, as though she should be shouting, 'Hooray, it's Sunday!' and waiting for something momentous to happen. Well, she did wait, and it never happened, which was why Sundays always left her tired, a bit jaded, less than satisfied.

Still, today was Friday. Wringing out the socks with vigour, she reminded herself that there was still enough money left to buy something nice to eat over the weekend, and that it was a really lovely day with a light breeze and warm sunshine. I'll have a roll and butter, a bit of ham and a tomato and an apple for afters and I'll eat them on the beach, she told herself, wringing away. I'll go down as soon as I've finished here and be really childish and paddle through all the low waters and catch shrimps in Posy's tin bucket. I'll tuck my skirt into my knicker-legs and go really deep. I'll draw Friday's teeth for it, that's what I'll do!

Back in her room she bustled about, hanging the washing out on a home-made line and spreading newspapers under it to catch the drips. She really should tackle Mrs Grant about being allowed to hang washing in the backyard, but the only time she had tried the old hen had promptly reminded her that there was something in the rules about there being no washing facilities available.

'But that's for holidaymakers,' Jenny had protested. 'We're here for months, we can't afford laundrettes all the time.'

'And you don't pay anything like holiday rates,' Mrs Grant reminded her. 'Try the laundrette up by the funfair; it's cheaper than the others.'

If she had only thought she would have explained about Posy's socks and all the little bits and pieces of school uniform which had to be washed every other day. They were both lamentably short of clothes since the fog of unhappiness in which she had left the farm had completely obscured the need to take clothing. She had snatched some underwear, a couple of thin dresses and some jeans and tee-shirts for herself and the same for Posy, so their clothes led a busy and active life, barely touching the chest of drawers for a brief lie-down before being snatched out again and worn.

She had spread the last of the newspapers and was watching, rather disheartened, as the print darkened with drips – she had wrung with all her might – when there was a clattering of feet on the stairs. They hesitated outside her door and then someone knocked. Could it be Sue, deciding not to work today after all? Or Anna, wanting a lesson on how to make apple pies? The heels were too high for either Mrs Twigg or Bernard.

She shouted, 'Come in!'

'Morning, Jenny.' It was Brenda, looking crisp and pretty in a white angora sweater and very pink, very tight jeans. Because Brenda was in full-time work and had such strange hours, Jenny did not see very much of her, but they were still on friendly terms and always chatted if they happened to meet. They had not, however, called on one another and Jenny, urging her to come in and sit down for a minute, wished fervently that she had cleared away the breakfast things before going up to the kitchen to wash the socks. They looked so bald, sitting there on the table, the milk in its bottle, the jam in its pot, even the loaf still in its waxed paper. Mrs Grant's bounty extended to a milk-jug (cracked) and a plate could have supported a few tasteful slices of the loaf, but at the time it had not seemed worthwhile to do anything so elaborate. I'm becoming a slut, Jenny thought with only moderate self-scorn. After all, she had been branded as an unwanted wife, why should she not be a trifle sluttish in her own time, so to speak?

But Brenda's thoughts, as soon became apparent, were not on the bottle of milk, the loaf in its wrapping, or the pot of jam. To be sure she was eyeing the table, but for another reason.

'I say – Rice Crispies! Can I have a handful? I never have breakfast, I'm generally in too much of a rush.'

'Have a bowlful, with some milk,' Jenny said hospitably, and Brenda immediately tipped the packet into Posy's (used) bowl, added a sprinkle of sugar and sloshed in the milk.

'Great, thanks. Gosh, I'd almost forgotten that they really do make a noise! I am awful, taking your food . . . oh, are you going to put the kettle on?'

'Naturally. It isn't every day I have a visitor. Tea or coffee?'

'Tea would be nice.'

Presently they found themselves sitting opposite each other at the table, sipping and chatting idly. Brenda, having called, seemed reluctant to divulge what her business was, if she had any, and merely drew Jenny's attention to the fact that there was a fat pigeon sitting on her window-sill.

'I know, it's Percy. He likes Rice Crispies too.' Percy was sitting with his huge blue-grey breast pressed hard against the glass, cooing in an agitated and strangulated fashion. You could almost imagine that he was watching the Rice Crispies disappear down Brenda's throat and was audibly regretting their passing. 'I'll put the window up presently and then he'll have the scraps. He always does. Posy started feeding him the day we moved in I believe, and now we both do it. I'm sure Bernard must wonder why the poor old thing's got so fat and lazy, but I'm certainly not going to let on.'

'I'm glad it doesn't perch on *my* window-sill,' Brenda said, with a shiver which made all her neat little silvery curls dance. 'I think they're filthy creatures, probably covered in lice. Bernard smells of them, haven't you noticed?'

'No, I've never got near enough. Are you working today, or is it your day off? Only I thought that was Monday.'

'It is, and I am working, only I don't start until ten. Actually, I came because my boss has listened to me at last. He says if I can get someone to come in from about half twelve until say a quarter to two he'll pay £2 a day, so I thought of you. It wouldn't affect your little girl, and you did say . . . you seemed quite interested . . .' Brenda was now scarlet and staring fixedly at her empty cereal dish. Considering where she worked she was very easily embarrassed, Jenny thought, and wondered how it affected someone when they were constantly going scarlet. She was still wondering when Brenda's words sunk in. She was being offered a job!

'Brenda, do you mean it? Do you really think I could do it? Gosh, you've no idea how I'd like to try and only yesterday Mrs Twigg was saying that if I did get work she'd keep an eye on Posy during half-term.'

'Of course I mean it. If you really would like the job then could you pop in to the shop today, at about noon? It's a formality more or less but the boss will be there and he'll make sure you really are the respectable person I've said you are. Will that be okay?'

'It'll be fine. What's the boss like, Brenda?'

Brenda finished her tea, stood up and adjusted her crotch. The jeans were every bit as clinging as the angora top, Jenny could see.

'Christ, these things are all but sawing me in two! Like? Well, he's . . . damn, look at the time, I really must fly! See you at twelve.'

'Oh, but Brenda, do tell me what he's like,' Jenny squeaked, as the younger girl flew across the flat and hurtled out of the door. 'I'll feel much better if I have some idea – is he young, old? Cross, easy-going?'

'Not very old, and very . . . oh, good morning, Mrs Grant, sorry, did I tread on your toe? I really am . . . byeee!'

'Don't shut the door, Mrs Sayer,' Mrs Grant panted, limping up the flight. 'I was comin' to see you, if you could spare me a moment.'

'Oh, well come in, Mrs Grant.' Jenny stood aside as her landlady heavily ascended the last three stairs and ushered her into the flat. 'Can I help you?'

'A man rang whilst you were off out this morning, dear.'

Mrs Grant managed to imply that Jenny had been gadding. 'He wanted to see you . . . he did leave a name . . .' She had a little pad in her hand and ruffled the leaves uncertainly, peering down at the pages, though so far as Jenny could see there was only one name written on the top sheet. 'Now where is it? I know I writ it down.' She looked up at Jenny through her stubby little dark lashes. 'Now what was the name? Would it be . . . ah, I'll get it in a moment . . .'

'Perhaps it wasn't for me,' Jenny said, determined not to put a name forward. When Mrs Grant had first spoken her heart had thumped with delicious anticipation – suppose it had been Dirk, ringing to ask her to come home – but the landlady's prevarications had put that right out of the question. Even Mrs Grant would scarcely forget that a Mr Sayer had rung for a Mrs Sayer!

'Oh yes, dear, it was . . .' Mrs Grant pretended to find the name on the pad, which had been staring her in the face for the last two minutes. 'Ah yes, it was a Mr Croft, he said would you please go and see him some time today.'

'I daresay I'll manage it,' Jenny said, rising to her feet and walking across to the door. 'Thanks very much, Mrs Grant, for bringing the message.'

'That's all right, Mrs Sayer.' Mrs Grant was looking at the makeshift clothes line and the newspapers beneath it. She shook her head and made a vague disapproving sound, a cluck of disapproval in fact. 'Now why don't you hang them socks out on the line, dearie, on a fine day like this? They'd dry in 'alf an hour, and smell fresh, too.'

'Thanks very much, I'll certainly do that,' Jenny said politely, and then as Mrs Grant lingered hopefully in the doorway she relented. 'Mr Croft is the family solicitor; I daresay it won't be important.'

'Ah, solicitor, eh? D'you know, I thought he sounded legal, like.' Curiosity satisfied, she swung round and began to thump heavily down the stairs. Over her shoulder she remarked, 'I daresay you don't know what he wanted yet, yourself?' It was a question, hopefully phrased.

'No, not yet. Thanks again, Mrs Grant.'

As soon as her landlady had wheezed down to ground level Jenny shut the door and began to whizz round the flat, clearing the table, shovelling food into cupboards, carelessly rinsing the crockery and spoons under the cold tap. She had kept her head in front of Mrs Grant, but there must be some good reason for Mr Croft to call. She had been in on Tuesday for her allowance and had received it from his clerk since he himself had been in court. But today was Friday; if it had been some small thing like a signature or perhaps information, then he would have waited, surely, until the following week, he would not have sent for her specially. Perhaps he had a message from Dirk, or possibly her sister-in-law had heard of the break and wanted to heal the breach, or . . . there were a thousand reasons why he might want to see her!

By the time she had tidied the flat and was walking down the road she had, of course, imagined a thousand bad reasons for the solicitor's call and was no longer walking on air. Suppose one of the boys had been taken ill? Or perhaps Dirk had decided to go for a divorce and wanted her to give him grounds. Or the farm might have been burned down . . . Dirk might have been seriously hurt . . . needing her . . . By the time she was within sight of the office she was running, her mouth open, her hair windswept.

Fortunately, at the door, common sense prevailed. What rubbish she had been thinking! If anything bad had happened the solicitor would either have called or have asked to speak to her, he would not have demanded that she call in and see him 'some time today', he would have been on her doorstep. Comforted, she tidied her hair with her hands, allowed herself to stand quite still for a few moments until her heart stopped its mad hammering, and then walked sedately into the general office.

The girls knew her now. The spotty typist smiled at her and pressed the button on her intercom without a word exchanged.

'Mr Croft, Mrs Sayer to see you.'

'Ah, excellent. Tell her to come straight up.'

Jenny climbed the stairs and halfway up found herself suddenly reluctant to go on. Stupidly, her knees were weak and she felt sure that her errand was for nothing. He was such an odd sort of man, he might easily have got her here just to lecture her on his various legal functions! However, having got this far she would go through with it. She climbed the last few stairs, knocked briefly on his door, and entered the room.

Anticlimactically, Mr Croft was on the telephone. He gave her his best crocodile smile though, and gestured her to a chair whilst speaking into the receiver: 'Yes, yes. Oh, yes, definitely. Mm . . . mm . . . I would agree with that. Yes.' Strangely, despite the repetition, he did not sound at all certain but rather as though his mind was miles away.

Jenny sat on the chair and then, for something to do, turned her head slightly and stared out of a small side window which overlooked a flat roof. A gigantic ginger cat was sitting on it, dozing in the sun, but as she gazed at him he opened first one yellow eye and then the other, staring at her, his expression so outraged at finding his quiet perch overlooked that she had to smile.

As if the smile had calmed his annoyance over her voyeurism the cat's yellow eyes slitted once more, his chin sank and presently he slept again, and Jenny's attention returned to the room she was in and to Mr Croft.

She glanced across at him, still on the telephone, and he was staring at her bosom. Absently? Jenny, shifting uncomfortably, decided that there was nothing absent about his regard, though he continued to talk meaninglessly into the receiver. His black eyes were fixed, somehow lascivious, as though he could see through her pale lemon blouse to the skin beneath. Jenny was suddenly visited by the bizarre and extraordinary thought that he was visualizing tempting mounds and this expression, when applied to her own modest proportions, seemed so funny that she began to giggle.

Soundlessly, at first, with the merest shake of the shoulders her mirth made itself felt, but giggles being giggles they became less and less controllable. When she realized she was shaking with laughter she immediately thought of blancmanges – tempting mounds – and of jellies – tempting mounds – and tried desperately to think sad thoughts. Suppose the ginger cat fell off the roof and died? Suppose she and Posy really were overfeeding Percy and he burst? Suppose . . . ah, suppose Dirk really did want to divorce her.

The giggles were gone like a bad dream and Jenny fixed her

attention on the solicitor. By this time Mr Croft, after more murmured agreements, was obviously trying to get rid of his caller, which he managed eventually after some nifty verbal footwork which, in other circumstances, Jenny might have admired. But since his eyes remained fixed on her bosom she felt only impatience with the caller and embarrassment that she might have a button undone or a seam about to come revealingly loose.

At last Mr Croft said goodbye and replaced the receiver, and his eyes at once moved up to hers. Any desire to giggle left Jenny abruptly. His eyes were glittering strangely and as he stood up and came round the desk she saw a sheen of perspiration on his forehead. It was warm in the small room to be sure, but . . . that warm? She stood up.

'Ah, Mrs Sayer, may I say Jenny? How nice to see you! I'm sorry I was in court on Tuesday. I wanted to have a word with you then, but alas circumstances prevented me.' He took her hand in a fatherly clasp, smiling down at her, quite pleasantly for him, and Jenny smiled back and told herself that she really must control her imagination. An unfortunate, absent-minded glance, a warm day, and she was ready to accuse Mr Croft of . . .

'Good morning, Mr Croft, my landlady told me you'd rung.'

Her hand, she was rather alarmed to see, was still tightly wrapped in Mr Croft's grasp, whilst his other hand proceeded to pat her shoulder with hearty, – too hearty, – pats. Lingering pats with just the hint of a squeeze. Jenny stepped back and he followed, his eyes fixed on hers with what he no doubt considered to be a sympathetic gaze, his mouth pulled into an unattractive grimace she had no desire to interpret.

'My dear child, you've been having a bad time, a bad time! I wanted to see you – without your friend – to tell you I'm making every endeavour, – literally every endeavour, to get you back where you belong, but Mr Dirk's an obstinate man and in the meantime any comfort, any help I can offer . . .'

Jenny took another step back and the chair caught her just behind the knees. She sat down quickly, lop-sidedly, seemingly off balance and then, just as Mr Croft bent solicitously over her, she got abruptly to her feet. His chin met the top of her head with a delicious tooth-clashing crunch. He grunted and gasped, the air whistling out of him sharply, and Jenny eyed him with false sympathy, ruefully rubbing the crown of her head – which did not hurt a bit – and smiling with a hint of hopeful anticipation. Had she shattered his upper set, splintered his jaw-bone or merely hurt his pride? He had turned and was retreating behind his desk but as he faced her she saw with pleasure that his eyes were watering and that his chin was showing the ghost of an incipient bruise. Good! That would teach him. Although she knew she looked slight and physically weak, she had not humped sacks of spuds round the yard and helped to stack bales of hay without becoming at least capable of fending off importunate males. The last time something similar had occurred she had pushed the offending, drunken neighbour into a plateful of cold Christmas pudding. This had had an immediately sobering effect on him and he had not quickly recovered from the experience. Despite his strenuous efforts in the bathroom, traces of pudding had still been visible on his elegant cream corduroys when he emerged some time later, and she imagined he must have had to indulge in some pretty deft explaining when he and his smug, huntin', shootin' and fishin' wife went home in the car.

But either Mr Croft was made of sterner stuff or he was used to being hit on the chin by his clients. He was sitting down again now, smiling urbanely and opening a file as though nothing had happened.

'Well, there you are Mrs Sayer; I'm yours to command, as the saying goes. Mr Dirk has asked me to keep an eye on you, to make sure you've got everything you want . . . money sufficient, eh? I could arrange for a little more, I daresay, if you can't manage. You must think of me as a friend to both parties, willing to do anything in my power to heal the breach . . . but between ourselves, I know where the faults lie. So if you need a friend . . .'

Could she have been mistaken? Was all that patting and squeezing and crowding, which she had always associated with an unwelcome pass, merely a perfectly proper solicitorial gambit for putting clients at their ease? But the glittering eyes and the overheated countenance were signs of something quite other, she was sure. No, she had been right to head-butt him; it would make him think twice before pawing her again, no matter how avuncularly. Right now she supposed he believed it to have been an accident but later, when he thought about it, he would surely see that it had been an act of aggression?

'Now, where was I?' He was hunting through the file diligently, as though he expected to find something delicious within. 'Ah yes, here it is.'

He handed over a letter; one glance was enough to confirm that it was from her sister-in-law. But why on earth had Ella not written direct to the flat, or even to the farm? Why was the letter addressed care of Mr Croft?

'Thanks.' Jenny slipped it into her pocket and with the movement caught sight of her watch. A quarter to twelve, and she was supposed to be in the sex shop by noon! She jumped to her feet; she was at the door and opening it before Mr Croft had done more than get to his feet. She had no desire to indulge in another hand-holding session, particularly when she was in a tearing hurry.

'Sorry, I must dash; I've got a job interview in fifteen minutes,' she said over her shoulder. Mr Croft had followed her to the door and as she began to go down the stairs he said: 'A job? Indeed? I'm sure Mr Dirk will be glad if you find work . . . but then I don't have to tell him, do I?'

'I haven't got it yet,' Jenny shouted. 'See you next week!' Wicked old devil, she told herself as she trotted down Wellington Road. She should never have mentioned the job because it was quite possible that Dirk would reduce her pittance accordingly. Not that it was a pittance but suddenly, with the possibility of earning twelve whole pounds each week to add to her allowance, it had become very much more difficult to exist without it.

She arrived breathless but composed on the dot of twelve, and because she was expected she pushed the door of the shuttered shop without hesitation. If she had had time to think she might have felt foolish going in there; as it was she simply opened the door and walked inside.

71

At first glance the cheerful normality of fluorescent lighting, brightly colour-washed walls and lino tiles were reassuring, as were the racks of magazines, the long counter, the clothing rails full of garments. And there was Brenda sitting on a high stool reading a paperback with an apple in one hand and a sandwich, still in its cellophane wrapping, on the counter before her. She put her book down and beamed as Jenny entered.

'Hi there, right on cue!' She slid down from the stool and pushed open a narrow door behind the counter. 'Simon, she's here!'

Simon emerged from the back room with a kettle dangling from one hand. He was tall and chunkily built, perhaps even tending to chubbiness, with a round cheerful face, brilliantly white teeth and a cowlick of dark hair falling across his forehead. He reminded Jenny of the pile of old boys' magazines which Dirk's father had owned; Tom Merry, Greyfriars, footer and tuck. A prefect-type, clean-cut and possibly even rather goody-goody. Not at all the sort of person one associates with rhino-hide whips, rude magazines and peculiar plastic gadgets.

For the whips and gadgets were there, if you cared to look. Jenny could see them out of the corner of her eye as she smiled politely at Simon. Under the glass top of the counter all sorts of things were displayed and, on the wall above Brenda's head, the juxtaposition of the flimsiest nightie in the world and the curl of what certainly looked like a whip did a good deal to off-set the wholesomeness which Jenny had first assumed.

'Hello, Jenny.' Simon's smile was friendly. 'We use first-names here, it's easier. I'm just about to put the kettle on so we can all have a cup of coffee; would you like to come into the back and be interviewed whilst it boils, or do you prefer to remain on the scene of the crime?' He waved his free hand at the shop.

'Go in the back,' Brenda advised. 'Customers often browse in their lunch-hours . . . here comes one now.'

Jenny went round the counter and into the small room behind it, noticing as she went that the shop door, which appeared from the outside to be of solid wood, was in fact made of thickly-painted glass so that the staff could see a

72

customer as he stood fumbling with the door handle. Simon balanced the kettle on a small gas cooker which stood against one wall, then gestured her to a creaky little chair and took the other himself. Jenny, glancing round, saw that this back room was mainly used for stock, every available surface, barring the chairs and cooker, being crammed with boxes, bags and bundles. There was a back door leading, presumably, out to a yard and possibly to a toilet, since she could see no other sign of one, and like the shop it was artificially lit, though there was a window, high up by the ceiling which grudgingly let in little light through its dusty and neglected panes.

'Now.' Simon leaned back and the chair groaned; hastily, he leaned forward again. 'Let's get this over with! What were your first impressions of the shop, Jenny?'

'Er . . . clean, bright, not too much stock . . . but I didn't have much time to look round,' Jenny admitted.

'Ever had shop experience – ever worked a till, for instance?'

Jenny shook her head. No point in prevaricating since someone was going to have to show her how everything worked.

'Hmm. What's your mental arithmetic like? We don't have an automatic till and to tell the truth we probably never shall, because what with discounts and loadings we prefer to employ people who can do simple sums themselves.'

'I'm quite good at adding up, probably above average, because we never had a till or anything at the farm and I sold a lot of goods in the summer,' Jenny said, glad to be able to air one small talent. 'Our prices varied quite a lot too, being seasonal stuff, but I don't think I ever made any mistakes.'

'Great. Add these up for me.' He reeled off a list of prices and Jenny totalled them quickly, smiling at his nod and the surprised look on his face. 'Well, that really *is* all right! Now tell me, what would you do if a customer came up to the counter with . . .', he rummaged in the nearest box and came up with a sinister looking object, ' . . . with one of these and asked you what it was used for?'

'I'd tell him he'd find directions on the box, or if it wasn't boxed I'd say it was up to the customer to decide how best to use it,' Jenny said promptly. Common sense dictated that if you did not know you flannelled round it.

'That's fine. What about size? If someone asks advice on sizes . . .'

'Women, you mean? I'd either make a guess, or . . . isn't there a changing room?'

'No. But suppose your guess was wrong, or you just couldn't guess? Suppose it was a man buying for someone else? Or for himself, for that matter.'

'The same, except I'd probably suggest the customer took the garment home, tried it on and brought it back immediately if it didn't fit. Would that be all right?'

'Yes, that would be okay. What I was getting at is that you never offer to take measurements. In fact since you're only going to be here for just over an hour a day it would be best if you advised customers to take stuff away to try (they pay first, naturally) and then bring it back after two, when a more experienced member of staff will deal with the exchange. The same goes for complaints – just ask the complainer to come back after two o'clock.'

'Does that mean I've got the job?' Simon's affirmative coincided with the kettle suddenly popping its lid and the water putting out the gas; Jenny jumped to her feet and turned off the tap, then lifted the still spluttering kettle off the hob. 'Where are the mugs, or cups? Shall I make the coffee for you as a first task?'

'Well, you pour the water in.' Simon had already put out three large mugs on the boxes which covered the table; now he spooned coffee into them, and stood back as Jenny added water. 'You'll get paid £2.50 a day for a five-day week – we only open until noon on Saturdays – and for that we'd like you to arrive at half twelve or just before and stay until two.' Whilst talking he had added milk to the three mugs of coffee and now he turned to Jenny, a brow rising. 'Do you take sugar?'

'No, no sugar, thanks. When do I start?' She knew her smile was far too broad, far too relieved, but . . . twelve pounds fifty a week! It would mean she could thumb her nose at Mr Croft's suggestion that he might ask Dirk for more money, yet she would still be able to manage.

'On Monday? Is that all right?'

'It's fine.' She picked up two of the mugs and headed for the shop. 'In fact, it's a life-saver.' She peered round the door but the shop door was just closing very softly behind a customer. She put the coffees down on the counter and smiled at Brenda. 'I start on Monday.'

'Good. And that chap just spent over a hundred quid, so you won't feel you're wasting your time here. I'm paid a bonus on my weekly rate, so what you take will go on my bonus.' She winked, slowly and flutteringly, at Simon. 'My boss doesn't mind me making a bit over, fortunately.'

'The more the merrier,' Simon said rather obscurely. He drank his own coffee in one long swallow, gasped at the heat of it, and then turned and disappeared into the back room. When he came out again he had a heavy sheepskin coat flung over one shoulder. Now he looked like a young farmer, Jenny thought despairingly – all he lacked were the wellingtons. Why couldn't people look like what they really were? It was quite impossible to reconcile Simon with sleaziness, yet there was something definitely sleazy about the idea of selling sex-aids.

'Right, girls, I'll leave you now. I'll order some more 224's, Bren, since you're nearly out and they're going so well. If you wouldn't mind, Jenny, I think it would be a good idea if you hung on with Brenda for an hour or so, whilst she puts you wise to where things are and so on. Okay?'

He swung out of the door, crashing it shut behind him. How different from the customer who had closed it softly as a whisper. In a week or two I'll probably crash in and out like that, Jenny told herself without much conviction. She finished off her own coffee and turned to Brenda.

'Right; where do we start?'

CHAPTER FOUR

'Hello! I thought my burnt toast must have put you off for ever! What's it to be, then? An early tea, a late lunch, or just a nice cuppa?'

Jenny had not been into the cafe in the Botanical Gardens since that first morning when she had left Posy at school, and was flattered and astonished to be remembered. She stood on tiptoe now to peer over the counter at what was spread out on the back surface. There were more sandwiches in preparation, but she was unusually hungry because she and Brenda had worked until well past two, and if he really did do something hot . . .

'Hello to you. What's available to someone who hasn't had any lunch and who's absolutely starving?'

'If you'd been ten minutes earlier you could have read my board.' He gestured to a blank blackboard leaning against the cooker. 'I wipe it clean around half two so that I can put high teas on it later. But I can do you a lovely fry-up – bacon, egg, mushrooms, fried spuds and a nice fat sausage – for less than a quid. Oh, and that includes a cup of tea and a round of bread and butter.'

'Crumbs! Right, I'll have that and probably burst on my way to school, but it'll be worth it.' She stood by the counter, watching as he got together the makings of her meal and began to slice up cold boiled potatoes. Her news had to be shared by someone, so she hissed at him.

'Psst! I've got a job!'

'Well, get you!' He turned, giving her a broad smile. 'Congratulations, no wonder you're splashing out. Told the little girl yet?'

It threw her, because she had never brought Posy into the cafe. The only time she had felt able to afford ices, Sue had gone in and got them.

'My little girl? How did you know I had one?'

'My daughter Dawn is in her class – Posy, isn't it? She

comes to the cafe most days after school and several times she's said, "There's Posy and her Mum" so I've looked up and there you were. Tell me about the job.'

'It's not much of a job, only relief during lunch-hours, but the money will make things easier and it'll get me out of the flat.'

He flipped sizzling bacon and sausage on to a plate and slid it into the warming oven, then began to fry her egg, mushrooms and cold potatoes; they fought gamely and the fat spat but she could see he was winning.

'Lunch-time relief, eh? Cafe work, is it?'

'No.' Jenny hesitated, then plunged. 'Actually, it's in the P-Private Shop. It sounds so awful, but I'm sure it isn't really, it'll probably be rather fun.'

'Well, good for you.' He began dishing up, then turned to her, the steaming plate in his hand. 'Odd, actually. I somehow imagined you living in a rather posh house, double-fronted, with a big garden at the back and possibly an orchard at the side.' He handed her the plate, then began to fizz coffee into a cup. 'Shows how wrong you can be about people,' he added, raising his voice above the coffee machine's hums, purrs and clicks.

Once again, Jenny felt a stab of pleasure that someone had bothered about her enough to imagine her home. After Dirk's casual dismissal she had not even expected men to see her, far less to think about her when she was not there. She supposed they would shun her, as Dirk had, seeing the thickly layered faults that had caused him to finally give up on her after nearly two decades of effort. Because Bill had been so kind, she said more than she otherwise would have done.

'I did live in a big house. My husband still does. But I'm in a flat now.'

'I see.' He came round the counter with her coffee and the slice of bread and butter and put it beside her on the table. He looked down at her for a moment, then gestured to the empty room. 'Mind if I bring my own cup of coffee over? I've not had one since about eleven and as it's quiet . . .'

'Yes, do.' He returned to the counter for his own coffee and then came and sat down opposite her. He was wearing a white, short-sleeved shirt open at the neck and dark grey

77

trousers. Was he ex-navy? She glanced at his arms looking for tattoos. They were lightly freckled and covered with very blond hairs, but there was not a tattoo in sight. Not that tattoos had to be in sight; she remembered a very rude joke which Dirk had told her when they were first married and which she had not, at first, understood. Something about Ludo and Llandudno, tattooed in what she had thought must be a most unusual spot. So Bill might be covered in tattoos from navel to kneecap and she would probably never find out.

The thought brought an involuntary smile to her face and, opposite her, Bill's face creased in sympathy.

'Go on, ask me – what am I doing running a place like this single-handed?'

Jenny laughed and nearly lost a very hot fried potato. She crammed it back into her mouth with her fork, shook her head at herself and then said thickly, 'Right . . . what's a nice fellow like you doing in a place like this? Is that what they say?'

'More or less. I'm separated from my wife and I'm bringing up my two little girls. So of course when I see a woman on her own, looking worried to death and counting her money before she buys a coffee, I can't help but wonder if we're in the same boat.'

'Only temporarily, I tell myself.' She kept her head down, eating with enjoyment despite the subject of conversation. 'What happened to you? My husband found me the flat so of course I came here, but you must have chosen the cafe.'

'We both chose it but unfortunately, after we'd been here a few months, Daphne decided that the work was too demanding and she was bored so off she went.'

'Alone?' Jenny noticed that his eyes were green, not grey or blue as she had supposed, and that he had faint lines round them. It could not be easy for a man bringing up children without a woman's help.

'No, she found a fellow.' He grinned at Jenny's expression. 'Don't feel sorry for me, love, it was the best thing that could have happened, both for me and the girls. She wasn't a very maternal woman, Daphne wasn't, which was one of the reasons I left my job and bought the cafe; I thought we'd make out better working together, you see. But it was no use, it made her feel caged, spied on, so off she went and left us the better for it. It may be hard work, but when I think of those last few months . . .', he blew out his cheeks and crossed his eyes expressively, ' . . . this has been heaven in comparison.'

'D'you think I'll feel like that, one day?' Jenny said curiously. 'If the worst happens and Dirk doesn't want me back, I mean.'

'Well . . . do you still dread each morning? Do you hanker and hanker for your old home, your old life? Is it as black as it was at first?'

Jenny sat and stared at him, and slowly there stole into her mind a thought so alien, so wicked, that she could scarcely believe she was thinking it. It was disloyal to feel, even for a second, that life in Beechcroft Road was livelier and warmer than life at the farm, yet if she were honest that was exactly how she felt.

'Oh, well, I . . .' She got to her feet, pushing back her chair with a screech on the polished tiles. 'I must go, I'll be late for Posy! It's been nice talking to you. I'll see you again.'

He got to his feet too; he looked worried.

'I'm sorry, I'm a tactless fool, I can't think what I said, but . . .'

Jenny forced a smile and stayed her flight for a second, one hand on the doorknob.

'You didn't say anything, in fact you made me see that – that life isn't all dark, not any more. Look, I fetch Posy every day from school and we always walk back past the gardens; would it help if I were to fetch your girls as well and leave them with you?'

'I say, that is good of you.' The anxious look disappeared. 'Tell you what, pop in later when you bring your Posy back and I'll introduce you to Dawn and Erica – then if I do get stuck, I'd be grateful for your help.'

'Right. Goodbye for now, then.'

Bill watched her as she made her way out of the gardens, her soft hair lifting with the breeze of her going, her step quick and bouncy, and it was not until she was out of sight that he turned and walked behind the counter once more. There was always something to do . . . he would split and butter some rolls ready for his after-school customers.

Once his hands were busy, his thoughts returned to his recent customer; a real little lady, his old mother would have called her. Softly spoken, with a sense of humour and no opinion of herself, though you could tell from her clothes and the way she behaved that she had never, until recently, been short of a bob or two.

He had thought about her a lot, right from that first time when she had come in early one morning, pale and uncertain, and had sat and had her coffee and toast whilst the old men rambled and boasted about bowls and gardening. Something, even then, had intrigued him because she did not seem to fit into her surroundings. Why should a girl like her sit in his cafe, idling her time away, when she must have a thousand better ways to spend a morning?

It was the broken marriage, of course. What had he done to her, that husband who had turned her out to fend for herself and for their little daughter? He remembered what Daphne had done to him, how she had made him see what a clumsy, ugly fellow he was, had even mocked at what other people would have found praiseworthy – diligence, loyalty, a love of order and cleanliness. Yet she had given him the children, and he loved Dawn and Erica so much that he could forgive Daphne most things because of them. Besides, she had done something else for him; she seemed to have extinguished even the faintest flame of sexual desire and in the circumstances that was a good thing. He was too busy and too tired to think about women. Indeed, the girl who had just left was the first female, apart from Louisa next door, with whom he had exchanged more than the most casual remark for months. Briskly spreading butter, he wondered whether it was the girl's simple, uncomplicated friendliness which had bridged the gap or their mutual – and bad – marital experiences. Whatever it was, he was glad of it. It would be a good thing to be able to look out for someone entering the cafe, to be pleased when they arrived and sorry when they left. Louisa, square, fresh-faced and freckled, was a good sort but she and her Rex had their own lives to lead. On sunny evenings Rex often leaned over the fence and they shared a grumble about Mr Backhouse, who lived on the other side of Bill and complained about everything Bill did – and a good few things he hadn't but simply might – , and when Bill needed advice over the girl's schooling or clothes he found Louisa a sympathetic listener and a sound counsellor. Apart from that, though, he saw very little of his neighbours.

Fetching some fillings from his fridge, he wondered what her name was, other than Mrs Sayer of course. When she came in later to meet Dawn and Erica he would ask her. He guessed a few names none of which sounded quite right, so he gave up, but it was nice to know that he would be finding out.

A group of bowls players, wives as well as their menfolk, straggled in through the doorway and up to his counter. Bill leaned forward and grinned at his customers as they began to size up their requirements.

'Afternoon, ladies and gentlemen; who's for a toasted teacake and a fresh brew of tea?'

Jenny hurried out of the cafe and down the road in the direction of the school. As she went, she wondered was it disloyal to Dirk to appreciate some of the things in her new way of life? Surely not! She still missed him achingly, but she had been rather friendless at the farm and here she had made quite a lot of friends already. Of course Mrs Ted and Mrs George had been very nice, but they were so different! Even in their most casual and gossipy moments – usually at coffee time – they had seemed poles apart from herself. Their daughters moved into town as soon as they could and married young, their sons worked on the land like their fathers but resented it, craving the bright lights and comparative sophistication of urban life. Yet they had helped her with the work of the farmhouse for fifteen years. She had gone with Mrs Ted when young Bob fell off the tractor and broke his tibia, and had sat for hours with her in casualty when Stuart mashed his hand in the old mangold chopper up in the loft. She had mourned with Mrs George when Helen found herself pregnant and had bought a whole layette of little clothes for the child, as well as attending the wedding, cooking for the wedding breakfast and trying not to stare at the bride's bulging stomach beneath the white satin of her not-before-time wedding gown.

Yet even so, she and Mrs George and Mrs Ted were not friends; when Mrs Ted said she'd sooner scrub floors than put up with her Ted's amorous attentions, when Mrs George, to cap it, said she'd sooner walk barefoot to London, Jenny herself had laughed and remained silent. The two older women had let it appear from their conversation that they spent most of their time at home vigorously repulsing the husbandly advances of their sex-crazed mates. To one who knew Ted – small, bow-legged and balding – and George – thin as a lathe, until you reached his stomach which stuck out like a mother-to-be in her seventh month – it was almost impossible to imagine either of them being amorous towards anything. Jenny could never have admitted to Mrs Ted or Mrs George that for many years she herself had been an eager participant in the act of love-making and that she could never have found it in herself to deny Dirk what he obviously regarded as his God-given right to her, even on the rare occasions when she really would rather have gone to sleep.

But now, thinking about it, she realized that even before Bronwen had come on the scene Dirk's love-making had grown more and more perfunctory; speed and his own satisfaction seemed to be the only criteria she recalled with dismay. Yet even so, there had been enjoyable moments . . . she still missed him physically, longing for the feel of his arms around her, his mouth on hers . . .

The thought was followed by another, which brought her up with such a jolt that she actually stopped walking for a moment. He had not kissed her during the course of making love for a good many years. Five? Ten? Surely not so long! But however long it was, they did not kiss. Guiltily, she told herself that it must have been her fault, she must have grown cold towards him, put him off in some subtle way – yet she knew she had not. Dirk's personality was forceful, he had always been the leader in their love-making, never the follower. The truth was that he had not bothered to court with kisses a woman who was already his, body and soul. It was not that he no longer loved her, of course it was not, it was just that he felt he no longer had to prove it with kisses, caresses or any prelude to the act of love. That was why she now thought of his love-making as having been somehow perfunctory.

She was breathing a sigh of relief when she realized that it was after she had caught Bronwen and Dirk kissing that she had first known about them. Just kissing, that was all, except that they had been . . . oh, almost encapsulated in one another, tangled, fierce, too far absorbed to hear the door open . . . or close.

Remembering, she felt sick again at the shock. She had longed to go back, accuse, weep, order Bronwen from the house, but she had done nothing of the sort. She had tried instead to tell herself that, if she ignored it, it would come to nothing. A stupid, head-burying attitude which was the result of being a dozen years younger than Dirk and of never questioning his actions. She still believed that Dirk was only trying to prove to the world that even at forty-seven he could attract a girl young enough to be his daughter, except that he had not reckoned with Bronwen. She had moved into the house and made Dirk behave so badly, so cruelly, that even Jenny's most determined head-burying could not blind her to certain things. Mrs Ted and Mrs George had eyed her with such bright-eyed, almost gloating interest, such determined pity, that she had been forced to tell Dirk, falteringly, that he must change his ways.

He had done so. He had driven into Rhyl and found her a flat, and had moved her into it without so much as telling their sons what he was doing, far less, she was very sure, his sister who . . .

The letter! Incredible, impossible though it seemed, she had totally forgotten it! She was nearly at the school but because she had left the cafe so abruptly she was early. She walked up the cinderpath a short way, selected a convenient wall to lean against, then took the envelope from her pocket, slit it open and pulled out the letter.

Dear Jenny,

Dirk tells me that you've moved out for a while, so that the pair of you can sort things out. My dear, what things? I've always thought you such an ideally happy couple, and I know Dirk worships you and would do nothing to hurt you, so why take such a foolhardy course? He's a very attractive man (I don't have to tell you that, naturally!) so leaving him does not seem a very wise course – suppose, dear Jenny, that he turns to Another, how would you feel then? . . .

Jenny stopped reading at that point, feeling a surge of real anger against Dirk. It was a rotten, cowardly thing to do, to tell poor old Ella that it was she, Jenny, who had left her husband. But when she thought about it, it was in character; he never admitted to a mistake, it was always someone else's fault, or the weather, or a quirk of fate. To tell Ella the truth would have been to admit to a fault, yet Jenny, understanding this, was still distressed by what he had said. It was shabby, unworthy.

Once, years ago, she had known Ella a good deal better than she had known Dirk, through the younger Sayer daughter, Freda. She and Freda had been at boarding school together, and, in the same year that Jenny's mother had finally decided to sever connections with her ex-husband and her daughter, Freda's mother had died. Jenny's father, with a hotel to run and money to make, had decided to leave his fourteen-year-old daughter at boarding school, just for the Easter holidays, he explained, until he had sorted things out. Freda, too, had been there for a few days until her sister, ten years her senior, had found time to fetch her. Freda and Jenny were quite different and would probably never have become friends but for the fact that Ella, swooping on the school eight days into the Easter break, had seen the two of them morosely circling the lacrosse pitch, talking, and had suggested it might be nice if Freda brought her friend along too.

Everyone had jumped at the chance; Freda, embarrassed by the prospect of changes at home and a sorrow she had overcome in a week, had dreaded going back to the farm alone and Jenny had dreaded another three weeks in the empty school building, with only the caretaker and the cook – who both resented her presence – to keep an eye on her.

So back to the farm she had gone, to be absently mothered by Ella whenever she remembered her new role, and to be bossed by Freda. But it had been worth it for three weeks of delightful country living, with plenty of hard work in the hay fields, the sheds and the milking parlour and lots to do in the house, but none of it boring and none of it obligatory. She had helped because she had wanted to do so.

Dirk had only been a large portrait in the dining room to Jenny, because the only son had been dispatched to Canada, via several other countries, and would then go on to study the sort of farming that was being done over there. Old Mr Sayer had married late. When Jenny first went to the farm he had been sixty-eight and set in his ways; she gathered, from talking to Ella when the two of them – Freda always disappeared at the clearing of the table – were washing up after high tea, that he had not got on too well with Dirk.

'He told Dirk if he wanted to preach fancy farming he should learn some first,' Ella had said, clattering china. 'Dirk's a grand lad, none better, but my, he and Father do have some rows! The house fairly shakes sometimes.'

It had been a wonderful holiday and, when they had invited her back again for the summer break, she had been delighted and had begged her father to let her go. He had only allowed her what she had described at the time as 'a measly month', but even that had been unalloyed delight. For some reason Mr Sayer had taken a great fancy to her and this had made Ella's life a good deal easier. Freda, who was a year older than Jenny, soon gave up even pretending that Jenny was her guest and went off about her own affairs from early morning until late at night. Jenny helped Ella, tried her hand at some of the cooking she had seen being done at home in the hotel kitchens, and worked in the fields whenever she could be useful. She returned home after her month, sun-browned, healthy and, alas, sulky at the thought of double-glazing, thick carpeting and all the other trappings of an expensive hotel on the east coast. She had always adored the sea and loved it still, but in summer the beach was so crowded and the white sand filthy with donkey droppings and the detritus of picnic lunches that her love was tempered by distaste.

Looking back on it now she could feel ashamed of her attitude, her long face whenever her father had asked her to perform some task or other. But the truth was she hated the hotel as violently as she had grown to love the farm and spent as much time as possible out of the place, slipping off early in the morning and rarely returning before ten at night. She behaved, in fact, very like Freda did, only she condemned Freda's behaviour as 'beastly and unfair' because she was fond of Ella. Her own behaviour she saw as perfectly natural in the circumstances.

When the following Christmas and Easter came and went with only Ella's short letters to enliven them, she thought that she had been dropped from the charmed circle and moped as much as a fifteen-year-old can, until in June Ella rang her at school.

'Jenny, dear, I'm sorry to tell you – Father passed away this morning. Your headmistress is going to break the news to Freda and she'll be catching the first train home . . . we've asked if you could come with her, just for a few days. I've rung your father, he's agreed.'

Jenny was sad for Mr Sayer but ecstatic for herself. It now transpired that Ella's father had been ailing for the best part of a year but Ella had said nothing, not wanting to upset her young friend. She might also have assumed that Freda would mention it but Freda and Jenny, back in the school environment and in different classes, scarcely ever exchanged more than smiles and a few words.

At the funeral Jenny had met Dirk for the first time. Tall, dark, serious, he had been tremendously impressive and the likeness which she could discern to his father was touching, for Jenny could see now for herself why father and son had not always seen eye to eye. They were too alike; both would have wanted to give orders, to run the farm.

She had stayed for a week in the end, helping Ella and making meals when Ella and Dirk had to go off on business connected with the farm. Later in the year, when the summer came and Ella wanted to get married her first thought, she said, had been to get Jenny to stay again, to show someone else how to run the farm once she, Ella, was no longer there.

Jenny, just sixteen, had arrived and taken over for the summer holidays. It had been terribly hard work for she had had no inkling as to how much Ella had done and how small her own contribution had been, but Dirk made every moment sweet. At first she merely thought he liked her in a brotherly, companionable sort of way, but soon his attitude towards her when other young men were present forced her to revise her ideas. He bristled, like a dog with a bone, when she so much as spoke to another man; to dance with one was apparently tantamount to mutiny on the Bounty, so sternly did he reproach her. He stressed always that she was in his care, so when she went to say a tearful goodbye at the end of her holidays, his kiss was stunningly unexpected and stunningly sweet. She had dreamed of nothing else during the following term and had gone back at Christmas for a couple of days only, dreaming more and more wildly and telling herself that she was a fool, that it would never happen.

Except that it did. He was very correct at Christmas, introducing her as 'a very old family friend' to his fat, rather bad-tempered housekeeper but, again, when she was in the car heading for the station he put his arm round her and, on the platform, kissed her in a manner which not even Jenny's innocence or ignorance, call it what you will, could construe as brotherly.

When her year ended in June, he more or less kidnapped her. He came up the drive in his latest sports model looking very black-browed and dashing, piled her luggage on the back seat and helped her into the front seat. Freda had left school the previous year, so there were just the two of them driving along the motorway, then on the quieter roads, then on the lanes. At the top of their lane he stopped the car and took her in his arms and told her he wanted to marry her.

She had been in ecstasy, there was no other way to describe it. It was as if a cinema idol had stepped off the screen and announced that he was going to whisk her off to somewhere exotic and make her his. The girls at school thought he was the best-looking man ever to cross the threshold, they were wildly envious of her and of the romance of the affair. Everyone she wrote to tell replied at once, clamouring to be a bridesmaid or at least a wedding guest. Jenny, too quiet and not athletic enough to enjoy a great deal of popularity, found herself suddenly besieged by invitations to stay and by vows of lifelong friendship.

Her father's attitude had shocked and upset her; he had

behaved as if Dirk were a wicked seducer just because he was twelve years older than she. He had almost forbidden the wedding, probably would have done so had he not been so busy, it being the holiday season when she had produced her bombshell. Dirk, naturally, had read her father's letter and had been incensed.

'You won't go back there,' he had announced, his brows meeting as he scowled down at the letter. 'No woman of mine is going to skivvy in a hotel, especially for her own flesh and blood. He disapproves because now that you're a big girl . . .' he squeezed the biggest part of her which was not in fact very huge, ' . . .he can see how useful you could be. Well, that's his hard luck, let him employ an extra barmaid or two.'

It had never crossed Jenny's mind until this moment, nearly two decades later, that the same might have been said of Dirk. Employ another housekeeper and you'll manage very well without Jenny, someone might have remarked. Of course, she would have had to be a very loose-moralled housekeeper, Jenny remembered, thinking of the delights of their honeymoon and their subsequently active sex-life, but she had worked terribly hard at the farm in those early years. Mrs Ywr-Evans, the housekeeper, had left the week before their wedding, and Dirk had not even suggested that Jenny get some help from Mrs Ted and Mrs George until she had given birth to Mark.

Abruptly, she remembered where she was; standing on the cinderpath with her back against someone else's wall, dreaming, and all because Ella had written to her. Dear old Ella! She had been a good friend until her husband, having bought a vast, tumbledown mansion in Ireland, had taken her off there with her brood of handsome, dark-haired little boys, to breed cattle as well as children. Ella was not a great letter-writer but they exchanged about two really long epistles a year, full of news and gossip. She wondered why Dirk had bothered to tell Ella anything, even lies . . . and hastily pulled the letter out from her pocket where she had stuffed it, and began to read more carefully. She soon reached the relevant bit: ' . . . *going to come over for a whole month, from the end of December to the end of January,*' Ella had written exuberantly. *'Naturally we'll spend most of the time in Cambridge with Paul and Felix, but we would have liked at least a long weekend at the farm. How sad I should feel, my dear, to arrive there and find no little Jenny waiting to greet me!'*

So that was it! That was why Dirk had lied, because otherwise he would find himself entertaining Ella, her husband Adam and possibly even his nephews with only Bronwen to help him. Jenny hugged herself at the dizzying prospect of Ella having to support her large frame on whatever Bronwen could produce in the way of meals, Bronwen being apt to boast about her inability to boil an egg without burning it. Now, probably, Dirk thought he could get away with blaming Jenny for the break-up and casting himself in the role of a wronged husband who, naturally, would go off that particular weekend (whichever weekend Ella chose) in search of his erring wife.

Only one thing remained unexplained and that was why Ella had written to her care of Mr Croft. Dirk must have said she had gone and only Croft knew her address. Why? It did not make sense, he surely would have guessed that Ella would write to her at once and since he had lied it was in his interests to keep her and Ella apart at all costs.

At this point Jenny heard the children's voices and had to cram the letter back in her pocket and make her way to the school gate. Posy would be last, she always was, but she would also be very distressed not to see her mother waiting.

Halfway home, with Posy hanging on her hand and telling her about the joys of playing fox and geese when Marty Sumner was fox, the probable reason for Ella's addressing the letter to Mr Croft occurred to her. Dirk could scarcely say he had let her go off without knowing where or how she was going to someone like Ella, who knew him very well for one thing, knew that Jenny had no money of her own whatsoever for another and would condemn Dirk for not making sure she was financially comfortable, no matter what her transgressions. No, he had been forced to say that she had gone to a secret destination but that Mr Croft knew where she was and was providing her with a weekly sum of money. Otherwise he would probably have had Ella round his ears like an angry wasp, demanding that every detective in the country be put on her trail.

Satisfied on that score, Jenny wondered just how much of the truth she should put into her own reply to Ella and soon realized, with a good deal of dismay, that she would have to back up Dirk's lie to a certain extent. Otherwise returning, when . . . if . . when Dirk wanted her back, would be very difficult indeed. And Ella would tell the boys the true state of affairs whereas, with luck and if Dirk's infatuation were not to outlast the autumn, she might easily brush through the whole thing without ever having to let Philip and Mark see how tenuous was her hold on their father.

'. . . and when Marty catches you he growls and roars and pinches,' Posy was saying enthusiastically. 'Not nasty pinches, but nice, hard, foxish ones. I do like Marty!'

She's getting awfully like me, Jenny thought anxiously, agreeing that Marty sounded an interesting boy. I used to let Dirk growl and pinch and roar just like a fox with a goose and never saw the connection! Perhaps if I'd roared back a bit . . .

But it seemed unlikely that any behaviour on her part would ever have caused Dirk to deviate one inch from his chosen path. She had never succeeded in changing his mind or his attitude once he had made his own feelings clear, at any rate not on important matters. On less important things he had allowed himself to be cajoled or pleaded with and sometimes he had indulged her whims, even if to do so did not particularly please him.

'Shall we go on the beach, Mum?' Posy demanded presently, as they turned into Beechcroft Road. 'It's a lovely afternoon, we could take our tea.'

'A good idea,' Jenny said absently, squeezing Posy's small hand. 'Here's the key; you run on ahead and unlock the door.' She had noticed how Posy celebrated her own grown-upness now by referring to her mother as 'Mum' instead of 'Mummy'; it had happened with the boys too but, though she had expected it, it was still a little sad when it happened.

Later, lounging on the soft dry sand whilst, a little further down the beach, Posy vigorously dammed a small pool and a stream, something else occurred to Jenny; she no longer had Dirk because he was with Bronwen. Bronwen undoubtedly had the kisses and cuddles but she also had the sweaty socks, the overalls decorated with cow-dung and his damnably heavy hands and legs. Nights during which she had spent fruitless hours trying to escape from the weight of a leg thrown across hers, or when her slumber had been constantly disturbed by a huge selfish elbow in the breast or an abrupt knee in the vitals, were nights to be remembered now that they no longer occurred. Things like that made separation a little less painful. And then there were the immense meals, always served on the dot, which she had had to provide. Jenny glanced at her watch; at the farm, right now, she would have been struggling with a three-course high tea; what the boys always called, rather revoltingly, gravy and custard meals because Dirk did not consider food to be a meal unless it was presented with all its frills: gravy with the meat and custard with the pudding.

Right now Bronwen would be struggling, Jenny thought with more than a touch of spite. Here was she, lying in the sun while watching Posy paddle, and Bronwen would be cutting and slicing and roasting and keeping a wary eye on the clock for fear of being a few minutes late. Of course she could get some help from time to time from either Mrs Ted or Mrs George, but they were what Dirk called plain cooks – they could cope with meat and two veg. and a boiled pudding but they could not roast the pheasants shot by Dirk in the autumn, stuffing them first with chestnuts and parsley butter, nor would they know how to steam asparagus so that it ended up firm enough not to collapse when picked up to dip into melted butter, yet soft enough to suck clean from the stem with the minimum of effort.

Glancing at her watch, Jenny saw that it was high time she and Posy started to think about their own tea; she got to her feet and, shoes in hand, wandered over the hard sand towards her daughter, absently bending to pick up a few perfect shells as she passed them and joining Posy in the water for a moment for the pure pleasure of hot feet enjoying the tingling freshness of the little pools.

'Come on, love, teatime,' she said as Posy turned towards her. 'We really ought to be getting ourselves something to eat about now.'

'Why?' Posy said baldly. 'Why must we have food now? Why not later, when the sun's gone in?'

Why indeed; seeing her mother's surprised pause, Posy

quickly followed up her advantage. 'Why can't we just have chips from the chip shop? You said they weren't too expensive. Or we could have ices, I don't mind.'

Jenny was laughing at her when she suddenly remembered she had promised Bill she would return to the cafe to meet his daughters, so that if she were ever needed to pick them up from school they would know her. Conscience-stricken, she jumped out of the water and began to scuff her feet into her sandals.

'Posy, you've reminded me, the most awful thing! You know the girl in your class, I can't remember her last name, Dawn something? Her father has the cafe in the Botanical Gardens and I told him I'd go there after school to meet the children, so that they can come back as far as the cafe with us sometimes when he hasn't arranged for them to be met. Would you mind awfully, darling, if we rushed straight back there? And . . .', struck by inspiration, ' . . .we'll have beans on toast and a milk shake there if you like.'

'I don't mind; I like Dawn,' Posy said placidly, padding out of the water and hurrying along beside Jenny. 'Are you going to work there?'

Jenny had told the child that she was going to work but had no intention of admitting where; now she stopped on the edge of the promenade, lifted Posy up and began to put her tiny sandals on to her wet and sandy feet, not an easy task even with Posy's co-operation.

'What? Oh no, darling, I'm working at a shop in town. They sell clothes and things. There, that's the last buckle done up, so shall we hurry?'

'Do you really enjoy working there, Jen? I must say, I've never seen anyone look better or fitter after a spell of shop-work than you do!'

Sue was doing what she laughingly called her relaxation exercises in the middle of the kitchen floor and Jenny, to keep her company, was sitting on the draining board with her legs drawn up out of the way, so that Sue could flail around as much as she liked without hitting anything. The kitchen table had been dragged across the door and the chairs stood outside on the landing. Sue was reclining at the moment on her back, her bump pointing defiantly towards the ceiling, but she was not simply lying there, she was gathering all her resources for the moment when she would lift her top half from the floor, grunt, strain, and grab hold of her toes. Looking not unlike a portly rocking horse she would hold the position for a few red-faced and breathless seconds, then she would release her feet, which would fly back on to the floor with a thump, and sag comfortably supine once more.

She had just caught her toes when someone pushed against the door.

'Hang on!' Jenny called, slipping down from the draining board and skirting round Sue's teetering form. 'Just sweeping the . . .'

The door opened, undeterred by the weight of the table, and a head poked round it. A strange head. Worse, for poor Sue with her maternity skirt flopping back and her bloomered bottom much in evidence, a male head. Caught at such an inopportune moment she released her toes and fell sideways, uttering an unladylike curse as she did so.

'Oh *shit*! Why the hell did you have to open the door? Didn't you hear Jenny shout? It takes me hours to get into that position and then you come along and ruin it all!'

The head was grinning but it pulled a rueful grimace and then pushed the door wider, revealing that the intruder was a young man in his middle twenties, dark, reasonably good-looking and with nothing on but a pair of maroon pyjama trousers and dark-blue slippers.

'I'm awfully sorry, though why you should want to get into such a painful and inelegant position is beyond me. Still, if it'll help . . .' He reached down as if to grab Sue's toes and she swore again, curling them defensively beneath her, and then began to scramble to her feet.

'Leave me alone, the whole point is that I've got to do it four times without help.' However, she accepted a hand to drag her to her feet and grinned maliciously as her full weight caused the young man to stagger slightly. 'Now! Who the hell are you and what are you doing in our kitchen in a state of nudity?'

'Semi-nudity,' the young man corrected, indicating his trousers. 'I'm the ground-floor flat, Dermott Hughes.' He held out his hand and Sue, rather grudgingly, shook it.

'Hello. I'm Sue Oliver and this is Jenny Sayer. So *you're* the mystery man.' She managed to make it sound a disappointing revelation. She and Jenny had long been speculating on the identity of a mysterious figure who had been glimpsed once or twice disappearing into the ground-floor flat. 'If the old hen sees you trotting round in that state, semi or no semi, she'll . . . she'll . . .'

'Lay an egg?' Dermott winked at Jenny. 'Actually, I've only just discovered there is a kitchen, and I only discovered that because the rubber pipe to my gas ring perished and when I went down and saw Mrs Grant about it she told me I could come up here. So I thought I'd just investigate, see if anyone else was boiling eggs or making coffee . . .' He looked hopefully at Jenny and then across to Sue. 'No? Had brekker, have we?'

'Brekker!' Sue, who frequently used the expression, still managed to sound disproportionately disgusted. 'We ate *hours* ago, young man. We may be pregnant . . . well, I may be pregnant . . . but we're not decadent.'

'I'm not decadent either . . . nor pregnant,' Dermott objected. 'But I didn't get back from work until three and I start again at eight tonight, so I tend to lie in, mornings. Look, I can't stay here chatting to you for ever, would someone be a love and put the kettle on?'

Jenny, used to the wiles of young men, obediently went over to the sink and ran water into the kettle, then stood it on the stove. Dermott promptly blew her a kiss.

'None of that nonsense,' Sue said severely. 'Off with you and fetch your bread or your egg or whatever and you can have the kizzie to yourself for a bit. Jen and I have better things to do than hang around in here watching you work.'

'I thought he was rather nice,' Jenny said, when Dermott had departed and the kettle was beginning to mutter. 'Why did you keep freezing him off? After all, a fellow might be quite useful around the place.' She was thinking of the creaking board which still managed to annoy her each morning, though oddly enough she scarcely ever noticed it for the rest of the day.

'I have only one use for fellows,' Sue said loftily. She clattered two mugs off the hooks and then, with seeming

94

reluctance, added a third. 'And that use, at the moment, is null and void due to a certain protuberance, young Timmy-tummy . . .' She prodded her bump and then beamed. 'There, he's a boy of character, that one, he kicked me right back! Incidentally, it's a rhetorical question, but should one indulge in fun and games whilst staggering around preggers?'

'I think it's what you would call personal preference,' Jenny said cautiously. 'I don't think there are any hard and fast rules.' She hoped fervently that Dermott would remain in his own flat until Sue's questions on the rights and wrongs of sexual mores during pregnancy ran dry.

'Well, we discuss it at the clinic sometimes and the girls reckon that if you *do* the baby probably gets born easier, which is hard on us involuntary non-doers. But there is a small hard core who say that a prod at the wrong moment – don't wince, Jenny-wren, where have you been all your life – as I was saying, a prod at the wrong moment could cause a precipitate descent, and there's another style of thinking which believes . . .'

The kitchen door opened and Dermott came in, with a saucepan, an egg and a loaf all clutched variously about his person. Sue nodded to him and continued unabashed.

'. . . a style of thinking which believes that you could cause the baby injury. Mmm,' she nodded vigorously, a certain sparkle in her eyes giving away the fact that she was enjoying Jenny's discomforture. 'Oh yes, Jenny, I know what you think, but I suppose women have to blame a less-than-perfect specimen on the man in their lives somehow!'

Jenny was about to reply innocuously when Dermott, running water into his saucepan, intervened.

'I say, your kettle's boiling; I'm afraid I didn't bring my coffee or anything, I suppose I couldn't borrow some?'

'No' and 'Of course' came simultaneously from Sue and Jenny. Dermott looked from one to the other, one brow rising.

'I say, unanimous! Who's the soft touch?'

'Her,' Sue said crossly, jerking her thumb at Jenny. 'I don't believe she's ever shared a house with a man before, and . . .'

'You obviously have,' Dermott said silkily, looking at her

bulge. 'You should judge people by their merits, Sue, not by their sex. I happen to be perfectly competent at household tasks so don't think I'll bring my washing down or skip my turn at the saucepans.'

'I have three children, but I know what Sue means,' Jenny said, unable to stop a broad grin from spreading across her face. 'As a general rule men don't help much in the house . . .' She stopped short. A picture of Bill making sandwiches behind his counter had flashed across her mind and another picture, of Bill's nicely dressed children, reminded her not to make snap judgements or wild generalizatons.

'She's remembered one who does,' Dermott said, smiling to himself. 'Now, who takes sugar?'

He was poised over the mugs of coffee, a spoon in one hand, Sue's brown sugar jar in the other. He looked a friendly person with his appealing smile, a lock of dark hair falling across his forehead, and . . . well, there was very little else to notice, Jenny thought, eyeing his smooth brown chest and wide shoulders. Good-looking she began to think, then killed the thought, horrified at herself. At this rate she would be cradle snatching, the guy couldn't be more than twenty-five or -six, damnation, nearly ten years younger than she.

'We none of us take sugar,' Sue said, but she smiled as she picked up her mug. 'Come on, Jenny, let's take our coffee down to your flat, then Mr Wonderful here can have the kizzie to himself.'

As they made their way down the stairs, Sue turned back to speak to Jenny who was bringing up the rear.

'Don't be fooled by apparent charm, duckie; the serpent has just entered Eden. Before you know it, Brenda and Mouse will be fighting over him, you'll be darning his socks and I'll be listening to his hard luck stories.'

Mouse was the tenant of the tiny flat at the top of the house next to the Twiggs. Her real name was Melissa Haggerty and she was half-Chinese, but since she had been born and brought up in London and had never met her Chinese father, she spoke excellent cockney English, enjoyed ordinary English food and was also a good cook. She was in full-time secretarial employment and had a bevy of boyfriends attracted by her small size, her creamy gold skin and the long silky black hair which fell, rain-straight, down her fine-boned back. Both these facts, however, meant that the tenants of No. 24 saw very little of her except on a Sunday, when she would appear in the kitchen at about ten in the morning and then reappear on and off all day. Sometimes during the week she could be spotted with a towel wrapped round her wet hair, or else occasionally she would be found making tea or coffee, washing out her undies or cooking some fancy dish; but Sunday was her home day and she very rarely went out.

'Brenda and Mouse seem to do all right without adding one itinerant tenant to their list of conquests,' Jenny protested, having made sure with a glance over her shoulder that the kitchen door remained closed. 'And why can't you and I fight over him, why does it have to be Mouse and Brenda? What about Anna? She'll like him.'

'She won't. She likes fellers with a bit of money and no one who lives here can be rolling in it.' They reached their respective doors and Sue opened hers and crammed herself in through the small space. 'I'll just get changed, then I'll call for you; we can have a wander round the town and I'll come with you to work, just long enough to share a peep at the latest stock.'

'You are a devil, Sue,' Jenny said appreciatively, letting herself into her own flat. 'Just don't embarrass Brenda, there's a dear. How a girl like her ever got to be an expert on sex shops I really don't know. Not that you ever see her blush on the counter.'

'What a way to put it! I won't embarrass her, I promise, and I won't embarrass you, either. We'll eat first, shall we?'

'Right. Ten minutes, then.'

Jenny closed her door, stood her coffee down on the table, then kicked off her slippers and hooked her sandals out from under the chair. It was still warm, though October was advancing, but she refused to go to work in flat walking shoes and she did not want to have to spend her money on court shoes. It seemed such a waste, just for a couple of hours, and her sandals though elderly were high-heeled and gave her, she felt, a touch of sophistication, or certainly a touch more than her brogues would have done.

97

She always dressed up to go to work, partly because she felt better and partly because she knew she dealt with customers more efficiently and coolly if she was neat and made-up. It was odd, she mused while applying a dusting of powder to her nose and flicking mascara on her lashes, how quickly she had grown accustomed to selling. She had been at the shop three weeks now, and she no longer dreaded it when she saw a shape through the painted-out glass door. Indeed she felt pleased, because Brenda needed all her sales to keep up her commission.

Watching her face gradually change and become somehow older in the glass, Jenny grabbed a handful of her soft, slippery, difficult hair and pulled it into a tail at the back, then let it swing forward again. It made her look awful, like a skinned rabbit she thought distastefully, perhaps it had been a mistake to grow it. But though she had worn it short for years she had suddenly decided to have it longer, partly from a sort of defiance – Dirk thought long hair untidy and decadent – and partly from economy, because haircuts were expensive.

Brushing her hair out and letting it fall smoothly to her shoulders, she noticed with pleasure that it was so lightened by the sun that it had become almost pretty, a soft shade of fawn overlaid with gold, quite different from the mouse-colour Dirk had been so scornful about. Oddly enough she spent far more time out of doors here than she had ever managed on the farm. There, she had been lucky to get an hour a day out of doors because there was so much work in the house. Here, with only the flat round which to flick a duster, she could – and did – spend hours and hours on the beach or wandering round the town.

The knock on the door came just as she was picking up her cream-coloured jacket. It was a cheap garment, but it was waterproof and really quite warm enough for the present weather. She went out and found Sue arrayed in the glorious splendour of her maroon maternity dress, which Jenny always felt pleased to see – partly because Sue had been wearing it when she first met her, and partly because it was such a cheerful garment which Sue looked so pretty in that you forgot her awkward shape and strange gait and saw her as she really was.

'Right on time, as usual, Sue.' Jenny locked her door and then the two of them started down the stairs at their usual comfortable pace. No need to hurry, they had the rest of the morning in front of them and not a lot to do. Now that Jenny was working their comfortable routine had inevitably been changed and they did not see quite so much of each other, but somehow it only made their meetings more fun. Jenny had grown fond of Brenda too, and had been to the cinema with her one afternoon when Simon had come down to stock-take. Often the three of them sat around in the kitchen putting the world to rights after Jenny had taken Posy to school and before Brenda had bombed off to the shop, and Jenny enjoyed the sessions immensely. It made her realize more than ever how starved of ordinary female companonship she had been at the farm. Perhaps that was why she had welcomed Bronwen when the girl first came to take over the bookwork; perhaps that was why she had felt doubly betrayed when she found that Bronwen had become Dirk's mistress.

'Well, love? It's Thursday, so we might as well go to Marks and to the market, see what bargains we can pick up. Oh, incidentally, how is Croft's chin?'

Sue had been fascinated by the story of Jenny's brisk self-defence and frequently asked after his injuries. She had prophesied with relish that that bonk on the chin would keep him at bay for about a month and, since this time was now up, obviously waited quite eagerly to see whether he would pounce again and prove her right. But Jenny was forced to disappoint her.

'The bruise has gone and I actually went up to his room to fetch my money, because the girls in the general office were rushed off their feet, poor dears. I've grown quite fond of the spotty one now – her eye had a knowing gleam when I went in the week after I smote her boss. But anyway, Mr Croft was perfectly polite, if a trifle absent. I was probably making a fuss about nothing, the poor man's not tried anything on since, not even a hand-squeeze.'

'Well, bully for him, but don't forget what your Auntie Susan told you!' They were turning from Beechcroft Road into Brussels Road and Sue's pace quickened slightly. 'Let's have an extra coffee at the place on the corner; mine was quite spoilt by that Dermott fellow turning up in the kizzie at that particular moment. I may have appeared quite blasé and calm in the encounter which followed, but actually my mind was not on my repartee. I was too busy praying to God that my knickers were the new ones and not the ones with unsightly holes in usually unseen places.'

Jenny giggled. 'And were they?'

'My dear girl, as if I could possibly tell, from up here, with the bulge between me and . . . and mine! I'll tell you tomorrow.'

Laughing, the two girls strolled on along the sunny pavement.

CHAPTER FIVE

Exactly a week after Jenny had remarked on Mr Croft's now unblemished chin, Sue's words came true: Mr Croft pounced again.

It was, however, only partly his fault and would never have happened, Jenny told herself, had she not gone down to the beach for a paddle and a wander along the shore before taking herself off to the solicitor's office. It had been a lovely, mild, sunny day but there was a stiff breeze, and what with the breeze tugging at her hair and the little waves creaming against her toes, the time had stolen past and all of a sudden it was a quarter past twelve, she had to be in work by half past, and she had not yet visited Mr Croft.

Panicking, Jenny flew up the beach, crammed her wet feet into her sandals and then ran with all her might along the promenade, crossed over the road, dived up a side street, crossed another road and reached the office, breathless, panting and wind-blown with only ten minutes to collect her money and get back to the shop. Since she had never told Mr Croft she had actually obtained a job, furthermore, she would have to pretend that she was in a hurry for some other reason and she did not feel capable of much serious lying, not when she was so breathless, so hot and so damnably untidy!

Poking her head round the door of the general office however, it became immediately obvious that something was up. The room was milling with people, several of them in coats or jackets, with the spotty girl the centre of attention, holding out her hand, exclaiming and blushing.

'Is he in?' Jenny shouted, catching the spotty one's eye.

'Yes, love, and he's got your envelope; I'm engaged! We're just off to the boozer, would you like to come, drink my health?'

'Well, congratulations and thanks, but I'm in a desperate hurry; next week, perhaps.' Jenny backed hastily out of the room and headed for the stairs, galloping up them two at a time, and arrived on the top landing positively streaming with perspiration and panting like a steam train. She grabbed for the door handle and pushed, and even as she did so it yielded and Jenny found herself catapulted into Mr Croft's surprised embrace. He staggered but hung on to her and Jenny, starting to apologize for her abrupt entry, felt avaricious fingers tighten on her, dragging her further into the room, pressing her close to Mr Croft's navy-blue pin-striped business suit.

'My dear Mrs Sayer, now what's all this haste in aid of?' His voice was breathless with a tremble in it, yet he had run up no stairs! Jenny tried to pull away, her heart hammering, but he only held her more tightly, muttering that he was glad she had turned to him for he had longed to comfort her, to show her that Mr Dirk did not appreciate her but others did.

Jenny reacted blindly but instinctively; she kicked and struggled but it was useless because he was too close for a kick to be effective and then, when he bent his head towards her, still muttering, she bit.

Her teeth met his bony chin and she bit harder, and it acted as an immediate deterrent. A turn-off, you could say. He made a sound which might have been described in a man less pompous as a yelp and he not only let go of her but actually pushed her, his body curling away from hers as though he thought she had teeth at regular intervals from mouth to kneecaps.

Jenny allowed herself to give one more lingering chomp before she, too, stepped back. She was very angry and what made it worse was that she could see Mr Croft was equally irate. Several possible courses of action rushed into her mind. Challenge him? Rush screaming down the stairs announcing that she had been attacked? But it would make life too hideously complicated afterwards.

'Do you have my money, Mr Croft?' she said crisply. 'Sorry about that little incident. I'm afraid you must have opened the door just as I did, so I came crashing in on top of you. Would you mind hurrying – I have an appointment in ten minutes.'

'Really, Mrs Sayer, I don't think . . .', but he was unsure of himself now, his hand still covering his spade-shaped chin, massaging it, whilst above it his eyes, which had burned quite hotly with hatred, now began to look calculating once more. 'All I was trying to do, to say, was that I'm your friend and that if you need me for anything . . .'

Jenny did not say anything but she clicked her fingers, a gesture she had never expected to use to one of the dominant . . . ha ha . . . sex. She could see he disliked it but nevertheless he opened his desk drawer and then held out the familiar brown envelope.

'Yes, you're in a hurry – I ought to warn you, perhaps, that if your husband were to find out you had a job, the money he gives you could quite legally be reduced by the amount of your earnings.'

Jenny took the envelope, tucked it into her jacket pocket and then turned back towards the door. She opened it, and then in the doorway and with her retreat secured, she turned back.

'Job? Who said I had a job? And since the money he gives me has never been settled in a court of law I fail to see how you can make such statements. However, since you have, perhaps you're right and we should settle matters legally. I'll get my solicitor to contact both of you.'

'*Your* solicitor?' She had shaken him rigid, Jenny saw with satisfaction. He had never expected the worm to turn so far or so fast. 'My dear Mrs Sayer – or should I say my dear Jenny – who else should be your solicitor but myself? Have I not always looked after your affairs as well as Mr Dirk's? Was it not I who sorted things out when your father died? My sole desire is to see your marriage reinstated and I'm in the best possible position to help, being close to both parties . . .'

'You're a little too close to one party for my liking,' Jenny said grimly, relishing the ambiguity of the remark. 'I may be alone, Mr Croft, but I am not without friends and I can find myself a different solicitor whenever I wish.'

'My dear child, why make difficulties for yourself?' He smiled, trying charm as an alternative tactic, but one hand still covered his chin. Jenny was almost sure she had drawn blood, she knew she had marked him. Serve him right, the bastard! 'Besides, I am a link with Mr Dirk, I've known the family for years, and he'll talk to me in a way he would hesitate to do with a stranger.'

'If he talks to you that doesn't affect me. If I decide to take legal action I'm sure it would be better if I were to use another solicitor.'

'My dear, the last thing Mr Dirk wants . . . the last thing you want . . . is to make this parting official, surely? Let it lie for a bit, let Mr Dirk get things out of his system, and . . .'

But Jenny could wait no longer whilst Mr Croft tried to talk himself out of the quagmire he had so confidently entered. She made for the stairs, calling over her shoulder as she went, 'Sorry, I'm late already. I'll have a word with Dirk before next week.'

Jenny rushed down the stairs. Indignation had made her bristle like an offended cat but, by the time she had run all the way to the shop, nothing mattered except the pain in her side, the possibility that poor Brenda might have locked up and left, and the horrible fact that she had been forced into a lie. She did have a job. If Dirk and Mr Croft knew about it, could they really take it away from her, or cut the money off? She remembered someone once saying that a divorced woman could not earn money whilst her husband supported her. She was not divorced, but did this simply put her in an even more precarious position? Did she have any rights, situated as she was? She supposed that, as things stood, Dirk could simply refuse to pay her anything, because he would say she could go back to the farm and live in as housekeeper, whilst he and Bronwen. . . .

The shop doorway loomed. Jenny shot through it and into sanity. Brenda was not pacing the floor nor even donning her coat or glancing impatiently at her watch, she was pricing a quantity of frilly briefs and putting them on tiny hangers to display on a rail. She looked up and smiled as Jenny entered.

'Hi – want to see the latest? They're edible knickers – d'you think they'll sell? Gone are the days when a guy pulls a pair of knickers out from his pocket to blow his nose and is consumed with embarrassment – now he'll just gobble 'em up.'

'Truly? You can really eat them? I don't believe it!' Jenny went closer to examine the tiny garments. 'My God, you can! What will they think of next?'

'I could tell you but I won't.' Brenda gave Jenny a long,

considering look. 'You're all red, duckie; what happened, get held up?'

'You could say that. Actually, that swine Croft made another pass at me and then topped it up with a few threats. I told him I'd ring Dirk but I'm not too sure I want to put the cat amongst the pigeons . . . suppose Dirk responds by cutting my money? Apparently he could do it quite legally if he knew I'd got a job.'

'Balls,' Brenda said placidly, continuing to write price labels. 'It's those passes you want to put an end to, so ring your old man and tell him to go and punch his solicitor's head. Don't worry about the money – if I'm asked I'll say you take your wages in kind and not in cash.'

Jenny giggled, went behind the counter and into the back room to hang up her jacket and park her handbag in a safe spot. When she returned she brought Brenda's light-weight anorak with her.

'Here, you go off now, I'll finish the pricing if you'll tell me what to charge. I don't want Dirk punching Croft – in fact I've marked him pretty obviously myself. No, what I'd like is for Dirk to pay me direct so I don't have to go within pinching distance of the chap.'

'Oh. Well, use the phone here, it's more private than the one at Beechcroft Road with the old hen always on the listen.' Brenda rose to her feet and took her coat. 'Just the one price, for once, the same as I've got on all the tickets I've done so far.' She slung the coat over her shoulder. 'Is it nice out?'

'Yes, lovely. See you later, then.'

Brenda shut the door behind her and Jenny picked up the nearest pair of frilly knickers, glanced at the price and then began to copy the sum on to another ticket. Presently, when she had finished doing these, she really would ring Dirk.

In fact, it was one of those hours; a continuous stream of people, not necessarily buying but browsing, so that Jenny's chance of getting near the telephone was slim. Every time the room emptied she summoned up her courage and headed for the pay-phone on the wall just as another customer would come through the door. So when she finished work she decided to walk to the call-box outside the Botanical Gardens.

She could make her call, pop into the cafe and tell Bill she would fetch the girls, and then she could go up to the school. The weather was still warm and sunny though the breeze had increased and could now justifiably be called a wind, and Jenny was feeling assured and self-confident right up to the moment of dialling the familiar number.

When the ringing started she had a sudden urge to put the receiver down, but she fought against it and was still fighting when someone answered.

'Two-six-two-four-two-oh, Sayers Farm.'

It was Bronwen, which Jenny might have expected but somehow had not. Jenny opened and shut her mouth twice but found her voice totally absent, so she swallowed hard, breathed deeply, and then put the receiver down.

She might have renegued had there been anyone else waiting but as it was she had no excuse. The box had no queue of would-be users, the road itself was almost deserted and reason told her she was unlikely to get such a good chance again. She glanced at her watch and was once more certain that Dirk would be in the farm office. She would ring back at once and ask to speak to Dirk immediately. She did not need to bandy even a 'hello' with Bronwen.

Her first call must have rattled Bronwen because the telephone was answered at once, and by Dirk at his most businesslike.

'Two-six-two-four-two-oh . . . hello yes?' He gabbled it off, barking out the last two words and Jenny nearly fouled everything up by not speaking again, though this time because of the lump in her throat. The number of times she had heard him saying that into the receiver and had smiled to herself when the caller had been someone he wanted to impress . . . how his voice altered, how his frown disappeared! In her mind's eye the picture was so clear, the way he sat on the corner of the desk to answer the telephone, the trick he had of running his hand through his hair whilst he talked so that it stood up in tufts. Even the looks which crossed his face were clear in her mind – absorbed or absent, depending on the caller. A pretty woman got the absorbed look and he behaved as though the telephone had a secret camera, laughing to show his teeth, pulling a surprised face, a shocked or a teasing face, whatever was called for by the conversation. A salesman got the baleful look, another farmer the absent one. Absent because he was seeing not the office but whatever farming problem was being discussed. It occurred to Jenny now that the only telephone face of Dirk's that she did not know, could not imagine, was the face he wore when it was she on the other end of the line. He would not bother with the charm, the gleam of white teeth, the slow, deep laugh. It would be shutters down, eyes cold, frown very much in evidence, she thought.

'Yes? Who's that?'

His voice was impatient but there was something more. Was he worried? But she shrugged the thought aside since conjecture was pointless. Force yourself to speak or he'll put the phone down and you'll lose another ten pence piece, she told herself fiercely.

'Dirk? It's Jenny.'

A pause. Impossible, now, not to see in her mind how he would swing round, mouth her name to Bronwen and swing back to face the window.

'Oh. Did you ring earlier?'

Tempting to pretend she had not, but pointless. Lying for no reason never helped anyone.

'Yes.'

'Why didn't . . .' He cut himself short, obviously realizing that the answer to the question could scarcely please him. 'What do you want?'

A thousand answers flashed into Jenny's mind. My home. My husband. My life. Pictures danced. Their bedroom with its wonderful view right down the valley, the walnut branches which tapped on the right of the square bay window, the vanitory unit she had been so proud of, the big, old-fashioned walk-in wardrobes. And the kitchen, where so much of the life of a farm is lived, with Belle under the big table and Posy curled up, thumb in mouth, against the dog's black and white side. Daddy's cup, so called because the Sayer father had always had it; Dirk had used that cup every day of their married life, even after an antique dealer had told them that it must be over two hundred years old and extremely valuable. Her own cup, with its gold rim, its wide shallow bowl, its design of primroses and white violets. Who used it now? Did Bronwen drink from it, or had she sensed its personal nature and thrown it away?

'Hello? Did you hear me?'

She heard the strain in his voice and suddenly she could have wept for him. She had not meant to frighten or worry, she had simply wanted to speak to him. But he cared nothing for her, so why should she care about him? And what a thing to say to the woman you had loved, or pretended to love, for so long! What do you want!

'Yes, I heard you. I want you to send my money through the post, please.'

It was a simple enough request and the answer was simple too.

'No. Nothing doing. It must go through Croft.'

'Why?'

She could *hear* him shrug, see it, and the impatient expression which would flit across his face because she had queried his decision. Dirk hated explanations.

'Legal reasons. Anything else?'

She could feel herself beginning to tremble, the hand holding the receiver suddenly slipping as she began to perspire. It had been the same throughout their married life. Whenever she found herself in a confrontation situation with Dirk he always managed to put her in the wrong, make her seem foolish, unreasonable, even when she was sure she was being sensible. But now . . . now he had no right to make flat statements and take her acquiescence for granted. She did *not* acquiesce. She had a good reason for her request and he would have to do better than a blanket refusal without explanation to get her off his back.

'What legal reasons?'

There was an astonished pause before he spoke again and when he did there was frank curiosity in his voice.

'What does it matter, they're only legal reasons, after all. Why shouldn't you get it from Croft?'

'Because he made a pass at me this morning,' Jenny said, keeping her voice steady with an effort. 'And I don't want to endure any more hand-to-hand encounters with him. It would be easier if you could post the money.'

'Croft made a pass at *you*?' The sneer would bring his mouth up on one side, pull it down at the other; she had seen that particular expression too often for comfort. 'Oh come along, don't give me that, he's a cold fish is Rupert.'

'I can't help the way he treats *you*, Dirk, – in fact I'd be very surprised if he'd made a pass at you.' She had never stood up to him before nor answered him back quite so bleakly, and found herself suddenly glad of the twenty or so miles of telephone wire between them. 'If you doubt my word go and see him and ask him to explain the marks on his chin.'

'His chin?' Dirk actually laughed. 'Good God, woman, what did you do? Hang one on him?'

That annoyed her; it was Bronwen talking, not a man in his late forties.

'Something like that. But it will make things difficult, d'you see?'

There was another pause, then Dirk said, 'Mmmm . . .' on a thoughtful note. She could smile again now, sure that the unpleasantness was over. He knew she would not lie, he was going to think up a solution to her problem, he would not want her to suffer more meetings with Croft.

'Tell you what, why don't you go into the general office and fetch it from there? Do you sign for it? No? Well then, why not?'

'That would be fine,' Jenny said, trying not to sound too grateful. 'Only you'll have to make sure he sticks to it, Dirk. So far he prefers that I go up to his office and he delivers it in person.'

'I'll have a word,' Dirk said, suddenly sounding brisk and businesslike. 'Another time, old girl, don't lead him on.'

She opened her mouth to protest but he put the receiver down, crashing it on to its rest. Jenny put her own down as well. It was slippery with sweat and she was glad to get out of the stale warmth of the box and into the freshness of the afternoon. Oddly, she felt quite proud that he had put the telephone down on her; it just showed that he had no faith whatsoever in his own ability to come off best. The old Dirk would have scorned to sink so low, to use a device both bloody rude and extremely childish, but presumably he had changed as much as she.

Despite her triumph, however, halfway to the cafe she found that she was still shaking and stood in pretended admiration before a bed of dahlias whilst she recovered. It had been an effort to ring Dirk and a greater one to ask what had amounted to a favour from him. It was strange to realize that hearing his voice had not been a thrill, quite the opposite in fact; had his attraction worn so thin? But she knew it was not that. The Jenny who was painfully emerging from the shell of Dirk's semi-protective, semi-bullying love was a stronger, surer person than the crushed and diffident woman who had been sent down to Rhyl in order that Dirk might openly acknowledge his mistress. She was beginning to realize, she told herself ruefully as she walked up to the cafe, that Dirk's feet of clay extended jolly nearly to waist level!

The cafe was fairly busy with eight tables filled, all with the elderly or frankly old, but Jenny could see that this was the tail end of the business rather than the main part itself, and that most of these folk had enjoyed a late lunch and were lingering over their tea or coffee. She walked over to the counter and Bill looked up, his face lighting up as he recognized her. He was slicing fruit loaf, buttering it and arranging it on a plate, and it occurred to Jenny that she had never seen him idle, unless you counted the ten minutes or so in the morning when he had joined her to eat his bit of toast and drink his coffee.

'Hello! Going to have a cup of tea and try my bara brith?'

'I'd love a cup of tea,' Jenny said. 'But that isn't bara brith, you barbarian, that's fruit loaf.'

'Well, the visitors like the Welshy name,' Bill said, unperturbed. 'The trouble is if you buy genuine bara brith it's expensive and it's crammed with dried fruit. Now my customers prefer something less rich, and bara brith is only Welsh for fruit bread, so what's the odds?'

'None, I suppose.' Jenny glanced at the customers; there was not a person present under sixty and mostly they were older. 'You do attract a fairly geriatric clientele, don't you,' she observed, lowering her voice discreetly, though given the loudness of the customers' voices and the gleam of their hearing aids it was probably a needless gesture.

'Only first thing in a morning and around now. I have a

110

thriving lunch-time trade from the offices and factories as you'd know if you came in sometimes. I've tried to lure you in with my cottage pie and lemon-sponge pudding, but it doesn't seem to appeal.'

'Yuck! But I'm at work then, you know I am. Why do the old people come in early and then again now?'

'They've got time to kill, I suppose, and then they're mostly bowls fanatics, so they have a game and then pop in here for tea or coffee. Later, on a sunny day, I get a lot of mums and their youngsters coming in for ices and cups of tea, when they've got themselves all hot and bothered on the swings. And after that I do quite a roaring trade in spaghetti on toast, hot Cornish pasties, baked beans and sausages. That's younger people, in their twenties, coming out of the factories and wanting a bite to eat before they go to the flicks. Or at least, I suppose it is.'

Whilst he talked he made her a small pot of tea with a couple of fat, expensive-looking tea-bags. Now he set it on a round tray already complete with a cup and saucer, sugar lumps in a tiny bowl and a small, dented jug of hot water. He raised his brows at her.

'Milk or lemon? Sure I can't tempt you to some bara brith? It's the best butter, as someone said to someone else in a literary way.'

'It was the March Hare,' Jenny said absently, pushing coins across the counter and picking up the tray. She turned to an empty table, glad to realize that the small encounter had turned her shakes into the memory of a shiver only and that the hands holding the tray were as steady as she could reasonably expect. She set the tray down, took her chair, then glanced back at Bill. He was arranging his slices of buttered fruit loaf in a pattern on a plate which he then put into the display case, to one side of his iced cakes. Having done that he glanced round the room, apparently satisfied himself that all his customers were happy, and then came over to Jenny's table. He hooked a chair out with one foot and sat down on it, astride, resting his arms on the upper rung of the seat-back.

'You all right? You looked a bit fraught when you came in.'

Jenny poured her tea sedately, then picked up the cup. Her hand, she noticed dispassionately, was still not perfectly steady but she sipped the tea and then stood the cup back on its saucer with only the tiniest rattle.

'I was a bit fraught. I'd just spoken to my husband on the phone for the first time since I moved out.'

'Oh?' He pulled a face. 'Not money trouble, I hope.'

'In a way.' It occurred to her that Bill, also separated, might be able to tell her a bit more about the legal position than Dirk had done. 'My husband pays me a sum of money each week through our family solicitor – that's to say his family solicitor. Only when I needed legal help, the chap Dirk uses – Rupert Croft – also acted for me. The problem is I don't like Mr Croft and I wanted to have the money sent by post, but Dirk said I couldn't because of legal difficulties. What does that mean, do you suppose? And why can't I get myself a solicitor? Mr Croft said I might get myself into trouble if I tried.'

Bill gave a derisive snort. 'Sounds just like a solicitor! You get yourself someone else, love, there's nothing to prevent you doing so and, what's more, if you're going to get divorced it's accepted that you'll be represented by different people. Once you've got a new solicitor then your husband can send the money straight to your chap, see?'

'Well, but suppose Dirk decides not to pay? Or stops paying the rent for the flat? He doesn't like being crossed you see, and I don't want to put him against me more than he already is. When he realizes he's made a mistake . . . if he does, I mean . . . then I don't want him to feel it's impossible to say so.'

'I don't see why he should object to you changing your solicitor, though,' Bill said after a moment's thought. 'What was his reaction when you suggested it? I take it that was why you phoned.'

'Well, no, I didn't mention changing, I just said I'd rather have my money through the post and he said no, legal difficulties.'

'Ah, I see. Well, he was probably just protecting himself. You see, if you denied ever having received the money it might be difficult for him to prove that he'd sent it, though I suppose he could send you a cheque.'

'As if I would! But I get the point. Then how do I go about

112

changing my solicitor? Do I have to write to the law society or something?'

He laughed, but just then the door swung open and a family group entered, talking loudly amongst themselves and wheeling a pushchair complete with fat rosy-cheeked baby. Bill got up and stood by Jenny's chair for a moment, still talking, whilst the family arranged themselves before the counter.

'You just walk into a solicitor's office in town and tell him what's happened. I don't suppose you're even the other chap's client, really – your husband's his concern. See you tomorrow?'

'Yes, of course. Shall I fetch the girls for you?'

'If you would.'

He went behind the counter and Jenny heard his pleasant voice, with its comforting homely Northern accent, beginning to extol his bara brith. She sat where she was until the teapot was empty; it made three respectable cups, if you didn't mind the last one a bit weak. Then she got up and made for the door. As she opened it Bill called, 'Goodbye, thank you,' and she replied, laughing, 'Thank *you*,' as she made her way out.

'Poached eggs on toast twice – right, got that.'

It had been a quiet afternoon and these were the first of Bill's early-evening customers. 'Tea for both? Right you are, shan't be a tick.'

He left his customers and went into the kitchen to fetch the eggs from the fridge. They were two teenagers, probably High School pupils by the look of them, bound for a night out, both a bit giggly, the boy's voice hoarse as a crow's because it had obviously just broken, the girl with hot eager eyes and pimples on her chin. Bill put the toast under the grill, broke four eggs into the poacher and pulled it over the heat. That done, he had only to keep his eye on things and could let his mind wander where it wished which, right now, was to Jenny. She was improving every day, getting less tense, more relaxed and easy with him. He liked her more than he had ever expected to like a woman again, and admitted that it was more than mere liking. When he fell

113

into bed at night, images of Jenny found their way into his dreams; he saw himself touching her baby-soft fawn-and-gold hair, or cupping her thin, little-girl elbow to help her cross some imagined road. They were innocuous enough dreams but a great improvement on the arid desert his mind had been before, containing only worries about what he should do if the cafe failed or the children, in some strange way, grew beyond his capabilities. He loved Rhyl, the town, the beach, the gardens; it had only needed someone like Jenny to come along to make his life rounded and complete.

He knew she liked him and was at ease with him, even though he realized that this was just because he was such a dull, ugly blighter, so she knew he was no threat, she only thought of him as a fellow parent. This had satisfied him at first but now he kept thinking that if she liked him, surely with nurturing, her feelings might ripen into something warmer. He was beginning, nervously, to imagine his next move, to plan what he would say, how he would behave.

The trouble was, he was scared of placing his bet and losing everything. Suppose he asked her out and she turned him down and stopped coming into the cafe? His heart sank at the thought. Perhaps he was a fool to think of saying anything; he knew she was right out of his class so why not leave well alone, be content with her casual friendship? But nothing venture, nothing gain. Perhaps he could arrange it so that he could leave himself an escape route? He would work on it.

Bill buttered the toast, then took the eggs out of the poacher and carried the tea tray over to his young customers. They were talking, heads close over the table; one of the boy's damp red hands was over the girl's smaller inky paw. Bill's heart lurched. To take Jenny's hand, to feel her cool, firm fingers on his! It would be worth a bit of risk, wouldn't it? He could make it sound casual, could just shrug it off if she refused.

He balanced the tray on the edge of the table and began to unload. He would ask her to go to the cinema with him and then, if she did not at once accept, he would pretend he had been including Posy as well and had planned to go as a family group. Satisfied that this would be the answer, he smiled down at his unattractive but starry-eyed customers.

'Poached eggs on toast twice and a pot of tea for two; there you go!'

Sue lay on her back on the creaky, sagging bed in her room, fingertips on ribs, eyes on the ceiling, practising her breathing.

Once, she would have laughed scornfully at the thought of anyone practising something they did automatically, even in their sleep, but not any more; now she knew that how you breathed made a difference to the pain, and she wanted to breathe the right way and not the wrong way, and to have as little pain as possible. After all, she reasoned, if she was not to enjoy the pleasure of this baby, then why should she have the pain? So she drew in her breath deeply and conscientiously, trying to fill her stomach and not just her lungs, telling herself to relax, to breathe slowly, and to clear her mind of all worrying thoughts.

The trouble was, the thought that worried her most was actually having the baby, and when you were practising having it, as she now was, it was virtually impossible not to think about the pain. They did their best in the relaxation classes to put the girls at their ease, deny that birth was painful, but for Sue at any rate it simply did not work. Because she was older than most of the other expectant mums, Sue, with a vague feeling of *noblesse oblige*, put a good face on her terror and always used her jolliest and most bracing tone when discussing the birth, but there were times, like right now, when the good face and everything else just fell away and plain fear stared her in the eye.

If only, oh if only she could have known she had Hugo's support, she was sure she would feel very different. She would not be afraid because if he was not afraid of the north face of the Eiger, the slopes of Everest, the terrible drops and the arm-cracking climbs, then how could she fear a little thing like childbirth? Oh, why should I fear being split in two, she asked herself sarcastically now, pulling up her knees, setting them wide apart as they had been told to do in class, and reaching down to grab her ankles, rocking backwards and forwards in this position for a count of ten.

She also had nightmares about Hugo's home-coming,

which was a cruel quirk of fate. Recently, it had started to occur to her, at any rate subconsciously, that Hugo might be able to tell at one glance she had given birth to a child. In her dreams he reproached her and then left her for ever; she knew it was for ever, even if he never actually said so in the dream, and she always woke with tear-wet cheeks and the pain of loss in her heart.

The other mums in her relaxation class were all buoyed up by the fact that their husbands or boyfriends would be present at the birth. Sue had fed them some story about a husband filming wildlife in darkest Africa but hoping to get back for the birth; they thought it marvellously romantic and told her what a wonderful gift it would be for him, should she have the baby before his return. Sue, smiling and agreeing, was glad that they would never know the truth – what a fearful coward she was, how she was sure she would scream the hospital down and disgrace womanhood by her behaviour. She wondered now whether it was possible to gulp down so much gas and air as to render oneself unconscious but concluded, miserably, that some interfering midwife would probably be present to snatch the supportive mask from one's grasp at the first sign of crossing eyes and lolling head. She had also thought of demanding painkillers by the score, but imagined that these too would have the desired (by her) and undesired (by them) effect of knocking her out cold, and so be forbidden.

Another thought which had come to haunt her was that she might die and in doing so betray her situation to Hugo, who would be totally crushed both by losing her and by finding out what she had done. He would believe that she had wanted the baby, had cheated on him and had then left him. He would think that she had found herself pregnant and been delighted; if she had not wanted the child, he would reason, she could have had an abortion.

Now, lying hugely supine and feeling her stomach stirring with the baby's movements, Sue could only marvel at her own stupidity. Why had she not had an abortion? At the time, with Hugo making his preparations to leave, exuberant, loving, an abortion had seemed a terribly foolish risk. Suppose she went off for a few days and he discovered what

116

she had been doing? It was odd how he could feel the way he did, but she was sure he would have considered an abortion just another name for murder and so would not have agreed to it. Yet she knew equally that he would not have wanted the child, which did not leave her with a lot of choice. This way, the child would have loving parents and a good life yet Hugo would not even know Sue had slipped up.

Her breathing exercises finished, Sue sat up laboriously and considered her evening. Often, she liked to walk in the dark, but she had been put off her usual solitary wanderings when a young girl had been knifed down by the Voryd harbour. Apparently there had been a quarrel one Saturday night between a crowd of young people up by the funfair, but the girl who was knifed had not been involved. She had been the bystander who sometimes gets caught up in such affairs. Sue had no desire to find herself in a similar position, so lonely wanderings had had to cease.

But there was Jenny – she never seemed to go out in the evenings, perhaps she would like a walk along the beach? They could even go into a pub and have a drink, something Sue found difficult in her present advanced state of pregnancy. It was not quite right for a pregnant woman to sit alone in a bar drinking gin, she supposed; certainly, on the one occasion when she had done so, she had been a cynosure of more eyes than she cared to remember. Even the bar's fat tabby cat had wandered over, staring curiously. Gin was mother's ruin, Sue had belatedly remembered; her second drink had been a tomato juice.

Sue waddled across her room and threw open the window; a wild, buffeting wind blew in, lifting her hair and giving her a moment of wild, unreasoning happiness. Perhaps she would survive the birth after all, perhaps she would be one of the lucky ones they kept telling the relaxation class about, who gave one push and produced 10 lb twins. But whatever happened in the future, right now she wanted to be outside in that wind with only the sky and the stars above her – the same stars that shone on Hugo, wherever he was.

Jenny waited until Posy was asleep, then slid out of bed, padded across to the door and unhooked her dressing gown from the back of it. She put it on, checked with another glance that Posy was not stirring, and went quietly out of the door and up to the kitchen, leaving the door wide open behind her and the landing light on.

One of the irritating things about living in one room was that, now Posy was so involved with school and needed to be in bed and asleep by eight, Jenny was very restricted in what she could and could not do. She could not watch television because Posy could not fall asleep as long as she could hear the set working. Even reading meant that she had to have a light on, which usually resulted in Posy asking every two minutes when the light would be going off, and as her sleep-drugged voice got more and more querulous Jenny realized she was being unfair. As a result, she had taken to going to bed when Posy did and then slipping off later to the kitchen where she sat in solitary splendour and read a book – with one eye on her flat door of course, which meant bobbing up and down to look, since the kitchen was on the half-landing above their room and by no means in line with their doorway.

At first she had let herself fall asleep whenever she could, but she soon realized that this caused her to wake up later and lie wide-eyed and resentful in the dark in the early hours of the morning, totally unable to even consider falling asleep again.

The kitchen seemed the only way out. She dared not go further than that for fear that harm should come to Posy, but oh how she dreaded the long, dark evenings when not even a book could totally absorb her. If she had had a room directly adjoining their main room she could have gone in there and read or watched television without disturbing Posy. She found she could not do anything much in the small bedroom which they did not use because its door opened straight out on to the landing, obscuring the view to the other room – and the house was open to almost anyone. Mrs Twigg did not have many friends visiting but Bernard sometimes brought fellows home and sometimes came home himself more than a little jolly. Not dreadfully drunk or anything like that, Jenny reminded herself, but merely what Dirk would have called market-peart; singing, jovial, apt to giggle and trip over

118

imagined obstacles. Brenda went out a lot but seldom brought anyone back, but the same could not be said of Anna. She brought different guys back every few nights – guys chance-met, guys from the funfair, guys from the big hotels. Though she was reticent in front of Jenny, Sue had told her that the guy from the funfair had captivated Anna for several nights with his athletic prowess.

'If they didn't have it while hanging from the light fitting it's only because the old hen doesn't buy strong enough ones,' Sue said. 'And did she tell you about the bath of cold water? I nearly died laughing.'

'Are you sure you've got that right? I thought . . . should have thought that cold water was a certain put-off,' Jenny protested, but Sue, though she laughed, shook her head.

'Ah, it depends what you do, and they made the water sizzle! Don't look so unbelieving, ask Anna.'

But that was more than Jenny was prepared to do – and the thought of one of Anna's men seeing Posy's door ajar made her shudder. A funfair feller keen on cold baths might be brought home one night; who could say the next would not be a deviant with a thing about four-year-olds? Jenny found that she spent more time listening for a step on the stair when she was sitting in the kitchen than she did reading her book.

On this particular evening she reached the kitchen, stood her bottle of milk down and put the tin of chocolate beside it, then switched on the kettle. Then she listened. Silence. Well, silence unless you counted the noise of the Twiggs' television, the sound of someone, somewhere, pedalling an exercise bicycle and the high-pitched wailing of a music centre. That would be Martin, trying in his desperate, mushroom-like way to act like a normal teenager. Shut away in some tiny, sub-terranean basement bedroom he had taken to playing a set of drums which all the tenants knew about but in which his mother steadfastly refused to believe. Martin, she insisted, was far too busy with his schoolwork to play about with drums; if they heard drums it must be from next door. One felt that, if pressed, she would blame echoes from Africa rather than admit that the mushroom could make a din.

However, there were no footsteps on the stairs and no sound of the front door opening or shutting, so Jenny sat down on the kitchen stool and tweaked out her latest second-hand paperback from her dressing gown pocket, found the right page and started to read.

Reading without interruption was another almost unknown pleasure, she reflected, as she stopped to listen. Dirk was not a reader himself and was absurdly suspicious of those who were. He honestly believed that time spent reading fiction was time completely wasted, if it wasn't otherwise filling the idle mind with subversive ideas. Reading in bed at night had been a sin: 'Am I so boring?' he had been wont to say peevishly, pushing her book aside. As for reading during the evening, she could do so if she wished against the background noise from the television set, but even so he would constantly interrupt her to point out something happening on the screen, to remind her of some household chore left undone, to comment on the weather to come, the state of the Middle East, or merely to remark that reading ruined one's eyes.

The loo had been the safest place to read so that now, sitting in the kichen, Jenny found herself vaguely embarrassed by the open door. It should have been shut and the seat she was sitting on . . .

The doorway was suddenly filled by Sue. Jenny squeaked, not only from force of habit (everyone squeaks when walked-in-on whilst using the loo) but also from genuine shock. It was too early for most of the tenants to be making their late-night drinks, too late for the evening meal-makers. But Sue, it appeared, had not come to use the kitchen in the accepted sense of the word.

'Hi there, I was about to snoop into your room – the door was wide open, did you know? – when I saw the light up here and came to investigate. The night's young, Jenny, will you come for a walk? I'm bored to tears and lonely and, though I'm constantly being told that by the time the birth is upon me I shall *want* to do the old bearing down bit, this is one of the times I'm hard to convince. Tonight I feel like telling the Almighty that I've changed my mind and I'll go back to being a virgin and forget the whole business, only something tells me He'd be hard to convince.' She smiled beguilingly at Jenny. 'Come out with me? Huh?'

'In my dressing gown?' Jenny said, just as the kettle boiled.

She leapt to grab it off the gas. 'To say nothing of Posy, sound asleep in bed,' she added over her shoulder, carrying the kettle over to her mug.

'Now come, don't say you can't go out in the evening just because you've got a child? That's ridiculous. Why can't you leave her snoring away? If she wakes up and needs a drink or a pee she can get the one and do the other without your help, can't she? She seems a sensible little thing.'

'It's not her behaviour I worry about, it's other people's. First, there's fire. If she was asleep and no one bothered to wake her . . . well, I can't even think about it. Then there's prowlers. Men have been known to attack children and you must admit we have a mixed bunch here, what with Anna's friends and all. Then there's an accident – she could get out of bed, sleepwalking perhaps, fall downstairs . . . I tell you, it just isn't possible for me to leave her.'

'Well, I'd never have thought of any of that!' Sue sank down on the other kitchen stool, eyeing Jenny with respect. 'Gawd, I'd make a lousy mother, I don't even know what I should be afraid of!'

Jenny laughed. 'I don't suppose I did, when my first was in the position yours is. And don't think I wouldn't like to go for a walk, because I'd adore it. Believe me, I lie there in the dark and wish I could sleep, or read, or do almost anything rather than just wait for morning. But responsibility for Posy comes first.'

'You lie there in the dark? What time do you go to bedkins, then?'

'When Posy does, at about eight. I wait for an hour and then sneak up here for some hot chocolate and a read, but I feel guilty even so.'

'You're mad! Why've you never told me this before?'

'Because there was no point,' Jenny said, stirring her mug of chocolate briskly. 'After all, what could you do? I did try using the little room for a bit, but it was worse than useless: the door opens outwards and, being between the two rooms, it completely blocks the view, so anyone could get at Posy without me really knowing at all. The kitchen is far better – all I've got to do is poke my head round the door and I can see our room easily.'

'What about a babysitter, then? When you go out where does the babysitter sit?'

'I don't go out, because I can't expect anyone else to hang around in the dark. Here, do you want a mug of hot chocolate?'

'Yes, I wouldn't mind. Look, this has got to stop and why you didn't tell me I can't imagine, considering that my door is directly opposite yours. You can sit in my room and read or watch telly with the door ajar and you can see exactly what your pride and joy is up to, which will be sleeping of course. And tonight, I'll go and visit Twiggywinkle and get *her* to babysit in my room for Posy. If I do that will you get dressed and come out with me?'

'It would be marvellous, if you're sure you don't mind and Mrs Twigg doesn't either.'

'Right. And in future if I'm out you can have my room all to yourself, and if I'm in, which is likelier, we can both sit there and knit or read or whatever. Is that clear? You mustn't get paranoid about Posy, Jenny love, she'll be no happier for it. Don't tell me you behaved like this at home?'

'No, of course I didn't, but then the house wasn't open to anyone, like this one is. A number of people I scarcely know have a perfect right to come up these stairs, and it makes me nervous.'

'Yes, I take the point. Now you go and sling some clothes on whilst I talk to Twiggy.'

It was the work of a moment to talk Mrs Twigg into babysitting; she came downstairs with Sue just as Jenny, dressed in slacks and sweater, was tiptoing out of Posy's room.

'Here we are, Jenny, just as easy to work down here as up there – easier this evening, since Bernard's got a friend in for a drink . . . a bevvy, they call it.' Mrs Twigg giggled and shook her grey head coquettishly. In her arms she carried a half-finished shell-box, a bag of assorted bits and pieces, and a portable radio. 'No use trying to watch telly when you're working with shells,' she said, waggling the radio. 'But a nice bit of classical music, now, and me thoughts . . . that's what I like of an evening.' She stood the radio down on Sue's table and turned to pat Jenny's arm. 'Any time you want me, dearie, I'll pop down and sit with the littl'un. No trouble. You off to stretch your legs, then? That's it, you go for walks whilst you're young, tire yourselves out, then you'll sleep like a couple of tops.'

'Thanks a million, Mrs Twigg,' Jenny said. 'I've made you some coffee and there's a packet of chocolate biscuits by the flask.'

'Well, now, you needn't have,' Mrs Twigg said, reaching for the biscuits. 'My, chocolate shorties – quite my favourites! Now don't hurry, just enjoy your walk.'

It was a marvellous night; the mild buffeting wind pushed them along to the harbour and then fought against them as they came back again, and the stars sprinkling the dark night sky seemed brighter than usual, more exciting, because this was a stolen outing. The sea surged up the beach and sighed down again, and Jenny told Sue all about Mr Croft's pass, her telephone call to Dirk and the talk with Bill about changing her solicitor.

'Bill's right, but what gets me is that you didn't realize that fellow Croft would try it on,' Sue remarked as they strode. 'Men, the conceited pigs, think women can't exist without them, so a recently separated woman is, to their way of thinking, pining to go to bed with someone.' She shook her head reprovingly at Jenny's incredulous snort. 'It's true, and your friend Croft has proved it.'

'Well, I don't see why anyone should think that. They must know you're still dreadfully hurt and depressed and unhappy, and spend all your time wanting the man who chucked you over.'

'There, you said it yourself! Wanting the man . . . that's the bit of the sentence they think about. If you can't have one particular man, then why not another? That's the way they'd see it if the situation was reversed.'

'Oh no, Sue, I'm sure . . '

'Not all men, goose, just some of the nastier ones. So anyway, if you're going to find a new solicitor – and I think you should – then choose one well-stricken in years. Or a woman, of course.'

'Crumbs. If you're sure . . .but then, if I can get my

money without being mauled, that will do for now. I mean a new solicitor will think I want a divorce, or legal things. If Dirk were to start proceedings . . .'

'Or if you were to start them,' Sue reminded her.

'Oh well, yes, if I did. But until then . . .'

'If you're happy with things as they are, then leave it. But I'll try and come with you, Monday, when you go in to collect.'

After that they talked on general subjects, bought and ate some chips, laughed a lot and thoroughly enjoyed their windy walk. When Jenny made her way to bed for the second time that night she was relaxed, pleasantly tired, even happy.

She fell asleep at once, for sleep comes easier to those who are counting their blessings. She woke only once in the night, and when she did so she woke with a pleasant glow, a vague impression of something good just out of memory's reach. A dream, perhaps? Just as she fell asleep again, she realized what it was: friendliness – Sue's, Mrs Twigg's, Bill's, Brenda's. They had all been so kind to her; people were nice when you got to know them. People were really very nice. She slept.

CHAPTER SIX

'Yes, I fink they're the best. I'll take 'em, Miss. Could you gift-wrap?'

Jenny smiled. Her customer was a large and hairy fisherman, judging by the strong odour of cod which clung to his person. He was spending a lot of money on some girl and had bought a number of glamorous garments. The last of these had been a dress and there had been some agonizing over a blue with sequins on the shoulder-tie or a pink with a froth of soft lace at the neck. He had come down in favour of the blue when Jenny had asked him what colour eyes his girlfriend had, and had pointed out, when he answered blue, that perhaps the blue dress would be a better choice.

'Yes, I'll gift-wrap them. She's a lucky girl to get so many pretty things. Is it her birthday?'

The man nodded, grinning bashfully and counting fivers onto the glass display top. Jenny hoped he was not looking beneath it; she usually tried to avoid eye-to-eye confrontation with the various contrivances under the glass and it seemed wrong that such a normal young man should be subjected to a close sight of them. However, he continued to count out his money without apparently noticing the display. Jenny concluded that he was not capable of doing two things at once and went on with her wrapping.

'There we are, twenty pence change. I hope she's pleased with them.'

The fisherman grinned again, produced a string bag from his pocket into which he loaded the prettily wrapped parcels, made for the door, his head ducked a little to one side, and disappeared from view.

Jenny sat down on her chair and picked up the sales book. She entered the sale carefully, complete with the prices of every article. She was sorry to see that Brenda frequently neglected to fill in prices when she sold something, though she had always done so by the end of the current month.

125

Sometimes the prices then entered did not tally with what Jenny had been charging, but that was Brenda's business. Provided that no one expected her to do likewise, Brenda's conscience, or memory, were her own affair.

It had been a quiet lunch-hour but she had still taken a good deal of money. She was glad, because she often took nothing, though Brenda always assured her that the browser of lunch-time quite often turned into the customer of the afternoon or evening. Even so, she did feel guilty when the till was no fatter for her presence.

She had been working here for long enough now to put up with the customers without feeling nervous, though they were an odd lot, really. A lot of men came in for presents for their girls, though Jenny did wonder what the girls said when presented with open-work brassieres, crotchless mini-briefs or edible knickers. One fairly regular Friday lunch-time buyer bought sensible things: sturdy shoes, severe dark skirts and plain white blouses. Jenny wondered why he did not get them in the town at half the price, but assumed that he was shy of the ladies' departments and preferred coming in here, where he was sure of only having to deal with Jenny, safe from the stares and giggles of teenage girls. Girls did come in from time to time, nudging each other and tittering, but they bolted if she had a customer there or if someone came in whilst they were wandering, pink-cheeked, around the shelves.

A man sliding through the door brought her mind back to her responsibilities. She smiled at him, but perfunctorily. Customers rarely met her eye for the first few moments, she had noticed. This one had been in several times before, pricing the Cindy and Julie dolls – at least he had looked at the pictures on the boxes and had then asked her for the prices. It was odd, but though the clothing was mostly priced, almost nothing else was. There was a list beneath the counter, but though Jenny consulted it religiously, Brenda looked shrewdly at the customer and then ignored the list. Anyway, on the previous occasions, Jenny had reeled off all the prices of the life-sized dolls – you could spend nearly £200 or as little as £75, if you could call £75 little. The man had grunted, looked again at the boxes, put his hands in and out of his pockets half-a-dozen times and then left. Now he was back – would he buy this time? Jenny refused to let her mind wonder what he would do with a life-sized doll; she considered, instead, how Brenda's eyes would light up if she sold an expensive model.

'Er . . . Miss?'

'Oh, I'm sorry . . . can I help you?'

'I'll 'ave 'er.' he pointed. A man of few words, evidently.

'The Julie doll?' She reached the sealed box down from the shelf. 'That's £150 please, sir.' She felt the 'sir' was justified in view of the money he was about to part with.

He fished out a big clump of notes, obviously pre-counted, and counted them out again, rather slowly but with that air of finality which meant, Jenny thought, that he had faced up to losing them some time ago and now it was merely a matter of form. There were other payers who counted out their notes as though they would personally miss every single one; *that was six trips to the cinema, six fish and chip suppers and ten rides home in a taxi,* she imagined them thinking as the money changed hands. Presumably, however, to this customer the Julie doll was worth every penny. The box described her as a superior life-sized doll and the man must agree.

Jenny slid the big cardboard box into a plain carrier bag as the last note fell on the glass, gathered up the money, and handed over the bag. She smiled at him, but he did not notice; he was staring down at his new possession with an expression she classified as downright horrible. She knew she ought to feel sorry for him, so diffident and unattractive that he needed a blown-up rubber doll for company, but she only felt disgust and guilt because she had sold him the doll and it was owning the creature which had brought that horrible look to his really very ugly face.

She reached for the book as he left, filling in the price, and was not surprised to find that her fingers trembled. However, she reminded herself sharply that she was thirty-six years old, had borne three children, and should be both broad-minded and even understanding about a bit of sexual deviation, especially if it meant the deviant would vent his feelings on blown-up dolls instead of people.

It crossed her mind that what he did to his blow-up doll

might give him ideas about doing things to people, but before she had given it much thought the door opened again and Brenda bounced in. She was carrying two large ice-cream cones, one of which she held out, dripping, towards Jenny.

'Quick, quick, I cleaned the floor this morning, grab it and start eating at once!' she ordered, frantically licking the other cone. 'I met Bernard at the pub – I was with Nigel, the chap who works at the jewellers in Crescent Road – and he bought me a gin! Had a quiet time?'

Jenny grabbed and licked; as soon as she had halted the ice-cream's tendency to drip everywhere she jerked her head towards the book.

'Three customers; one a Julie doll.'

'Smashing.' Brenda was biting off ice-cream in big mouthfuls now, so that she could wiggle out of her coat. 'That'll do wonders for our sagging economy; trade falls off after the summer, then builds up towards Christmas. Crumbs, someone's bought a lot of clothing!'

'That's right. A chap buying for his girl. A nice, normal chap.'

Brenda gasped over a particularly big mouthful of ice-cream and looked more closely at the book, then up at Jenny.

'Nice? Normal? My dear girl!'

'Well, what's wrong with buying presents? I admit she's a strapping girl but all the clothing was respectable and quite pleasant, if a bit gaudy.'

'Oh, yes? When a guy buys clothing like that, I always . . .'

'Bren, do stop it, he was a great hairy fisherman covered in cod scales and he said . . .'

'Oh, yes? That'ud be the one Simon calls Barnacle Bill.' She finished her ice, slung her coat into the back room and then came round the counter, digging Jenny in the ribs with an elbow. 'He gets them for himself, you fool! If they were really for a girl he could get them in town for half the price.'

'Well I'm damned,' Jenny said slowly. 'But what about the lads who come in for rude knickers and bras with holes in them? I don't see how . . .'

'Oh, they're buying for girls all right. It's the ones who buy sensible stuff in large sizes you want to watch out for. Well, not watch out exactly, they're harmless enough. I daresay most of 'em only put the things on in their rooms and then dream a bit. And then there are the ones who buy for their Mandy or Julie or Cindie or whatever. Some of them spend a lot of money on huge wardrobes.' She smirked at Jenny's popping eyes. 'Aye, we get all sorts, we do.'

'They buy *clothes* for plastic *dolls*?' Jenny's voice rose to a squeak. 'I don't believe it! They wouldn't fit, would they?'

'Course they would. I'm not saying the dolls would fool anyone but they've got proper arms and legs and boobs and things. Haven't you seen one inflated?'

Dumbly, Jenny shook her head.

'Well, I suppose you wouldn't have. Sometimes we inflate one for a display of some sort but for the most part they stay boxed. You should read the instructions and details sometime.'

'I will,' Jenny promised, finishing off her ice-cream. 'Not that I intend to get knowledgeable about our products, mind you! And now, if you'll pay me, I'll go and splurge on some knee-socks for Posy; this sudden change in the weather is here to stay, if you ask me, and I want to be prepared. As fast as I buy one thing we seem to need another, that's the trouble.'

'That's life,' Brenda observed, watching Jenny put on her little light-weight jacket. 'What about you, though? You must have clothes at home which would do for winter – why don't you get Dirk to make up a parcel and send them on to you? I suppose he could take them in to Mr Croft, come to that.'

'Yes, I suppose he could. He comes in once a week now, I believe. He gives Mr Croft my money and then goes shopping – it's a lot cheaper to shop here than in the village. Yes, I could ask him to bring some clothes.'

But, as she wandered out of the shop and made for the promenade, she knew she would not. It would be another door closing, another bit of her ousted from the farm and brought down here. At home the right-hand side of the big walk-in wardrobe was hers, not overfull because she had never been terribly interested in clothes, but full enough. Practical things, good stuff, thick, glossy corduroy slacks and matching tops, tweed skirts and fine wool sweaters, a few good dresses, coats, shoes, brogues. Not at all Bronwen's sort of thing, unless she was changing her image, trying to fit into some imagined picture of a farmer's wife.

The thought was an idle one but unfortunately it presently created a picture in Jenny's mind of Bronwen dressed in Jenny's greeny-blue tweed skirt and the jumper that went with it, and the smart mid-brown court shoes which she had purchased the previous spring but had never found time to wear. Bronwen was wearing a smug smile in addition to all Jenny's clothes, and she was handing a plate of scones to a select crowd of friends and neighbours in the drawing room.

A cloud of red-hot fury passed across Jenny's vision for a moment so that promenade, idlers, beach and sea disappeared. She could see Bronwen clutching more clothing in her arms, standing before the dressing-table, obviously about to put her clothes into the drawers. Another mental picture of Bronwen being thrown out of the bedroom window, closely followed by a quantity of the lilac, pink and primrose plunge-necked dresses the girl had favoured, brought a good deal of satisfaction in its train.

Her subconscious apparently satisfied, the red mist cleared and the promenade appeared once more. Jenny set out phlegmatically to walk its length, deciding as she did so that she really must find a face-saving way of obtaining a good supply of winter clothing from home. Posy would have needed new things anyway, so quickly did she grow, but Jenny's clothes were the type that lasted for years. It would be ridiculous to spend money on herself when she needed every penny for Posy and for food, and when her wardrobe at home was stuffed with winter gear.

There was a telephone kiosk ahead; why didn't she just give Dirk a ring, ask him to bring the stuff down to her? Or speak to Mrs Ted or Mrs George, ask them to parcel it up and send it off? But that would never do; Bronwen might accuse them of theft, or Dirk might take exception to such an action. She refused to consider asking Dirk because it would widen the gap between them. How about ringing Bronwen, then? She could ask her to parcel up some of the stuff in the wardrobe . . . Bronwen would do it without a word to Dirk, she was sure.

But that would not work either, because once all her clothing was out of the way, the wardrobe would be more Bronwen's than hers, she would be out of sight as well as out of mind. However, an idea, hazy but hopeful, was beginning to form. Although she did not have as many clothes as some, the wardrobe was still fairly full. She could remove most of her favourite things and no one would even notice. There were times when Dirk left the farm, probably taking Bronwen with him; all she had to do was to find out when they would be away, go quietly to the farm and take what was, after all, hers.

It was a long way off, though. The nearest bus route went to the village, the farm was two miles further on. Two miles was no distance unburdened, but coming back, laden with shoes and skirts and things . . .

She had never learned to drive and anyway she had no car, but she could, presumably, hire a taxi. The back door of the farm was never locked, but in any case she had a key.

By the time she reached the flat the dilemma was still unsolved, but the problem seemed less urgent due to the fact that the sun had come out and was shining, warm but watery, on the town. She could manage with what she had for a while yet. Going up the stairs, she decided to put all thoughts of a winter burglary out of her mind until conditions justified it. In the meantime, she wanted to peel the potatoes for supper and count the money in her purse. Today was Friday, which meant that she would be taking Erica and Dawn back to their father and that she and Posy would pop in for half an hour. She would buy everyone ices because it was her payday, and then Bill would buy everyone tea and biscuits to celebrate, he would say, the coming weekend. After that the three little girls would play on the swings and roundabouts whilst she and Bill, in the kitchen, washed and wiped up and watched the children through the small back window which overlooked the playground.

She called for all three children most days, now. Bill's neighbour was very helpful but it was easier for Bill, who was rushed off his feet these days, if his daughters came straight to the cafe.

'We'll hold Louisa in reserve for the times when we want all three kids picked up and brought here,' he had said the other day. 'You wait, one day you'll have a dentist's appointment, and it'll be the day I have a coach-party booked in for tea. Then we'll be glad of Louisa, and she'll have the kids all the more willingly because we haven't overstrained her good nature.'

He had said 'we', and Jenny was glad that he could do so. They were good friends despite their very different backgrounds. He had done lots of things – her guess about the navy had been right – and his last job had been driving huge long-distance continental lorries all over Europe. He told her he had given it up not only because he realized Daphne was being unfaithful to him but also because she neglected the children when he was out of the way and unable to check up on her. In fact, he had taken on the cafe in a last-ditch attempt to save their marriage.

It had not worked. When Daphne had realized that he really expected her to be faithful and to stay with the children she had been at first sulky and then wildly accusatory and bitter. That, and the sudden change in their financial circumstances, had driven her to go off, sometimes for days at a time, to return without explanation until the day when she had calmly announced that she was going for good.

'Was there a scene?' Jenny asked, fascinated by thus seeing her own situation in reverse. 'Did you beg her to stay?'

'No, we were both extremely civilized, which I suspect showed plainer than anything else that it was for the best,' Bill told her. He was washing up and he suspended operations for a moment to gaze down at the bubbly water, slowly swishing a plate up and down in the soapy foam as he did so. 'She said she was going for good and I said, right, I'd take care of the kids, and she said she'd come back now and then to see everything was going all right, and then she picked up her suitcase and went. Not a tear was shed by either of us.'

'What about the kids?' Jenny lowered her voice, not that she needed to do so since the three of them, clearly visible, were descending the long slide in a tangle of legs and knickers. 'Were they upset?'

'No. She left one evening and it was a good fortnight before Ricky realized she'd been gone an unusually long time and asked if she was coming back. I said no, and she just nodded and wandered off. Kids are unbelievable, but of course Daph had gone off before for longish periods.'

'I see. Did she divorce you?'

'No. Not that I know of, anyway.'

'Why don't you divorce her, then?'

'I don't know her address and anyway, what's the point?' He turned from the sink to grin ruefully at her. 'I'm not exactly fighting off the women, you know. Two kids, a third-rate caff, and me. Not much of a catch.'

'Well, what about her? If you aren't divorced . . .'

'It won't worry her.'

Jenny took up the remaining handful of cutlery left to dry and began to polish it as Bill moved from the sink and started to replace the plates and cups back on the dresser. How odd it was that a woman could just leave the father of her children without a thought. Bill was moving quietly about the room, whistling under his breath, but there was a tenseness about his shoulders which made her wonder if it had hurt him more than he either acknowledged or recognized. Yet if he had loved Daphne, if there was any residue of that love left, surely he would not have been prepared to discuss their parting so matter of factly?

'Would she marry again bigamously, then? Is that what you meant? Is she pretty?'

Bill shrugged. He was sliding plates on to the racks, each one just touching the next. He spoke without turning his head.

'Very pretty, very charming. The exact opposite of me, in fact. It's fairly clear that I shan't remarry.'

'You don't need looks or charm to attract women,' Jenny said severely, brandishing her checked tea-towel at him as he turned away from the dresser. 'Look at Bogart, or those awful scarecrows on the telly with painted faces and wild hair that girls swoon over these days. What have they got that you don't have more of?'

'Money?'

'Well, yes, but it really isn't that . . . money isn't important to most women. It's something else, I'm not sure exactly what, perhaps it's as simple as leanability or as complex as . . .'

'As simple as *what*?'

'Leanability,' Jenny giggled. 'You know, someone to lean on.'

'Ah. And you think I have it?'

'Let's not get personal.' But she examined him carefully, a

smile hovering. He was not good-looking, he was right there; his nose had been broken twice and looked it, he had a chipped tooth, his eyes were green and fringed with lamentably light lashes and his hair was really ginger. Freckles and a rather too-heavy waistline probably did not add to his charm . . . yet Jenny was sure that women would want Bill. 'Well, Daphne married you, didn't she?'

'Well, yes. But . . . yes.'

'Stop being a gentleman; pregnant, was she?'

'That's it.'

'Well, you did the decent thing and so did she. Erica will be grateful one of these days,' Jenny said, stacking dinner plates.

'Erica? It was Dawn, actually.'

'*Dawn*? But . . . how stupid of me, I assumed they were both yours since Daphne left them with you. So Erica's your stepdaughter?'

'That's it.'

'Gosh! Who was her father, then?'

'I daresay even Daph didn't know that, though she covered up pretty well. She had long enough to think of a good story, but during our short courtship and married life she told me at least six different tales and afterwards I found that my six stories were nothing like the ones she told to other people. I figured in several myself and I didn't even meet Daphne until five years ago.'

'And Dawn's four. Did you . . . was she . . . had she . . .'

'Don't stutter, I told you she was pregnant when we married. She told me it was my child and I fell for it. That's all there is to it.'

Jenny, sorting cutlery into the drawer, turned and frowned at Bill.

'You aren't trying to say you've any doubts about Dawn's paternity? She's the image of you, quite apart from that bright red hair.'

'Oh, I'm convinced, but I don't think Daphne was. She must have given a great sigh of relief when Dawn arrived. I was an easy touch, I believed everything she told me until Dawn was about a year . . .' He shrugged and returned to the sink, getting out the bleach and beginning to clean. 'Oh, it's a common story and it's over thank God, so let's forget it. And we'll stop trying to convince each other that I've got any manly charms, too.'

'You've got leanability,' Jenny began, just as the back door flew open to admit three flushed little girls. 'Gosh, you three *do* look warm!'

The discussion had ended there but Jenny's thoughts on the matter had not. He was a nice bloke, Bill, struggling to bring up two little girls, only one of which was actually his. He was likeable, friendly and reliable. We're two parents trying to bring up our children, not a man and a woman, she told herself. Right now, a friend was what she needed, not a man who might make a pass or might need her to build up his ego. She knew herself to be too emotionally bruised to want anything other than friendship. Time might heal her wounds but she still could not imagine wanting any man other than Dirk. And I don't want him much, not in that way, she said to herself, surprised. At first she had yearned for his touch; now this no longer applied. She would not want to start up all that bed-behaviour again, which could equally well have been called bad-behaviour since it was all geared for Dirk's satisfaction with only a very absent-minded sideswipe at hers. It was odd really, because when they had been living together his demands had always seemed perfectly fair and justified. To be content with sexuality and not to expect sensuality, to settle for nothing more than the violent clash of body on body, was not really a perfect marriage as she had once believed. It was very weird when you thought that three months of separation had taught her more about marriage than nearly twenty years of married life, but she saw that it was true. It had something to do with distancing oneself from a problem or a situation, she supposed. Taking a longer view. Being detached. If she and Dirk were to make things up tomorrow and she were to move back to the farm, she would be unable to sink back meekly and uncritically into her former self.

She found she had been staring at the peeled potatoes for ten minutes or so, not moving, simply letting these new and rather disturbing thoughts wash around in her brain. I'm a different person, she thought wonderingly, as she took the potatoes out of the dirty water and began to cut them into pan-sized pieces. No, better than that, I'm more of a person. When . . . if . . . Dirk gets me back he's going to get quite a surprise as well!

'Well, I've got a complaint, like.'

It was an intelligent-looking, dark-haired young man wearing what Jenny's first startled glance had taken to be a clerical collar but later identified as a white tee-shirt with a black sweater over it. A third glance was enough to confirm that it was the man to whom she had sold one of the cheaper dolls a mere three days before; a Cindy, so far as she could remember. Now she tried to put a look of interest and sympathy on her face, though it was not easy. How did one complain about a Cindy-doll? Did it not show enough interest in his hobbies? Did it not mutter love-words into his ear whilst he was doing . . . whatever he did . . . to it? He had seemed an unlikely buyer for the doll when he had bought it, Jenny remembered; now he was complaining, probably with cause. She tried to tug sympathy down over her reluctant distaste.

'Yes, sir? I'm sorry if the goods weren't quite . . .'

Her voice tailed away. Because Brenda had insisted, on the very day she had sold this young man his doll she had blown up and regarded one of the Julie dolls. Or rather, Brenda had blown it up and Jenny had been forced to stare into its open-mouthed, pop-eyed, soundlessly-shrieking rubber visage. She had been shocked by the anatomical completeness of the thing and, when she told Brenda so, had been even more shocked by Brenda's response.

'Well, of course they've got to have all their bits and pieces,' Brenda said impatiently. 'How else can the customers be perverted with 'em?'

It was a fair enough point, Jenny had supposed, for no matter how much one tried to tell oneself that the dolls were only company, a dog or a cat, or even a goldfish, would have been more responsive. But she hated the doll, which Brenda had made even worse by over-inflating so that the creature's gigantic boobs had bulged like organ stops, making Jenny fear a two hundred quid explosion any minute.

Now the man was leaning on the counter, his eyes

flickering round the shop in the way eyes will when their owner is embarrassed by what he is about to say. Well, he can't be more embarrassed than I will be to hear it, Jenny thought, straightening her shoulders and preparing to be positively overcome with humiliation. Damn the thing! Why couldn't it have done its duty, just for my sake?

'It lets me down. She does . . . my Cindy does,' the man said in an aggrieved tone.

'I don't think . . .' Jenny began uncertainly. Was he *really* going to complain that Cindy didn't nibble his ear at the psychological moment . . . or that she couldn't make a decent fry of chips to save her life? But the customer, having started, was not to be easily stopped.

'Yes, she's let me down four or five times,' he said with increasing relish. 'I call it shocking – well, I was shocked, I admit it. All that money and she lets me down . . . a shocking crack I took, the first time, before I was prepared, like.'

'I don't think . . .' Jenny began, and was again silenced.

'She's got . . .' The man stopped and sucked his teeth, looking rather red and self-conscious. 'I daresay you don't know, being just as how you work here, but she' got . . . well, a hole.'

Jenny, having only three days before made the same shocking discovery – though she would not have put it in quite those words – felt her face begin to burn. Poor man, he had obviously been as shocked as she, but at least this was one problem she could understand and sympathize with. He must genuinely have bought Cindy for companionship, perhaps for the odd cuddle, and been as shattered as she to find all those . . . those unnecessary anatomical details.

'I'm awfully sorry but I'm afraid . . . well, they're all the same, they've all got . . . hmmm hmmm . . . the same.'

'The same?' Indignation brought his voice up to eight decibels but he sank it quickly as the door opened and another customer sidled in. 'The same?' he repeated on a lower note. 'Well, love, there's going to be complaints, I can tell you; it isn't all of us what'll take that sort of thing lying down. I was going to say I'd swop 'er for another, but if they've all got . . . well, if they're all the same . . .'

'I'm not certain, mind,' Jenny said quickly, mindful that

137

she had only seen one doll inflated. 'Look, I think what you'd better do is come back after two o'clock, when the full-time staff will be here. I'm sure they'll arrange something.'

'Right, I'll come back about half two,' the man decided. He heaved a massive sports bag onto the counter and through its gaping top Jenny saw, with some repulsion, a pink, semi-flatulent arm and a bulging, flaccid bosom. Cindy, obviously, was coming home to roost in a not entirely flattened condition.

'Um . . . I don't think you'd better leave the doll here . . .' she began, but was overridden once more.

'You don't think I'm carting 'er round the shops, do you? With people thinking I've got a corpus on me 'ands? No, Miss, I'm not denying that if she's one of a bad batch it's no fault of yours, but tek her a step further I will not.' He gave the sports bag a dismissive push and turned towards the door. 'I'll get some chips and be back later.'

Jenny had no time for more than a faint bleat of agreement before her other customer, with a handful of magazines, was at the counter holding out his money. After that someone else came in, so her complainant, if not forgotten, had at least been put at the back of her mind by the time Simon walked jauntily in.

'Hi, Jen; how did it go? I bought Brenda an expensive lunch and told her to go shopping this afternoon; I'll hold the fort here for once.'

Damn damn, *damn*, Jenny said to herself, telling Simon that she had been quite all right, thank you. Now she would have to explain to him instead of Brenda about the unsatisfactory Cindy!

'Oh by the way, Simon, before I go . . . there's a chap coming in later.' She pushed the sports bag towards him with one toe. 'He's brought back a Cindy doll – I'm afraid he isn't very pleased with her. He said she wasn't . . . what he expected. He didn't think . . . well, I do agree that . . .'

'Come into the back for a second,' Simon said, going over and locking the shop door. 'Let's straighten this out before the hordes pour in. What did he actually say? And remember what I told you, when a customer seems rather crude it's not that he wants to be, it's because that's the only way he knows how to express himself.'

'Oh, it wasn't that, he was quite pleasant really and very

reasonable. You see, he wanted a Cindy without . . . without . . .' She could hear her voice fading and, in desperation, repeated her customer's words in a loud, clear voice. 'He says she's got a hole.'

How crude that sounded! But Simon merely picked up the sports bag and peered distastefully in at the contents.

'Oh dear, no wonder he was annoyed. What did you tell him?'

'I said they all had . . . they were all made the same so far as I knew, and . . .'

She was interrupted by a shout of laughter. Simon was going red in the face.

'Good God, Jenny, what a mind you've got! He meant . . . look, tell me his exact words this time, not your interpretation. Think, then speak.'

'Well, he started by saying Cindy let him down,' Jenny said, after a mystified pause. 'Then he said he'd taken a shocking crack, and then he said she'd got a . . . what I just said . . . and he wanted to change her for another.'

'That's understandable, don't you think?' He gave Jenny a brotherly shove. 'She's got a hole all right, you goofy girl, in her knee or her shoulder or somewhere, so when he . . . er . . . climbs aboard she lets him down. Got it? – She's punctured. All he wanted was a puncture-mending outfit. There are some on the shelves over there.'

'My God,' Jenny said hollowly. She knew that the shade of crimson all over her face and neck must be unsurpassed. 'Simon, what a fool I was! I'm so sorry, but the way he said it . . . honestly, all I could think of was . . . he seemed quite . . .'

'They often do. But anyway you did the right thing, even if it was by accident. If he's had it a day or two and you say it's let him down, then obviously he must have used it, and we don't change things someone else has punctured, for obvious reasons, so I'll make him a present of the outfit.'

'Used?' Jenny backed away from the sports bag as yet another unsavoury penny thudded into place. 'Oh, my God!'

'Quite. You didn't say we'd change it, did you?'

'No, because . . . anyway, I said to come back later and see the full-time staff.' Her sense of fair play overcoming distaste she added, 'But surely you'll have to change it won't you, Simon? It must be faulty.'

'No way. But he'll go off with his adhesive and his little pink patches quite satisfied, you'll see.'

'I wonder if he'll feel the same about his Cindy,' Jenny mused as she buttoned her jacket, 'when he knows she's kept together by puncture patches? When he said she'd let him down I should have taken him literally, shouldn't I?'

'You should, because planks are a literal lot,' Simon said, going across to unlock the door for her. 'Don't worry, there won't be any trouble. By the way, how do you feel about full-time work in the run-up to Christmas? I'll be drafting an advert in another few weeks, if you're interested.'

But Jenny, murmuring a noncommital answer, knew that the last thing she wanted was a full-time job in there, particularly as Posy would be getting three weeks off over the holiday. If only she did not need the money so much then she need never walk through that door again! But she would keep plugging away at the job centre; you never knew, a nice, respectable job might come up any day!

Jenny told Brenda about the Cindy doll with the hole and then, because they both laughed so heartily over it, she told Sue. Sue laughed a lot, but when she had recovered she took a more serious view as well.

'It's no job for you, love,' she said, as the two of them hung over a pan of steaming tea-towels which they were boiling up on the kitchen stove. She stirred them with the wooden spoon, then straightened, pushing a lock of steam-lank hair out of her eyes. 'It was fun at first, I know, but half the time you're on edge over what might be said, aren't you?'

'I am a bit,' Jenny admitted. 'And Simon wants me to put in more hours now that the weather's getting colder – he says now all the voyeurs and peeping toms have to look at is the sand and seagulls instead of other birds, and consequently business will hot up. He says indoor games thrive in winter. He says cold brings out the beast in men.'

'My goodness, I must meet your Simon some time. But you don't want to work longer hours there, do you?'

'No, I don't, but I need the money. It's this awful feeling I

140

have that Dirk might suddenly stop my allowance, and legally I wouldn't have a leg to stand on. And then there's winter clothing, and Christmas, and feeding Posy the right things. I keep meaning to pluck up my courage and go back to the farm and get my clothes, but it's difficult to actually go ahead and do it.'

'Hasn't he ever suggested he might have Posy? Oh, not for good, I realize you wouldn't want that, but for a weekend or something? If so, you could . . .'

'He wouldn't want her, he doesn't like small children, particularly girls,' Jenny admitted ruefully. 'As for Posy, she was always more frightened than fond of him. No, it's no use hoping he'll call into the flat to see how she is and bring my clothes on the way. Mind you, Bronwen had quite a good relationship with Posy, comparatively speaking . . . not that I expect her to pop in either.'

'Well, find out when they're in town and we'll do a snatch.'

Sue spoke with relish; plainly even a half-hearted burglary attempt thrilled her, but Jenny shook her head.

'No, I couldn't do it quite like that. Taking you there would be . . . oh, sneaky, I suppose. But if you'd take care of Posy for me, then I suppose I could go by myself, one day, when I'm certain Dirk's not around. So if I give you the word . . . you see, it's a long bus journey, and I can't go until after two because of the shop, so if you really could pick Posy up . . .'

'Of course I could, and the other kids. I can take the lot down to that cafe in the gardens for you.'

Agreeing, Jenny found to her shame that a pang of something very like jealousy shot through her when she thought of Bill meeting Sue, sharing a pot of tea and a chat. But it was absurd, because it was Dirk she wanted, Sue wanted . . . well, not Bill at any rate, and all Bill wanted was to bring up his two children successfully. But of course Sue was so very lovely and Bill so very nice . . . Irritated with herself, Jenny picked up the wooden tongs and began to fish the tea-towels out of the boiling water, slopping them untidily into the red washing-up bowl which stood handy. Petty, that's what she was being, downright petty. It was not as though she and Bill were anything but friends . . . it was just that good friends

141

were at a premium with her at the moment, and if Bill did find he fancied Sue it would be natural for her friendship with him to become cooler. As would her friendship with Sue.

But she was being absurd, she knew that really, she told herself, carrying the bowl over to the sink and returning for the huge, double-handled pan, with which Sue was already struggling. Ridiculous, to think that just because Bill would meet Sue he and she would take to each other and exclude Jenny!

'Leave that pan alone,' she ordered Sue; even to her own ears her voice sounded unnecessarily sharp. 'You know you aren't supposed to lift weights.'

'Weights? It's not heavy, it's just awkward, and . . .'

'Leave it!' Jenny snatched at the pan which slopped over, drenching the floor and both girls' feet. 'Oh Sue, look at the floor! Just let me do it alone, will you? You can fetch the mop.'

'You take one handle and I'll take the other,' Sue suggested peacably, though she shot Jenny a shrewd look. 'That way neither of us will strain anything and then, when we've got it tipped down the sink, we can easily mop the floor.'

Jenny sighed but agreed and between them they carted the pan to the sink, emptied it, and then Jenny went for the mop which was the only piece of communal property no tenant ever leched after, for it remained in its cupboard getting balder and less attractive every day. Jenny pulled it out and carried it over to the sink where she ritually washed its thinning string curls, frowning at the dark grey water gurgling down the sink.

'This is a magic mop; every time I use it I clean it thoroughly and put it back in the cupboard, yet every time I get it out it's full to the brim with murky filth.'

'Perhaps the old biddy is telling the truth for once; perhaps she really does clean this floor once a day,' Sue said, watching Jenny scour the mop's pathetic locks. 'That reminds me, I need a wash and set. Shall I book myself into the hairdresser or would you care to do the honours?'

'I'll have a go,' Jenny said doubtfully. 'Your hair's natural though, isn't it? It doesn't look permed but it always looks very nice.'

'It's natural in that it waves, but every now and then I have it professionally done, just to keep my spirits up. Tell you what, if you do mine I'll do yours. We'll have a session. Brenda's rather good with hair, though she has a perm. She'll give a hand and offer advice.' Sue was still staring at the mop with its pathetic burden of thinning string – every day a little smaller. 'I wonder if I should go blonde?'

'Blonde? For heaven's sake, why? Or do you think that since it suits the mop it will suit you?' Jenny giggled, squeezed the excess water out of the mop-head and began vigorously mopping up the spilt water which had formed puddles in the creaky brown linoleum. 'Not that it does suit the mop – I wonder how much new mop-heads cost? But they might be difficult to fit on and I don't really see why I should have to buy it, just because the old hen doesn't seem much inclined.'

'She'll tell you it's you who wears it out so it's you who should buy a new one,' Sue said. 'I wonder what would happen if you stopped cleaning the bathroom? Having once given up she'd never do it again, I bet. And as for the loo . . .'

'Pooh to the loo,' Jenny agreed, finishing off the floor with a fine swirl and returning the mop to the sink, where it proceeded to lose yet more strings in its final wash. 'It's the tiniest room in the house – in any house, I should think, since my knees touch the door when I sit down – yet she still never gets it clean. She must empty pints of Harpic down it, or none, I'm not sure which – but it still pongs to high heaven.'

'That bolt worries me,' Sue confessed. 'Shall I put the kettle on now the tea-towels are off? Yes? Right, as I was saying, it's the bolt that worries me most. I swear I have nightmares about it sheering off and me being stuck there and . . . heavens, suppose the fright started the baby off?'

'Don't lock the door,' Jenny suggested practically. 'After all no one can get in without ramming your knees, so you aren't likely to be disturbed.'

'Oh? It wouldn't disturb you, then, if you had the door shot open, ramming your knees as you so delicately put it and probably causing you to fall backwards down the loo, where you – or I, at least – would probably wedge immovably? I can

143

almost see the headlines – *Pregnant woman gives birth in loo; baby's first cry a gurgle*.'

Jenny giggled. 'Don't make difficulties. Why did God give you feet, woman? You simply wedge the door with a toe and hum loudly (yes, I know, like the loo does) whilst you work. See?'

'In theory, that's grand, but in practice we mums-to-be need peace, quiet and a locked door behind which to function. I don't wish to bring down the tone of this meeting but don't forget my samples; how can I provide a first-thing-in-the-morning midstream urine sample whilst humming with one foot wedged against the door? No, I think I'll invest in a good little modern bolt. I can use that and you can use the old rusty one if it makes you happier.'

'Or you could break the old one,' suggested Jenny with a cunning which would once have been foreign to her nature, 'and tell the old hen it's bust; she'd have to buy another, then.'

'Huh! And three weeks later we'd still be crossing our legs. Do you know how long it took her to mend Dermott's gas ring? No, nor do I, because she hasn't done it yet. I may be careful but I'm not mean – when I get round to it I'll get a new bolt and damn the expense. Do you suppose Dermott will screw it on for me? I'm rotten at screwing.'

'I shan't rise to your tempting bait,' Jenny said loftily, as Sue smirked at her own words. 'Now, shall we have tea or coffee?'

'Coffee – have you seen my latest wheeze?' Sue dug around in her packet of detergent and presently produced a very tiny jar of coffee. 'See that? It's old-hen-proof – at any rate it's still there. Now, today's Monday which means you'll be off money-hunting. Shall I come with you? We could make a few innocent-seeming enquiries whilst we're there.'

Jenny glanced at the window. It was raining with the sort of relentless steadiness which means it does not intend to stop in a hurry. It was also very windy; the few remaining yellow leaves which still clung grimly to the lime tree outside the window were fighting a losing battle, and beneath the tree a soggy pile of their defeated brethren testified to the fact. Like the mop, the tree would soon be a mere skeleton of its former self. With a sigh, Jenny remembered the weather of a mere two or three weeks ago – the perfect Indian summer, blue skies, crisp bright leaves, yet a chill in the air which brought out every scent and a clarity which showed the autumn colours in all their detail. There had been evenings when the sunset had dazzled, when the dusk came bluer and the nights starrier as a result of the unexpectedly prolonged autumn.

'Can you face the rain, though? I quite agree that, if you're with me, we could find some excuse to go up and see old Croft and dig a bit – I'd never go on my own. Only it seems a bit mean to get you soaked just to fetch my money.'

'I'll do a lot for money, even other people's. Look, suppose we go at about half past ten instead of noon, then old Croft might tell us that your man's in town but hasn't yet delivered the cash. And with a few more quessies you might even find out if he lunches here, and so on. Then, armed with that knowledge . . .'

'Quessies! Really, what's wrong with questions? But I do get the point. Very well, if you're on, we'll go and ferret for information.'

'Good girl. I do feel you must be forced to seize your opportunities. You haven't even got a proper mac, have you, only that horrid see-through plastic thing and that sweats so you get wet anyway. Go home, little sheba, and steal your own clothes!'

'That mac cost fifty pence and it's good value, even if . . . all right, all right, I'm not changing the subject. If you're game, I am. But I'm in the shop at 12.30, don't forget.'

'I don't suppose you'll find out much today, except the sort of hours he keeps,' Sue said, glancing at the low cloud and shivering. 'If you find out he's always away on a Thursday, for instance, then I'll stand in for you at the shop just for once, or if you think that isn't proper, Brenda will and I'll supply her with a packed lunch and sit and eat it with her. Now, any more reasons for delay?'

'None. Let's go.'

The two of them clattered down the stairs and into their respective rooms, leaving their doors wide open. Sue's room, unlike Jenny's, was neatly partitioned off so that, though you could see her living part, the sleeping part was out of sight behind colourful floral screens similar to those found in a hospital ward. As Jenny came out of her own door, Sue pushed the screens aside and joined her, revealing a glimpse of the dressing table and bed, the bedside table and a picture, rather a big one, on the wall. It was a photograph, a man and a mountain. Jenny rather thought she had seen the picture before somewhere, but Sue was already snatching at the great, primrose coloured cape she favoured in the wet and saying with her own inimitable gaiety, 'An umbrella each, or shall we share?', and everything but their expedition faded from Jenny's mind.

'One each, I think,' Jenny said. It made conversation more difficult but what with Sue's bulge and her happy disregard for other pavement-users, Jenny decided it might be better to travel singly than together. Sue's lovely smile and frequent cries of 'I'm *awfully* sorry!' when she impaled a passer-by placated all but the most injured of her victims, though Jenny was always embarrassed by the tilted hats, scraped cheeks and lacerated dignities which Sue left in her wake.

'Coward,' Sue said, smiling at Jenny and making it plain she knew just why her offer of a shared umbrella was being shunned. 'Buttoned up? Weatherproof? Then let's go!'

'Mr Croft's in – he said if you came before twelve, would I ask you to go up,' the spotty girl at the typewriter said. She looked neat and smug with her engagement ring sparkling and her hair combed and dry; compared with the way Jenny felt – soaked, wind-tossed and slightly storm-battered – she looked like the Queen. 'Would you like to leave your umbrella down here, in the hall?'

'She's seen his chin,' Sue said in a clearly audible aside. 'She thinks you'll deflower him with that brolly!'

'Er . . . I've only called for my money,' Jenny said, digging Sue harshly in what might have been her ribs had she been less distended with child. 'Shut up, Sue!'

'I'm afraid it hasn't yet arrived this morning,' the typist said. She looked alertly from one to the other. She gave Sue what could only be described as a knowing grin, then turned it on Jenny. 'Both of you, of course,' she added making it perfectly plain to Jenny at least that the staff had noticed Mr Croft's dishonourable scars.

'Okay, we'll go up; would you ring him please and say we're on our way,' Jenny said, making up her mind. After all, she and Sue had agreed that they would see Mr Croft, it just seemed rather odd that it should be as much his decision as theirs. 'Come on, Sue.'

'You leave your brolly if you like, but I'm taking mine,' Sue said, digging Jenny in the back with it just to make her point. 'Who knows, he might be the sort of guy who takes a special fancy to large . . .'

'Shut *up*,' growled Jenny, torn between a desire to laugh and another to scream. 'Let's get this over with.'

Even with Sue's bulk to contend with, climbing the stairs was the work of a moment. Reaching the office, Jenny tapped, entered and was shutting the door behind Sue before Mr Croft had done more than half rise to his feet. Despite their last encounter he smiled quite urbanely at Jenny, though she thought she could see a glint of dislike in his eyes. Her bite-mark was still disguised by a piece of sticking plaster though it should have hardened into a decent scar by now, but on the other hand it would look very obviously like a bite. Serve him right!

'Good morning, Mr Croft; sorry we're making a mess of your floor but it's raining cats and dogs out there. May I have my money, please?'

'Ah, Mrs Sayer, nice to see you and your friend.' Charm oozed a little less freely, perhaps, but it was still evident if somewhat stilted. 'No, I'm afraid I shan't have it today until around five o'clock. Your – Mr Dirk I mean – usually comes in early, but today there's a big cattle sale in Abergele and the beasts he wants to bid for are scattered; he rang up and warned me he might not get here until four or five, possibly even later.'

'Oh? Then might it be safer if my friend came back tomorrow morning for her money?'

Jenny could see Mr Croft would have liked to ignore Sue's remark but did not quite dare to. Calculations were almost visibly clicking through his narrow head; she might be married to someone important, she might even be important herself. The possibility that she might be about to give birth to someone important was the only one which had not yet registered, Jenny found herself thinking. What a horrid man he was! Opportunist, egoist, would-be womanizer . . . but a list of his bad points would be endless as well as pointless.

'Yes, it might be better. Unless . . . let me see, what time do you finish work, Mrs Sayer?'

Jenny smiled demurely; no more *Jenny dear* with Sue around!

'Goodness, Mr Croft, whatever makes you think I have a job? I can come in any time but I'll probably leave it until tomorrow morning, now. It's pouring with rain still and I don't fancy hanging round the town until pretty nearly evening. And would you leave the money downstairs, please, to save time?'

'Now Mrs Sayer, you know very well that Mr Dirk likes me to keep an eye on you, to see that everything's going well. Indeed, if it would help I'm willing to forward you some money right away, on your allowance tomorrow.'

'No thanks; but if you'd like to run down with the money tomorrow morning I'm quite willing to wait,' Jenny said with saccharine sweetness. 'And you've seen me now, of course. I trust I shan't deteriorate a lot overnight.'

She and Sue left the office whilst Mr Croft was still trying to find an answer to that, both glowing with victory. There might have been no money in the visit, but success had been theirs. Mr Croft had been not only beaten but routed.

However, Jenny was not allowed to savour her success for long; Sue hustled her up the road to the cafe they had visited before and sat her firmly down at a window table.

'Come along, let's plot. Oh, I know you didn't get your money, but you got all the info you could possibly need.'

'Well yes, but . . . oh, all right, I could do with a coffee.'

The unsmiling waitress came over to them, looking as though she had recently lost her front teeth and so dared not part her lips. She even managed to say 'Yes?' without showing any teeth whatsoever.

'Scones and coffee twice, please.' Sue turned her most dazzling smile on the waitress and got a grudging lip-stretch in return. 'Now, Jen, do you know the times of the buses?

you'd better find out the times of the buses back to Rhyl as well, you don't want to find yourself stranded at Dirk's till tomorrow, though I'll look after Posy beautifully. In fact I'll stand in for you all night, if necessary.'

'Stand in for me? Well, yes, but . . .'

'I know all your arguments, flower, but they won't wash. You are going today and you are going now and you won't come back without a suitcase bulging with winter clothes. Right?'

'Oh but not today, I've had no time to prepare, if we leave it . . .'

'Jenny, I'm warning you! I know it's raining – all the better for a bit of burglary – and I know he's gone to Abergele market, but you know full well that he must come in to market quite often, and this is the only time he's not managed to get your money in early. This may well be the only time you *know* you're safe, because Ferret-Face said your Dirk wouldn't be in Rhyl, even, until tea-time. I'll see you off on the bus, take a packed lunch to Bren and I'll call for Posy and guard her with my life . . . but you're going to get your clothes!'

As the coffee and scones arrived Jenny leaned back in her seat and conceded defeat.

'All right, I'll go. You're absolutely right, of course; if I don't go today I'll never get another chance quite so good. I daresay he and bitch-Bron are making a day of it, lunching somewhere expensive and doing a show in the evening. Once, ages ago, when we hadn't been married long, we used to do that before the weather closed in.'

'There you are then.' Sue smiled at her and began eating a scone at a great rate; butter ran down her chin and she dabbed it off with a hanky. She jerked her head towards the dumb waitress, leaning against the jukebox whilst it played something with all the tune and verve of a moron shaking a tray of cutlery. 'Do you suppose she puts more butter on because we're regulars? She might have favourite customers.'

'Her favourite customers will be the ones going out through the door by the look of her,' Jenny said sourly. 'She wouldn't last long in the shop! Where do the buses leave from, anyway?'

149

'From the bus station, I suppose. It's only a couple of minutes from here. What's the procedure?'

'I'll get a bus to Ruthin . . . well, it'll be heading for Ruthin, anyway, and get the chap to drop me off at the top of the lane. I'll walk the two miles and I'll ask the driver to warn the chap who drives the three-fifteen or whatever that someone will be getting on at the end of the lane, then he'll wait for me and won't just steam past if I'm not right at the stop.'

'Two *miles*? My God, and with a loaded suitcase? Jen, I really do think you should ring for a taxi, you can leave the ten pence on the shelf if you feel guilty but you can't possibly walk all that way with your arms full of clothes.'

'It's all right, I'm quite sturdy despite my looks, I'll manage the walk easily. Oh, by the way, do you like perfume? The boys used to buy me heaps at Christmas and Easter, and I hate the thought of Bronwen getting her sticky little hands on my hoard, so if you'll tell me what you like best I'll try to bring you some.'

'Perfume? Gosh . . . do you run to Chanel No. 5?'

'I'm almost certain I do. Why, do you have an ill-concealed passion for it?'

'It reminds me of better times,' Sue said, smirking, 'when men drank champagne out of my slipper and wrote sonnets to my eyebrows. Unfortunately, due to various deficiencies, I now have to make do with Opium.'

'Oh? What do you do, inhale it and pretend men are drinking champagne out of your slipper, or smoke it, like Sherlock Holmes?'

'Fool, Opium's a perfume. It costs a million pounds an ounce which is why I'm always penniless but Chanel, of course, costs two million. I didn't know Sherlock Holmes smoked opium though. Finished your coffee? I'm sure you're making it last ages to put off the evil hour. You have? Good, then let's blow.'

'Isn't it odd that you go on using perfume when there's only us to notice,' Jenny said presently, as the two of them hurried along the gleaming pavement, umbrellas at the charge. 'Mind you, I do use talcum powder but only the baby sort I buy for Posy.'

'Force of habit; the hope that some handsome man . . .'

'An obstretician, of course,' Jenny nodded. 'When's it due, Sue? Tomorrow?'

'Oh ha ha, very funny. Actually, it's only another six weeks. What number bus are we looking for?'

'Don't know, can't remember. You see, from the farm you can catch any bus going towards Ruthin to get into town, and any bus leaving by our road to get home. But I can ask.'

'I'll ask,' Sue said as they entered the bus station. She hailed a man in uniform as he walked by. 'Excuse me . . .'

In the end it was such a scramble to catch the bus that Jenny scarcely had time to have second thoughts. The uniformed man pointed out the vehicle, bade them hurry and shouted to the driver, who was already revving his engine, to hold it for another passenger. Jenny hurtled up the step, paid her money and was halfway down the aisle when the bus lurched, roared and they were off, snorting out of the bus station, down the High Street, along the promenade and then inland, heading for the blue mountains.

Not that you could see the blue of the mountains, she reflected, as the rain drove against the windows. Only the foothills were visible before the cloud covered them. But being so closed-in gave her the thinking time that Sue's abrupt action had denied her. She began to be pleased that she had taken the bull by the horns and was actually on her way to the farm at last. She had a thousand pictures of it in her mind and had been conscientiously trying to banish them for weeks, but now she sat back and let them flood in; the farm in summer when the glorious creamy-gold roses round the dining-room windows were in full bloom and the flower-beds bright with begonias, pansies and campanulas; or in autumn, when the Virginia creeper was at its best and brightest; or spring, when the bulbs under the windows braved the cold, and the daffodils' yellow was like a trumpet blast heralding the spring; and winter, when the ivy which grew on the back of the house was at its glossiest, each leaf dusted with snow or outlined by frost.

It was, she thought, a cosy-looking house with its small, leaded windows set deep in the ancient stone blocks of its construction. The very roof tiles were mellowed with age and bore, at the back where the lean-to scullery came within four feet of the ground, fat cushions of yellow stonecrop, moss and even the odd clump of toadflax. Dirk was always threatening to have the tiles cleaned, to tear down the ivy and root out the Virginia creeper but he never did, being as fond, she believed, of the shaggy look as she herself was.

What would it look like now, her home, as she came up the long drive between the limes? They were another threatened species as far as Dirk was concerned, since the lime trees dripped their sticky fluid all over his cars and made cleaning them a chore. Now of course they would be leafless, but would the house wear a welcoming smile for her or would it seem to frown, as at a stranger, when she emerged from the trees? She would not of course enter by the front door, which was invariably locked; she would go round the back, through the farmyard with the buildings built protectively round three sides and the back of the house forming the fourth.

Two seats in front of her, a man was smoking; it was a pipe, not an unpleasant smell, and it reminded her of apple-wood fires in the living room on winter evenings, when the curtains were drawn against the chilly dark and Belle, privileged by her age and past glories, lay on the hearth rug snoozing and twitching and now and then waking to gaze at the flames. There would be no fire there now; it was not yet cold enough and in any event she had always got Mrs George or Mrs Ted to light it some time after three. Did Bronwen do the same? Or was it Dirk's job now to remember things like lighting fires and cleaning grates and bringing in supplies of wood? He would hate it if it were, but then as she had changed so might he.

Shrugging, she turned to the window, trying to see through the downward trickling drops exactly where they were, but all she could make out were the wildly whipping hedges and the blurred grass of the verges as they thundered and jolted onward. The noise of the downpour on the roof drowned out all but the most determined conversation, but even so she caught a few words now and then from her fellow-travellers:

'Beautiful it was, and only ten quid, but would 'e buy it for me? No, not 'im; didn't fit in with 'ow 'e sees us, like.'

'She'll be thinking of getting her own place, come Christmas . . .'

'We've not spoke a word in ten year, and then to find ourselves working for the same firm . . . there's shocking!'

For a moment Jenny wished she had let Sue come so that this could have been an adventure, something to laugh over and talk about, but she knew it would not have worked, not really. Her attitude would have been wrong. When you first took a friend round your home it had to be your home, not a home that had been wrested from you. What pride could she have had in a living room cleaned for Bronwen, in a flower-arrangement done by Bronwen? None, of course. It would have made the trip a miserable might-have-been instead of an amusing visit.

Presently the bus drew up with a great spray of water on a stretch of road that Jenny was able to identify as being no more than a mile or so from the end of her lane. She waited until the bus had disgorged three or four passengers, then got up and walked back to where the conductor was leaning against the luggage rack, eating an apple, and addressed him.

'Could you stop at the top of Sayer's Lane, please? Otherwise I'll have a long walk back through the rain.'

Strictly speaking, there was no stop at the top of the lane; one was supposed to walk another half mile. Jenny knew that sometimes conductors could be disobliging but this one looked young and cheerful and perhaps he hated long walks through the rain himself. He nodded, tossing his applecore carelessly over the nearest hedge.

'Sure. You coming back, later? What time d'you want the bus back to watch out for you?'

Jenny glanced at her wrist-watch. It was half past one and there was a bus out from Ruthin at 3.05. That should be long enough; if she made an effort and strode out her fastest she should arrive at the farm by two o'clock.

'If you could ask the chap on the 3.05, please? And perhaps if you could mention it to the 4.05 as well, just in case I'm held up?'

'Sure.' He swung out on to the platform as the bus gathered speed and gazed ahead, his eyelids screwing up against the driving rain. 'This it, coming up?'

153

Jenny peered as well and, nodded though she could see nothing. 'Yes, I'm sure this is it. Thanks very much.'

The conductor tinged his bell, the driver drew in, a trapped sports car veered out, gave a triumphant toot-toot-de-toot-toot and flashed past them, and then Jenny was standing alone on the verge with the wet grass coldly ticking her shins, and the bus was disappearing along the shining ribbon of road.

Jenny had already put up her umbrella but it seemed a puny defence against the raging downpour, the wind and the spiteful clutching of the wet and whippy grass. She began to walk up the lane on the verge, then left it and took to the middle of the carriage-way. What was the point of keeping out of the way of traffic when it meant becoming even wetter and when, on such a day, it was doubtful if so much as a tractor would come chugging along? She regretted her walking shoes though, as already they were squelching with each step, and decided to steal some wellies for the return journey. They would be useful for beach walks and for meeting Posy from school; yes, she would take some wellies.

Jenny plodded on, trying not to think of a warm, dry towel, a fire and a hot cup of tea. Since the master and mistress (ha ha) were out, there would be a fire in the range but nowhere else and she could scarcely help herself to towels and then leave them drying in the kitchen. Or could she? No point in dying from pneumonia, and anyway one would do as much for a storm-tossed friend or even an acquaintance who came to the house: give them tea, dry them off and send them into the storm again capable, for a while at any rate, of withstanding the worst that the weather could throw at them.

Jenny trod in a huge puddle, which sent waves of water sloshing over her ankles, and used a word she had heard the farmhands utter when trodden on by beasts. Presently, thinking that she heard a car coming up behind her, she turned to glance over her shoulder and her umbrella blew inside out with a spine-cracking jolt and proceeded to disintegrate before her eyes as the wind ripped it apart. Another curse did almost nothing to help and since the umbrella was now useless Jenny threw it crossly into the ditch, where it flapped like a wounded vulture, and turned her steps towards the farm once more.

The rain did not stop but it did ease a little, though it did nothing to improve her frame of mind, for as the rain eased so the wind increased. Jenny began to think wistfully, not of the comforts of the farm ahead, but of the flat behind. The glow of her small electric fire, the cosy faded chairs and the cushions that Mrs Twigg had given Posy. It would be lovely in the flat now, making toast before the fire. What was wrong with light clothing, anyway? She could have managed somehow. Darn that bossy Sue Oliver!

But then she rounded the corner of the lane and there was the drive, and she was walking up it, treading carefully – almost on tiptoe – though she knew Dirk and his latest fast car were in Rhyl or Abergele and unlikely to return for hours. Even Mrs Ted and Mrs George would be minding their business in their own cottages; they would not hang about up at the farm once the morning's work was done when everyone was away. Jenny continued to plod along, knowing that the house would remain hidden until the drive forked in two, left for the front door and right for the back. She would go to the back but would take a look at the front first. She reached the fork, turned left, then emerged from the dripping trees and stood, looking. Four-square to the wind and rain, the house faced her, the creeper already beginning to lose its gold and crimson leaves. Oddly enough, the house looked different. Grimmer? Less welcoming? But it was only a house, it could not really change its aspect just because she no longer belonged.

Did Dirk clip the creeper every autumn? She thought not, but it had obviously been done this year. That was why the house looked different, more formal. The windows were no longer overhung but were neatly hedged. Previously, the creeper had resembled curly hair clustered appealingly round a face; now it looked more like a severe perm, with the stone visible round the windows giving them a wide-open rather accusing look. Jenny turned away, a small, dripping figure, and headed for the farmyard. Never mind, it probably looked all right really. It was just . . . strange.

She entered the farmyard and stopped short. The house had been totally altered; it looked like a whited sepulchre she thought wildly. The ivy had been stripped off and the big stone blocks had been whitewashed. It looked at once younger, brasher and colder, standing there bare-faced in the rain, looking at its reflection in the huge puddles and trying not to sneer too obviously. Jenny glanced sideways then quickly away, but she had still seen that the cushions of stonecrop and moss had been stripped from the lean-to roof and that someone had put up Venetian blinds in the scullery and the office. They gave the lean-to a very odd expression, like eye-shadow and sequins on the face of one's grandmother.

But it was silly to be standing here in the rain, staring. Jenny checked that Dirk's car was still away – it was – and then bolted for the back door. She tugged it open and was about to erupt into the kitchen when she heard a smothered yelp from behind her and someone – something – hit her in the back of the knees so that the pair of them entered the kitchen precipitately, one on top of the other.

It was Belle. But what a change in her! She was thin, bedraggled and soaked to the skin – Belle, who had been in gracious retirement, was caked not simply with farmyard dirt but with old farmyard dirt and thick in her coat. She must have been sleeping in the barns and outhouses for weeks – months!

Jenny knelt on the floor, regardless of drips and mud, and put her arms tightly round Belle. The dog whined and nuzzled up to her, her whole body shaking with what seemed to be a mixture of fear and delight – the fear, Jenny realized, because she had come indoors where she was allowed no longer, the delight at seeing a friend.

Presently, their first rapture over, Jenny checked over the kitchen. The fire was lit in the range and there was a kettle pushed to the back of it which was still respectably hot. She dragged it over the hob, careless now of anyone coming in. Let them come! How *dared* Dirk treat Belle this way, how dared he! She fetched the roller towel off the door and rubbed Belle dry, then filled a pan with milk, sweetened it, heated it to blood temperature and put it in a dish on the floor. Belle dared not touch it at first, then she bent her head and drank every drop, cleaning the dish thoroughly afterwards with great sweeps of her long, pink tongue.

The kettle boiled quickly. Jenny made herself hot, strong tea and drank it down, then fetched a clean towel from the cupboard by the range and dried herself thoroughly. When she finished she pushed both towels back into the cupboard and turned her attention to the kitchen. It had not changed at all so far as she could see, but she was still so furious over what had happened to Belle that the kitchen, indeed the house, had almost ceased to matter. Belle had worked hard for the Sayers all her life and Dirk had acknowledged it. Now . . . but it was no use thinking about it, she had too much to do in her short time here. She should go straight up to the bedroom and start packing her clothes, but a glance at the kitchen clock confirmed that it was only ten past two; she could take a quick look at the rest of the house.

There were changes, more changes perhaps than she had expected in a few weeks. A large colour television had been put in the drawing room and a black-and-white in the dining room. There were no flowers in the big bowls in the front hall and in what they had always called the garden room – because it had one wall made entirely of glass, with double doors that opened onto a small terrace – all Jenny's precious plants were either long-dead or dying. Things that she had valued . . . a small but sturdy orange tree, grown from a pip, a sizable grapefruit tree, grown the same way, a couple of grape vines which twined their way right up to the ceiling . . . had all been allowed to die, obviously because no one had bothered to water them.

Jenny stood there for a moment whilst sadness and rage fought and were conquered. Instead, in a cool place in the middle of the whirlpool of her mind, she found a very odd thought stirring: *I have no friends here.* How could she say such a thing, or think it rather? Yet was it not true? It was not only Dirk who knew how she loved her plants, what time and affection she lavished on them, there were also Mrs Ted and Mrs George and the boys and Bronwen. Whenever she had gone away she had detailed someone to come in, to water and in the event of hot sunshine, to move the more delicate members of her family into the shade, to turn the plants daily so that one side did not receive more sun and warmth than the other and cause uneven growth . . . even the farmhands knew about her garden room, laughed at her over her pride in her fruitless orange tree, her grapeless vines. You would have thought that Mrs George or Mrs Ted might have watered them, if only in her memory; might have kept her little trees green.

She had read of the iron entering someone's soul, but now she knew, a little, what it meant. A coldness, a hardness of purpose, had entered hers. Dirk had been proud of the garden room, or had pretended to be so; yet he had not had sufficient love for growing things to spare a few drops of water to a little orange tree which had given him much pleasure over the long years.

She could not take them away with her; they were too bulky and anyway there was no room at the flat. It seemed foolish to water them, as though deliberately prolonging the life of someone terminally ill, but she could not help herself. She soaked every plant, even those which were plainly past help, and then went very slowly up the stairs with Belle, who had never climbed the stairs to Jenny's knowledge in her life before, dogging her heels.

Together they reached the bedroom. It too had changed. There were no plants on the wide window-sills, not even dead ones, and there was a grey line round the pink hand basin. The taps were grimy and the mirror had dust on it. Jenny played with the thought of writing 'Jenny was here' in the muck, then dismissed it as childish. She went over to the wardrobe and slid back the door.

The first thing that caught her eye was her pale-green wool suit with the lemon jumper she had bought to go with it on the hanger and a striking gold and black scarf loosely hung across one shoulder. But – she stared, unbelieving – the antique gold brooch which she had worn on the lapel was there no longer. Taken? Fallen off? Quickly, she checked along the row but could see nothing else obviously missing, so she stood on tiptoe and opened the topmost cupboard, then climbed on to the pink and grey stool and hooked out a couple of suitcases. Opening them, she put them on the floor and began systematically to go through the wardrobe. What riches she had once owned, she thought, and how odd that she had forgotten all these things. Dark jeans jostled with thick sweaters, corduroy slacks and tops hung alongside heathery tweed skirts and lilac and lavender jumpers. But it was no use standing there admiring her own past taste and fingering the lovely warm materials; she was here for a purpose and must get on with it.

She packed the first case to bulging and then went to the dressing table and pulled open the top drawer, for underwear – a stranger's possessions met her eyes. It frightened her almost as much as the first sight of an intruder would have done. She shut the drawer, her heart thudding, and abandoned hope of finding her own possessions, then thought of the cupboard under the vanitory unit. It had not been much used, perhaps . . .

Yes. No underwear, but many other things. Bronwen had not dared or perhaps had not wanted to throw away Jenny's talcums, perfumes, scented soap. Jenny selected the best, including the Chanel, and chucked them into the second suitcase, then began to take shoes out of the wardrobe and pile them in on top. Some brogues, her sturdy green hunter wellies, a pair of black court shoes she had always rather liked and another pair, dark-green, which went with her light-green wool suit. Her comfortable fluffy mules were greeted like old friends and tucked into the side of the case.

She shut the second lid and Belle, who had not moved an inch from her side, whined on a high, alarmed note. Jenny picked up the case, reached for the other one . . . then put them both down. She ran to the window . . . damn damn *damn*, if you leaned to the side you could just see the old cartshed where Dirk garaged his cars and the bloody sports car was back! She dithered, suddenly certain that if she were caught here Dirk would see that she regretted it. He would stop her allowance, have her evicted from the flat, hurt her in some awful, unimaginable way. She ran back to the suitcases, tried to lift them, and realized that she could not run with them. She pushed them right into the very back of the wardrobe, her mouth dry with fright, just as she heard, from far below, the kitchen door open, voices, the kitchen door shut. But they would not come in here; she knew what Dirk would want the minute he arrived home, he would want some tea. He would hang about the kitchen whilst it was made and then he would take it through to the drawing room so that he could turn the television on. She would wait until he did that and then she could get the cases out, sneak down the back stairs and leave.

She was actually in the wardrobe reaching for the cases when she heard footsteps coming up the stairs. And voices. One male, one female. Panicking – and not without reason – she grabbed Belle, pulled her inside the wardrobe, and slid the door across as far as was possible from the inside, leaving an inch-wide gap.

She had imagined some awful situations but none quite so ghastly as the one she now found herself in. Quiet amongst the muffling coats and skirts she heard Bronwen's giggle, high, young, possibly even nervous. Then a few words, impossible to make out, in a masculine voice – Dirk, of course. They had come home early after all, probably because of the awful rain, and now they were going to change out of their towny things into older and more comfortable clothing whilst she, an unwitting voyeur, was stuck in the wardrobe! Well, perhaps voyeur was not quite the right word since she could see nothing but a slit of light from the bedroom, but nevertheless she was, albeit unintentionally, spying on them.

The very thought was frightening; she tried to move back, one hand on Belle's collar, the other held out behind her, and so strong was her fear of discovery that she was sharply disappointed when her fingers met the back of the wardrobe and she did not find herself emerging into Narnia, pine-trees, snow and all. No saint, she felt, had ever prayed quite so hard for roses and found her prayers unanswered. She remained in the wardrobe, an unwilling listener, whilst outside in the bedroom her husband and his mistress proceeded to change their clothing.

Presently, she heard a familiar sound which brought her heart into her mouth; it was bedsprings, creaking. She bent down so that her hot face was pressed against the side of Belle's head and begun to pray in a fast, hissing gabble: 'No, not that, please not that, I'll be good, I'll never steal my own clothes again, please, after all the other humiliations, not that, not here, not now.'

She had closed her eyes tightly, screwing them up so that she saw patterns on the inside of her eyelids, a childhood trick to make something unbearable retreat. She opened them, suffered a swirl of mad colour and light, and saw through the slit in the wardrobe door a pair of frilly blue knickers lying on the maroon carpet. They had not been there two minutes earlier. Oh God!

Somewhere in the swirl of sick emotions which began to curdle her guts as the bedsprings creaked was a small cool voice telling her that she knew all about it and that she was being a fool for caring, but reason was not enough. She was on all fours now, still clutching Belle, and she crept forward, unable to stop herself, though she knew that what she was doing was despicable as well as dangerous.

She applied her eye to the opening just as the bedsprings reached a crescendo and then, suddenly, were quiet. She saw Bronwen lying on her back with her lilac and white dress, all ruffles, hoicked up round her neck somewhere and sweat streaking her young acquisitive face. She saw Dirk, his trousers round his knees but with everything else in place, moving off her, rolling on to his back, dragging Bronwen across so that her sweaty face lay on his chest.

Bronwen's face was just as it had always been, though her hair was a little more yellow, and for the first time Jenny realized she was not a natural blonde. But the man's face had indeed changed . . . for a moment, Jenny merely thought dazedly that Dirk had become amazingly youthful; then she realized what she felt she should have guessed from the start. It was not Dirk at all. The young man lying on Dirk's bed, with Dirk's mistress draped across his chest, was Jenny's eldest son, Philip.

Jenny, not surprisingly perhaps, missed the 3.05 bus back to Rhyl. Indeed, it was a quarter past three before she established that the coast was clear and, burdened with two suitcases and with Belle in close attendance, crept down the stairs.

She had remained in the wardrobe throughout the lovers' tryst there, if it could be so described, an interested listener to what began as a slow, semi-amorous conversation and ended in something closer to a row. Philip had started, lazily curious.

'What's happened to the garden room? It looks different.'

161

'It's a bit of a mess at the moment, I agree. But sometime we're going to do it all out completely, so it isn't worth bothering with right now.'

'Do it out? What's wrong with it?'

'I think it's dull, and besides it reminds me . . . well, it reminds Dirk more, of . . . of other times. He's as keen as I am to get it changed.' Bronwen sounded defensive.

'Dad, keen on change?' Philip snorted. 'First I've heard of it. I suppose it reminds you of Mum and you don't want to think about her.'

'Not *me*; why should I care about her, or think about her for that matter? She's nothing to me.'

'She made this house what it is.' A pause. 'She made *me*, for that matter. For what you've just received may the Lord make you truly thankful.'

'I don't see that! I think she made a mess of the place anyway, and Dirk must have agreed. He pulled the ivy down, didn't he?'

'At the back? Oh, aye. How did you get him to do it?'

Bronwen giggled. 'I please him if he pleases me; it's the only way with someone as pig-obstinate as your dad.'

'You mean . . . scratch my back and I'll scratch yours?' Philip's voice, which had been slow and drawling, sharpened. 'What d'you want from me, then?'

'Oh, Phil, it isn't like that! I don't want nothing from you except to have you, now and then. After all . . .'

'Forget it.' The bed creaked violently and Jenny heard a thud as Philip's feet hit the floor. 'Come on, or Mrs Ted will be coming in to light the fire and start the tea.'

'She won't, not for ages,' but there were more creaks; Jenny guessed that Bronwen was, reluctantly, dressing. 'What's the matter with you, Phil? Men are all alike, as soon as you've got what you want you forget a girl's human, with feelings.'

'Are you? Human, I mean. You saw off Belle fast enough and she'd done nothing to offend you. I told Dad last night if someone wanted to walk into this house and steal everything in it, there'd be nothing to stop them any more. Mrs Ted and Mrs George aren't in for more than an hour in the mornings and another before tea, you go gadding off half the time, and you've kicked Belle's arse out of the place so she couldn't stop anyone taking things.'

'Useless, dirty old bitch.' Bronwen's voice was vicious. 'What good was she, anyway? Stuck under the table half the time, or sprawled in front of the fire keeping the warmth off everyone else. And she barked at me and kept growling, even after your dad had shut her up. She's too old, she should have been put down ages ago, it would be a kindness, I told him.'

'What a nasty girl you are!' But Philip's voice did not sound particularly serious. 'One thing, Dad soon discovered there was only one use for you! Your cooking stinks, did you know?'

'I'm not a bloody cook.' Her voice was flat now, sullen. 'I'm a farm secretary I told him, not a bloody cook. If he'd wanted a bloody cook he should have kept *her*. One thing she *could* do was cook . . . the only thing, I grant you, but she could make the sort of meals your Dad keeps on about. If he wants them that bad, he should get her back. She'd come running, he knows that.'

'He will get her back.'

Jenny did not know how Philip meant the words, because she could not see his face; very probably he was just being irritating, but if so, he succeeded. Bronwen's next words came out high and fast, with the suspicion of a hiss.

'That's just where you're wrong, Mr Philip bloody Sayer, he won't get her back, not even if he starves! He's mine, now, till I choose to let him go, which I shan't, because we're in love, but even if you went and told him what we just did, that wouldn't do any harm because he'd never believe you. He's in too deep. And I'd say you were jealous and that you'd had a go at me and I'd had to fight you off. He'd believe that too, with your reputation.'

'Why you lying . . .' Philip broke off but Jenny knew from his tone, now, that he was really angry. 'Why do I bandy words with you? Your reign, my dear, will be short. I knew it the first day I came home, when I saw him looking at the bills for the new carpets. It isn't the money, though he must hate spending it like that. It's *you*. He's still slightly besotted, but not enough. He sees you pushing now, and he's beginning not to like it. You won't last, dear Bronwen, until Christmas.'

'Oh, no?' They were making for the door, their voices beginning to fade. 'I only have to rub up against him and he's willing to do . . . oh, whatever I want. He's got the hots so bad . . .'

Jenny, unwilling to miss the rest, stole out of the wardrobe and across to the bedroom door. Philip and Bronwen were going, slowly, down the stairs. Their voices floated up the stairwell to her ears, each word clear.

'It isn't enough, dickhead. You're grabbing, and he doesn't like it. Mum made his life very comfortable, you never even consider his comfort if it gets in the way of your own.'

'Comfort – what about mine? If you think it's comfortable being screwed flat on your back on the dairy floor, or bending over the bloody sink and nearly braining yourself on the taps . . .'

Philip began to laugh. Bronwen began to shout. The noise faded as they turned, together, into the kitchen.

Jenny waited a moment and then ran to the blue room, whose windows overlooked the yard. Five minutes passed, then the two of them emerged. Even from above you could see that they were still furious with each other. A stiffness in their gait, the way they spoke without turning their heads, made it clear.

They crossed the yard and got into the sports car. Of course, Jenny realized, Dirk would never have taken the sports car to market, what had she been thinking of? He would have taken the Land Rover, because he might be bringing stock back, and even if he were to buy nothing else he would be unlikely to come home without animal feed or seed or something.

She waited, watching from behind the curtain, until the sports car roared off up the lane, then she descended, accompanied by her suitcases and Belle. As she put on her mackintosh and turned up the hood – her light-weight jacket was now in the case with her other clothes – it occurred to Jenny that she might make life more pleasant for Belle by staging a robbery in the house, so that Bronwen would let the dog live indoors once more – but then it might not work, it might merely make Bronwen insist that Belle was truly useless and force Dirk to install a burglar alarm.

It was still raining, and heavily too. Jenny closed the kitchen door behind her, not regretfully, and stumped across the yard. She had passed beneath the dripping limes and into the road before realizing that Belle was still with her, silent, persistent, her nose no more than an inch from the backs of Jenny's calves.

Jenny stopped with a sigh. She could take the dog to Mrs Ted's cottage, beg the other woman to give her a home. But the Batley's were farming people, they did not have much use for old dogs who could no longer earn their keep. She could ring Philip and tell him he must insist that Belle be looked after, perhaps that would be best. Only . . . suppose they had the poor old girl put down? She was not that old, only twelve, it was just that she was old for a working dog.

Jenny and Belle continued to trudge down the lane through the downpour.

CHAPTER SEVEN

'My goodness, you poor soul!' Sue, who had been sitting in Jenny's chair in Jenny's flat, with Jenny's daughter in the chair opposite, both staring obsessively at the television, had jumped to her feet. 'My dear, you're positively *sodden*, what happened to your brolly? Don't say you walked from the bus . . . my God, those cases . . . they weigh a *ton*, it can't be just clothes you've brought . . . my God! What's that?'

But Posy had no need to ask; she and Belle were in each other's arms, both making very similar whimpering noises, both kissing, both panting. A reunion of the very best sort was taking place on Mrs Grant's meagre and dusty carpet and Jenny felt privileged to watch the outward show of such love.

'It's Belle. I didn't ask her to come, she just got on the bus with me and I couldn't turn her off,' she explained now, to Sue's astonished eyebrows. 'Dirk . . . no, Bronwen . . . had turned her out. She was sleeping in the sheds, not allowed into the house any more. I couldn't just leave her there. She's old, she needs to be taken care of.'

'Yes, love, but *here*? I'm darned sure there's a no pets rule and the old hen's bound to find out. She'll prate on about health and her licence or whatever it is and insist you get rid of it.'

'I'm not meeting trouble halfway, not tonight,' Jenny said. She caught hold of a handful of her hair and wrung it out; a satisfying stream of water cascaded onto the carpet. 'Look at that! No one, not even the old hen, would turn anyone out on a night that produced such wetness.'

Posy turned from her fascinated searching of Belle's features, though her arm was still firmly locked round the dog's thin shoulders.

'Who's the old hen? Why won't she love Belle?'

'She will, of course,' Jenny said hastily, shooting a loaded look at Sue. 'And if she doesn't, we'll have to move to somewhere who does. If you see what I mean. And . . . oh, darling, Belle's awfully wet, don't hug her too hard . . . and, if you don't mind, don't say *old hen* because some people might think it was a bit rude. I think Sue was being a bit jokey about Mrs Grant, actually. Landladies can be a bit funny about dogs.'

'But not about Belle,' Posy protested. 'Belle's special, isn't she, Mum?'

'Very special. That's why, if Mrs Grant won't let her stay, we'll go somewhere else.' She turned to Sue. 'Can we leave these two lovebirds here whilst we go up to the kitchen? Then I can make us all some tea.'

'We had tea at Bill's,' Posy remarked from the floor. 'A super tea. Hot chocolate whip to drink and beans on toast with a fried egg on top and then ice-cream, the pink and brown sort, my favourite, and then an iced bun, only I couldn't finish mine and Dawn said eyes bigger'n stummick and Ricky said she was rude, to a guest, and Bill put the iced bun in a bag for later and . . . oh, Belly, Belly, see what I've got for you!'

Jenny and Sue left the two of them, Belle eating the bun small piece by small piece, Posy contentedly shredding it.

'And for afters,' they heard her say as they climbed the stairs, 'for afters you shall have some lovely hot milk with the rest of Sue's loaf in it, and my Mars Bars. And tomorrow Mum will get real dog food, some in a tin and some, the bicky sort, in a bag; won't that be lovely?'

'Was that a hint?' Sue asked darkly as they entered the kitchen. 'I did mention my loaf had gone stale and Posy remarked you had a whole pint of milk over and wouldn't need to have any for breakfast tomorrow.'

'Not a hint so much as a takeover, I think,' Jenny told her. She had undone one of the suitcases whilst they talked and abstracted a towel which she now proceeded to use, vigorously, on her head. 'Gracious, I never knew a human being could get so wet, I'm sure it's got through my skin and thinned my blood, I'm certainly cold enough!'

'You poor thing! My sympathies, like your blood, were thinned by the surprise of finding you'd acquired a furry friend – if it is fur, the poor creature's so wet it could be an otter.'

'I'm a lot more of a poor thing than you know. If you'll put the kettle on, and a pan for a boiled egg or something, I'll tell you my whole grim story. It's not for young ears, mind, so if you hear Posy coming warn me and I'll stop.'

'Why won't you hear her yourself?' Sue enquired reasonably, filling the kettle at the sink. 'After all, there will be three pairs of feet, not just one, because I don't believe those two will be parted again, not for a while.'

'True. But I've got streaming catarrh and I'm not hearing anything too clearly,' Jenny said. 'Oh, how I wish I could just go and flop in the bath but, knowing the old hen, either someone's already in occupation or there's no hot water or she's saving it for Dermott.'

Dermott was a high favourite at the moment with Mrs Grant because he had been in the summer show at the Coliseum and would be in the pantomime when they started rehearsing in a few weeks. She dismissed with scorn the idea that she was a theatrical landlady, however. She let her flats to Stars only, she explained when Sue asked. Dermott was a resting Star perhaps, since he was working in a nightclub until the panto rehearsals started, but even so, to Mrs Grant he was Star quality and that, apparently, was what counted. When the show started, no doubt he would be a real pain as Mrs Grant would insist that he had priority for everything, not just the bathroom, but at the moment, as Sue put it, he was merely twinkling and not blazing, so they were only reminded about five times a day that Dermott needed the bathroom between seven and eight.

'Tell you what,' Sue said now, thumping the kettle rather untidily on to the gas stove. 'I'll live with my unbearable curiosity for twenty minutes whilst you have a bath and, what's more, I'll get you something hot to eat. Then, when you've finished, we can pop Posy into bed and sit in my room and have a jolly good natter; does that appeal?'

It did.

'Only what if Dermott really does want the bath?' Jenny said forlornly, standing on the top stair with her towel and her soap and her flannel all at the ready. 'Once he's in there, I can't even have a good strip-down wash.'

'Dermott's got a very kind heart, especially when a pretty

woman's in distress. Go down to his room, not the old hen's, and ask him straight if you can grab the tub first. He'll take one look at that pale face, that draggly hair, that streaming snout, and he'll let you go ahead. No offence,' she added, grinning at Jenny's watering eyes, 'but you do look like death!'

'Pretty woman one moment, death the next,' Jenny grumbled. 'Right, I'll go throw myself at Dermott's head.'

'Well, no, because . . . but throw yourself on his mercy, by all means.'

'Don't quibble,' Jenny shouted, as she reached the ground floor. 'Just you be glad . . .'

'Hello, Jenny! Everything all . . . Christ, what have you been doing? Swimming? Or a failed suicide attempt?'

Dermott, leaving his room quietly with his bath things in one hand, almost gave Jenny a heart attack so firmly was her attention fixed on Sue at the top of the stairs. She jumped and squeaked, a hand to her heart, and sponge-bag, towel and soap descended all over the dirty hall floor. Jenny groaned and bent to pick them up.

'I've been out in the rain, that's all. I was coming down to throw myself on your mercy and ask if I could have the first bath, but I suppose it's too late.'

'No, carry on, I can wait half an hour,' the cheerful Dermott said, picking up her soap and handing it to her. 'Your need is obviously greater than mine. Just give a bang on my door when you're out, will you? And don't let Martin beat me to it,' he added, sinking his voice to a breathy whisper. 'He's taken to bathing, you know. God knows why, – it can't be a woman, not with all his spots.'

'Oh, Dermott, you really are a dear,' Jenny said gratefully, heading for the bathroom. 'A thousand thanks, if there's ever anything I can do for you . . .'

Dermott grabbed her arm, spun her round, and smiled down into her eyes.

'Give us a kiss, gorgeous,' he said inexplicably. 'Come on, just one little smackeroo because I'm so kind.'

He kissed her, his mouth gentle and undemanding, tasting of toothpaste and clean living, then released her with a pat on the bottom to take her bath.

How odd, Jenny thought drowsily as she ran hot water and tipped Sue's bath salts into it until it was tinged with blue and smelt divine. Now why on earth should Dermott give her a kiss when she was looking unbelievably grotty and he was looking extremely toothsome? She had not registered much at the time but now she thought about Dermott bound for the bath. A dark-green silk dressing gown open to the navel, a good deal of tanned, muscular chest, untidy dark hair, the gleam of his teeth . . .

The bath reached a respectable depth and Jenny turned off the taps and stepped into the water, then, by degrees, lay down until only her head was above the surface. Lovely! Warm! Relaxing! Gradually, she ceased to think at all; thought could come later, when she was back in the kitchen with Sue.

'And you were in the wardrobe the whole time? My God! What on earth would you have done if it *had* been Dirk and not Philip?'

'I don't know. For a little while, I thought it *was* Dirk, I suppose because he and Phil are awfully alike. That was awful, so bad that it was like a physical pain eating me up. I don't suppose you can possibly understand, but when you love someone . . . or *loved*, which I think may be true . . . when you've felt very special about them, to see them . . . to think they're . . . oh, I can't explain.'

'You don't have to.' Sue was sitting opposite Jenny at the kitchen table, toying with a pancake whilst Jenny ate her way through a four-inch pile of French toast with bacon on the side. Jenny looked at Sue through her flattened hair and saw Sue's face was wistful, her eyes full of the same sort of longing which Jenny had once known. 'Just because I'm having a baby by . . . someone . . . doesn't mean I don't love someone very much indeed. Oh, I can imagine seeing him with someone else, but I can't imagine what it would do to me. Kill me, probably.'

'Sorry. Stupid of me,' Jenny said gruffly. 'Take it as read that I felt awful and then, when I realized it was Phil, felt quite different. Oh, I knew I was spying, and on my own son too, but it was an accident, I hadn't meant to do it so it didn't count. It would have been worse for everyone if I'd popped out of the wardrobe and said "cooee", wouldn't it?'

'Gosh, much worse,' Sue agreed. 'And then. . . ?'

'Then there was the row, which I told you about, and then I came home. I left in a hurry, as you can imagine, but I did check round, and I don't think I left any signs. I filled the kettle and rinsed the pot and my mug, I shut the wardrobe door and the cupboard under the sink, and the towels which Belle and I used might have been similarly grabbed by anyone who'd been out in the yard and come in to answer the phone or something. No, I don't think they'll know they've had an intruder.'

'And Belle? You don't think they'll notice she's gone missing?'

There was a hollow pause, then Jenny shrugged and heaved a sigh.

'They will, of course, and eventually I may have to admit I went home and took her, but they'll more likely think she's been killed by a hit-and-run driver and dumped in a ditch. Things like that do happen to farm dogs, particularly if they're underfed and hunting for themselves.'

'Then that's grand. All you need worry about is how to talk Mrs Grant into letting Belle stay here.'

Jenny, finishing up her plateful of food, shook her head, chewed very fast, and finally spoke.

'No, I'm not going to worry about it. I'm going down, right now, and I'm going to tell Mrs Grant either Belle stays or Posy and I go.'

'That could do it, of course, because it's getting late to find people who want winter lets. Tell you what, I'll nip up to see the Twiggs and Anna and then down to see Brenda, and we'll present a united front. The house is too open – that's true, you've said so yourself – we'll all feel safer with the dog, and if she can't stay we'll all go. It may not be true, but it'll make the old hen think.'

'You're the best thing that's happened since sliced bread,' Jenny said, getting to her feet. 'I'm going *now*, before my courage fails.'

'Now? Oh, but Jenny, you know what she says about her sacred evenings, and about the mushroom's homework and about her telly. Wouldn't it be more tactful to leave it until tomorrow?'

'More tactful perhaps, but tomorrow my nerves mightn't be as strong.' Jenny opened the kitchen door. 'Keep an ear out for Posy, will you? I won't worry about her, not with Belle, but I won't disturb them. They were both sleeping like angels when I came up from having my bath.'

She hurried down the stairs, passed the flat, across the familiar hall and on to strange ground. She had gone calling on Mrs Grant once or twice before, but somehow during the day her footsteps scarcely had to sound on the basement stairs before Mrs Grant was halfway up, edging Jenny back to the ground floor where she belonged. But now, with the television blaring away in the background and the mushroom's music centre broadcasting Boney-M to the world, Mrs Grant would have needed to have been psychic to have heard a flock of sheep descending the stairs, far less one not very large woman.

At the bottom of the stairs was a small square stairwell, covered by a huge, curly rug from wall to wall, and a blue door with a brass door-knocker shaped like a dolphin suspended from it. Jenny lifted the dolphin's head and dropped it again, and the resultant bang brought, sooner than she expected, the sound of approaching footsteps.

Only they came from behind her – someone was descending the stairs from the flats. She looked over her shoulder and there was Dermott, properly dressed and with a carrier bag in one hand. He looked rather put-out to see her, she thought, though he covered it quickly with his pleasant smile.

'Hi again! Visiting?'

'More or . . .' Jenny broke off as the blue door opened a crack. A face hovered, she could not identify it at all against the light which streamed out from behind it.

'Yes?'

'Oh . . . could I speak to Mrs Grant, please?'

The head made no reply. It simply withdrew and the door closed again. Jenny gave Dermott a startled look but he only grinned.

'Usual practice,' he murmured. 'That was probably her old feller. She'll be out in a minute.'

He was right. Far less than a minute had passed when the

door creaked open again and there was Mrs Grant. She had combed her hair out rather nicely and was wearing a brown and fawn dress with a big gold brooch pinned above one breast. However, her expression was not pleased – or not when her eyes fell on Jenny. When she looked past her and saw Dermott she smiled and held the door open.

'Come in, then. Now what can I do for you? I was just watching *Dallas* – my, that J.R.'s a card, I wouldn't want 'im as a tenant!'

She ushered Dermott and Jenny into what Jenny realized must be a tiny parlour or best room, because it was so clean and tidy, so cold and cheerless, from the ice-blue paper on the walls to the electric blue of a two-seater sofa and a couple of very new-looking easy chairs. The curtains were not drawn and now Mrs Grant bustled across to close them, shutting out the sight of the rain falling on the paving stones of the back yard which was about all you could see. Then she turned on the electric fire and urged them, quite hospitably, to take a seat. Jenny hastily went for a chair and Dermott did the same; the couch looked a bit small to share with Mrs Grant, a large lady.

'Now!' Mrs Grant, setting herself on to two-thirds of the couch, turned to them with a bright, social smile. 'Are you together, or did you want to see me private, like?'

'Jenny was first, let her have first go,' Dermott said, smiling from one to the other. 'It's nothing private for me, at any rate.'

'Nor me,' Jenny said hastily. 'Mrs Grant, I went home today and discovered that my husband has turned our dog out. She's an old dog, quiet and good, but a marvellous house-dog. I've brought her here, I had no option but to do so, and I'd very much like to keep her. She's house-trained, of course, she'd be no trouble, and . . .'

'A dog?' Mrs Grant stared very hard at Jenny as though she were secreting the dog somewhere about her person. 'There was no mention of a dog when you first come, Mrs Sayer, no one said there might be a dog.'

'No. Well, no one knew that Belle would be turned out,' Jenny said, trying to sound reasonable without sounding condescending. 'If you would just let us keep her for a few days you'd see for yourself that she'd be no trouble. She's very intelligent – a working dog – and once she knows everyone's footsteps she'll only bark when a stranger comes into the flats.'

Mrs Grant's eyes had been getting beadier and beadier, closer and closer together, but for some reason Jenny's last remark gave her pause for thought. She held up a hand, a bit like a traffic policeman, then smiled graciously.

'She? It's a lady dog, then?'

'Yes, she's called Belle. She's twelve years old.'

'And she'd bark if a stranger came in?'

'Oh, yes. She'd stop anyone coming into the place if she didn't know them, but that needn't worry you because, if I make it clear to her it's only my room that she's to guard . . .'

'No indeed, Mrs Sayer, that won't be necessary. If you'd be kind enough to let her have the run of the lower hall and stairs say between midnight and seven o'clock, I'll say no more about our house-rules. We do have dogs in the summer, now and then, and it hasn't always been a good idea, but as it happens . . . yes, that would suit.'

Jenny was stammering her thanks, not sure whether she should do so or whether Mrs Grant should be thanking her, when the landlady turned to Dermott.

'Now dear, having settled Mrs Sayer's little problem, what can I do for you?'

Jenny stood up as if to go but Dermott gave her such a pleading, hunted look that she sat again. What on earth was he going to say? Dermott, the favourite, could surely get away with anything if she, Jenny, far from being the favourite ever since Mrs Grant had decided her cleaning activities in the communal rooms amounted to criticism, could get away with a dog!

'I had a letter this morning, Mrs Grant,' Dermott began. 'It was from an old friend of mine – a colleague, actually, Solomon Kant. He's a stage manager and he'll be coming down to Rhyl in a week because he's got the stage manager's job at the Coliseum, and I was wondering . . .'

Jenny looked at Mrs Grant; she was wondering too, you could almost see a cash register clicking.

'Yes, Dermott? You was wondering. . . ?'

'If it would be possible for Solly to share my place? It's got single beds, and though it might be a bit of a squeeze at meal times I think we could manage.'

Jenny knew at once that Dermott had put his foot in it there, and Mrs Grant speedily made it plain. Her face, which had been looking quite soft and receptive, tightened and hardened.

'A bit of a squeeze?' she repeated slowly. 'A bit of a squeeze, Dermott? In the season that flat takes a family of three, let me tell you!'

'Oh, I'm not suggesting that it's *small*,' Dermott said hastily. 'It's quite . . .' Danger signals flashed from Mrs Grant's narrowing eyes. 'It's quite huge,' he concluded. 'It was only the dining area . . . though there's plenty of space there really, only as you know I've got quite a few of my own things in there, which has meant . . .'

He was obviously going to sink in a mire of his own making if someone didn't say something quickly. Jenny smiled brightly at Mrs Grant.

'Another young man, Mrs Grant, that'll be nice for all us women! We are a rather female-dominated society at the moment, so if Mr Kant joins Dermott we'll be a bit more balanced.'

'Well, I suppose there's no harm in one more,' Mrs Grant said at last. 'Seeing as how he's your friend, Dermott, so won't be noisy nor no trouble, I trust?'

'Not a bit noisy, and no trouble at all,' Dermott said at once, blinking rather too rapidly; Jenny saw that he had been genuinely anxious that Mrs Grant accede to his request. Presumably, for all Mrs Grant's talk about her tenant's stardom, Dermott was as short of money as the rest of them and would be glad to have someone else sharing the rent.

'Very well then, that's settled.' Mrs Grant smiled graciously on them both and rose to her feet, indicating that the interview was at an end; from the room next door a well-known theme tune swelled, making it clear why Mrs Grant had decided to end the discussion.

Just as they reached the stairwell, however, and Jenny was three steps up on her way back to the ground floor, Mrs Grant cleared her throat.

'I won't make a *large* additional charge for your friend,' she said rather stiltedly, 'Just a pound or two . . . should we say three? Because of the extra use of the communal kitchen, the bathroom and so on.' As both her tenants turned to stare she added a trifle defensively, 'One more will make more work for me, cleaning and such.'

Jenny, outraged, opened her mouth to give Mrs Grant a piece of her mind, but Dermott dug her in the back and spoke over his shoulder, propelling his fellow tenant up the stairs more by force than anything else as he did so.

'That will be fine, Mrs Grant. I'll tell Solomon that he can move in as soon as he likes, then,' he said. He dug Jenny in the back again. 'Many thanks . . . you'll find a small token of my regard . . . for the family, naturally . . . in the back of my chair.'

'So that was what the carrier bag was for, a bribe,' Jenny remarked as soon as she had heard the blue door close below them. 'You should be ashamed, Dermott Hughes!'

'A few chocolates for the poor old dear doesn't break me and pleases her,' Dermott said righteously. 'Why should you grudge me giving them? After all, she'd have got them anyway since I left them in the chair, and if I hadn't, that three quid might have been six, or nine. Tell you the truth, I was prepared for her to suggest we both paid full rent, and I was going to beat her down. It was a good job you were there; she isn't too sure of you.'

'Not sure of me? Whatever do you mean?'

'Oh, honey, you aren't the type for a winter let! I know you and your husband are separated, but usually someone like you has a home and a family to fall back on. The old hen thinks you know people who matter, so she never quite dares to treat you the way she would if she thought you were just like the rest of us.'

'I am!'

'Of course, but she doesn't know it,' Dermott said un-answerably as they arrived outside his door. 'And if you were surprised by your own success over the dog, I can explain that as well.'

Jenny, about to climb the stairs back to her own floor, stopped short.

'You can? Go ahead, then. I'm intrigued.'

'Didn't you hear the racket at midnight last night? You must sleep like a log.'

'Racket? What racket?'

'Hell, a drunk got in, or so Anna claimed. Others thought it was one of her less successful fellers. Apparently she came home late from some dance or other and she thinks he must have followed her. She didn't lock the door, or so the old hen claims. Anna admits she might not have done, but of course you aren't supposed to lock it until after midnight, and Anna swears she was in at five to the hour and thought she was by no means last. Anyhow, this chap came burbling in, fell up the first flight and down the second and was routed, believe it or not, by the old girl from the top floor armed with a bloody great saucepan. Honestly, how you can have slept through it is beyond me but of course I didn't hear anything because I was at work, and Sue and Brenda claimed they just lay there and wondered what was going on but never even peeked.'

'So did that decide Mrs Grant to get a dog? I can't believe it!'

'You needn't try, because it didn't, of course. But Mrs Twigg's a permanency and she was so irate she threatened to go, which didn't suit madam because I believe they're quite thick, aren't they, those two? And when you came along talking about how Belle would bark and drive intruders off . . . well, it must have seemed like manna from heaven to Mrs G.'

'If I'd known I'd have charged *her* three quid for the privilege of housing Belle,' Jenny said. 'Really, Dermott, you should have stood up to her and refused to pay. You pay for the flat, you're entitled to have someone share with you without paying extra.'

'Oh go on, don't be so bloody tight, she's got to make a living too, you know, and Solly won't grudge the extra. Goodnight, love.'

He disappeared into his own room leaving Jenny to climb the stairs, still unsure whether to be elated or annoyed. It was marvellous about Belle, of course, but how the old hen dared to charge extra for cleaning which she did not even do was beyond her.

But Sue, when Jenny told her the story, shared Dermott's opinion.

'A landlady's got a lot of power over her tenants,' she said when she had heard Jenny out. 'It's her house, when all's said and done. I pay for my flat, you pay for yours, but if she chooses to put up the rent tomorrow there isn't really much we can do about it. Dermott was right, at least he'll only be paying half as much in future, plus an extra one fifty, which isn't so bad. Better that than a refusal and ill-feeling on both sides.'

'I suppose so. Thanks for holding the fort, Sue, I'm off to bed now. See you in the morning.'

Jenny went slowly back to her own room and left the door slightly ajar, so that Belle could get out during the night if she so wished. Not that she thought the dog would want to explore, not when she was curled up so comfortably, close to Posy, with the child's fingers tangled in the thick ruff of fur round her neck.

Climbing into bed, she thought what a long day it had been, but also how successful. She had reclaimed her winter clothes and saved herself a lot of momey, she had brought Belle back with her and would no longer need to worry about Posy's safety if she left the flat for ten minutes. But best of all, she knew that her mind was a good deal clearer over her own situation. It had seemed a very hard situation until that afternoon, but now she was not so sure. Dirk had landed himself with a very unpleasant young woman, but she had known that right from the start. What she had not known was how badly Dirk was prepared to behave in order to keep Bronwen. And now that she knew, her opinion of him had sunk lower than she had believed possible; the idol's feet of clay reached right up to his elbows!

Her own lot, too, had seemed rather hard, her path stony. Not any more. She had revisited the farm kitchen she had once loved so much and had remembered, not only the happy times but also how lonely she had been over the years, most of the time without being aware of it. Why had she found it so difficult to make friends? The fact that Mrs Ted and Mrs George had let her plants die rankled terribly. The answer had to be that Dirk had prevented her from making friends of her own age and type, and that Mrs George and Mrs Ted had regarded her simply and solely as an employer. Here, in the flats, she had good friends, people she could laugh with, go out with, weep with if necessary. She was earning money by her own hard work, she fed and clothed her child from an allowance which was insufficient for her needs but which she stretched out to cover its job. She had dreaded being alone; it was not so terrible!

Afterwards, Jenny tended to think that her visit to the farm had been the big turning point in her life, a catalyst which started everything moving. Perhaps it was because she stopped looking back wistfully and began to look forward optimistically, perhaps because she no longer wondered before taking an action what Dirk would have done. From the time that she visited the farm, almost imperceptibly to her, her attitude began to change.

That did not mean to say, however, that she stopped loving Dirk, though she most certainly stopped respecting him. Love, she discovered, was not a thing which just stopped for the asking, not even when you knew the object of your love was unworthy of it. Love continued, grimly, doggedly, to bestow itself where it was neither desired nor deserved.

But the urgent longing had quietened down to an acceptance of being content with what she had, which was friendship, family love and an enjoyable work and social life. She had little time to grieve for her lost marriage and, as time went on, little inclination. Jenny was doing very well alone.

A week after her visit to the farm, Jenny resigned her job. She had little option as she explained to Sue afterwards.

'Fool that I am, I'd totally forgotten Simon had said I could have a day off,' she said, pacing the kitchen. 'They – he and Brenda – were going to close because they had a big consignment of stuff coming in and they wanted to do a stocktake.'

'So you went in – why resign?'

'Shut up and stop spoiling the flow of my narrative. Have you ever noticed, by the way, that when something peculiar happens to you it tends to keep happening, over and over?

You know, like you hear someone use a word you've never heard before, and you look it up in the dictionary, and after that you find it in everything you read, all your friends use it in casual conversation, people on television keep repeating it . . . d'you know what I mean?'

'Yes, I know. What's that got to do with it?' Sue was peeling onions which she and Jenny were presently going to pickle. Jenny sighed, sat herself down and reached for the next pile of onions. When your eyes were streaming it was a good idea to get a break for a moment, but her break was now over; she settled down to the niggling, fiddling, eye-watering task once more.

'Rather a lot. As I said, I'd forgotten I'd had the day off . . . well, I hadn't forgotten being off, of course, what I'd forgotten was that the shop was closed. So I went waltzing over there with the jeans I'd bought at the end-of-season sale in Annette's, because they'd got quite a lot in Brenda's size and I thought she might like to know. And I walked into the shop without even noticing that it said closed on the door – they'd forgotten to lock it – and it was empty, but the door was open and there was a light in the back room. So in I walked.'

'And what did you see? Brenda in Simon's hot embrace? Dear Jen, you certainly do live dangerously, and you with no wardrobe handy to jump in! What did you do, sneak out again?'

'Unfortunately I'd entered talking, as it says in plays. Oo-ooh, Sue!'

'Look, it's all right, people are far more broad-minded than you'd believe. I know you think you'll never be able to face Brenda again, but . . .'

'It's not Brenda . . . it wasn't Brenda. That's the trouble. Sue, it was stock!'

'Stock? Who's she when she's at home?'

'She's Cindy, or Julie, or possibly even Mandy! Stock!'

There was a pause during which Sue's eyes and mouth both got rounder and rounder and even in the midst of her own embarrassment Jenny found time to be glad that Sue was not as unshockable as she liked to appear.

'*Stock*? Jesus H. Christ! You mean he was having it off with a rubber doll?'

'Well, I wouldn't have put it quite like that . . . yes, I suppose there's no other way of putting it, really.'

'Cor!' Sue had been a study in suspended motion but now she began to peel her onion again and to giggle steadily, despite the tears which were pouring down her cheeks.

'What's so funny?' Jenny said suspiciously. 'If you're getting a mental picture . . . well, it wasn't funny, I tell you, it was one of the worst things that has ever happened to me. I liked Simon, I thought he was a decent guy, I encouraged Brenda when she tried to get him to take her out, I thought they'd make a nice couple.'

'A threesome, you mean! All right, all right, I'm sorry I laughed, I suppose it's not that funny really. Only . . . don't you think you could put it down to one of those mad things one does when totally alone? I've done some pretty stupid things in my time behind locked doors. The fact that he forgot to actually lock the door was very unfortunate, but . . . do you have to give in your notice?'

'I think I do,' Jenny said half apologetically. 'I wouldn't want Simon to feel he had to sack me, and even if I could bring myself to face *him*, there's no knowing whether he would be able to bring himself to face me!'

'Then what'll you do? Twelve quid doesn't sound much until you lose it.'

'Actually, it's so nearly Christmas that I should be able to get a job pretty easily, I think,' Jenny admitted. 'I've seen adverts in shop windows and all sorts, but since they mostly want you from ten until three I've not done anything about it, being semi-employed. And, you know, Simon's been on for weeks now about wanting me to do more hours. Well, they won't have any trouble filling a job of that nature, it was just the lunch-hour that was difficult because it meant breaking into someone's day without actually paying them a worthwhile sum, or that's what Brenda says, anyway. So I can leave without having to tell Bren a thing.'

Privately, she thought that perhaps it might save a lot of heartache later if she did tell Brenda everything, but as Sue had said, Simon had believed the door to be locked. She had had no right to tell Sue, she supposed, but there are some things that have to be shared if only to take the horror out of them. And she had not told Sue what she privately considered the worst part; it had not been a Cindy or a Mandy or a Julie, it had been a Bobby, or a Shane or an Alan doll.

Telling herself that Simon had merely grabbed the first doll which came to hand, inflated it and got to work, only partially calmed her. The experience had put her off the little back room in the Private Shop for life; it would have an aura of nightmare for ever. No, she would tell Brenda, regretfully if untruthfully, that she had been offered a job by a friend in an ordinary shop and felt that it would suit her better than . . . no, that wouldn't do, that the *hours* would suit her better than those Simon was offering.

Sue peeled the last onion in her pile and poked her finger into the mass of skins and peel in front of Jenny.

'Finished? I have, and it's about time you cleaned yourself up and set off for Posy. Have you actually given in your notice yet?'

'Yes. Coward that I am, I wrote it out and posted it. Simon will get it tomorrow morning.'

'And what'll you do tomorrow, pray? It wouldn't be very fair to leave without notice, no matter how hard you find it to face Simon.'

'I know. I've said I'll hang on till they replace me, but I've already suggested to Anna that she might step into the breach and she's willing. I've not said anything about Simon to her, of course – you won't tell a soul, I know that.'

'True.' Sue began to giggle again, holding up a hand to ward off Jenny's incipient swipe. 'I'm sorry, it's just that I can't see myself confiding in the nurse who gives us our relaxation classes or one of the other mums, can you? And, apart from them, my chances of exchanging idle gossip are pretty small.'

'If you told your relaxation class they'd probably all give birth on the spot,' Jenny remarked. 'I'm off, now.' She raised her voice. 'Belle!'

Belle enjoyed company and would have been quite happy sitting under the kitchen table but for the onions; after a few moments she had got up, sneezed a couple of times and taken herself firmly back down to the flat, where she was probably illegally curled up on Posy's bed. But now, a few seconds after hearing her name, she appeared round the kitchen door, her tail wagging doubtfully. The smell still lingered and you could see she did not care for it at all.

182

'Going to get Posy, lass,' Jenny said briskly. She had rinsed her hands, but with very little success since the smell of onions can take days to dissipate. 'Want to come?'

Belle danced and gave a muted whine; she had never been a noisy dog and, as Jenny had promised, was no trouble at all in the flat.

'Right. Cheerio, Sue, see you later. I'll get my coat and boots.'

'You three going on the swings? Well, be careful, because there's a cold wind. I'll give you ten minutes, then it's back in here and hot chocolate and fancy cakes all round. Fair enough?'

Bill always treated the children sensibly, Jenny thought, watching as the three girls ran out of the cafe, chanting 'Fair enough'. He never said 'Don't,' without explaining why not, a thing which many parents seemed to find too much trouble. Jenny had always scorned the 'because I say so' approach, but she had heard it often enough to know what a convenient escape route it could be for some adults.

Now she walked round the counter to give a hand with the hot chocolate and to see whether there was any washing-up which still needed doing. It was a chilly day, the wind far too brisk for idle strolling, and as a result the usual sprinkling of elderly customers was missing, though one or two parents with children would be rushing in presently, having stoically done their duty on playgrounds and clock-golf.

'Well, Jenny? How's life?' Bill looked at her closely, then again with concern. 'Love! You've been crying. What's the matter? Not husband trouble, I hope?'

'No, onions, actually. You know the pickling sort. Mind you, I've resigned from the shop, so I shall probably be crying for real in a couple of weeks.'

'You're leaving the shop?' Bill hesitated, eyeing the half-dozen or so advertisement attempts he had spent the afternoon composing, now crumpled up on the counter. For some time he had been struggling to cope single-handedly with the extra work generated by his hot lunches and the increasing number of Christmas shoppers who were dining at the cafe. Would it be an awful cheek? . . but nothing venture,

183

nothing gain, he reminded himself and anyway, she did need work, she had said so often enough. 'Look, I suppose . . . you wouldn't think of helping out here? I was thinking of advertising, but if you could do it you know where things are kept, you . . .' He gulped. 'You could come whenever it suited you,' he finished lamely.

Jenny stared at him. 'But do you want more help?' she asked uncertainly, 'You seem to manage awfully well.'

'I'm run off my feet,' Bill assured her. 'Look at these if you don't believe I was desperate.' He handed her the draft advertisements.

Jenny took them and read them slowly and carefully, then looked up at him. A smile dawned on both faces.

'Oh Bill, if you think I could do it – you aren't just saying it to be kind? No, of course not, you really were advertising. But I've never been a waitress or a cook, so . . .' She stopped short, then laughed. 'What an idiot I am, I spent the last ten years of my life being waitress, cook and general dog's-body to three thoroughly selfish men. Right, here we go. I apply for the position of . . . of general worker at this cafe.'

'And I appoint you my manager,' Bill said promptly. 'Gosh, what a difference it will make to the work to have two of us tackling it.'

'Great! When do I start? And the very nicest and best thing is that you've made me truthful instead of a liar.' She explained how she had planned to tell Brenda that a friend had offered her a job. 'I've found a replacement for me, the girl in the flats I was telling you about, Anna, so they may let me go almost at once. Or even at once, if I'm lucky.' She could not help thinking that if she were in Simon's shoes she would gladly see the back of her immediately.

'Well, start as soon as you can,' Bill said. He was grinning from ear to ear, looking terribly pleased. 'I can't tell you what a relief it will be to have you here, I was dreading the idea of some chit of a thing who'd spend all her time making up her face or upsetting the customers, or else some old biddy who'd hobble round complaining about her feet and keep telling me I was doing it all wrong. But just what made you decide to leave the shop? I've always been careful never to suggest it . . . I told myself you liked it there.'

'I didn't, not really, I just put a good face on it,' Jenny admitted. As they talked, she had been setting out the cakes and piling crockery on to a tray whilst Bill filled the children's mugs with chocolate and then made cheese and tomato-ketchup sandwiches, a colourful mixture much admired by Dawn and Erica and one to which Posy was becoming reconciled. 'Anyway, I took my courage in both hands and decided to leave and try for something else.'

'Any particular reason? Dirk come up with a bit more money, seeing that Christmas is only weeks away?'

'No, not really. Just that they wanted me to do more hours and . . . does it sound priggish and snobbish to say it really wasn't my scene?'

'Not a bit. Neither. If you were a prig or a snob I'd scarcely ask you to come and skivvy in here!'

Jenny laughed and carried her tray out from the kitchen and into the cafe proper. Through the glass door she could see two mums, five children and a red setter she knew to be both brainless and incontinent approaching the cafe. She put her tray down on the table the children usually used and called to Bill.

'Customers, Boss!'

It was trying to turn over that woke Sue up. One minute she was wrapped in velvet sleep, secure and snug, positive that a few inches from her curled-up and recumbent form Hugo also lay sleeping; the next minute she was conscious, desperately trying to heave her vast pulsating stomach from its left side to its right whilst cramp needled at her calves and the chill of knowing herself alone in bed pricked her into wide and uneasy wakefulness.

Sometimes, once she was settled, she could drop off to sleep again without trouble. She was on her right side now, so she straightened her right leg and pulled her left leg up obediently, as she had been taught in her classes, so that the weight was properly distributed. The baby, who had not apparently wanted to turn over, kicked out fretfully, curling and uncurling like a little shrimp, giving Sue a bad moment when she wondered whether this was the start, because until you had started how could you know what it felt like? But then the baby settled again and Sue shrugged the covers well up and told herself firmly that insomnia was imagination, that she was really extremely tired, and that she was about to plunge into dreamland once more.

Ten, slow, dragging minutes later she knew she lied. Sleep had gone to visit worthier people and she . . . oh, damn, damn, *damn*, she had heartburn! Boiling hot acid rose in her chest, up and up, until it was sour in her throat. She moaned and swallowed, trying to will it away, cursing the frivolous appetite which had attacked her when Dermott had said he was going down the road for chips. What a fool she had been, why on earth had she not remembered what hell heartburn could be? On her bedside table there were some tablets, horrid little pink things made out of chalk and sour milk, or so the taste led one to believe. She found the tube in the dark, fidgeted one free and put it in her mouth, grimacing. She began to suck, but they were horribly drying, so she cheated and chewed, crunching briskly, wishing she had thought to put that marvellous medicine Dermott had recommended closer to hand than the mantelpiece.

Miraculously, the heartburn receded to mere indigestion. Sue slid another tablet into her mouth and crunched that too, just for good measure. Perhaps, if she lay very still and forced her mind into a blank, the fickle God of expectant mothers would let her fall asleep again, perhaps . . .

Cramp straightened out all her toes in an agonizing spasm, then curled them all under in another, more painful one. Despite her size, Sue found herself on her feet, swaying and stunned, still in the dark, trying to stand on her heels, to lift up her foot in order to physically uncurl her toes and to stand on the balls of her feet, all simultaneously and unsuccessfully. She snatched at her right foot, overbalanced and fell on to the bed. The bed slid squawking across the lino, defeated by her weight, and crashed against the wall or a chair, she could not tell which.

She reached for the bedside light, found it more by luck than judgement – cramp made fools of the wisest, she reflected bitterly, still trying to balance on her heels – and breathed a sigh of relief as the room sprang to life. That was better, she felt a good deal more sane with the light on.

Hugo's photograph smiled down at her from the wall and she smiled back at it; your confounded seedling is giving me gyp, she told him affectionately. Why else should I be standing on my heels in the middle of the night, chewing indigestion tablets and unable to sleep?

Sleep had always come easily to her. Rich and delicious slumber had been her right, taken totally for granted. Hugo had sometimes teased her about her ability in that direction, telling her long and probably apocryphal stories of how he had fancied a bit of love in the early hours and been unable to provoke any response from her whatsoever, save for a string of muttered gobbledegook accompanied by a more determined curling up and deeper slumber.

Yet nowadays she rarely got an uninterrupted night's sleep, and she resented that more than anything, more than her shape which was so hideous that she shut her eyes when approaching full-length mirrors, more than the heartburn which followed almost all remotely enjoyable food or the cramp which attacked so unexpectedly, even more than the dark throbbing vein which had suddenly appeared, running the length of her left leg from ankle to crotch and ruining her pleasure in walking.

Still on her heels, she tottered across the room to the hand basin, where she kept a bottle of milk for breakfast or early-morning tea or both, depending on how late she slept. She lifted it up and took an experimental swig; it went down smooth and cool, without causing her stomach or any other part of her to bunch and growl. She sighed and stood the bottle gently back on the porcelain. It seemed that the tablets had done the trick and dispelled the heartburn, and although she dared not stand normally quite yet, the cramp had left her. Since she was now wide awake though, she could light her gas ring and have a cup of tea. It was . . . she glanced at her travelling clock for confirmation . . yes, it was only three-thirty, and she knew from bitter experience that it would be at least an hour before she was permitted to sleep again, so she might as well have a cup of tea and a sit down in front of her electric fire, then with luck she might climb back into bed and sleep till morning.

It was the work of a moment to fill the kettle, light the ring, and slump into her easy chair, from which she examined her room by the light of the bedside lamp. I've done wonders with it, she told herself complacently, it's really rather homely. She had bought a few brightly coloured scatter cushions which made the chairs and the little sofa both comfortable and brighter, and then she had put Hugo's rugs down, and they were so big they covered most of Mrs Grant's horrible browny-grey carpet, and then there was the standard lamp with its rose and gold shade and the matching bedside lamp, and her precious pictures plus the photograph of Hugo, only that was not visible from the main part of the room. She did not want someone recognizing him and putting two and two together, though the chances were that a visitor, glancing at her pictures nearly all of which had a mountain in view, would merely think that she had a crush on Hugo who must be one of the best-known mountaineers in the country.

Her screens had been made up from one of Hugo's presents, so she loved them very much, but when she had decided to bring them she had not realized what a boon they would be. They were made of Chinese silk, hand-painted, and were probably worth more than all the rest of the furniture in the house put together – which was not, reflected Sue wryly, putting much of a value on them – yet no one had recognized them for what they were, which was a work of art. Jenny had called them pretty, Posy, touching one with her cheek, had praised it as 'smoother than Belle' and Mrs Grant had stigmatized them as 'them things that attract the dust', so one way and another it did not look as though anyone was going to wonder what she was doing with works of art dividing her bedroom from her living quarters.

The rugs, on the other hand, had been much praised. Hugo had brought them back from Tibet and she thought they were goat's hair, unlikely though it seemed – or had he said llama? Anyway, they were the most glamorous colours – a deep and dramatic shade of cream fading to parchment, a lovely chestnut fading to gold and a dark, rich charcoal which ebbed to shimmering pearl. They made even the hardened Mrs Grant gasp when she first set eyes on them and Mrs Twigg, touching the cream-coloured rug, had said wistfully that if it were hers she wouldn't tread on it, no indeed, it should be hung on the wall, high up out of reach of feet or fingers, where she could feast her eyes on its beauty all day.

Sue's kettle boiled and she got to her feet, her toes enjoying the silky floss of the nearest rug, and made a pot of tea, helped herself, then waddled back to her chair. She fancied . . . a biscuit? No, not a biscuit. A slice of bread and butter? Certainly not, how mundane! Cake, then? There was some cake in a tin under the saucepans; it was a chocolate one, not terribly indigestible, perhaps . . ? Her stomach, which had always had a mind of its own, growled a refusal to the suggestion of cake. It wanted a great big hunk of bread spread thickly with peanut butter and on top of that it wanted good, big slices of a ripe tomato. Sue groaned and shook her head at her stomach; you'll be sorry in another two hours, she warned it silently, but it only persisted in its demands. Peanut butter and tomato, it reiterated stubbornly; you shan't sleep until you've eaten peanut butter and tomato.

Hoping to silence it Sue drank tea, but it was no good and she knew it. Cravings, they had been told at the clinic, were just an old wives' tale without a word of truth in them. Well, I've got news for you, Clinicians, Sue said to them silently, my stomach hasn't been told cravings are old wives' tales and so it's either provide it with peanut butter and tomato or forget sleep until tomorrow night.

She finished her tea and got to her feet; one thing you did have to say for a determined stomach, it had never been so mean as to demand something she did not have somewhere in the flat. Oh, it had craved kippers one day, smoked salmon another, had announced it fancied roast lamb when faced with pork chops and stewed apple when peaches were on the menu, but it had never done the dirty on her at night by urging her to stuff herself with something totally unavailable.

She had a food cupboard over the pans and crockery cupboard and now she reached into the back and extracted her loaf of wholemeal bread, the bag with two rather squashy tomatoes and the peanut butter jar. She knew as soon as she touched it, of course, that it was empty, remembered that she had forgotten to buy a refill as she wandered round Kwiks with her trolley.

Still, empty? . . . it couldn't be completely empty, there

must be some left, a smear, enough to kid her stomach that it had been fed on the desired food. Sue dug out a knife from her cutlery drawer, opened the jar and moaned. Not a smear! The last time she had fancied peanut butter she had fancied it good and proper, there was not enough left even to get a scraping on the knife. She slammed the empty jar into her rubbish bin, then got it out and stood it, reproachfully, in the middle of the table. That would remind her to get a refill; but what to do right now? She looked at the clock and it was still only three forty-five. No one else would be around; even in a lively place like Rhyl the number of shops open at three forty-five for the sale of peanut butter were likely to be few. Her fellow-tenants were undoubtedly all in bed and asleep and probably peanut butter-less to boot; it was not a common taste, Anna had never heard of the stuff until she had walked into the kitchen and seen Sue, Posy and Jenny making peanut butter sandwiches for tea one afternoon. With, Sue remembered slowly, Jenny's jar of peanut butter.

Jenny's jar. Had they finished it? She squeezed her lids closed and tried to visualize the jar; no, it had not been empty when Jenny left the kitchen with it, it had been a huge jar, much bigger than Sue's miserable little one, and it had still been well over half full.

However, it was three forty-five in the morning and Jenny's jar of peanut butter, along with Jenny and Posy and of course Belle, would all be tucked up in bed, or cupboard or whatever. Impossible for a person with any sort of conscience to wake them just for peanut butter!

Five minutes – five peanut butterless minutes – later Sue padded out of her own room and on to the landing. Jenny's door was ajar of course, so that Belle could roam the house to discourage unwanted visitors. Not that Belle was wandering; by applying her eye to the slit in the door Sue could see her, quite clearly, curled up on the bottom of Posy's bed, apparently fast asleep. Posy was fast asleep too, on her back with her thumb in her mouth and most of her out of the covers. Jenny, in the double bed, was just a small hump, all curled down and cosy. She was not snoring but she was very obviously dead to the world. Lucky Jenny! From where she stood, Sue could see the food cupboard and by pushing the door a bit wider she could also see that there was an un-obstructed path across to it. She could go in quietly, smile and pat Belle if she awoke, burgle the food cupboard of its peanut-butter, and be back in her own room, spreading, in no more than half a minute.

Sue pushed the door wider. It yawned without so much as a sound. She stepped into the room.

'I don't know what came over me,' Sue said tearfully, sipping the hot chocolate which someone had made her and taking a big bite out of her peanut butter sandwich. 'I don't think theft runs in the family or anything like that, it was just as if my stomach had suddenly turned communist. All I could think of was how Jenny had that huge jar of peanut butter and poor Sue had a tiny jar and that was empty, and how if life were fair peanut butter should be divided equally. And . . . and your door was open and I knew whereabouts in the cupboard it was kept, and . . . and Belle and I are old friends . . .' She stopped to stare accusingly at Belle who was seated demurely, paws together, tail out straight, by the kitchen door, '. . . when she suddenly let rip with those awful, screaming barks, I nearly had kittens . . . well, no, I nearly had *it*,' she amended.

Her audience, which consisted of Jenny, Anna, both Twiggs and Dermott, were all smiling sympathetically. Posy had slept through the entire affair and, since the basement door had remained firmly closed throughout, everyone assumed that the Grants, too, had heard nothing.

'I'm awfully sorry about Belle, I can't think why she barked at you,' Jenny said. They were all sitting around the kitchen on a variety of chairs, drinking hot chocolate though no one else, not even Bernard, had succumbed to the lure of peanut butter sandwiches; Sue chomped on alone. 'I think you probably scared the life out of her, as indeed you did out of me.'

'And me,' Dermott said. 'I thought, my God, someone's raping one of the girls and I just made straight for the stairs. And of course when I got to the girls' floor . . . well, I wondered just what had been happening.'

'Why?' demanded Anna, a late arrival on the scene. 'By the time I'd arrived it was all giggles and gin. So to speak.'

'When Dermott came bounding up the stairs – in the pyjama

trousers he favours and no jacket – Sue was screaming, I was out of bed still asleep I swear, taking swipes at Belle to try to shut her up, Bernard was halfway down the flight shouting that he was on his way, Mrs Twigg was a few stairs behind him ringing the biggest handbell I've ever seen, and then Dermott slipped, cannoned into Sue, who flew across the room and knocked me off my feet, and I started to laugh . . .'

'It was the knife that worried Belle, I imagine,' Sue said, sipping hot chocolate. 'I'd intended to plunge it into the jar of peanut butter but from the way that dog shrieked murder you'd have thought I was a madwoman on the rampage.'

'That's dog's perspicacious,' Dermott said dryly. 'What d'you think I thought? Well, Bernard, you're not a giggling girl, what did *you* think?'

A tide of crimson flowed over Bernard's face at being directly addressed, but he stood his mug of chocolate down and answered promptly enough.

'Same's you, Dermott. 'Cept I thought . . . you din't 'ave no pyjama jacket on, remember . . . I thought it was you creepin' about and makin' the gel scream.'

'Crumbs, he thought I was a rapist,' Dermott said, grinning and hitching up his pyjama trousers with one hand whilst adjusting an imaginary tie at his throat with the other. 'But why did you think I was coming *up* the stairs, Bern?'

'You'll laugh,' Bernard warned, going a shade redder. 'I thought you was being clever, going down 'em backwards.'

When the shout of laughter died down Mrs Twigg announced that she was going back to bed.

'I'm glad the dog barked, 'cos that just shows what would happen if a real intruder came in,' she said, putting her cup down on the draining board and brushing biscuit crumbs off the lapels of her baby-blue dressing gown. 'And Sue, dear, if you get peckish another time or can't sleep, just you come up and tap on my door, very gentle, so's not to wake Bernard, and I'll come and keep you company.'

'Another time I'll suffer in silence, or take a sleeping pill,' Sue said, also rising to her feet. She was wearing a voluminous white cotton nightie and now she picked up the hem and curtsied gracefully to them all. 'I'm truly sorry for waking you, but at the time I wasn't quite sane. Now all the peanut butter's finished, I'll . . . Oh, Christ, no!'

'What's the matter?' Jenny called, hurrying after Sue who had shot out of the kitchen like a scalded cat. 'Are you ill?'

Sue turned a white, agonized face towards her.

'Oh, nothing. Only I've got the most awful heartburn!'

CHAPTER EIGHT

'Jenny, where on earth have you *been*? Some man's been ringing you, he wouldn't leave his name, and of course I said you'd be in around four, because you usually are, and so he rang back and rang back . . . and here it is, half past eight before you step over the threshold!'

Sue was standing just in front of her own door; she had popped out, like a spider from its web, the moment she had heard Jenny's feet on the stairs. Jenny halted and a hand flew to her mouth.

'A man? For me? What did he sound like?'

'Middle-aged, rather cross. Not Mr Croft, I'd have recognized his voice. I wondered whether it was Bill, wanting to leave a message for you about work tomorrow, only he wouldn't leave a message, if you understand me.'

'Well, I know what you mean. It wasn't Bill, though. He asked us back to his place for tea and then we took the kids to see *The Jungle Book*. It was good, wasn't it, Posy?'

'It was lovely,' Posy said, rubbing her eyes. 'Only they wouldn't let Belle in, so she had to stay in Bill's kitchen with some Spillers shapes and a bowl of milk. She was glad when we got back, weren't you, dearest love?'

'Dearest love' wagged her tail politely, glanced up at Sue and then, pointedly, at her own door. Sue laughed.

'Belle wants to go to bed, poor love, and I expect you two want the same. I wonder who it was phoning, though? When you weren't in at seven he really sounded cross, as though you'd no right to be out so late. Have you an elderly uncle who bosses you about?'

'No. Well, whoever it was will probably ring later. Thanks for telling me, Sue, I'd best get this sleepy couple to bed, now. See you in the kitchen in half an hour?'

'Certainly. Too tired for walking?'

'No-oo, though it's been a long day. Can Mrs Twigg oblige?'

'You know she will. Ever since I got the colour TV she's been down like a streak of lightning at the mere mention of babysitting. If you're going to be half an hour, then I'll go up and check with her. Okay?'

'Yes, fine,' Jenny said, eyeing her sleepy daughter whose cheeks were still flushed with the excitement of her very first cinema show. 'Make it twenty minutes. I don't think we'll lie awake long tonight.'

She was right. Posy slept within moments of her head touching the pillow and Belle, curled up at the foot of the bed, wagged her plume of a tail and yawned when she saw Jenny slip into her coat again but made no effort to accompany her.

'Here we are,' Mrs Twigg called, as Sue let her into her room. 'I'll be happy here until close-down if you girls want to be late.'

'We shan't be late, I'm pretty tired myself,' Jenny said, pretending not to notice Sue's long, blue-tinged eyelid flutter and close into a wink. 'Thanks very much, Mrs Twigg.'

But they were not even halfway across the hall when the telephone rang again. Jenny, with her heart jumping up into her mouth, answered it. She gave the number briskly, trying to sound like someone else.

'Jenny? It's me.'

Stupidly she almost reacted by putting the telephone down, so strangely did Dirk's voice affect her. Her hands began to shake and her voice, when she spoke, came out too high with an almost hysterical note.

'Yes? Was it you earlier?'

'Yes. Where were you?'

Her self-control came back with a rush at that; how could he ring her after weeks and weeks of silence and then dare to sound condemnatory because she had not been waiting by the telephone for his call!

'Out. And I'm on my way out again, you were lucky to catch me.'

'Oh, really? And just where were you going at this time of night?'

'Dirk, I'm sure you didn't ring me after all this time just to talk about my whereabouts. What do you want?'

'To see you. If you're ever available, that is.' Heavy sarcasm, with overtones of impatience. Jenny smiled. If he had wanted to discuss divorce or legal separation she was sure he would have contacted her through Mr Croft, so he must want a more personal discussion. Perhaps it was about Ella's visit, or possibly it was about Mark's Christmas holiday which must start any day now.

'Oh yes, I'm available. Is it urgent, though? I'm quite busy during the week, what with . . .'

'Tomorrow? I'll come into town, meet you for lunch if you like.'

Her heart sang, then dropped. No matter what happened, she would not let Bill down at lunch-time when the cafe was at its busiest. And anyway, it would not hurt Dirk to be told no for once. But when she started to say no, she felt the trembling begin again, for suppose he just said 'Right, forget it,' and put the telephone down? What would she do then?

'Oh no, sorry, not tomorrow. Do you want to see Posy too, because if so . . .'

'No I don't. Look, just what are you up to? You were out all evening and now you don't want to meet me tomorrow, just what are you playing at? If you've got some . . .' He cut himself short. 'I'll come to the flat and pick you up tomorrow, about seven o'clock. Get someone to sit with the child.'

She opened her mouth to say that she could manage seven o'clock but Dirk was taking no chances. He crashed his receiver against its rest and cut the connection. Very slowly, Jenny put her own telephone down, then turned to Sue. She put her hands up to her hot cheeks; her fingers were trembling still, but she felt so excited, so triumphant, that it no longer mattered. He wanted to see her! He had actually sounded jealous; Dirk, jealous of her! Then all his affection could not be dead, he must still care!

'He put the phone down on you,' Sue said slowly. She looked white, shocked. 'He dared to ring you up, shout loudly enough for me to hear, and then hand you an ultimatum and put the phone down. Jenny, you aren't going to be here at seven o'clock are you?'

'Not be here?' Jenny's hands fell to her sides. She frowned.

'Not be here? Sue, he wants to see me! It's the first time he's rung or got in touch or . . . Sue, I couldn't stand him up.'

'No, not if that's how you feel – but ring him back and tell him you're busy, you can't make tomorrow night. Jenny, if you let him get away with it, if you just knuckle under to such appalling bad manners, then he'll despise you. Don't cringe. You'll despise yourself too one fine day.'

They were still standing in the hallway. Before Jenny could reply, however, a door opened and Dermott appeared, talking to someone over his shoulder as he emerged.

'. . . on the next floor up,' he was saying, 'and the kitchen's on the half landing above that. So if you want to make a big meal . . .' he broke off, having seen Jenny and Sue. 'Oh, sorry girls, I didn't see you . . . look, you've not yet met . . .' Something about their stillness caught his attention. 'What's the matter? Jen? Don't say you two best buddies have been quarrelling?'

'No, not quarrelling, just not agreeing,' Sue said swiftly. 'We're on our way out for a walk, actually. Coming, Jen?'

'Oh, I . . . Dermott, that was my h-husband on the phone, he . . . oh, I'm sorry.'

A man had followed Dermott out of the room and now stood looking a little uncertainly from one to the other. He was of medium height, stockily built and very dark, in fact rather foreign-looking. His hair curled tightly like the fleece on a lamb, his skin was smooth and olive-toned and he had a large, curved nose. But when he smiled you saw he was attractive, and his eyes, dark and liquid, were both sympathetic and intelligent.

'Oh bless you, you wretched girls, this is my room-mate, Solomon Kant. Solly, the tall dark elegant creature on my left is Sue Oliver, and the small fair pretty one is Jenny Sayer. I think they've been fighting.'

'Nice to meet you,' Solomon said. He looked at Jenny. 'Go on, get it off your chest, you were about to ask Dermott's advice.'

'Well, Sue says . . . the thing is my h-husband rang up and wanted me to meet him here tomorrow evening – at seven. Only he was . . . he was rather cross with me because he'd been ringing all day and I wasn't in, and h-he put the phone down before I could reply, and Sue thinks I should stand him up.'

'You should have heard him shout at her,' Sue said hotly. 'Honestly, Dermott, he spoke to her as if she were a dog or a deaf child.'

'Oh Sue, that's just his way! Please don't despise me, but I can't not be here, you don't know what you're asking.'

'If that's how you feel, of course you'll have to be waiting for him at seven,' Dermott said slowly. 'But really, love, you must tell him that he'll have to mend his manners if he wants to see more of you. You do see the common sense of that, don't you?'

'Oh yes, of course,' Jenny said eagerly. She would have agreed to anything provided she was allowed to meet Dirk next evening. 'He is a little overbearing, I know it, but . . . not to meet him would be unendurable. I would never know, would I, just why he wants to see me.'

'Right, if that's how you feel . . .' Sue headed for the front door. 'Come on, once right along the beach and back, then we'll be tired out and ready for bedkins. 'Night, Dermott, 'night, Solomon.'

Out on the beach in the windy dark, with the sound of the breakers making conversation difficult, Sue reached out and took Jenny's arm.

'I'm sorry, love,' she bawled, 'I shouldn't have tried to interfere; you know your own business best. But I'm very fond of you, I'd hate to see you just knuckle under and become a doormat again.'

'It's maddening, because I know you're right, I really should have told him to get knotted, but I'm not a bit strong, when it comes to Dirk,' Jenny shouted back. 'You've no idea how I've longed to see him, just to see him! I keep imagining I've spotted him in the street, only it never is him, and now perhaps, if we can talk, we can be together again.'

'You didn't even ask if he'd ditched Bronwen,' Sue shrieked. 'You really should . . . oh damn it, let's just walk, my throat's beginning to hurt.'

They fought the wind in silence all the way to the harbour and then, returning back again with the wind behind them, they talked on other, less contentious subjects. When they

198

parted neither had had their say but both were aware that the decision was Jenny's and hers alone.

Whether it was the prospect of seeing Dirk the next day or the near-row with Sue that was making her so restless, Jenny did not know; all she knew was that sleep completely eluded her. She lay wide-eyed and waiting for morning, all the excitement and pleasant anticipation which had followed Dirk's call now dissipated and gone. She was a fool, she had let him get away with abominable behaviour, for all she knew he might turn up tomorrow night to talk to her with Bronwen on his arm or waiting for him in the car. Jenny cursed herself; she had behaved like some sex-starved over-eager kid and he would probably treat her like one, with contempt.

The maddening thing was that the telephone call had come at the end of a near-perfect day. She and Bill had been run off their feet in the cafe; because the town was so full, Christmas shoppers were using the big car park near the gardens, walking into the centre and returning with their arms full of loot, and then coming into the cafe for a cheap but substantial lunch.

Tiring though it was the takings had been excellent, and Jenny, already very nearly as involved with the cafe as Bill, had rejoiced with him when the money in the till mounted and mounted. Because of the short afternoons, an older child now brought Dawn and Erica and Posy to the cafe on her way home, and Jenny and Bill would settle the three at their favourite corner table, provide them with drinks, biscuits, colouring books, jigsaw puzzles and pencils, and leave them there whilst they served the few customers who still popped in between three and four.

At a quarter to four the door was locked against more customers, an unlikely event since people were usually keen to get away when darkness fell, and Jenny and Bill cleaned up. Sometimes the children helped, though Dawn, still very much a baby although she was four, did not contribute much. A round, freckled, cuddly little creature with the sweetest temperament despite her ginger curls, Dawn was the sort of child that everyone loved, including her teachers, yet she was unspoiled by it. Posy petted her and shared sweets with her, though she also greatly admired Erica, who, at six, was rather old for her age and whose air of being bowed down by cares worried Jenny. Erica was also bossy and conceited, however, forever glancing at herself in any reflective material, patting her thick, straw-coloured hair and tugging down her miniscule skirts. She could be helpful though, and this afternoon, when nudged by her father, had set to with such a will that the place was tidy in excellent time.

And then, out of the blue, Bill had invited Jenny, Posy and Belle home for tea.

'You've never seen our place,' he said. 'And after tea I thought we might go out somewhere.'

'Are you trying to date me?' Jenny had blurted out, feeling her face flame. 'Because if you are, it's silly – we're such good friends, must we spoil it?'

Bill had not known where to look; instead, he had turned his back on her as he pulled down the kitchen blinds, speaking over his shoulder in a friendly but resigned manner.

'Forget it, I didn't mean to upset you, I was a fool to ask you back. You see far too much of me as it is. It's just that *The Jungle Book*'s showing at the cinema and the kids want to see it and I thought . . .'

'Bill, I'm sorry, you must think I'm the most conceited bitch alive,' Jenny had said, filled with contrition. Poor man, he only wanted her company at a children's cinema show! 'Of course we'll come, we'd adore it, but what'll we do with Belle?'

'She can stay at my place.' He turned back to her, beaming. 'You're a sport, Mrs Sayer, think what an idiot I'd have felt going to a kid's show without moral support!'

It had been interesting, visiting Bill's home for the first time. It was small, as Bill had said, and semi-detached, but it was clean as a new pin and gleaming with loving care. Bill told her he had picked up nearly all the furniture second hand, but Jenny would never have guessed. The living room was delightful, with old-fashioned prints on the walls, a brilliant all-over patterned carpet and a china cabinet full of delicate porcelain. The chairs and sofa were saggy and comfortable – but had bright chintz stretch-covers which made them look presentable – and Bill had placed a low round table on the hearth rug for the girls' jigsaws, Monopoly games and other pastimes.

The kitchen was large and airy; the floor was tiled in yellow and white and the walls were covered from floor to ceiling with the children's paintings. It overlooked the vegetable garden, or would have done had Bill not built his rockery there, right outside the window, a miniature Everest lovingly planted with everything Bill could persuade to grow in it. The front garden was a delight with its tawny chrysanthemums and great clumps of Michaelmas daisies smelling of autumn and woodsmoke, but the rockery, Jenny decided when they reached it, was unusual and rather special. There were ferns in every nook and cranny, tiny miniature roses still blooming, and at its base a thick hedge of small but prickly, healthy-looking shrubs, to discourage, Bill said, any would-be mountaineers amongst the neighbouring young.

'It must have been a lot of work, whatever made you do it?' Jenny said, as they circumnavigated it in order to admire the neatly planted lines of winter vegetables. 'It must have taken weeks just to get the rocks to look so natural.'

'Yes, but I like gardening – and it improves the view no end; hides the winter cabbage.' Bill pointed down the garden. 'There are raspberries further along, and a young strawberry bed.'

But Jenny lingered for a moment, admiring the rockery.

'Look at that heather; most of it's over now. Oh, and that dear little cyclamen. I didn't know that flowered as late as this either.'

'Come into the front garden and I'll get you some chrysanths to take home,' Bill offered. 'We'll cut them now and put them in water, then when you come home for Belle after the cinema you can take them back with you. How's that?'

Jenny said that would be lovely, and meant every word of it. He was so kind, yet he wanted a friend as badly as she.

Even after the film, when they had gone back to his house to pick up Belle and he had told her, a trifle shamefacedly, that he had arranged for Louisa's sister to come in and babysit whilst he took her home, she had enjoyed herself.

Walking along with Posy's hand in hers and Belle a shadow at their heels, she had suddenly felt Bill take her hand and it had been natural and pleasant, not the pass she had feared but a sensible way to make sure that they all kept in step in the dark streets.

At the door of the flats he had squeezed her fingers, kissed Posy on the nose, said, 'See you in the morning,' and gone off down the street, whistling. She had known Bill was her friend; now she knew he was something more. Reliable? No, she had always known that. Fond? Ah, that was putting it a bit too strongly. No, she knew now that he wanted her to be a real friend, someone who could wander into his house, make a cup of tea, share a joke with him, help with the kids, and yet never feel in any way compromised by the friendship.

Perhaps it had been that which had made her say no to Dirk's offer of lunch. A real friend would never let another down. Of course she would never have let Bill down anyway, in any sense of the word, even had he only been her employer. But she would have asked for a lunch-hour off, despite knowing it would cause inconvenience. As it was, she would see Dirk tomorrow evening and Bill would not have to know anything about it.

She knew, then, that she was ashamed of herself for giving in so easily to Dirk. She frowned into the darkness, biting at her knuckles, suddenly furious with her own stupidity. How could she have let herself down so? And not only herself but her friends. They had been staunch allies when Dirk had been missing. For their sakes, as well as for her own, she should have let him see that she was no longer dependent on him, simply waiting for him to throw her a word, and not even a kind one.

I'll not be there when he calls tomorrow evening, she vowed to herself; I'll take Posy and Belle and we'll have a meal out, or we'll go for a long walk, or take a bus ride. But I will *not* be hanging round waiting for his ring on the bell tomorrow at seven!

By half past six she had finally decided on jeans, a checked shirt and a pale grey sweater with a deep V-neck. She had first put on and then discarded every article in her wardrobe more or less and had finally decided on the jeans and shirt more as her solitary gesture of defiance than for anything else. Dirk thought jeans were sloppy and rather unfeminine; when they went out anywhere he always liked her to be in a well-cut suit or a pretty dress. So tonight, when it was so important that she evoked the right kind of memories, it had been tempting to dress to please.

By twenty to seven Posy and Belle were safely lodged with Mrs Twigg, one making a shell picture of great intricacy, the other watching with an indulgent eye. By ten to seven Jenny had combed her hair up and tied it in a pony-tail, let it loose, put it in a bun and then let it loose again. By five to seven she was idling about down in the hall, as if waiting for a telephone call – or for someone to ring the bell.

At a minute to seven the bell rang and Jenny, suddenly shaking, opened the front door. It was Dirk and for a moment they just stood and looked at each other. He made no romantic move to sweep her into his arms, he just stood, slightly belligerent, and stared.

Jenny's first thought was that he had aged; her second that he had put on weight. She had always considered him extremely handsome and had, she supposed, seen him in her mind's eye as he had once been – dark, slim-hipped and broad-shouldered, somehow supple.

Now he was merely solid, and his once black, wavy hair was grey and had been recently – and badly – cut. It stuck out over his forehead in a little shelf, lending him a fleeting resemblance to a gnome.

'Well, Jenny? Going to invite me in, or will you come out for a coffee whilst we talk?'

It was very strange, because she had taken pains with the room, cleaning and dusting it, and had bought biscuits and the same type of coffee she had used at the farm. She had borrowed one of Sue's rugs, too, and Mrs Twigg had lent a great many brightly-coloured cushions and a very beautiful tapestry cover for the bed, yet now she realized she did not want Dirk in her room. He would look round and think it a poor place when it had been a good little room to her, a refuge, somewhere cosy when the wind howled outside and the rain drove against the window panes.

'No, we'll go out,' she said. 'Can you wait here whilst I fetch a coat?'

'I'll come up, shall I?'

He moved into the hall and stood there, rain gleaming on his hair, legs apart, still managing to look like a farmer who owned everything his eye alighted on. Alarmed, Jenny shook her head.

'No, stay there, I've got a babysitter – I don't want Posy disturbed, she doesn't know . . .' She had been running up the stairs as she spoke, and now she stopped and shot into her room, grabbed her coat from behind the door and hurried downstairs again. He had not moved. She was struck by another resemblance, this time to a bull they had once owned; Dirk was looking at her with his head lowered, just as this bull had done when it was feeling irritable. Jenny's heart skipped a beat, and she scolded herself. Don't be a fool, woman, she said inside her head, he can't do anything worse than he's done already!

The thought was comforting. She smiled at him and slipped the coat over her shoulders; after a moment he smiled back, though the smile did not reach his eyes which remained the bull's eyes – hot and angry and somehow tricky, as though the owner of the eyes knew no more than she what his next move was to be.

'Come on, then.' He led the way out of the flat, down the short tiled path, rainwet and reflecting the streetlights, out on to the pavement. The Land Rover was parked outside; she peered at it, trying to see whether Bronwen was with him, but it seemed to be empty and he was ignoring it, turning to her.

'Well? Where's the nearest place? You live here, after all.'

'I'm sorry, I thought you must know Rhyl pretty well – you chose this house for me to live in, after all.' She set off along the pavement at a brisk pace, her flat brogues silent save for a spongy squelching sound as she strode through puddles. He kept pace with her, making no move to touch her nor to speak. They continued down the length of Beechcroft Road and then turned into Russell Road, still without speaking. Jenny was silent because she was afraid that if she did say something he would not answer and that would be so hurtful that she might easily burst into tears, which would, naturally, annoy him. She had no idea why Dirk said nothing, though he had never been particularly garrulous. Still in silence they turned into the big cafe on the corner by the church. She had not been in here late before and it was full of teenagers, cheerful, colourful, with pleasant background music and attractive-looking waitresses. She looked round hopefully for an empty table and, even as she looked, a group of peroxided spiky-haired boys rose up in a body and made for the door. She motioned to Dirk and they slid into the still-warm seats. Dirk looked about him, rather like a Martian might look around if he found himself suddenly set down in the middle of Piccadilly Circus. This was new ground for him, Jenny realized. When he came into Rhyl he would go to a pub or hotel, not a cafe favoured by teenagers.

'Yes?'

A pretty waitress had approached them; she smiled, first at Dirk and then at Jenny.

'Oh, two coffees, please. Want anything to eat?'

Dirk spoke with his usual assumption of authority; Jenny immediately wished for tea but decided not to argue. The sooner the waitress brought their drinks the sooner she would know just what it was that Dirk did want.

'Nothing else, thanks,' Dirk said as Jenny shook her head. The girl went away and Jenny relaxed in her seat, though inwardly she was as taut as a bow-string. She longed to say, what do you *want*, but knew he might well remain silent just to upset her and make her more vulnerable. He would have to tell her in the end, so waiting quietly was best.

The coffees came and Jenny stirred a spoonful of sugar into hers, purely in order to give her courage and to occupy her hands. Dirk stared morosely across the table at her, took a deep breath, stirred his own coffee, and finally spoke.

'Mark's home in five days.'

'As soon as that? Well, he's always been a help round the farm, so that'll be nice for you.'

He shrugged, impatient with small talk.

'What am I to tell him?'

It was Jenny's turn to shrug. 'Whatever you like. What did you tell Phil?' She could have bitten her tongue as soon as the words were said, because she was not supposed to know her eldest son was home, but Dirk appeared to notice nothing.

'Philip's older, more understanding. He likes Bron. But Mark doesn't like her, or so she says.'

'Then it doesn't really matter what you tell him if he's already formed an opinion of her, does it? Tell him the truth, he can come and see me if he feels like a day at the seaside, though I won't pretend it's the best time of year.'

'Bron thought you might like to have him here, in the flat I mean. She thought . . .'

'That wouldn't do at all, I'm afraid,' Jenny said politely, but with fury only just held in check. 'There's nothing for him here, nowhere to sleep – Posy and I live in one room you know. And Mark would be absolutely miserable, Dirk, away from you and the farm. How could you even suggest such a thing?'

He had the grace to look a trifle shamefaced, and defensive.

'I didn't, it was Bron. She doesn't understand that the boys are closer to me, perhaps, now that they're older. She thought you'd like to have your son with you.'

Truth must out on this occasion, Jenny thought wryly. She shook her head. 'No, I don't think even Bronwen could have been foolish enough to believe that Mark would enjoy a month of living in a one-room flat in a seaside town in wintertime. She doesn't want the extra work and the extra antagonism, but frankly nor do I. It's hard enough to manage with Posy and . . . and myself, I really could not cope with Mark as well.'

She had nearly mentioned Belle; sweat pricked on her forehead. She must be careful!

'I'd double your allowance.' Dirk was eager now, thinking it was merely the money that stopped her from taking on Mark. 'I'll treble it for that month if it would make things easier. Look, Bron's only a kid herself, think what it's like for her with those great lads of yours . . .'

Jenny slid out of her seat, not without difficulty, and stood up. She buttoned her coat, trying to stop her fingers from trembling, then looked down at him.

'Thanks, but no thanks, as the saying goes. Goodnight,

Dirk. I can see myself home. God knows I'm used enough to doing so.'

She walked out on him; behind her she heard him curse as he tried to squeeze out of the small space between the leatherette-covered seats and the table, then heard the waitress's voice and knew he was being forced to pay for the coffees before he could follow her.

Outside, it was dark and cold and the rain had started again, but Jenny's heart was light. She hurried, putting as much distance between herself and Dirk as she could, and soon she could see Beechcroft Road, and then she was slipping through the gate and pushing open the front door. She hurried up the stairs and knocked on Sue's door. It opened and she shot inside, a finger to her lips, waiting to speak until Sue had closed the door once more.

'He may be following me – in fact he'll have to since he's left his car parked outside. Could we possibly turn the light out and then watch from behind your curtains, do you suppose?'

'Sure,' Sue said eagerly, clicking the lights off. 'Pull back the curtain wide enough to let me take a look as well, idiot! All I can see is the back of your head.'

'He isn't going to come,' Jenny said presently, in a voice of deep irrational disappointment. 'How odd!'

'This isn't him, then? The square chap, in the light mac?'

'No, it's . . . golly it is! Look, Sue, if he comes here do you mind going down and saying I'm out? There's no way I'm facing him again tonight.'

But the request was needless; Dirk strode up to the Land Rover, climbed in, roared the engine, and was gone in a spray which lashed across the pavement and with a noise loud enough to wake the dead.

'Someone's in a nasty mood,' Sue observed, when the vehicle's tail lights had disappeared into the distance. 'What was that all in aid of? You couldn't have been with him more than a quarter of an hour!'

'It felt like several decades,' Jenny said gloomily, drawing the curtains across again as Sue switched on the light. 'You'll never guess what he wanted! When I think of it . . . the cheek of it . . . my blood boils, it positively boils!'

'Your blood, Jen, should have been boiling last evening; mine was. However, I'm glad it's warmed up at last.' Sue's kettle had been simmering when Jenny had rushed in; now Sue filled the teapot, stirred it, and poured them both a cup of tea. 'Right, let's settle down by the fire and you can tell me all.'

Jenny was only to eager to oblige but when she had finished Sue merely laughed.

'Your Dirk really has to be the archetypal male chauvinist pig, besides being almost totally insensitive to the feelings of others,' she said at last. 'Fancy expecting his wife, who he has chucked out to scrape a living in digs, to act as a gaoler on his behalf, to his son, because that's what it would amount to. A lively seventeen-year-old would go mad cooped up here, as well your Dirk must know. He is the very worst.'

'I do think he's pretty awful,' Jenny admitted, chuckling now, seeing the funny side of it. 'He referred to Bronwen as "a poor kid", you know, wanted me to take Mark for her sake.'

'Well, at least you told him no pretty plainly, from the way he drove off,' Sue said, chuckling again. 'He was in a rage, wasn't he?'

'Yes, he was. I only hope he doesn't decide I was biting the hand that feeds me and so need to be kept short for a while,' Jenny said, suddenly feeling apprehensive. 'That would be just like Dirk, and Christmas is coming up too.'

'I shouldn't worry. If you're right and he doesn't want to make a complete break, then he must realize that if he doesn't pay you enough to live on you'll go to court and get it legalized. And if he tells Mark the truth the lad may turn up here anyway; it wouldn't endear Dirk to his son – nor Bronwen, for that matter – if he found you and Posy starving.'

'You're probably right.' Jenny drank her tea quickly and stood up. She rubbed her eyes with fingers that trembled again, now that the ordeal was over. 'I'll fetch Posy down and we'll both go straight to bed; I don't know why but I'm absolutely knackered, I feel as if I've run a marathon.'

'Mental exhaustion,' Sue informed her. 'Right, off to bedkins with you; see you in the morning, little lion-tamer.'

Jenny, halfway through the doorway, looked back.

'Little what?'

'Lion-tamer. You walked out on him; that must have taken courage after all the years of being a good girl.'

'It did. Oddly enough, though, it's given me a taste for doing it again; I feel downright exhilarated.'

'Good. And he didn't eat you up or disinherit you either.'

'No, because I moved very fast! Goodnight, Sue, and thanks.'

After the encounter with Dirk Jenny half expected another telephone call but nothing happened. When next she called for her money the amount was still the same. Mr Croft made no reference to the affair and indeed asked her if she would like a bit extra with Christmas approaching. Jenny said no, thanks, but she could manage, and he gave her one of his chilly, suspicious under-the-brow looks before accepting what she said and telling her that Mark had accompanied his father to market that morning.

'I tell you because he may come in and see you, the boy may,' he said, as he headed for his own office once more while Jenny made for the front door. 'I told him you called for the little girl at about three and would be available from then on.'

Jenny thanked him from the heart for that piece of information, since she had formed the habit of lingering in the cafe with Bill and the children and often did not get back to the flat until five; now today she would be forewarned and could go straight home.

She did so, which was as well because Mark was lying in wait for her in the hallway. He grinned awkwardly at her, gave Posy a hug and then gasped as he recognized Belle.

'So you've got her! Dad said she'd run off and Bronwen said she'd been run over. They don't know, I take it, that she came to you?'

'No, they don't know. Please don't say anything, Mark. Bronwen doesn't care for Belle – she'd probably have her put down if your father insisted on taking the dog back.'

'Over my dead body,' Mark said grimly. 'Mum, when are you coming back?' He sounded, for a moment, like a little boy once more, begging for reassurance and wanting his life to resume its even tenor.

'I don't know whether I am, dear. Your father . . . well, he turned me out because he wanted to live with Bronwen. He may change his mind, men do I believe, but that doesn't mean he'll want me back. He may just feel like another change.'

'He's sick of *her* already,' Mark said confidently, following them up the stairs. 'You should hear them in the evenings, snapping and snarling at one another. And she's a lousy cook, she undercooks things or burns them, Dad says she hasn't yet found a middle way, and we keep getting shop pies and cakes and Chinese take-aways.'

'Chinese take-aways? Where from, for goodness sake?'

'There's one in Ruthin, stupid, didn't you know? Dad hates it, he never has liked foreign food, and Phil moans and gets into the MG and roars off and doesn't come back until the early hours, and Bronwen nags and nags at Dad and she's had a row with Mrs George so Mrs George won't come in any more, and she was a better cook than Mrs Ted and anyway Mrs Ted doesn't talk to Bronwen, much.' Mark paused for breath as Jenny unlocked her door and ushered them all in. 'I say, this is a bit of all right, how bright and cheerful it looks! Mind you, I'd go mad cooped up in here after the farm. Don't you?'

'What, go mad? No, I rather like it. At first it seemed cramped and dusty but I've grown very fond of it, and of course I don't have to do much housework and I only cook for Posy and myself, so I wouldn't need a lot of room.'

'When you come back, the first thing Dad'll want will be a good meal,' Mark said, with no intention either to hurt or amuse, though Jenny felt the stab and the giggle virtually at the same moment. The awful part was that he was right, Dirk would have been getting plenty of the other, it was only the cooking that Bronwen couldn't manage! Well, perhaps it was better to be loved as a housekeeper than not to be loved at all.

'I shouldn't say "when", Mark, it's safer to say "if",' Jenny commented, going over to the cupboard where she kept her food supplies. 'Are you staying for a meal? We didn't know you were coming but as it happens it was my turn for the bottom shelf in the oven – we have this oven rota, you see – and so we've got some beef in red wine simmering; Posy loves it and it lasts well. I've done the potatoes, so all I'd have to do would be three or four more and we could eat. But if you'd rather, we'll go out.'

'Actually, I was going to buy you a meal – Dad gave me some money,' Mark said gruffly. 'But if it's all the same to you I love your beef casserole, could we have that? And I'll leave you the money and then you can take yourselves out one evening.'

'That's very sweet of you, but we can manage a meal out now and then,' Jenny said, trying not to sound stiff and formal. 'Right, I'll just peel some more spuds.'

In the end they had a pleasant evening, and Dermott popped into the kitchen where they were spooning out the food and asked Jenny if she'd like free tickets for a rehearsal the following week.

'I've got four going, and I thought you, Sue, Posy and Bren might like them,' Dermott said, eyeing Mark curiously. 'Though come to think, there'll be Solly's spare tickets too, if you want to invite the Twiggs and Anna along as well.'

'We'll arrange something, I'm sure. Dermott, this is my son, Mark. Mark, Dermott Hughes, who has the ground-floor flat.'

The two men shook hands and Jenny was interested and rather amused to see her son positively bristling, eyes wary, whilst she and Dermott exchanged small talk. When they had the kitchen to themselves once more, Mark asked bluntly, 'Who's that?'

'I told you. Dermott Hughes, who . . .'

'I know *that*; what is he to you?'

'Goodness, Mark, what a thing to say! He's nothing to me, except a friend.'

The rest of the evening went well: the meal was praised; Sue, despite her condition, was flirted with; Anna received an invitation to go to the funfair, and Mark, who had never taken the slightest notice of Posy, offered to come and meet her out of school sometimes, to help Jenny.

It was quite a surprise when, at ten o'clock, the bell rang. It was Philip arriving to fetch his younger brother home. He came in, almost swaggered in, to the party which had congregated in his mother's room – Posy had long since gone to sleep with Belle in the tiny spare room – and said hello all round, gave Jenny a hug and a kiss on the cheek which somehow managed to be just that little bit patronizing, and gave all the other women a slow practised smile and all the men, especially poor Dermott, a cold and suspicious stare.

'That boy of yours is handsome,' Sue remarked, when all the men had left and the girls were making their hot drinks in the kitchen. 'Mark will be handsome as well but your Philip's already there.'

'Yes, he's the spitting image of Dirk when I first knew him,' Jenny admitted, pouring milk into the little pan and setting it on the stove. 'Weren't they funny with Dermott, though? You'd have thought they were jealous, the fools.'

'They were, in a way,' Anna said, nibbling Jenny's shortbread biscuits. 'You're their mum, they don't want to see you as a woman who could get another man; that'd unsettle 'em.'

'That's very perspicacious of you, Anna,' Sue said sounding unflatteringly surprised. 'I can see what you meant, Jen, when you said your sons were very self-centred. Their father has upset their comfort, that's how they see the break-up.'

'Oh, not break-up,' Jenny protested, still warmed by the knowledge that the boys had talked of it as a temporary thing. 'Mark says Dirk's miserable with Bronwen, he's sure it won't be long before his father's down here begging me to come home.'

'Will you go? Just like that?'

The question, which she should have expected, rocked Jenny back on her heels. She stared at Sue, the 'of course' which she longed to say suspended for a moment by truth. Would she run back to heel? Just like that?

'I couldn't, could I? Not until Bill's sorted things out at the cafe, and not until your bouncing boy puts in an appearance. Not that I think Dirk will admit defeat quite so soon.'

Sue nodded, as if the answer satisfied her.

'You're learning, girl. You say Dirk's like Phil, or Phil's

like Dirk if you prefer. Neither of them values what comes easy, if you ask me. Make yourself rare and you become precious. Think about it.'

Jenny did, though not for long. After such a satisfying day, sleep came quickly.

The cafe was decked with paper chains and holly, and Jenny and Bill worked at top speed. Jenny began to make a special Christmas cake for the customers, so that she and Bill could wish them a merry Christmas. Mark had brought her the recipe, which had been handed down from Dirk's mother and which, he said with a grin, would probably have whole generations of Sayer women spinning in their graves if they knew it was being sold for gain.

Jenny had also taken over the cake-making in general for the cafe and consequently Bill's profits had soared, since he no longer had to pay out for a finished product but merely for the ingredients that Jenny needed. During the last week before Christmas itself, they produced a traditional Christmas dinner on the Monday, Wednesday and Friday, retaining an alternative of course, and were packed out, almost everyone choosing turkey and plum pudding and obviously enjoying the festive atmosphere and the Christmas trimmings which accompanied the meal – crackers, a balloon for each child and a piece of Jenny's Christmas cake to take home.

And Dirk rang. Every evening, about seven o'clock, when Jenny and Posy had eaten and were settling down to their evening's television, reading or games, Mrs Grant would call up the stairs, 'It's 'im, Mrs S., for you.'

Jenny had longed for Dirk's attention yet she soon discovered she did not enjoy the telephone calls. He was obviously trying to sound interested and friendly but did not quite manage it. Suspicion and something very like jealousy crept over the line in waves, and it was not a straightforward healthy jealousy but the dog-in-the-manger sort. He might not want her himself but he was damned if anyone else was going to get her!

School finished and Posy, home all day, spent the mornings until half past eleven pottering round the flat with

Jenny, making Christmas presents, wrapping secret parcels, fetching Sandra so that the two of them could deck the tiny artificial Christmas tree which Jenny had bought, or make more sticky paper chains to hang up in the flat, or admire the sugar mice that Jenny was making for stockings. At eleven-thirty she might go off up to Mrs Twigg for more exciting shellwork, or else go shopping with Sue; otherwise, Jenny took her round to Bill's house where the sister of Louisa-from-next-door, Sian, babysat happily – and moderately cheaply – for an increasing number of small children. Bill was perfectly willing to have his house used as a day-nursery provided that his own children were taken care of, Sian was going to be a teacher and genuinely had a way with small children, and Posy adored both Sian and the set-up.

Jenny had always loved Christmas at the farm, but now she realized that she had not known how much fun it could be. At the farm it had been just family, the boys enjoying the food and the presents but having little time for what she now realized was the true spirit of Christmas, and it was that spirit which she found at 24 Beechcroft Road. It was a spirit which had Jenny tramping the shops looking for gifts she could afford for the other inmates, gifts which would please them and also be useful. It made poor Anna shut herself in the kitchen and try to make fudge which she intended to put into pale pink boxes and decorate them with satin ribbon to give indiscriminately to all her girlfriends and her men. It even made Mrs Grant think about having the party.

'We've cleared out the big room,' she explained, when she came up to the kitchen one evening, apparently drawn by the laughter and shrieks of participants in a corn-popping session. 'We're going to re-paper it later but for now, 'e thought we might 'ave a bit of a knees-up, just for friends, like, before we all go our ways for the 'oliday.'

'That sounds fun,' Jenny said rather cautiously. 'Um . . . what sort of a knees-up did you have in mind?'

'Well, a bit of dancing, refreshments, a few drinks . . . it'll be like a bottle party, bring your own bottles,' Mrs Grant explained hastily. 'A game or two, p'raps, and prizes . . . there's a good few of us, if you count me and 'im, our Martin, all you lot and the Griffiths next door. We could 'ave a good time. That Dermott, 'e's a card, we could get 'im to bring some of the cast along, mebbe.'

'It would be great, thanks very much Mrs G, I accept,' Sue said suddenly and grandly. Jenny quickly followed suit and so did Brenda and Anna, though Brenda, blushing, did ask if it would be possible for people to bring friends.

'If they bring a bottle I don't see why not,' Mrs Grant said, her eyes glittering behind her glasses; it was plain she was envisaging her big room stacked from floor to ceiling with booze. 'Dermott's got lots of them nice discs or tapes, the sort you can dance to, not them 'eathen screeches our Martin calls music.' She gave a loud sniff. "Eavenly Medals some of it's called: screechings, that wot I calls it.'

'She means Heavy Metal, I think,' Brenda said when Mrs Grant had left them, as she noticed Sue's and Jenny's round-eyed astonishment at their landlady's impassioned outburst. 'Well, I'll ask Simon, he should enjoy seeing Mrs G. in full swing. What about you two?'

'Us?' Sue smoothed a hand proudly over her lump. 'There are two of us already, we can't be greedy. What about you, Jen?'

'I'd love to ask Bill, because I've accepted so much of his hospitality,' Jenny said. 'I'd provide his bottle as well as my own – that'll be two bottles of ginger ale – and I'll get him to lend me his stove and do some cooking for the old hen. Otherwise I can just imagine the refreshments – half-a-dozen Marie biscuits and a sardine split into eight.'

'Right, you ask Bill, Bren will ask Simon, and Anna and Mouse will ask the Treorchy male-voice choir,' Sue said, smiling at them. '*My* bottle will be milk, of course – very appropriate. Can't you just see the old hen's face?'

'Does this mean we'll have to buy Christmas pressies for "'im" as well as for Mrs G. and Martin?' Jenny chipped in. 'Because if so, we'd better get hunting. And what did she mean . . . before we go our ways?'

'Jenny, how daft can you get? Mrs G. likes her house to herself over Christmas, though she's never said it in so many words. She's hoping that everyone will take off on Christmas eve, for a family Christmas somewhere far from this place. So far as I'm concerned she's way out, because I don't go a step from this town until Tiny Tim's put in an appearance, but you . . . what are the chances of getting asked back to the farm?'

'Me? With Bronwen still in occupation? You must be joking! No, Posy and I will be here to sing carols with you and cry over the Queen's speech.'

'I'm going home,' Brenda remarked, dipping into the popcorn and speaking rather thickly through her mouthful. 'My Mam would be really upset if I didn't go home for Christmas. And I reckon Anna will probably go home as well, and even Dermott may go home for the day itself. To say nothing of Solly. Although Jews don't celebrate Christmas, do they?'

Jenny had never known a Jew well before and was intrigued by Solly and by his religion, almost as intrigued as was Posy by the little cap he wore, apparently sewn on to his curly fleece since it never seemed to move, not even under the most severe provocation.

'No, I don't suppose they do; well, I like Solly, so perhaps I'll ask him up to the flat to share my lonely Christmas repast. Will you tear a turkey with me, Sue? Just a tiny one? Or possibly a chicken?'

'I will, love, if you aren't otherwise occupied. Brenda Crisp, if you eat any more popcorn you'll pop and there won't be any for hanging on strings.'

Two days after Mrs Grant issued her invitation, Jenny realized that she was being followed. Twice in the crowded street she had had the oddest feeling, almost as if she had been lightly stroked along her back, and turning quickly she had seen a familiar figure trying fairly unsuccessfully to blend into the crowd.

Her first thought was that Dirk suspected that she had a job and was trying to catch her actually working, and this infuriated her. God knew he gave her little enough money, would he grudge her earning a bit more to give herself and his small daughter a good Christmas? But after she had seen him three or four times she absolved him from that particular motive. He knew she was working, he did not have to prove anything, yet he had not mentioned her job on the telephone.

She had been flying round the cafe with her tray loaded with dinners and she had seen him skulking outside, peering through the misted glass; presently, he came in, looking very self-conscious, went over to the counter and bought a cheese bap from the unaware Bill, and left with his coat collar turned up and his shoulders hunched. The great booby, she thought with mixed affection and irritation, how could he imagine her unaware of his presence after all the years they had shared together?

So if he was not trying to catch her earning money, just what was he doing? But before she had done more than decide that when she had the chance she would turn suddenly, grab his arm and shout 'boo!' into his face, the shadowing stopped. Whatever he had wanted to find out he had apparently done it and Jenny suddenly found herself too busy and too happy to wonder just what that something was. The excitement of pre-Christmas was building up. Bill had accepted Mrs Grant's invitation and had insisted on providing a bottle of whisky. Sue, despite her remarks about milk, had bought gin and four large cartons of orange juice, and Jenny herself, having spent one whole Sunday baking sausage-rolls, vol-au-vents, mince pies and other delicacies, got a litre of white wine from Marks and Spencer's.

Because of the party, Posy had been invited to spend the night at Bill's house, with Sian and the other children, Sian to sleep in the spare bedroom with Posy whilst Bill would walk the child home in the morning. This innocent outing was the cause of great excitement, Bill buying a party-type spread for their tea and Sian inviting her best friend, Nesta, round for the evening so that the five of them might have a little party of their own.

Sue went out to the shops with Jenny and bought a splendid new maternity dress specially for the occasion. She looked like a queen, Jenny assured her, though she spoiled this by adding, ' . . . the Queen Mary, I fancy, or possibly the QEII,' which did rather take the edge off the compliment.

Sue got her own back by assuring Jenny that she, in her slim, black, sheath-like dress with its floating chiffon overskirt and sleeves, looked like a merry widow – the type that lurks in banana trees and eats the male of the species after he has performed his marital functions.

However, when the great day arrived at last, both girls were pleased with their appearance. Jenny's dress was by no means new, but it had been extremely expensive in its day and its day was by no means over. Sue's dress had been extremely expensive only a couple of days ago, and it lent her a demure air whilst the colour reflected the blue of her eyes and the swirling line of it diminished her hugeness as much as was sartorially possible.

The party was due to start at eight; at ten minutes to the hour Sue knocked on Jenny's door and entered.

'Hi there, honeybunch! Hell, babe, we're goin' to slay 'em,' she announced in a ghastly mid-Atlantic accent. 'Have you seen our Brenda? She's determined to have Simon punch-drunk with her charms; she's got herself all up in pale pink, even her shoes are pink. She looks like one marshmallow and Anna looks like another – she's all in white.'

'And I'm the stick of liquorice, I know,' Jenny said, grinning. 'Are we waiting for Brenda and Anna, or shall we go down now?'

'No use waiting for them, they've gone off to collect their fellers,' Sue said. 'How about Bill? Making his own way here?'

'Rather! He's not at all shy, he's used to people in the cafe I suppose.'

'I'm looking forward to meeting him again,' Sue said, rather obscurely, 'and I can't *wait* to meet Simon. Do you think, dear Jenny, that I look a bit like an overblown rubber doll?'

'You're awful,' Jenny scolded, remembering the last time she had seen Simon. 'Come on, let's go down; d'you know, I'm nervous?' She could not help reflecting, as they descended the stairs, that if Simon's taste in people was reflected in the rubber dolls he chose, then it was not Sue but Dermott and Solly who would have to look out!

Jenny had not seen 'the big room' before, but from what Mrs Grant had said she expected it to be large and bare.

By the time the party started, it was nothing of the sort. There were borrowed chairs all round the walls, the entire ceiling was a forest of garlands, and a very large artificial

Christmas tree filled up most of the end wall. Solly and Dermott had rigged up loudspeakers in each corner and one of the cast, presumably the electrician, had brought a set of multi-coloured light bulbs which he strung up all round the room and set to flashing at intervals. One particular ultra-violet light caused all the whites to stand out; Anna looked spectacular and so did Jenny, for her black chiffon was not proof against the light's brilliance and you could distinctly see the line of her bra and briefs through the material.

'Never mind,' shouted Bill above the thudding of the music, 'you look charming, even if a trifle undressed when the blue bulbs take over. And you're amongst friends.'

It was true; everyone was warm and friendly and they were all asking each other to dance, even Sue was gyrating around the floor in the electrician's arms. She was amazingly light on her feet all things considered, and Jenny found that Sue was not the only one. Bill, grasping her lightly round the waist, quickstepped and foxtrotted like a professional.

It was odd to find herself in his arms, though there was nothing amorous about it; it was just odd, like seeing someone from an entirely different angle. She danced with Dermott too, and that was very smoochy but even less amorous than Bill's dancing, strangely enough. Dermott snuggled, so why was she not slightly embarrassed by him? Was it the weight of her years? But she thought not since Solly, grabbing her and whisking her into an extremely athletic and giddying polka, managed to positively exude sexual awareness and made her feel young, attractive and ever so slightly naughty.

A good deal of drinking was going on as well. Bottles kept arriving to be placed ceremoniously on the big table at one end of the room, whence their owners soon ensured that they were removed, emptied into various glasses and dropped into the big laundry basket standing ready to receive them.

By ten o'clock, when the food put in an appearance, Dermott had gone out for fresh supplies of beer and Anna's friend, who had arrived with sherry protruding from one pocket and brandy from the other, had given Dermott the wherewithal to buy another bottle of brandy and what he termed 'A decent brand of whisky'. Anna's friend was a surprise to everyone; he was middle-aged, grey-haired and rather respectable-looking. Not at all Anna's type, as Sue whispered frankly to Jenny during a quick rush up to the kitchen to fetch some hot sausage rolls.

'I bet he's married with grandchildren,' she said, piling cheese straws on to a dish and then sprinkling them with parsley and chopped-up radishes. 'He's Anna's sugar daddy and she's his little bit on the side.'

The food was good and plentiful and Mrs Grant had made a huge urn of coffee to accompany it, or hot punch as an alternative. By this time you could have believed the entire assembly had been bosom friends for years, Jenny thought, watching Brenda sitting on Simon's lap whilst he discoursed with Solly on the idiocy of crowd behaviour at football matches and occasionally slid his hand up and down Brenda's marshmallow back.

Bill ambled over to where she and Sue were sitting; he had captured one of the few dinner plates and had piled it with an assortment of food. Now he set it down on the floor between them and raised a brow.

'Who's going to get up, so's I can sit down? Then the lucky girl can sit on my lap, like Brenda's sitting on Simon's.'

'I've a bloody good mind to take you up on that and watch your thigh bones groan and bow beneath my thirteen stone,' Sue said severely. 'Jenny, are you into lap-sitting?'

'No, my years won't allow it. However, you can sit here, Bill, and I'll sit on the floor.' She slid off her chair and then, when he sat down after some natural diffidence about taking her place, she leaned back against his knees. 'Now isn't this nicer for us both?'

'Well, it'll do.' He leaned over and picked up a sandwich. 'I say, is this home-made pâté?'

'It is. With lots of onion, so no one will want to dance with you afterwards.'

'Oh, to hell with it, I can't resist home-made pâté. Have some yourselves and then we can dance the night away, oblivious of each others' niffy odour.'

Dermott wandered over to them and began to chat to Sue, and, presently, with her tummy pleasantly full and the white wine beginning to loosen her inhibitions, Jenny agreed with

Bill that the best way to get them both dancing again would be a breath of fresh air. She rose to her feet, let him take her hand, and went with him out of the basement, up the stairs and across the hall, and out into the sweet cold of the night air.

Hand in hand, they wandered up Beechcroft Road to the sea-front; the tide was out and far in the distance they could see the white line of the little waves, for it was a mild December night with only the faintest breath of breeze.

'Want to go and paddle? Or is that too far?'

'No, let's go right down to the water,' Jenny said, jumping off the edge of the promenade and setting off over the hard wet sand. As her eyes grew accustomed to the faint starlight she could see the shells embedded in the hardened sand-ripples, the channels and the little sea-water pools almost as clearly as she could see them by day. She found that she was filled with enormous happiness and excitement, so that it was hard not to swing on Bill's hand, act the fool, kick off her shoes and run barefoot across the sands.

But then . . . why not? She kicked off her shoes, jerked her hand free from Bill's, and began to take off her tights. Presently she straightened, stuffed the tights into Bill's pocket, since her beautiful dress was not a particularly practical garment, and they set out for the distant line of surf.

When they reached it, Jenny let go Bill's hand again and ran right into the little waves creaming against the shore. The water was tinglingly cold and fresh and her feet sank into the softness of the sand, while all her old love of the sea came flooding over her; she wished she could bathe, she wished it were summer and that she were eight years old again, all set for a day on the beach.

Then Bill joined her, shoes and socks left neatly behind, his trouser legs rolled inexpertly up to his knees.

'You're a madwoman,' he scolded. 'I'm a sober citizen, or I was until I met you!'

'It's cold,' Jenny said, kicking the spray, 'But it's wonderful! I feel like a kid, I can hardly remember feeling so carefree before.'

Bill reached for her hand, Jenny, she hardly knew why, eluded him, and they began to chase each other in and out of

221

the waves, with disastrous results for the hem of Jenny's dress and Bill's right trouser leg, which speedily fell right down and got saturated. Bill shouted at her, Jenny laughed and ran . . . and then he grabbed her, had her in his arms, both breathless and panting, with Jenny held so hard against his chest that she could feel his heart hammering right through her.

The kiss was inevitable but her response to it was not. She clung, oblivious of the water washing round her calves, her draggled dress, the breeze tugging her hair. His mouth knew what pleased her, knew it better than Dirk ever had, she marvelled. Gentleness and wanting, tenderness and desire were combined in that kiss. It lasted for longer than a casual kiss should have done, and Jenny encouraged it. She moaned under his mouth, knowing that this was a dreadful way to behave and not caring; she pressed close, closer, lost in him, her mind absorbed as was her body.

Presently, he lifted his mouth from hers and muttered her name in questioning tone, then lifted her up and carried her out of the water and stood her down on the hard sand. He still held her close.

'Jenny? Do you know how I feel about you? Do you want to know?'

He sounded as breathless as if he had been running and beneath her cheek his heart was pounding. Jenny meant to draw back; instead, she snuggled closer.

'Oh Bill, you are so cuddly!'

'So are you. Did you hear what I said? Jen, I want you.'

'That's a wonderful compliment, Bill, and I . . .'

'It's a statement of fact. It's not mutual, though, is it?'

'I . . . no, I suppose . . . I'm not free to want people, I'm married, as you are.'

Bill drew away from her, but slid his arm round her waist and began to lead her up the beach.

'You think it would complicate matters? Is that what you think? Or is it even simpler?'

'It would complicate matters, wouldn't it, since we're neither of us free to . . . well, to . . .'

'You could say we were both pretty free to do what we wanted to do, since our spouses . . . spice? . . . no, spouses

222

had left us. I'll accept that you don't want a closer relationship though, if that's what you're trying to say.'

'I think that's what I mean,' Jenny said gratefully, rubbing her head against his shoulder in a way which gave the lie to her words had she but known it. 'I know people do go in for affairs even when they're married to someone else – look at Dirk and Bronwen – but I'm so *involved* with Dirk still. And you know, don't you, that I think he'll take me back? I wouldn't want to spoil that by having to admit that I'd been unfaithful.'

'Why not? Hasn't he?'

Abruptly, Jenny saw the sheer stupidity of her own argument; it was ridiculous to pretend that Dirk had any right to expect her to remain spotless and pure for his sake, considering what he was doing probably at this very minute. But, she reflected wryly, you either have a natural bent for adultery or you do not; she did not. She said as much to Bill.

'Right, no adultery.' His tone was indulgent, as to a small child. 'But there's no harm in a few cuddles.'

When they reached the promenade they sat down on it and kissed again, very sweetly, Jenny thought, and cuddled for a bit. Just as it was becoming rather intense, when Jenny's breathing had speeded up and her long-married body was preparing itself, with every sign of enjoyment, for the next move in a game it had known so well, another couple came along the promenade behind them, arms entwined. Jenny and Bill sat demurely enough until the pair had passed, but then, to the disappointment of Jenny's body though she hoped her mind had more sense, Bill pulled her to her feet and turned her in the direction of Beechcroft Road.

'We'd best be getting back; you don't want people to talk.'

'Yes, all right,' Jenny agreed docilely. Her body's awakened expectations died away in rebellious mutterings, or so she felt. A certain part of her – several certain parts – were calling her a prig and a spoilsport in no uncertain terms.

They arrived back in the basement just as a game of Blind Man's Buff started, with 'im wearing the scarf. Jenny realized that the main point of the game for Mr Grant, at least, was the chance to fondle any female figure which came within arm's reach, so she kept well clear. She and Bill were making for the

drinks table, in fact, when Jenny suddenly realized that Sue
was nowhere to be seen. She cast an eye over the others; who
had Sue sneaked off with, the dreadful girl, and her still
tank-sized after her last sneaking-off? But there did not seem
to be anyone else missing.

'Bill, where's Sue do you suppose?' she asked, as they
reached the drinks. 'I can't see her anywhere.'

'Gone off to her room with someone I expect,' Bill said
with unimpaired cheerfulness. Jenny found she was half-
hoping he would look deprived and sour over her own de-
fection, but instead he simply looked like Bill pouring out
two glasses of shandy. Oh well, his half-proposal had probably only been the result of the romantic starlight and the
amount they had both drunk. She wrenched her mind away
from her own business to that of her friend.

'No, if she's gone she's gone alone. I wonder if she's in her
room, not feeling too good? Do you think I ought to go and
see?'

'Sure; I'll keep your drink safe.' Bill, however, made no
move to accompany her. Following his greeny-grey gaze,
Jenny realized with considerable rancour that he was looking
at Brenda, pink as a piece of Turkish delight and probably as
sweet, sitting rather uncomfortably on the arm of a chair
and gazing into space. Simon was dancing with Anna, and
Mouse, looking tortured, was being patted and prodded
around the room by Mr Grant. The nice young clerical
assistant she had brought with her from the office was busy
fetching drinks and had his back to the action, so could do
little to help her.

Jenny cleared her throat. 'I think I'd better go.'

'Yes, you should, really. If she's in trouble, come back and
I'll come up with you.' He smiled rather absently at her, then
turned his head so that he was looking towards Brenda once
more. 'I'll go and chat with little whatsername whilst you're
gone.'

'Right, I shan't be a moment.' Jenny marched out of the
room, willing herself not to look back, because if he were
talking to Brenda she would not be responsible for her
actions. She looked back. He was talking to Brenda; as Jenny
stared, Brenda tilted her head back and laughed. She looked

adorable, her silvery curls gleaming, the column of her throat very white and slender.

Jenny shot out of the room, cursing Sue for being so awkward as to disappear just at that particular moment. Not that Sue could have known she would worry. Jenny took the stairs two at a time, crashed into Sue's room without knocking and found it empty, tried her own room with the same results, and was about to see if Sue had, for some unknown reason, taken herself off to the attic when she heard a plaintive mew and a bumping noise. A *cat*? She looked in through her own open door again and there was Belle, lying on Posy's empty bed looking very comfortable and not at all as though she were mewing for amusement. She wagged her tail twice when she saw Jenny looking in, thump thump, then closed her eyes meaningfully; Belle wanted to sleep even if others did not mind being wide awake.

Halfway down the flight, the mew and the bump were repeated and Jenny suddenly realized they were coming from the loo and knew, in the way one does, that she had found Sue. She hurried down there and found it occupied, judging from the light visible under the door. She tapped gently.

'Sue? Are you in there?'

'Yes; forever,' Sue said in a sepulchral tone. 'Oh Jenny, I'm glad you've come – that bloody bolt's sheered through and I've got ever such a funny pain in my back.'

'Oh, Sue! Can't you fiddle the bolt back with your fingers? I *told* you not to lock it!'

'And I told you I had to. There's nothing to fiddle back, that's the trouble. I've tried and tried, but it won't budge an inch. Oh hell, here comes that dragging pain again.'

'A dragging pain?' Jenny had been telling herself it was just another of Sue's alarms, but the words rang horribly true to one who had experienced the pangs of childbirth within the last few years. 'Look, love, I'm going to get some help, we'll knock the door down if there's no other way in . . . stay where you are, I won't be long.'

'And little chance I have of leaving, unless I dive down the loo,' Sue reminded her bitterly. 'I got up and stood on the seat and looked through the window and it's tiny, quite ridiculous, only a midget could get through it in either direction. Do they grow very small firemen, perhaps?'

'Or tiny midwives?' Jenny giggled as Sue moaned. 'No, I don't think so, I suppose they pass things through the window for the undoing of bolts. Hang on, shan't be a tick.'

She got back to the basement to find Bill dancing with Brenda; it said a lot about her feelings for Sue that she scarcely noticed and went straight across to him.

'Bill, Sue's stuck in the toilet; the bolt sheered off. Can you come and see if we can get her out?'

Brenda promptly shouted to the whole room, gaining immediate attention.

'Hi, everyone, Sue's stuck in the loo; any volunteers to break the door down?'

'Stuck in the *loo*? Not that bolt? Hell, we've been warning each other for weeks that it was going to bust off – trust it to choose this evening.' That was Dermott, one arm round a member of the chorus to judge from her make up and false eyelashes. 'Come on, let's take a look.'

The entire party, buzzing, surged for the door; Bill shook his head reproachfully at Jenny.

'Daft! Too many cooks spoil the broth.' He raised his voice to a bellow. 'Don't all cram up the stairs, you won't be able to help. Leave it to me, Dermott and Solly, we'll get her out.'

The party surged back again and Jenny slipped out with the men and grabbed Bill's sleeve.

'Bill, you won't be able to break it inwards without risking Sue, and she thinks the baby's started.'

Bill stopped, stared, then shook his head. 'I doubt it; she's just panicking I expect and who can blame her? It's not due for a fortnight, is it?'

'No, but babies do put in early appearances sometimes.'

'Oh I know, but not first ones surely? Anyway, no point in worrying. I'll take a look at the door.'

Dermott and Solly were up the stairs first and, began bombarding Sue, through the woodwork, with different instructions; stand back, get on to the seat, mind yourself. Bill was more practical. He looked long and hard at the door, then spoke with his voice deliberately slow and his mouth inches away from the panel.

'Sue? What are the screws like that hold the bolt in place? Old and rusted, or quite new?'

Pause. Heavy breathing before Sue answered.

'Old and rusted. Even if I had a nail-file I'd never budge 'em.'

'I see. What about the hinges?'

'Hinges? Well, they're just sort of barber's poles, not un-doeable.'

'Right, I get the picture. Now how about if we got you a pair of pincers to grasp the bolt, could you draw it back then, do you think?'

Sue's voice, when she answered, was lighter, less gloom-laden. 'Yes, I'm sure I could! Oh Bill, you're a genius! But how will you get them in to me?'

'There's a good gap under the door, but if they won't go through it, it'll have to be the fire service and the window, I'm afraid. Unless someone's got a very long ladder.'

'We could always break a hole in the door panel,' Dermott said hopefully; he was plainly longing to use some of his boundless energy.

'Don't let him!' Sue squeaked. 'There isn't room in here to swing a cat, he'll hit me.'

'It's all right, we won't let him,' Bill said soothingly. 'Jenny's just going down to see if Mr Grant's got a pair of pincers.'

Jenny took the hint and rushed down the stairs, arriving dramatically in the basement. Mr Grant was still blindfolded and fumbling about amongst the dancers but Mrs Grant was quite willing to go and fetch him.

''e's had a drop too much,' she said quite indulgently. 'A pile of tools 'e's got, in the back. I'll get 'im to fetch 'em out.'

And eventually Jenny was able to return to the crowd outside the loo door, complete with various pincer- and grabber-type tools.

'That'll do very nicely,' Bill said, pushing the smallest one under the door. 'Got it, Sue?'

The hospital smelled, as all hospitals do, of floor polish,

antiseptic and, faintly, of pain. Jenny had been allowed to travel in the ambulance and, as the stretcher-men carried Sue in through the big double doors, she sniffed the air and felt a cringing sensation begin in her toes and work rapidly up to the top of her head. A healthy person herself, in Jenny's mind hospitals were associated either with childbirth or with accidents which had happened to the boys – assorted agonies of crushed toes, broken limbs and torn flesh had been a regular feature of life with the Sayer boys when they were small. But this was Sue's first visit to a hospital as a patient, so no doubt she felt differently. Jenny looked at Sue, lying very pale and wide-eyed on the stretcher. Or perhaps not, perhaps hospitals by their very nature called forth the gibbering coward in most people.

'Jen?'

'Yes, love?'

'Stay with me?'

'As long as I'm allowed.'

Almost as she said the words Sue was swooped on by a porter and a couple of pretty nurses. They cooed over her, telling her that she'd be on the ward in a brace of shakes . . . how far apart were the contractions, had she eaten recently . . . gracious, was that whisky they could smell? Nice girls, Jenny thought approvingly, as some of Sue's fear dissipated in this informal atmosphere. But then they swung her off the ambulance trolley on to one of their own and Sue's face turned piteously towards her friend.

'Jen? Don't go!'

'No, don't go,' the older of the two nurses agreed, giving Jenny a charming smile. 'Since this is Mrs Oliver's first child she may have a bit of a wait; be nice if you're there to chat to her.'

'I'll be happy to stay for as long as you don't need the space I take up,' Jenny said, walking along beside the stretcher, her arms full of Sue's coat and handbag and overnight bag. 'But I'll go as soon as I'm told.'

She guessed that they would not want her once Sue went into the second stage of labour; she would probably be home to say cheerio to the party guests.

* * *

'Breathe deeply, Sue, remember what you told me, and then pant. If you stop breathing altogether and screw your muscles up, you'll slow things down besides giving yourself the maximum amount of discomfort.'

'Pain you mean,' Sue snarled. 'I don't want to be hurt like this, you know, it's just happening.'

'Yes, I remember how I felt the first time; cheated describes it best. The way they said it was a natural bodily function! It's about as natural as plastic knickers if you ask me.'

'I don't ask anybody,' Sue said. 'Aaargh! Bloody hell! Count, damn you, Sayer, don't just sit there!'

'I'm watching the second hand,' Jenny promised, waving a hand soothingly in Sue's general direction. 'Tell me when it's over . . . and do stop holding your breath!'

Sue let out her breath in a long, whistling sigh and relaxed all over, then sat up on one elbow and tried to examine Jenny's watch upside down.

'My God, it's two o'clock in the morning! Why don't they *do* something to get it born, it shouldn't be allowed to take its time like this! Where are the nurses? And doctors? If the buggers are in bed, kick them out of it – go on, don't sit there gaping at me, get some attention!'

'I'll ring,' Jenny said diplomatically, pretending to press the bell. She had been here with Sue now for three hours and the night was beginning to fall into a pattern. Sue would get fed up and tired and shout for the medical staff, they would appear briefly, scold her, tell her that it would be a long while yet, and disappear again. Jenny was glad for Sue's sake that she was here, because otherwise her friend would have been going frantic. Not that she wasn't going frantic anyway, but at least she did not feel totally abandoned and ignored.

'Oh, damn, here comes another,' Sue said presently and Jenny, looking at her watch, realized that the contractions were getting closer; every four minutes – shouldn't someone really be called for this time?

She reached for the bell-push and pressed it full in, holding it down. That should fetch them!

'It's a dear little boy, Sue,' Jenny said softly, smoothing the soaking hair off her friend's white forehead. 'Just like you said it would be, a dear little boy!'

Sue was lying with her eyes shut; now the long lids flickered up and big pain-darkened eyes looked sombrely up at Jenny.

'Really? I hope he and his mother will be very happy.'

'Yes, I know, dope, but don't you want to look at him?'

'No. What's the point?'

The doctor and nurses were cleaning up, the baby lay wrapped in what looked like a piece of green canvas in a hammock-like structure. He had been born, had been hung upside down by his feet and slapped, had given his first cry. Jenny had marvelled over the fresh redness of him, the tiny fists with their extraordinarily long fingers, the elderly peevishness of a face that was younger and more innocent than any face she was likely to see again. She understood that Sue did not want to see the baby because she was going to have him adopted but she also knew, with the side of her that had been and still was a mother, that Sue needed to see the baby, even to cuddle him. If she refused to have anything to do with him it would scar her in a way that giving him up to another woman could never do. It was illogical, even to herself it sounded all wrong to try to make Sue look at the child, but she was borne up by a strong conviction that she was right. If Sue gave her son away without a look or a touch, she would be in some way crippled by the experience.

'Sue? Do take him. It's Tiny Tim and he needs you still, even though he's not actually a part of you any more. Tiny babies need love you know.'

Very slowly, Sue's long lids lifted. Jenny had picked up the child and held it in the crook of her arm, absurdly small and light, and sending out a warmth that penetrated the green canvas of his wrapping as well as the black taffeta and gauze of Jenny's dress. Such life-giving heat, such tenacity! The small, Churchillian face with its puffed lids and its unused, pursed lips, the ears, delicate as newly unfolding flower petals, the soft down of the silky black hair were all objects of wonder. Jenny, glancing down at him, had to smile, to love him for his milky newness, and then she looked at Sue and held the baby lower so that the new mother could gaze into the new face.

Sue looked, gasped, looked up at Jenny, then back at the baby. A hand stole out and touched the child's soft cheek, then, slowly but very deliberately, Sue took him in her arms, took off the green wrapping, and cradled him against her bare breast, looking down at him with such marvelling surprise that Jenny felt her eyes fill with tears.

'You're just exactly like Hugo,' Sue said, in a very different voice from the one which had greeted the baby's arrival into the world. 'You're a teeny, weeny, cross Hugo, when he's lost a bus or a plane and thinks the world's against him. Well, young man, your mother had plans for you which have just crumbled into dust. I could bear the idea of another woman bringing up my son – she'd probably do it a good deal better than I would – but I couldn't give Hugo away, not for anyone or anything. Tim Oliver, you're going to become a one-parent family.'

It seemed to Jenny that the baby understood and snuggled closer. It was very quiet in the delivery room. Outside, the beginnings of the new day were making themselves felt; a milk float hummed past, someone clattered over a grid on a bicycle, a cockerel announced that it was morning. Inside, the hospital was waking up. Trolleys rattled, china and cutlery clinked, voices began to speak above the night-time murmur.

Presently, Jenny heard another sound. A low, contented, bee-like sound. Sitting up on the hard delivery couch, Sue was singing to her new-born child.

CHAPTER NINE

'They're keeping her in for a week, becuse of her being so alone,' Jenny explained later in the day when she, Brenda, Anna and Mouse were sitting in the kitchen, watching their vegetables come to the boil and savouring the delicious and interesting smells of their various Sunday dinners. The oven rota was a marvellous idea and today, because Jenny was sharing the top shelf with Mouse, she and Posy were having a small chicken with all the trimmings which was roasting away beside Mouse's guava lamb.

'What will Sue do when she comes out?' Brenda asked. 'I mean she told the old hen – and everyone else – that she was having the baby adopted. Can you see our Mrs G. putting up with a squalling brat day and night? Especially one with only a single parent to cater to its whims.'

'But is she really going to keep it, or was it just an idea?' Mouse asked. 'She wanted the best for the baby; surely she must see that this place . . .', she waved an expressive hand round the tiny, crammed kitchen, '. . . cannot be the best.'

'Perhaps she's come to her senses,' Jenny said rather tartly. 'I have. Once, I'd have agreed with Sue that adoring parents and all the money you want and an easy life were ideal conditions in which to bring up children, but now I know better. Posy's happier here than she ever was on the farm.'

'I think kids don't take a lot of notice of places. It's more people,' Mouse observed. 'I was born and brought up in the Smoke, but you couldn't call me deprived. Pavement games, days out at the sea down at Clacton or Hastings, going to the zoo, the parks . . . you name it, we did it, my Mum and my Nan and myself.'

'Then where'll you go for Christmas, Jenny?' Brenda asked curiously. It was common knowledge that Jenny and Posy had received several invitations but intended to stay in the flats because of Sue. Now that Sue was in hospital, however . . .

'Bill asked us first, so we'll go there on Christmas day. But I do think perhaps I'll go back to the farm for Boxing Day. Dirk wanted us to go for the whole holiday, once he knew Bronwen was going back to her parents that is, but I wouldn't do that. Although the boys said to go, said I'd be surprisd how eagerly their father was planning for it . . . so I think we will spend Boxing Day at the farm.'

'Did he ask Posy by herself first?' Brenda asked. 'Or has it always been both of you? You'd think he'd miss his little girl terribly; she's his only one.'

'The inference being that he's got a substitute wife, I suppose,' Jenny said wryly. 'No, the invitation came for us both. I've told you before, Dirk isn't keen on little girls.'

'Not until they get to be sixteen or so,' Anna remarked. She had the bottom shelf today, which meant a casserole or a pot-roast. 'I've never seen your Dirk, but I fancy your Philip like crazy!'

'Hmm. Looks aren't everything. Tell yourself he'll grow up just like his father and maybe you'll be a bit less fanciful.'

'I don't keep 'em for long enough to care what they're going to turn into,' Anna said honestly. 'I just like 'em whilst I have 'em. Who's cooking cauliflower? Something smells burny, like.'

'Oh, hell!' Jenny jumped down from her perch on the draining board and grabbed her pan off the gas, then groaned. 'Damn the thing, it's caught inside on the bottom and I absolutely hate cleaning off burnt food.'

'When are you going to visit Sue?' Mouse asked, after Jenny had laboriously transferred her cauliflower to someone else's pan and was chipping off the burnt mess with a knife. 'After dinner? If so, I'll come along.'

'Lovely. Why don't we . . .'

'All go? Fun for us, but what about Sue? Do you think she's up to a crowd? And what about Posy? Won't she want to go?'

'No children allowed in maternity wards, and anyway she and Mrs Twigg plan an assault on the beach since it isn't raining. Do come along, all of you, Sue will love to see you. It isn't as if she's ill; they spend so much time telling everyone that childbirth's a natural function, now they can prove it!'

'Yes, but isn't visiting for husbands only?' Mouse said belatedly. 'I know Sue's husband isn't here, but will they let us just barge in?'

'Sure to.' Anna poked a fork into her tiny milk pan with its one potato bubbling away and pulled a face. 'Still like a rock! Let's see if Dermott wants to come as well. And Solly.'

'We can say one of them's the father but they aren't sure which,' Brenda giggled. 'And if the hospital won't let us all round the bed at once we can go in relays.'

'Right. We can walk round, it isn't far, and visiting starts at three. Who's going to ask Dermott?'

'Me,' Anna said promptly. 'I'll go down now.'

When she had disappeared, slamming the door behind her and clunking down the stairs in her latest absurdly high heels, Brenda dug Mouse with her elbow and grinned across at Jenny.

'Poor old Anna, can't take no for an answer! Though I'm sure he'll come to the hospital, he rather likes Sue.'

'We all do,' Jenny said. 'I'll go and shout Posy now; I'm about ready to dish up.'

Sue lay in her bed on the ward, surrounded by women, re-reading Hugo's latest letter. He, lucky blighter, was surrounded by men: little yellow ones – the porters; big hairy ones – the other climbers; intense bespectacled ones – the two photographers. His letter was pages and pages long, and was covered with tiny sketches no bigger than a thumbnail, some in the form of cartoons, others little scenes, drawn for her amusement or interest.

She knew, of course, that he was loving every minute of it; frostbite might nip, the cold might be cruel, they might be so high that water would not boil for some obscure reason that she had never quite managed to grasp, but he would be happy. He had an affinity for the frozen wastes which amounted to a craving for them; he could not be happy unless he knew that sometime soon he would be returning to the high mountains of the Himalayas or the Alps, or most of all to the Caucasus where he was now, which was his favourite mountain range.

Yet when he was away he longed for Sue; his letter was full

of it, sometimes merely visible between the lines, sometimes explicitly said. He loved her as she loved him, totally, without holding back, He was not ashamed of his passion for the mountains and the snows because it equalled, but did not surpass, his passion for her.

When Jenny had first put the baby into her arms, Sue had made the astonishing discovery that he was not just a baby, he was Hugo's image. She had thought then that she must keep him, could not let him go to someone else, because, as well as Hugo's features, he would also have trapped inside him Hugo's fears and strengths, his sensitivities and needs. Another woman might mother an ordinary baby but it would take her and her alone to understand the complex little creature who was Hugo's son. She could not hand the child over; he would be misunderstood, alienated because he was different, and finally, perhaps, put into a children's home because his adoptive parents were unable to see why he was the way he was. She would put up with anything rather than that.

Anything but losing Hugo. She could not live without him, could not bring up a child who had cost her his love.

And then she had pulled out the letter and read it, and in her mind the conviction had grown, steadily, surely, that Hugo would love the baby. He might be upset and reproachful at first, but then his good sense would take over; after all, he had very much enjoyed conceiving Tiny Tim, and he loved her very dearly, she knew that. Had they both been born in an earlier age, before the pill was available, she would not have been able simply to choose not to give birth to a child. All right, so she had dragged a little boy into this vale of tears, to grow and suffer, love and hate, but it had happened and she did not believe for one moment that Hugo would refuse to take his share of responsibility for that happening. The baby would have Hugo's daemon, but he would also have something of Sue. She hoped she had passed on some of her optimism to Tiny Tim to counter Hugo's pessimism, and some of her enjoyment of people to counter his deep mistrust of humanity in general.

So she would keep Tiny Tim and she would write a letter to Hugo explaining his existence. Lacking Hugo's artistic ability, she would enclose a photo of herself and the child, or possibly just of the child; he could not fail to love the baby once he had seen a photo, she thought, with a mother's self- deluding fondness. Such a wonderfully beautiful child, who also looked so like him, could not fail to find a way into Hugo's generous heart.

Lying in bed, she found Hugo's image growing in her mind's eye until he was almost by the side of her. Was he good-looking? She could never tell because when one loves besottedly one can no longer judge, but she knew she had once thought him handsome. He had floppy hay-coloured hair, a thin intellignet face with blue-grey eyes beneath straight dark brows, and a nose which was just short of being Roman. His mouth was determined, and when he smiled, and the firm, resolute lines of his countenance tilted, into amusement and friendliness, he was irresistible. Now, of course, his face would consist largely of fair beard and moustache, because no one shaved halfway up enormous snow-clad mountains, but even when bearded the strong line of his jaw showed, and the firm planes of his cheekbones.

The girl in the next bed leaned over towards her. 'Sue, it's five to three; is your husband visiting?'

Sue put her letter down and shook her head. Her hair was lank and felt horribly greasy; tomorrow she would try to wash it. She knew Jenny would come, but that was all. Never mind, she had Tiny Tim and her letter. They would suffice, even if no one visited her at all.

Christmas day was everything that Christmas day should be; Bill bought a turkey, Jenny provided a Christmas pudding and, of course, the cake for tea. Everything else they shared. Posy woke early, before it was light, and investigated her stocking with Jenny's bleary-eyed assistance, then slept soundly until Jenny woke her for a cooked breakfast. After breakfast, they put their presents into Jenny's shopping bag and set off for Bill's house.

It was a fine but cold morning, just right for Christmas day, with the sun shining on the wet dark gold of the sand and making the waves twinkle and dance. Passing the gardens they saw the grass untouched, heavy with dew, and

Jenny felt a tiny pang for the farm where untouched grass heavy with dew was the norm rather than something to exclaim over. But there were roses still in bloom in the gardens and that did not happen at the farm.

When they arrived at Bill's gate Jenny paused, wondering for one awful moment if they were too early – after all a good many people slept in on any holiday, even this one. But then she reflected that Erica and Dawn were excitable little girls, just like Posy, and were unlikely to have allowed Bill to snooze late, no matter how tired he might have been. So she walked up the short, brick path between the frail pink-and- yellow roses and rat-tatted on the door.

Dawn and Erica were fighting to be the first to open it, their slippers skidding on the lino, squeaks and giggles competing with the radio or the television, Jenny did not know which. Through the frosted glass pane, she saw Bill's large figure loom up and then the door was open and she was bending to pick up first Erica because she was the oldest and also too heavy to hold for more than a moment, giving her a hug and a Christmas kiss, then Dawn; then of course Bill kissed her under the mistletoe – how light, how casual a kiss – before leading the way into the living room. Wonderfully appetizing smells came from the kitchen; dinner was well under way and the bread sauce was in the process of being made, hence Bill's tear-filled eyes.

The little house was warm and brightly decorated. There were bunches of holly on the picture rails, cards on every available surface, many of them home-made by children at school, and in the corner opposite the television there was a big Christmas tree, a real one smelling of pinewoods, complete with lights, tiny crackers and parcels.

'This is more like it,' Bill cried, as the children grabbed Jenny's bag and up-ended it, adding the presents inside it to the pile beneath the tree. 'This is a real Christmas! Who wants a drink of pop, or a dry sherry? Who wants nuts, raisins or salted peanuts? Who wants to help me with the dinner?'

Posy danced about, imploring that they open presents first, before they had drinks or even crisps. Bill teased her with threats of empty boxes if she did not help him peel the onion for the bread sauce. Ricky and Dawn were showing off their stocking presents and Posy described her own amazing good fortune. Christmas reigned.

Jenny and Posy were walked back home by Bill and the girls, everyone wrapped up well against the cold except for Belle who trotted sedately along with the children. She had a new collar, and a magnificent rubber bone which she would destroy, casually, the next time she was left in the house alone and became bored. Posy was wearing the scarf, mittens and pom-pom hat which Bill and the children had given her; Dawn and Erica were wearing the scarves, mittens and pom-pom hats which Jenny and Posy had given them.

'A bit dull, I daresay, after Christmas at your farm,' Bill said quietly, as they strolled behind the three small girls. 'No flames on the pudding, no brandy liqueur, no expensive presents.' He had given Jenny a big shoulder bag which had delighted her; with her job and Posy and Belle to look after, she frequently needed more space than her shabby red leather one could possibly provide. She had given Bill a gorgeous chunky sweater, dark blue with a roll neck. She had bought the wool and Mrs Twigg had knitted it up for her, so it had not been nearly as expensive as it looked. Bill had insisted on slipping it on then and there and had preened himself in front of the mirror, pointing his toe, holding out the hem of an imaginary skirt and pretending to be a model to make the children laugh.

'Not a bit dull; marvellous,' Jenny said equally quietly. It was that kind of evening. The sky was brilliant with stars, and the nip in the air and the frost on fences and grass simply served to make it more exciting. 'I haven't had such a lovely day for years.'

'Nor me. I wish I could ask you over again tomorrow, but I mustn't be greedy. You are going back to the farm?'

'Yes. Dirk's calling for us at ten and he'll bring us back in the evening. I expect it will be quite a strain for us both, though obviously I'm hoping . . .'

'What? For reconciliation?'

Jenny sighed and lifted one shoulder in a shrug. 'Oh, I

don't know. Perhaps. Perhaps just . . . just a better understanding.'

'What about Belle? You're taking her, of course?'

'No, that's why we bought her the bone. She'll be alone all
day, and I'd rather she spent her time chewing up that bone
than wandering around whining. The Twiggs are there, and
the Grants of course, but everyone else is either away or busy.
Dermott and Solly are at home in the morning, but
pantomiming in the afternoon and evening – first show, very
important.'

'Would you trust Belle with us? We'd love to have her. You
know how the kids adore her, and it would give me . . . could
we take care of her for you, just for the day? We'd bring her
back to you first thing the following morning.'

'Oh Bill, would you? It wouldn't be asking too much? I've
felt horribly guilty over leaving her, though I can take her out
for a walk before we leave and again when we get back. But
it's a long time for her to be alone, with virtually no one else
in residence – the Grants do keep themselves to themselves
down in that basement.'

'Great, that's settled then, we'll take you to your door and
then bring Belle back home again. If she'll come, of course.
To tell you the truth, it'll make my Boxing Day.'

'Oh Bill, you aren't *that* fond of her, surely?'

Bill grinned, she could see the flash of his teeth even in the
dark. 'I like her all right, but it's not that. It's just that I know
you wouldn't ever abandon her. You'll come back for her, if
only to explain that you've moved back in with Dirk.'

'You didn't think . . . you couldn't think that I'd just
abandon all my friends here and quit?' Jenny asked, outraged. 'Bill, I'm not like that, really I'm not! What about Sue,
and Brenda and the others?'

'No, I know you wouldn't leave them without a word, but
I'm only the chap you work for. It would be easy to intend to
let me know and then . . . well, just get swept back into your
old life and not get in touch again. I might even be an
embarrassment; the party . . . I didn't mean . . .'

'Oh, shut up,' Jenny said roundly. 'As if you could ever be
an embarrassment; you're the best friend of the lot!'

She took his hand and squeezed, deliberately hard. He

squeezed back; it became a silent contest in which, she suspected, Bill was withholding at least three quarters of his strength.

Ahead of them, the little girls had linked arms and were singing a carol, one of the new ones. The words floated back to them, reminding Jenny sharply of Sue.

A boy is born at number four, I heard the milkman say,
And Angels sang a song for him, born on Christmas Day,
Yes Angels sang a song for him, born on Christmas day.

'And as for leaving Beechcroft Road, I'm committed to them all, as I am to the cafe,' Jenny said, while the carol died away on the still air. 'I'm not saying I don't love Dirk or wouldn't like my old life back, but it isn't straighforward any more. It would be a hell of a wrench to leave Rhyl.'

Bill gave a sort of muted whoop which brought Belle's head round, though the children, immersed in talk, did not appear to notice.

'Good,' he said, lacing his fingers companionably in hers. 'Good!'

'What time did Daddy say he was calling for us?'

Posy, washed, brushed and ready except for her coat, was standing at the window, peering down into the street. It had tried to snow, earlier, which had excited her, but now it was merely chilly and overcast with a brisk breeze. If you listened hard you could hear the surf building up down on the beach.

'Ten o'clock, love. It's just on the hour now, so he should be here any minute. Are you excited?'

'Yes . . . no. I'm not sure. Will Phil be there? And Mark? Will they be in the car, d'you suppose? I expect there'll be presents, won't there? Do I have mine? Will they each give me something, or will it be between them? Will Daddy's young lady be there? Will she buy me a present? Have I got her one?'

'Crumbs darling, what a list! You've got presents for Phil and Mark of course, just small things, and for Daddy. I don't think the boys will be in the car but they'll be at the farm, of course. They didn't have their Christmas day yesterday, they've saved it for today so I expect there will be crackers and the tree and all sorts. You'll have a lovely day.'

'Will I?' But a good few of Posy's doubts had been laid to rest by being allowed to wear her brand-new winter dress, which was made of warm scarlet wool with a full skirt and long sleeves. That was courtesy of Sue. Posy was also wearing knee socks instead of tights, which pleased her, and of course the locket on a gold chain from the Twiggs would probably accompany her everywhere for the next six months, including to bed.

To complete the picture, Jenny had tied her hair into two bunches fastened with scarlet satin ribbons and allowed Posy to use her new American cloth bag to carry her presents. It was a pity about her coat which, though new in October, was only a cheap navy-blue duffle with a hood, but Posy would not mind that. New coats were beyond Jenny at present.

'Here's a car! Mum, is it him? It's red with a silver hood, it's slowing down . . . it's stopped! A man's got out! Is it Daddy?'

'Darling, it isn't that long since you saw him; is it Daddy?'

'It's coming up the path!' Posy shrieked, diving for her coat. 'Get it on, Mum, quick, or we'll be late!'

'Don't be in such a rush,' Jenny said laughing as she fed Posy's arms into her coat. 'Oh, all right, you go and let Daddy into the hall, I'll be right down.'

She still did not want Dirk in here; it would be better to meet him on neutral ground downstairs.

The bell rang, hard and long, the way Dirk always rang bells, and Posy's feet could be heard scampering downstairs. There was a pause whilst she struggled with the lock – they would be the first ones out this morning – and then a deep voice spoke. Jenny picked up her own coat, checked quickly that she had left things as they should be, then went out, shutting and locking the door behind her. Below her in the hall she could hear Posy's small voice and guessed that she was describing every gift she had received. She began to descend the stairs and there was Dirk, big, somehow awkward, bending down to hear Posy as she reeled off her list. He looked up as she came into view and half smiled. His face was ruddier than she remembered, his hair greyer.

241

'Morning, Dirk. Right on time. Posy's been watching for you since nine,' Jenny said, trying to sound cool and unconcerned. 'We're all ready; shall we go?'

'Yes, of course.' He glanced up the stairs; he expects me to invite him in for a drink or a coffee, Jenny realized. Well, he would be disappointed because she had no intention of doing any such thing. She knew the boys had not mentioned Belle to their father but there were many signs of the dog in her room, and, in any case, she did not want to take Dirk up there and there was absolutely no reason why she should.

Dirk opened the front door and Posy hurried ahead of them down the path. When her father opened the passenger door she climbed quickly into the back seat, hugging her bag of presents, looking excited and yet still a little apprehensive. It occurred to Jenny that Dirk had almost certainly not tried to kiss his daughter or hold her hand or touch her in any way. She wondered if he had actually spoken, or whether Posy's gabbled list of 'I got' had started as soon as the door had opened half an inch. The thought made her smile as she slid into the passenger seat. What a father! Yet had Posy been a boy Dirk would have grabbed her, hugged her, played a-let-and-a-wing or some other riotous game with her, talked non-stop . . .

Dirk started the car, revved up the engine and pulled away from the kerb, all without a word. He drove along the promenade. He was a good driver, always in full control of his machine, changing gear smoothly and fast, accelerating just at the right moment so that the engine never roared unnecessarily. But then, remembered Jenny, he never kept a car for longer than two years and they were, as he was fond of remarking, his one big extravagance, so perhaps he was just an average driver with a better-than-average car.

She glanced sideways at him as the car turned away from the sea and headed for the distant hills. It was ungenerous to suggest, even to herself, that it was the car and not he who was good. He held the wheel lightly but authoritatively, his eyes steady on the road ahead; he was humming beneath his breath, she could not recognize the tune but she knew it was a good sign. Dirk was not musical but when he was very happy he did sometimes sing or hum to himself. Was he happy because she was at his side, or because the car purred beneath his hands like a contented cat, or because it was not raining? It was rather daunting to realize that she had not the slightest idea.

After a couple of miles she spoke to Posy over her shoulder; something innocuous about the farm. Dirk slid a quick look at her and then said, to no one in particular, 'Gilly's got a litter of kittens. They're in the big barn. Mrs Ted wants the ginger one, but you might like to take a look at 'em. Pretty little blighters.'

Gilly was short for Gilbert, which just proved that no one was ever right about cats; Dirk had sworn that the little red-and-white kitten with the chestnut eyes was a tom, when Jenny had taken a fancy to it three years ago. Gilly had been proving him wrong a couple of times a year ever since, but she had attractive kittens and there was never any difficulty in finding homes for them, since Gilly was the best rat-catcher the Sayer family had ever known.

'We really ought . . .' Jenny began absently, and changed it quickly, flushing. 'You really ought to get her speyed; one of these days we'll . . . you'll run out of people wanting the kittens.'

'Oh well, wait till it happens,' Dirk said. 'She only has two or three, not like some of 'em. And No. 54 dropped a pure cream-coloured calf a week back; never seen anything like it, not a coloured hair on its body.'

'Cream-coloured? Wasn't Tex the father, then?' Tex was a Hereford bull, a great, deep-chested, easy-going creature with a passion for any form of sweets, particularly polo-mints. He had been serving the Sayer herd for five years now and had never had a bad calf, Dirk was wont to boast.

'I put him to her, but I have my doubts. The Charolais was supposed to be well fenced and away from the herd, but either No. 54 got in with him or . . .'

He grew technical. Jenny followed the conversation with half her mind, keeping her end up when necessary and watching the meadows and woods flash past. How long this journey had taken on the bus, and how quickly the miles flew by in Dirk's car with Dirk at the wheel! Talking about farming he became easier, less stilted. She was glad he had thought to tell them about the kittens or this entire journey might easily have passed in silence. Dirk, she knew, was a stranger to small talk except on farming matters, and she would not have dared to instigate a topic of conversation which might annoy him in case he spoiled Posy's pleasure in her day out.

The car slowed, Dirk indicated left and turned into the lane. The two miles which Jenny and Belle had almost swum six weeks earlier now flashed by in seconds. The car turned left again, into the drive. They reached the fork and swung right, into the familiar farmyard. Jenny remembered she was not supposed to have seen the house since she left, but did not wish to give anyone the satisfaction of knowing the horror she had felt six weeks before. She said nothing until they had drawn up and Dirk was opening her door for her, and then she merely said, as she lifted Posy out, 'Quite a change without the ivy; well, at least it'll make the back bedrooms lighter, I suppose.'

'Ivy's filthy, creeping stuff; better off without it.'

Having made his position crystal clear, Dirk set off towards the back door.

'I rather like it,' Jenny said mildly. 'The birds do, too.' Having made her feelings equally clear, she followed with Posy's hand in hers. Posy was staring round her, not commenting, just staring. This had been her home for the whole of her short life until twelve weeks ago, Jenny remembered. It must be quite a moment for her, returning here after the flat.

'Hello, Ma; hi, Posy.' Mark was in the kitchen, sitting at the table with a newspaper and eating buttered toast. He grinned at them but did not get up. 'Want a cup of coffee? There's a pot, but this is the last of the toast.'

'Pour me one,' Dirk said briefly; to whom Jenny had no idea. Shrugging, she took down two blue-and-white mugs from the dresser, poured two coffees and pushed one across the table towards Dirk. He picked it up, sipped it and put it down again.

'No sugar.'

He's ill at ease, that's why he's being so rude, Jenny told herself, silently adding two spoonfuls of sugar. Since Mark had now disappeared behind his paper again and there was no sign of Philip, she cleared her throat, sat down on one of the kitchen chairs and spoke directly to her husband.

'Is there anything I can do? Towards lunch, I mean.'

'Oh, the turkey. Yes. Well, Mrs Ted did the vegetables the day before yesterday – they're in the big fridge – and she said there was a bowl of stuffing too, and bits and pieces. If you'd like to put the stuff in the oven, I think that's all you'll have to do.'

Jenny hesitated, then went over to the walk-in pantry where she began to look through the fridge and the shelves. The potatoes had certainly been peeled; they lay half in water and half out of it and the halves that were out were grey and shell-like. A cauliflower had been cut into four large chunks but nothing else had been done to it that she could see, and there was a paper bag full of sprouts, untouched by either human hand or knife. The bowl proved to hold two packets of stuffing, the shop sort – Jenny had always lovingly made her own stuffing at Christmas – a very stale loaf and an onion. A bought Christmas pudding, of a size that Dirk could eat in one mouthful, sat nearby. On the bottom shelf of the small fridge squatted the turkey. It had not been part-cooked and must weigh, Jenny judged, something between eighteen and twenty-one pounds. She emerged from the pantry, trying not to look as angry as she felt.

'The turkey's raw, Dirk.'

He looked surprised, even slightly indignant. 'Well, of course it is, I told you we were saving our Christmas day until you arrived.'

The words he had left off, *to do the cooking*, seemed to hang unspoken in the air between them.

'I understand that. But it's a big turkey. It will take at least eight hours to cook, probably longer.'

'Eight *hours*!' Dirk's jaw sagged and Mark actually lowered his paper. 'Oh come on, Jenny, you've cooked bigger turkeys than that on Christmas day!'

'Well, yes, but I part-cooked them the day before; didn't you know?'

'No. How on earth should I? That wasn't my province, the cooking.'

'True; you did yeoman work at the eating however, as I

recall.' She could not help smiling a bit, though she knew it was mean of her; poor Dirk adored his food and particularly relished a Christmas dinner with turkey and all the trimmings, but unless he was willing to put up with a considerable wait, he was not going to have this one today.

'Well, it's eleven o'clock now. So it would be seven o'clock this evening by the time it was cooked.' He brightened. 'That's not impossible, then. Do it for this evening, we'll have bread and cheese or something for lunch instead. Save ourselves for later.'

'That won't be much fun for Posy, though,' Jenny said as gently as she could. 'I'll have to leave at half-past seven, she goes to bed at eight – and I don't want her eating a heavy meal late at night.'

'Well, couldn't you roast us a piece of beef for lunch? Yes, why not, there's a nice big piece in the freezer. Then we can have that at about one o'clock and the turkey tonight.'

'Well, I could, only the turkey's too big to share the oven, so that would mean putting the turkey off until one o'clock, which will mean it won't be ready until nine. And if the beef's frozen I doubt it will be ready to cook under about three hours.'

'You're just being difficult,' Dirk muttered, hunching a shoulder discontentedly. 'You know bloody well I'm no cook, but I should have thought . . .'

'Look, you had the right idea in the first place,' Jenny said, keen to avoid the open conflict she could see looming. What on earth was the point of squabbling at their first meeting for ages? 'I'll cook the turkey, we'll have a cold lunch, and you can run me home a bit early, say at half six, then I can make Posy a light supper before she goes to bed.' Hearing herself making the suggestion she was astonished at the eager feeling of anticipation which overcame her. She would be able to leave here an hour earlier than she had planned – how nice! But that was all wrong, was she mad? She had longed for this moment, this home-coming; was she going to throw it all away just because of one damn great turkey?

Dirk, too, seemed to think this not quite right. He looked doubtfully across at her. You could almost see the wheels whirling; *that would mean I could have my delicious turkey dinner, but there's something wrong, she can't be willing to make such a sacrifice, there's a snag here somewhere if only I could spot it!*

Mark put down his paper. He was grinning.

'It won't hurt Posy to be late home for once, Mum. Let her have a cold lunch with us and then a hot dinner tonight. It's Christmas, after all. I went out and bought crackers because I remembered we used to have them when we were kids, and Dad got the lights and the tree down from the attic even when Bronwen said . . .' He stopped short – the forbidden name! Dirk was scowling.

'That's settled then. There's a ham and a lot of salad stuff, and Mrs Ted half-baked a lot of bread which she said we only had to put in the oven when it was hot and leave it for twenty minutes to have it as good as new.'

'And twice as indigestible. Right. Look, you three go through into the living room or the garden room, put on the telly or play games with Posy whilst I get on here.'

Looking remarkably sheepish, Dirk headed for the living room, then stopped and addressed his daughter.

'I forgot, the kittens. Shall I take you out to the barn, show you where Gilly's hidden them?'

Jenny went and took the sprouts and a sharp knife. She heard Posy scraping one foot against the other, as she did when she was embarrassed. Poor little girl; Dirk had never attempted to be fatherly towards her, so she did not know how to take it. But Jenny underestimated her daughter.

'No thanks, Daddy. Mark'll take me, won't you Mark?'

Jenny stayed tactfully in the pantry until she heard the back door close, then she emerged into the kitchen once more. Dirk was standing in front of the Aga, staring at the back door. His face was very flushed. Out of the corner of his eye he saw her moving and swung round to face her, his expression accusing.

'You want to teach that kid some manners; thinks she's somebody, does little Priscilla. Speaking to her father like that.'

'She doesn't know you very well, Dirk,' Jenny said bluntly, not mincing words. 'She's more at ease with youngsters.'

'Huh!' he grunted, but he moved away towards the living room. 'Well, since she's gone off with Mark I might as well . . .'

He was gone. Jenny tipped the sprouts into the colander and began, crossly, to prepare them for the pan.

'You run up to your bedroom, Posy, I want to talk to your Mummy for a minute,' Dirk said as he drew the car to a halt outside No. 24. 'I won't keep her long – tell you what, do you have a friend in the place?'

'Yes, they're all my friends, but Mrs Twigg is my best friend,' Posy said. 'Shall I go up and show her my presents? And what about the bicycle? I can't ride it up the stairs.'

The bicycle had been Dirk's gift to his daughter and had been well received, for Posy had been enviously watching other children doing wheelies and other tricks ever since she had started at Ysgol Maesydre. Jenny, startled both by the size and imagination of the gift, had looked at Dirk with new respect; if he wanted to be looked upon with favour he had got off to a good start!

'The bike's in the back; I'll wheel it to the foot of the stairs. Mummy thinks you'll be allowed to keep it there but, if not, she says she can carry it up and down.'

'Oh; right. Mrs Twigg might like to come down and see it,' Posy said hopefully, letting Dirk help her out on to the pavement. It was very late, after nine o'clock, but she was wide awake and very obviously still excited. Jenny, on the other hand, was desperately tired and worn out and wanted nothing more than her bed, but although she had spent most of the day cooking, serving and then washing up and clearing away, she did not really blame Dirk for any of this. He thought she liked it; he had no idea that she considered it unfair and an imposition, and how could he possibly guess how she now felt? She had been content for years with little other than housework; he could not know that in twelve short weeks she had changed so completely.

She watched Dirk carrying the bicycle up the path. I should be grateful to him, her thoughts ran, for showing me that life on the farm had never been all beer and skittles; in fact, for showing me that life there had been dull, repetitive, lonely and something not to be hankered after. His desertion no longer seemed quite so unforgivable; after all, if he had not tossed her aside in favour of Bronwen she would never have known that she was missing a whole different and exciting way of life. Earning her own living was fun, mixing with her fellow tenants was fun, meeting all the oddities who came into the cafe was fun; being with Bill, both at work and socially, was fun. Of course it was dreadful to know that the man you loved no longer loved you . . but then she had begun to question her own feelings for Dirk. They were – or had been – so totally uncritical, so dumbly accepting, that she felt quite ashamed of them. She had continued to behave like a be-sotted sixteen-year-old many years after she should have matured enough to question his attitudes instead of simply accepting them.

But he was coming back to the car, striding out. She got out of her seat and walked up to meet him. She *was* tired; whatever he wanted to say had better be said quickly or she would simply yawn in his face!

'Thanks for a pleasant day, Dirk,' she began, but he cut across her sentence.

'Look, I want to talk. Not in your room in case Posy comes down. Can we walk? Down to the beach if you like.'

'Oh.' She did not feel like walking nor like discussing life or divorce or whatever he had in mind. But it would be churlish to refuse, she supposed. 'All right, we can stroll on the beach but not for long; I want to get Posy into bed and, to tell you the truth, I shan't be far behind her tonight. I'm awfully tired.'

Having said he wanted to talk to her, however, he proceeded to say nothing all the way down Beechcroft Road and across the promenade. It was not until they were on the hard wet sand that he finally spoke.

'Jenny . . . are you sure you're all right? Not mixing with the wrong sort of people . . . getting into bad company? I worry; Posy's an odd little thing, and I'm not sure that the life she's leading is good for a child of her age. If you ever feel . . . if you want something . . .'

'We're fine thank you, Dirk.' She did not want to hurt his feelings when he had just done his best to give them a pleasant day, but she would not be criticized obliquely, which was what his so-called worrying would seem to amount to. 'Posy's a good girl doing nicely at school and I'm making plenty of friends. Please don't waste your time worrying about either of us.'

'Well, it isn't just . . . not just Posy. You're used to a better life than that place,' he jerked his head vaguely in the direction of Beechcroft Road. 'I feel I acted too hastily, putting you into a holiday flatlet. After all, it was only . . . damn it, I can't explain, but I want you to know that I'm right on the end of a phone, if you ever need me.'

She had dreamed of hearing him say it. Now she heard her own voice, quite calmly and pleasantly, denying him.

'That's nice of you, Dirk, but I don't think I shall need you. I'm becoming remarkably self-sufficient and, as I said, I've a lot of friends. Was that all you wanted to say?'

'Why you . . .' He grabbed her shoulders hard and turned her to face him. In the moonlight she could not see whether he was flushed or pale but his eyes sparkled with anger and his mouth was tight. 'Why, you . . .'

She thought he was going to hit her and stiffened, trying to pull herself free; instead he pulled her into his arms and tried to kiss her mouth.

It was very odd. Abruptly, the new Jenny decided she did not wish to be mauled and kissed against her will on the moonlit beach. She kicked and then ducked and wriggled free. She said breathlessly: 'If you want to carry on like that, Dirk, go back to Bronwen right away, please!'

He grabbed her arms again and shook her. He was very angry. 'You don't say that to me, you're my wife, you're mine, I'll do what I like, I'll . . .'

She had always been a fast runner. Now she twisted away from him and set off up the beach, running her hardest, hearing him panting along in the rear and using some ugly language, knowing he would not be able to catch her up.

She hurled herself at the gate, up the garden path and in at the front door. Then, despite the midnight rule, she locked it. No one tried the handle, and presently she went up to her room, where Posy had still not put in an appearance, and drew back the curtain to peep.

Dirk had reached the Land Rover and was leaning against it, breathing heavily. He looked ill and old. Abruptly, remorse caught at her throat. That was Dirk, who had once courted her and loved her. That was the man whose life she had shared for more than half her entire existence. He had been angry but he would not have hurt her. She padded down the stairs again and out into the garden. He did not look up. His chest was heaving and his breath was coming in rasps. She slipped through the gate and put her hand on his, as it lay on the Land Rover's wheel arch.

'Dirk? Are you all right? I'm sorry I ran off but I have to take care of myself now, and you . . well, you shouldn't have done that.'

'Shouldn't I?' It was the old arrogant Dirk speaking, even though he could hardly get the words out. 'Anyway, I only said what's true.'

'Did you? Well, I'm off to bed now. Goodnight Dirk.'

He did not reply but merely went on staring down at the Land Rover, breathing stertorously.

Jenny walked slowly back indoors. She went into the flat and prepared Posy's things, put some milk to boil on the gas ring and then ran up to Mrs Twigg to fetch her child.

It was at least ten minutes before she went again to the window; he was still there, still leaning against the Land Rover in exactly the same position. Irresolute, she stood there watching for a moment, then the milk began to hiss up the sides of the saucepan and Posy asked if she had to wash again and whether she might wear her new nightie with the pink ribbons that Mrs Twigg had made for her.

By the time these vexed questions were settled and Posy tucked up, Jenny was so tired that all she wanted was her own bed. But she went back to the window for one last look.

He and the Land Rover had gone. The road was cold and empty. Not knowing whether to be glad or sorry, Jenny began to undress.

'Two eggs, bacon and so on, one cottage cheese salad, one child's sausage and mash,' Jenny gabbled, going into the kitchen where Bill was poised over their new cooker. 'I'll do the salad.' She began to dive in and out of the fridge, collecting her ingredients together. 'Gosh, the price of tomatoes! Wouldn't it be worth our while to buy wholesale? And what about us having a rest after Christmas? Where did that idea go?'

'We did have a rest for a few days,' Bill protested, cracking eggs into a sizzling pan. 'It's the sales, I hadn't reckoned with the sales. But the takings are getting near summer proportions.'

'I thought we must be doing well. At this rate, you'll be needing me until Easter and once Easter gets here there will be old people again, and weekenders, and the coach trips . . . Gosh, it's getting to be a permanent job, isn't it?'

'Yes, it is. Full-time too, or pretty nearly.' Bill dished up his first two plates and smiled at her, pushing them on to the working surface nearest the door. 'How d'you feel about it?'

Jenny was making her salad look beautiful by adding some tiny radishes, then placing the cottage cheese in a pile in the middle of the plate and decorating it with sliced onion rings. She picked up the plate and then added the two that Bill had just completed. He was preparing the child's sausage and mash so she waited a moment until it was ready; four plates were still impossible to carry, but Bill would bring the last as far as the counter for her to pick it up.

'Still love it. It's awfully convenient, too, having different days off, so that on mine I can keep an eye on our three, and on yours you can.'

Bill grunted. 'We need someone to relieve the pair of us from time to time, though. The business could afford it if we could find someone we trusted. Anyway, school's back on Monday, which will ease things a bit.'

It was true that the school holidays did complicate things, though Sian was still coping manfully at Bill's place. Sue and her Tim were home, Mrs Grant had not made any complaint about the baby since apparently she had expected Sue to keep him for a while, and Sue was only too pleased to have Posy in the flat with her when Jenny wanted to leave her at home.

'And the sales ease off after another week,' Jenny reminded him. 'Then it'll be back to office and factory workers I suppose, and you'll be able to manage without me. Or will you? We're rather a good team, I think.'

252

'I told you, the job's permanent so long as you want it to be,' Bill said, taking the last plate out of the counter. 'Ah, here come the welly brigade; are they early or are the other customers late?'

'They're early. Never mind, we can manage,' Jenny winced though as the gardeners trooped in, their boots shedding great chunks of earth on the floor. They made an awful mess but they were permanent and the younger ones who were on community service or work experience and so had their meals paid for them really appreciated a well-filled plate. They always sat at the same tables, which had a little reserved notice stuck up on them; now she smiled brightly at them.

'Hello, fellers! What's it to be?'

'There we are, into the water and Tim's swimming for the shore . . . slosh with your arms as well as your legs, little noodle . . . and he's going to make it, he's winning, this will be the first cross-Channel swim ever completed by a man under twelve weeks old! And the crowd's cheering, they're waving their Union Jacks, the French are putting a good face on it but you can see they're furious – Tim Franklyn WINS!'

Sue swooshed her son energetically up and down in the big bath whilst Posy, representing the crowd, hung over the side waving the flannel and cheering with surprising shrillness.

'Ooh la-la, a kiss for the winner! Both cheeks, please, madam, you're a stunning French beauty now, mad for love of this great cross-Channel swimmer.' Sue held Tim, dripping, above the water whilst Posy kissed his small face and then Sue kissed his bottom, once on each cheek of course, and sat him down on her knee, snuggling him up in the big white towel.

'There, another bath-time over, and all that swimming gives you a big appetite, doesn't it young Tim?' Posy, ever-attentive, had gathered up Tim's garments and was now holding out a nappy, correctly folded earlier by Sue. 'There, your trainer's got your gear, as soon as you're dressed you can have a lovely long guzzle.'

She was not yet slick, she was still at the careful stage when a nappy is a work of art to be frowned over, but she got it on sufficiently straight at her second attempt, then slid the little vest over his big head and puny shoulders and pinned the nappy to the vest so that it didn't slide down and let air in round his waist.

'Of course he doesn't have a waist yet, just a round, bulgy tummy,' she explained to Posy as she put his nightgown on and added a cardigan which had crouching blue bunnies for its buttons. 'Next problem is to mitten or not to mitten? If I leave them off he scratches his own nose . . .', she tickled Tim's round tummy, making him belch noisily, '. . . but if I put them on he can't suck his thumb and soaks them by trying. I'll leave them off for a bit. Now, where are his trainers? Sneakers? Bootees, poppet, that's what I mean. They're blue ones tonight, to go with the forget-me-knots on the nightie.'

She finished dressing the baby and held him up so that his soft mossy head rested in the tender place just beneath her chin. 'Oh, we make a cissy of you with embroidered night-gowns, don't we? But when you're a *big* boy, in about three weeks, you can have teeny-weeny trousers and blouses and you'll be ever so proud, ever so macho!'

'Shall I clean the bath?' Posy asked, as Sue stood up to leave the room. 'I'm in next though, and I don't mind Timmy's filth.'

'He does get dirty, don't you, ducks?' Sue snuggled the baby with her mouth, blowing gently into the fold of his neck. 'Yes, he's a filthy blighter, it's all the cross-country training he has to do for his Channel swims. Swish it round for me, there's a love, and then no one will know I haven't cleaned it properly.'

'I wee in my bath,' Posy said reflectively as Sue and Tim turned to leave the room. 'I wonder if Tim does?'

'I'll ask him and let you know,' Sue promised. She walked carefully up the stairs with her precious burden, tapping on Jenny's door as she passed to let her friend know that the bathroom was clear for Posy. In her own room she settled down, with a sigh of pleasure, for the most rewarding part of her day. The six o'clock feed was lovely, with Timmy night-gowned and sweet-smelling, eager for her milk, quick to sleep afterwards.

She adored feeding him and could not begin to understand

254

the girl in the hospital who had had hysterics the moment they put her baby to the breast, shrieking that it was like being attacked by a little animal, that she could not, would not, bear it. Now, with Timmy weaving his head as he searched for the nipple, Sue felt rich with a totally undeserved, unexpected happiness. She had so much! The most beautiful baby in the world, enough milk to feed twins – the breast which was not being very efficiently emptied by her son insisted on a sort of sympathy drip, so she put a spare muslin nappy into the cup of her very large nursing bra in order to keep her clothing dry – and a clear conscience.

She had composed and written a letter to Hugo which was waiting to be posted. Dermott had a friend, a professional photographer, who was coming in to take a few shots of herself with her child. She was going to have lots of copies made, but she would not send them round to friends and relatives until Hugo had not only received his but had also replied to her letter. She did not worry that he would not welcome their son, not after she had written the letter. Her explanation of what she had meant to do, and what she now intended to do, seemed utterly rational in view of Tim's charm and potential – she had decribed his cross-Channel swims, his cross-country runs (taken in the pram at the moment, to be sure, but later he would surprise them all, she had written), his exercises on the most beautiful of his Daddy's rugs. Press-ups, side-to-side rolls, bouncing on his toes, he was a natural at them all with only minimal help from his proud mother.

She thought him a little young yet to start climbing, she confessed; actually, in view of her own aversion to heights it might be better if Hugo were to take him climbing when he returned, but in the meantime she frequently held him high above her head and the closest scrutiny of his small, Hugo-like face had not shown a trace of vertigo or fear. In fact all he did was dribble on to her, which she thought a charming reaction.

Her work had not suffered either, because she would have to feed Timmy with real food one day and in the meantime needed a good well-balanced diet herself. So she still wrote her articles and features from the flat, and would continue to do so until the winter was over and spring forced her back to London. What a surprise for all their friends to find that Hugo and Sue were parents – and of a prodigy, to boot! She had no doubt that Tim was exceptional if only because of his father, and by the time Hugo got back, which should be early April, she thought the baby at nearly four months old would probably be beginning to talk as well as swim and walk and eat.

There was a light tap on the door; Sue called 'Come in!' and smiled as Jenny's face appeared.

'Hello! Thanks for keeping Posy occupied; she's been telling me about Tim's latest crossing, it sounds pretty good!'

'I expect it sounds like the ravings of a madwoman,' Sue said frankly. 'However – oh damn and shit, I forget to time him! Did you time yours?'

'Bless me, I believe I did. Five minutes a side or something, then burp 'em, then another five minutes. I think it's so that they don't keep draining one and leaving the other half full. How do you get him off?'

'I just pull,' Sue said, suiting action to words. Little Tim and his six o'clock feed parted company with a sound like a cork escaping from a bottle. Jenny giggled.

'You aren't supposed to do that, you're supposed to pinch his nose so that he lets go to take a breath.'

'I know. That's the cruellest thing I ever heard! No son of mine is going to get inhibitions about breasts from his mother, even if it means I end up with nipples a foot long. Now don't just stand there laughing, what can I do for you? I assume you're here for a purpose, not just to lecture me about the correct way to breast-feed?'

'True. I'm on the cadge, though it's your time I'm after, not peanut butter. Is there any chance of you having Posy one evening this week? There's a play Bill and I both want to see and it seems a pity to go alone. As you know, Mrs Twigg would willingly sit for me, only you're in during the evenings now, and if you could . . .'

'Of course, Jenny, don't make a thing of it. When Tim's a bit older I'll be going out again myself, and Twiglet can babysit for us both. Only right now, what with his six o'clock feed and his ten o'clock one . . .' Timmy, draped across her shoulder, gave a huge burp and a tiny trickle of milk dribbled down his chin. 'Now who's a clever boy, then? Not every baby can do that! When's the best night for a spot of cuddling in the back row?'

'Hey, come off it, I'm a married woman, Bill and I just enjoy each other's company. Dirk rang, he wants Posy and I to spend a weekend at the farm. He said Bronwen's going away for a few days, and it might be nice for Posy . . .'

'Oh? What did you say?'

'Well, I said we couldn't, not this time. Bill needs me on a Saturday and a whole weekend would be a bit of a trial for Posy . . . but probably, next time he asks . . .'

'Did you say you would only consider it if Bronwen were no longer living there, like I told you?'

'No, I didn't. If he's going to send her packing, and all the signs point to it, then I want it to be entirely his decision. Don't you think it would be better, that way?'

'Yes; on reflection, you're right. And when he kicks her out you'll go back and live there again, forget us and give up your job?'

'Well, I . . . let's not cross bridges before they're hatched! In theory I'll be back there like a shot but in practice I believe I'll want some changes made.'

Sue lowered Tim into her arm and he latched on to the full breast with every sign of juvenile satisfaction including some very squelchy noises. Sue laughed.

'Just like a man, no inhibitions! Tell Bill it's fine by me and I hope you enjoy the play.'

Because it was holiday time and his mother had begged, Bill had dispatched Erica and Dawn to York for a three-day stay. He had put them on a train, in charge of the guard, taking them all the way to Chester so that they would not have to change, and was feeling, as a result, both footloose and slightly drunk with the sudden easing of responsibility. His mother, who was in her seventies, might not have been allowed to take charge but she lived with his sister Liz, and Liz adored the girls and managed them every bit as well as Bill.

Of course, his mother had wanted Bill to go back as well,

just for a few days, but Liz had perfectly understood that a cafe could not simply be abandoned for a period of time. She had soothed their parent by promises of a trip to Rhyl in the summer, had soothed Bill's conscience by telling him frankly that it was time he had a break from the children, and had rung the previous evening to let him know that Erica and Dawn were in their element and having a marvellous time.

He had decided to take Jenny home for a meal before the theatre, without revealing the fact that it was to be just the two of them in the house, but then at the last moment his courage had failed him and he came clean, admitted that the girls were away and suggested a visit to the Ocean Beach. The funfair and all the other promenade amusements were opening for a weekend and he thought that, if they closed the cafe at four, it might be possible to make a long evening of it – funfair, meal out, theatre trip. Afterwards . . . he could go back to her place . . . only Posy would be there. Would he be able to entice her back to his home if he promised to return her, shaken but probably not stirred, by midnight?

The trouble was that he did not want her to see through his friendship to the desperate wanting which lay beneath – and not all that far beneath, he mused, as a seduction scene flashed through his mind, bringing the inevitable physical reaction. So my sex-drive is not dead but sleeping, he thought guiltily; down boy, down!

Jenny left work before Bill, since she wanted to go back to Beechcroft Road to change and to check that everything was all right with Posy and Sue. Bill was wearing a cream wool sweater and slacks and had hoped that he might get Jenny to say he ought to wear his dark suit, which was in his wardrobe at home. And then . . . oh, oh, kissings on the couch and cuddlings on the carpet, Bill thought incoherently but blissfully, letting himself out of the darkened cafe and setting off for Beechcroft Road. Not that I would, he added hastily, walking briskly to offset the chill of the wintry sunshine, not that I would! Nevertheless he could not help thinking wistfully of his careful preparations: wine cooling in the fridge, the table set for two with red candles in borrowed candlesticks, the fire laid in the grate with Louisa on a promise to light it promptly at four. But now, because he had not quite dared, all these innocent preparations would go unseen, because Jenny would undoubtedly opt for a meal in town. But still, you never knew, if she liked the idea they could have a take-away; Jenny adored Chinese food and they would be able to have a slap-up meal for half the price of a restaurant dinner.

He reached the flats and Jenny was waiting. She had dressed up in a full blue skirt and white polo-necked sweater over which she wore a smart camel-coloured hip-length jacket. Bill's chest swelled with pride, because a woman does not take the trouble over her clothes to go out with a man she despises, or so he told himself, and her eyes were glowing with excitement and her lips curved into a smile of great sweetness when her glance met his.

'All set then, Jenny? You look sizzlingly smart, you make me feel very dowdy. Tell you what, if you don't mind a wait I can rush home after we've done the funfair and change into my dark suit.'

She took his arm and smiled up at him, teasingly but with affection. Her lovely hair was loose and looked pure gold beneath the light of the streetlamps.

'Why not? Oh Bill, an evening out is a treat!'

It was a charmed evening. As they walked slowly up the promenade, the sun sank into a bed of flame and lemon clouds whilst overhead the blue of the sky gradually darkened and turned, as it neared the horizon to a pale, singing green. A fishing boat, with lights fore and aft, came creeping up the channel of the river into the harbour, stark and black against the brilliance of the water, and behind the jumble of red and grey roofs the mountains loomed, a dark and misty blue, against the deepening sky. Stars pricked out and a slender moon. The beauty of the scene was so astonishing that the crowds on the promenade were quiet for a moment, and then the sun sank a little further, sucking the colours out of the sky, and the youngsters began to shout and boast whilst the girls giggled and called. Bill, glancing down at Jenny's head so near his shoulder, felt a pang of such desire, mingled with such tenderness, that he was surprised she did not sense it and turn to him, either to slap his face or at least to wag a warning finger at his presumption.

'Oh Bill, the candyfloss place is open; can we have some?'

For an hour they wandered in and out of amusement arcades, eating rubbishy food, taking turns on the shooting galleries, changing their notes into coins so that they could lose them on one-armed bandits, on the penny-falls, the space invaders, the driving games. Bill, who had taken Daphne on this very funfair several dozen times before, marvelled at Jenny's innocent enjoyment of something he had supposed to be good for ten minutes before boredom set in. Jenny, however, was plainly not bored. She gasped, shrieked, jiggled handles, aimed her gun all cockeyed, laughed helplessly at all the vulgarities, and made him feel one hell of a guy to entertain her so royally.

When they wandered out into the night again, dusk had fallen; the brilliant sunset had become a thin line of blazing gold on the horizon and Ocean Beach was lit up, tempting them to walk yet further with its garish music, its barkers shouting their rival attractions, its roundabouts, swing-boats and rides. Bill looked down at Jenny's face, tinted pinky-gold by the lights. She was holding his hand, swinging along beside him, totally absorbed.

'Want to go on the Mad Mouse? We can just about make it if we hurry . . . Then we could pick up a Chinese take-away and go back to my place. Unless you'd rather eat in town, of course.'

'I'd love to go on the Mad Mouse – I haven't been on a roller coaster since I was a kid. I bet the town will look wonderful from up there.'

It did. The promenade was garlanded with lights from the Voryd to the bandstand and the reflected gleam from the brilliance stretched right out to the white-capped waves as they surged up the beach. Inland, the town was quiet, the everyday streetlamps in the side streets wearing their fairy-like haloes in the frosty dark, the little houses crammed higgledy-piggledy one against another calling up images of a children's book illustration straight from Dulac. As Bill and Jenny careered madly up and down in their small car, Bill felt Jenny's warmth cuddling close, her hair fanning out in a fine floss against his cheek. He knew a moment of wild and deeply satisfying happiness. Daphne might never have existed, his worries faded into insignificance beside this perfect moment.

'Isn't it beautiful?' Jenny was shouting against the wind of their downward rush. 'Isn't it the most beautiful thing you've ever seen?'

She indicated the huddled town and the great expanse of beach and sea but, though Bill nodded and tightened his arm around her shoulders, he was looking not out at the night but down at her face.

Walking home, with Bill carrying their Chinese meal in two brown paper carriers, Jenny was still filled with the wonder of the night and spoke very little. The streets themselves seemed enchanted still and the night wind softer, because of her happiness. When they reached Bill's house she saw the preparations he had made solely on the off-chance that she might go back with him and squeezed his hand but they were soon ladling the food out on to his preheated plates and teasing each other about their childish delight in the funfair.

'We'll take the girls, next time,' Jenny said as they carried their plates to the table. 'They would have loved it, though of course the play we're going to see would be miles above their heads.'

Bill sat down, then rose again to pour the wine. He smiled at her.

'Let's forget our kids for one evening and think about ourselves! We enjoyed it much more because we could act daft, just for once. Now come on, get stuck in or we'll be late for the theatre.'

He was already wearing his dark suit, having changed the moment they got indoors and this, as Jenny later pointed out, was really rather a waste, for they never reached the theatre.

After the meal they piled the dirty plates into the sink and returned to the living room to sit by the fire, whilst they digested, as Bill put it. They had an hour before they needed to leave, since the play did not start until eight and Bill intended, he told Jenny grandly, to ring for a taxi to take them there in style.

Bill sat down in his chair and Jenny took the opposite one; then Bill got up, walked over to her, lifted her out of her chair and carried her back to his.

'I know the rules, just a friendly cuddle,' he said as he sat her down on his knee.

Five minutes later, he reached up and clicked off the standard lamp; the fire would give them all the illumination they needed, he said in a voice which trembled slightly.

Cradled in his arms, Jenny knew only the blissful pleasure of being tenderly and then fiercely kissed, of feeling his hands moving across her, carefully undressing her, never trying to hurry or grab or squeeze too hard, stopping the moment she muttered to him that he mustn't, he really mustn't, and not starting again, what was more, until he had kissed and caressed her into accepting that it was a good idea, after all.

She had never imagined for a moment that she would let any man other than Dirk strip her down naked, but then she had never imagined any man who could make love the way Bill did, so that she was on fire with the anticipation of his next move long before he made it.

In the firelight, when she was quite bare, he looked at her for a long time before he touched her and then he buried his head in her breasts and said, against her skin, 'You're the most beautiful thing I've ever seen.'

It was a lie, of course it was, Daphne was very lovely, he had said so. But perhaps it was the firelight, or perhaps he preferred dark women to blondes, or perhaps . . . she looked down at her body, painted rose and blue in flame and shadow, and then at his head with its hair gilded by the light, and tugged hard at his ear. He raised his face at once, to look up at her; a smile trembled on his mouth but there were tears in his eyes.

'Why do you say that? It can't be true.'

'Not *true*? You must know you've got the most beautiful body, your skin's like milk and your breasts are firm, you look like a sculpture. Other women sag – didn't you know? Surely he must have told you over and over.'

'I don't think he ever looked at me after the first year or so,' Jenny said unsteadily. 'Bill, I've never been unfaithful to Dirk even in my mind, would you mind very much if . . . if we pulled ourselves together now, and went to the theatre?'

'I'd mind *very* much, but then so would you,' Bill said calmly. He pulled her close to him, beginning to kiss her neck, then into the hollow of her shoulder, then across the swell of her breast to her peaking nipple. She did not know how she came to be lying on the couch with Bill on top of her, she just knew that he was right; she wanted him blindly now, without reasoning or thought. She grabbed his shoulders, pulling him down on her, moaning and moving against him, but he was not to be hurried, not even by her urgency. Slowly, lovingly, he led her through all the phases and different faces of love until the final, inevitable, moment of truth, when the oldest emotion in the world took over.

Afterwards, Jenny sat up cross-legged and leaned against him, turning her face towards the warmth and brightness of the fire.

'I suppose I'm an adultress,' she said dreamily, pinching Bill's thigh. 'And it's your fault, you sexy beast, but I don't feel a bit furtive or guilty. I just feel comfortable and warm and well loved.'

'You have been,' Bill said with more than a touch of complacency. 'That was really something, wasn't it?'

'Mm hmm. Will you get horribly swollen-headed if I tell you it was the best ever? The most wonderful, world-tipping, mind-boggling experience ever? I must sadly conclude that Dirk was a very poor . . . hell, how do I say what I mean without using four-letter words?'

'You say lover, and don't think my head will swell exactly, though other parts might gain an inch or two.'

'Bill!' She moved her head caressingly up and down on his chest, then put up a hand and slid her fingers round the back of his neck. 'Was it . . . was I . . .?'

'Heavens, woman, you're not in any doubt, are you? If you felt the world tip, how do you think I felt? The whole damn universe slid sideways and the stars rattled in their sockets.'

'Golly! It wasn't because we're both married to someone else, was it? I mean guilt adding to the fun? Only I'm sure it wasn't, because I didn't feel in the least guilty as I've said before. Just . . .'

'Warm and well loved; which is truthful. Never feel guilty for giving or receiving love, darling, if in doing so you're hurting no one. Love enriches, it doesn't take.'

'Them's lovely sentiments,' Jenny murmured, tipping her head back and smiling at him upside down. 'Only I've always been terribly conventional. Marriage made everything all right but having it off – if you'll forgive the expression – was wicked out of wedlock. Do you mean I've got to unlearn all my previous convictions?'

'Well, it won't half cramp my style if you don't,' Bill murmured. He slid his hands down from her shoulders to her breasts, held them tenderly for a moment, then began to move his fingers caressingly across and beneath them. 'Is that nice? I can't tell you how it thrills me to feel your bare skin; if I told you how I'd dreamed of it you'd think me a dirty old man.'

'Think? You are a dirty old man; you've debauched me. Is that the word?'

'Well, I tell myself it was mutual.' He was doing things that made Jenny's breathing quicken, made his own voice shake a little. Jenny shot out her legs and turned towards him in one quick lithe movement. They lay there for a moment, breast to breast, and then he put his arms round her, drawing her close.

'Bill, don't start again, we really ought to get our things on and ring for that taxi. Oh Bill, you really shouldn't . . . no, don't . . . aaah!'

She had protested too much; Bill released her and Jenny rolled backwards off the couch to land with a thud which knocked all the breath out of her body. Bill promptly descended on top of her and, laughing, turned her defenceless, breathless body over and smacked her bottom.

'There you see, you can't escape me! When you're black and blue tomorrow don't blame me, blame my living room couch for being too narrow and yourself for trying to wriggle away. Oh, Jenny!'

They spoke no more. Their bodies were already beginning to know the strength of feeling that they could engender; they looked at the clock, then at each other. Then they made love with trembling intensity and a degree of haste which did not spoil things but seemed, if anything, to improve them.

CHAPTER TEN

'She's going around looking like a cat that's got at the cream, that's all I know.' Anna sucked her milk shake, swallowed and sucked some more. 'So of course I thought your Dad had asked her to go back, except that she didn't mention leaving. And now you say she's asked for a divorce?' She shrugged, eyeing Philip with open curiosity. 'Are you *sure*? It doesn't make sense.'

They were sitting in a little cafe on the promenade and Anna was only waiting for the milk shake to finish before suggesting that they go back to her room. She fancied Philip madly; even his unexpected appearance at her flat on Christmas day, and the way they had fallen on each other like sex-starved wildcats, had not done more than whet her appetite for his handsome, take-it-or-leave-it style of love-making. But now he was frowning, plainly thinking about his mother and not about her, and this augured ill for the next few hours unless she could convince him that all was well with Jenny.

'Look, you want her back, right?' She waited and presently Philip jerked himself out of his frowning abstraction and nodded.

'Yes, we do. All of us, not just me and Mark. Dad's a sour old cuss in a lot of ways – his idea of modern farming is to buy another tractor and pension off an octagenarian – but he wants Mum far more than he ever wanted that nasty little slut he picked up. The trouble is he won't admit it, won't ask her to come back, because, damn him, he's never admitted to a mistake in his life and isn't going to start now.'

'She'll never go back then,' Anna said with unimpaired cheerfulness. 'You couldn't expect it, not after he chucked her out. Besides, she's happy, I think, she likes her job and her friends . . . I can't see her begging somehow.'

'No, I suppose not.' Philip spoke grudgingly, as though he would have been quite happy to see his mother begging, provided she came back to them as a result. Anna, no fool

266

despite her healthy sexual appetite, looked at him shrewdly; they missed Jenny's cooking, that was one thing, and her housekeeping for another and the warm, efficient way she ran her life. From what Philip had said, they were out in the cold now that Dirk had thrown Bronwen or whatever her name was out, and they had expected Jenny to replace her without a word. Anna had never seen the house but she could imagine it, big, imposing and unfriendly, with chilly rooms and stiff ugly furniture. Last week she had been invited into Jenny's place and had been struck by the changes. It had looked really warm and cosy, really friendly. Jenny had been about to go out, not with anyone who mattered, merely the fellow she worked for, but she had asked Anna in to see a picture she had bought in a jumble sale. It was nothing special, a country scene made up out of bits and pieces stuck on a backing of some sort and then set behind glass and framed; but it had plainly taken Jenny's fancy and so Anna had looked closer and had seen that it was rather nice. The house had been made, very cleverly, from pieces of old nylon stocking, shaped and stitched to look like blocks of warm goldy-brown stone, and the roof was of some grey, felty material. But what particularly tickled Jenny and what she had pointed out to Anna was some flower, a yellow flower which apparently bloomed on old roofs, and which had been put on to the roof in the picture. The woman who had done it had used tiny yellow beads – real pretty, they'd looked, Anna thought, and Jenny had stroked the glass with her finger and for a moment that house had looked really real.

But Philip was staring at her; it would never do to say that Jenny's room was nicer than his home, even if it were true. She had better say something, offer to help, or he'd storm out of here without even paying for her milk shake and go off home in that little sports car he ran. She knew his type; you had to humour them.

'Well, look, would it help if I put in a word? Mentioned that the girl had gone, that you were missing her? Jenny, I mean . . . your Mum.'

'No, for God's sake, don't do that!' He looked really alarmed. 'What you *could* do, sweetheart, is to tell me a bit

267

about her; does she have a boyfriend? That's what Dad thinks only I'm sure he's wrong – I mean who'd fancy a woman of her age, with kids?'

'She does go out with men now and then,' Anna said carefully. She did not intend to admit that Jenny hardly ever went out unless it was with Sue or Brenda or the fellow she worked for, who had two little girls and probably a cosy wife at home. Jenny was not the type to go out with a married man, so presumably she went out with both him and his wife. Anna's heart bled for Jenny . . . but if Dirk played his cards right, made a fuss of her, let her keep the dog indoors, she was sure they could all be happy again, the way they had been before that Bronwen came.

'Which men? Anyone from Beechcroft Road? Not that little Jew-boy down in the basement, I hope?'

If he had not been so good-looking, Anna would have smashed her handbag across Philip's face and walked out of the cafe. Jew-boy, indeed! Solly was as handsome as Philip in his own way and a good deal kinder and with better manners! Besides, Solly was only twenty-seven, a bit young for a woman of Jenny's age, and Philip had no right to refer to him like that!

'Certainly not, Solly's not a bit like that, he doesn't hang round after older women, especially when they're married. I think you should wash your mouth out, Philip.'

He shrugged, elbows on table, one fist gently beating time against his cheekbone.

'I don't like blacks, Asiatics or Jew-boys, so why should I pretend to? If I catch anyone like that sniffing round my mother I'll smash his face in, and don't think it's just talk, I'd do it too. That is, I'd do it if Dad didn't get there first.' He pushed back his chair and stood up. 'Come on . . . is she in, by the way?'

'If you mean your mother, no she isn't. She works until late on Saturdays.'

'Right.' Apparently he had got what he wanted, or thought he had; he took Anna's elbow in his hand, then slid his fingers down until he held her wrist, just above her palm. His forefinger slid into the centre of her palm and began to make little circles. The rest of his fingers held her wrist hard.

268

Anna shivered; she knew the language he was talking and she liked it, but just for a second . . .

'I'll see you home; right home. In fact, I'll see you right into bed.'

He spoke in a low, intimate murmur, looking down at her with an expression on his face which she recognized as being the before look. When a man has made up his mind that he's going to have a woman, his face sometimes wears just that sleepy, lustful, knowing look. The after look, in Philip's case, was one of total indifference as she knew well. She braced herself to say no, to tell him to take a running jump, to go break someone else's heart.

'Oh, well . . . all right, Philip.'

She let him pull her down the road to his car, let him slide his hand up her thigh and only shook her head at him. Back at Beechcroft Road she let him hustle her indoors and upstairs, knowing that he was afraid of meeting Jenny, wishing she had the courage and resolution to tell him not to be, that he had every right to come into her, Anna's, room if he so wished.

And once inside her own room, lying on her scruffy pink counterpane, Anna just let him.

'Jenneeee! Telephone!'

'Oh drat and damn it, just when I was settled!' Jenny uncurled herself from the big chair in Sue's room, blew a kiss to Sue and the baby, said, 'Shan't be a moment, sweetie,' to Posy, and ran down the stairs. She glanced at her watch; seven o'clock. It would be Dirk.

It was and he wasted no time with conventions, even ignoring her polite 'Hello?'

'Why won't you bring Posy back for a weekend? She's gone and you must know it.'

'Gone? Bronwen, do you mean?' She was surprised but what was even more surprising was her indifference; she nearly said *so what?*, which really would have shattered Dirk.

'Oh come on, one of the boys would have told you . . . Philip's been into town a couple of times since I kicked her out.'

269

'No one's told me. But you said she'd be away weekends anyway, so I don't see that it makes much difference.'

'No difference? Good God, are you mad? She's gone I tell you, and there's nothing to stop you coming back. For a weekend.'

'I will come back some time, only right now I'm terribly busy at weekends. I've got a job, you know I have, and any spare time seems to be fully occupied somehow.'

'Croft said you'd talked about divorce.'

'Oh Dirk, of course I have – you must have talked about it too, but I've not done anything about it yet. Only . . . wouldn't it be better for both of us to get it all cleared up, settled? Who's doing the bookwork, anyway? Did you sack Bronwen?'

'I told her to go and she went. I've got some girl coming in each day to help with the books and paperwork. Margaret, her name is. Don't worry, I haven't laid a finger on her.'

Yet, remarked a voice inside Jenny's head. *And if you do, you won't admit it like you did with Bronwen. You've discovered the world is not necessarily well lost for love, and you'll do all your carrying on the way other married men do, on the quiet.*

'Jenny? Are you there? I spoke to Croft, he said you're legally bound to bring Posy to see me if I want her.'

'Dirk, what a thing to say! You could apply to the courts for access, I think that's what it's called, and that would mean I'd have to let Posy come to you for so many weeks a year, but it wouldn't tie *me* in any way at all. I'm not part of the bargain. Look, if you're very keen to see Posy, you could come into town on Friday, pick her up, and bring her back on Sunday night. Only I couldn't make her go if she didn't want to, I don't think.'

'How could I have her here?' His voice was sullen. 'There's no one to keep an eye on her when I'm working, no one to cook or light fires . . .' He broke off. Jenny's lips twitched. His reason for wanting Posy – or rather herself – was all too clear.

'I see. If I were you, Dirk, I'd advertise for a housekeeper.'

'I can't afford it.' The farmer's answer to everything, Jenny reflected ruefully, unless it directly concerned the farm of course.

'I'm sure you can! After all, you aren't feeding me or Posy – Mr Croft said your allowance stopped a fortnight ago – so all you're doing is paying our rent here, which isn't exactly a fortune.'

It was not, either. When the allowance had stopped she had panicked, imagining herself homeless, but it soon became obvious from Mrs Grant's attitude that she was still receiving the rent every week. And then her earnings from the cafe were proving enough for her to live relatively comfortably, unless a very unexpected expense occurred. She had never mentioned the allowance to Dirk before, but now she had a shrewd suspicion why it had suddenly stopped. Dirk had thrown Bronwen out and had decided to make things so difficult for Jenny that she would have to return to the farm. What a charming person he was! How could she ever have loved him?

'Oh, the allowance. That was a mistake, you'll get it again this week. Croft misunderstood . . . it was you, talking about divorce.'

Jenny bit back a hasty retort because she kept envisaging the farm without a fire lit or a meal prepared. She had looked after him for so long, seen to his clothes, his food, his general well-being. Was she now prepared to let him suffer? A man could not make a home . . .

She shook herself briskly; could they not? Then why was it that Bill's little house was so much a home, so warm, so loved? Dirk had more money and a more promising house; let him have a go!

'It doesn't matter, actually, I can manage without the allowance. Look, use it to get some more help in the house, you could ask Mrs Ted's eldest girl to . . .'

'Jenny, that isn't the point! This is your place, you belong here, and I want you to come back for the weekend, then you'll understand. I'm not begging, I'm telling you.'

She had dithered, now she dithered no longer.

'Sorry I'm too busy. Don't keep ringing with this one suggestion please, Dirk, because . . .'

For the second time in their lives, he put the telephone down on her.

It was a cold winter. On the mountains at the back of the town snow lay deep and thick and 24 Beechcroft Road was filled with howling draughts and shivering tenants. It was impossible to keep warm because of the draughts and for the first time everyone envied Sue her screens because, strategically placed, they kept her room the warmest in the house. Baby Tim could have his kick and do his exercises whilst the screens kept off the draughts which came through the windows and under the doors, and the beautiful Tibetan rug saw to it that no chill seeped up through the floorboards.

The Twiggs' room was also snug, because Mrs Twigg and Bernard were old hands at draught exclusion. Their windows were sealed with a mixture of cotton wool, Blu-tac and Sellotape, their window-sills sported a thick layer of Mrs Twigg's cushions, all their doors were equipped with curtains which could be drawn across them and fat knitted snakes which could be kicked against them. They also had a larger electric fire than that supplied by Mrs Grant and a gas cooker of their own, which Mrs Twigg occasionally ran just for warmth.

At first Jenny tried to tell herself that it was healthier to be a bit cold than too warm, but that attitude did not last. She soon joined the other tenants in their endless search for a means of conquering the cold. She bought a second electric fire which she placed strategically between their beds and the window so she could leap out, switch it on, leap back, and not get up to dress until the fire had at least warmed up the draughts a little.

'But when the wind's off the sea, which it usually is, it's just about impossible to stop it coming in,' she told Bill as they washed up and cleared away after their lunch-time customers. 'You'd think it actually penetrated the glass, the curtains blow right out like yacht sails in a force-eight gale.'

'I'll come round at the weekend, see what I can do,' Bill said, clattering plates. 'Our bedrooms are chilly, though it's snug enough downstairs. But then we're a mile further inland than you and sheltered, too. Still, I can fit some decent draught excluders.'

'I do worry about Posy. She's got a beastly cough – it just goes on and on, and no medicine seems to touch it. I keep

272

telling myself that if I could get her warm and then keep her that way . . .'

Unspoken between them hovered the thought that there was central heating at the farm, a doctor who had treated Posy since her birth, a leisured life for her mother or, if not leisured, at least a life with more time to spare to tackle childish ailments.

'She's always dressed warmly, anyway,' Bill said absently. 'Last evening when you took her off she looked just like a bundle of knitting!'

'I know, I tell myself I'm doing everything possible . . . and she's happy, you know, trotting up to Mrs Twigg, overseeing Timmy's bath, playing with Ricky and Dawn, or with little Sandra if we're at home on a Sunday. If I could just get rid of that cough . . .'

'Have you tried old-fashioned methods? I've got some linctus made with lemon and honey and stuff like that, I bought it from a little village shop last time I was up north . . . it worked when Ricky was poorly. There's half a bottle left, you're welcome to it.'

'Great, I'll try anything! Sue's got a theory that if I could stop that niggling little cough at night Posy'd get rid of the whole thing; she says coughs get to be a habit. So I thought I'd give her some baby aspirin tonight and she can have your linctus tomorrow.'

'Rubbish! I'll walk round with it later this evening, she can have it tonight. And I'll take a look at your windows and doors at the same time, so I can buy anything I need before the weekend.'

'Who's a treasure, then?' Jenny took a quick look round, then stood on tiptoe and kissed the back of Bill's neck. He turned, took her in his arms and kissed her properly, undeterred by a tea-towel in his right hand and several plates on his left. Like all his kisses, it was a satisfying one, the sort of kiss, Jenny thought dreamily, that made you want more, turned the mind to thoughts of bed, or couches or carpets for that matter. But Bill was not one to take advantage of the fact that they worked together. He gave her one, last, lingering squeeze and stood back.

'Mm-mm, that does me more good than a double whisky! Is there much cooking to be done this afternoon?'

Admirable man, to be able to think about cooking whilst Jenny's mind was still, so to speak, throwing back the bedcovers! She knew, what was more, that he had a perfectly normal sex-drive, it was just that they had agreed after they had first made love that they would not let this new, delicious relationship enter their working lives. They never misbehaved in the cafe, not even when a rare opportunity occurred . . . but boy, we've misbehaved in other places, Jenny thought with some awe. Bill made her laugh by insisting that he was a typical Englishman and needed time, and it was true that their best love-making had been taken leisurely, but twice he had startled and delighted her by beginning in the middle, so to speak, and finishing at a gallop. Once had been during the course of a late-night walk along the deserted beach after a trip to the cinema – she thought she would never forget the upsurge of passion which had terminated so gloriously, nor the sensation of being driven rapidly into the soft sand, which had made her laugh at quite the wrong moment. And the sand, she reflected now, had been pretty unforgettable too; they had both been removing it from unusual places for two or three days.

The other spur-of-the-moment loving had been equally bizarre. They had strolled up to the deserted funfair, found an innocent and unchained swing-boat, had climbed into it for a giggle, really . . . and when it had begun to swing really well, requiring only an occasional pull on the tasselled rope, Bill had put his arms round her, kissed her neck, and . . . wham! The stars had been whirling anyway but she and Bill had made them whirl so fast they simply merged into a brilliant blur in the sky.

'Penny for your thoughts, love? I asked about the cooking.'

'Ah! No, there's not a lot of cooking; I made enough teacakes on Monday to last us the week, and I did fancies yesterday, and the gingerbread was in and out of the oven before the welly-men arrived.' The welly-men had proved discerning despite their muddy boots; they adored Jenny's home-made cakes and bought them in great quantities.

'Then I think we'll close early, pick up the girls and go straight back to Beechcroft Road. I can measure up for draught excluders and so on, and you and the girls can bag the kitchen to make us all some tea. I'll nip out and tell the welly-men to come at three or not at all; they're just about our only post-lunch-time customers at the moment.'

It was true. The severe cold meant that no one ventured out of their own homes for longer than they had to; fortunately the office and factory workers still had to eat, and when they came in they ate better than ever, but the mums hustled their little blue-faced children past the gardens and ignored pleas for the swings, and the bowling green was deserted even by the hardiest ancient.

'That's fine by me. What do you think the kids would like for tea? It'll have to be something which doesn't need too much cooking, because of the time factor.'

'Did you make steak and kidney pie for the customers tomorrow, when you baked the pastry? Well then, steal a hunk of pie. We all need our stomachs lining in this sort of weather.'

'Oh Bill, but that means . . . no, I'll pay for it! Then it will still be my treat.'

'Right. Cost only, mind you, because it was your own labour. Oh, hell, Jen!'

She knew him well enough to know just what he was thinking; if things had been different they would not have this constant urge each to pay a fair share, to take an equal burden regarding the children. They would have pooled everything without thinking about it. But, Jenny thought comfortably as she cut five squares of steak and kidney pie and put them into a cake-box to carry home, they were getting that way. They might move slowly, but they were moving forward, and moving in step what was more.

'Yes? Come in!'

Sue was typing, spectacles perched on her nose, the keys of her little portable zipping down on to the paper. When she saw Dermott she stopped working, pushed her spectacles up into her hair and raised her brows.

'Fancy seeing you! What's up?'

'Sorry to stop you working, but I shan't be a tick. I'm hiring a mini-bus to take some of the company up into the mountains in search of some decent slopes for skiing. I wondered if you'd like to leave the baby with one of the other girls and come along. You keep on about your figure and exercise, but it's difficult with the weather so bitter.' He paused, eyeing Sue half shyly, half hopefully. 'I know you can ski, you said so when Jenny was talking about it. Solly can't and he won't come, he hates the cold like a cat does, so that leaves a spare seat.'

'It's jolly nice of you, Dermott, and I'd love to come, but I don't see how I can leave Tim,' Sue said regretfully. She was uneasily aware that she would never regain her figure without taking exercise, yet it was so hard to leave the baby! When she had first emerged from hospital and discovered that, despite giving birth, she still weighed over a stone more than she should have done, she had cried for an hour. Not even Jenny's bracing remarks about the same thing having happened to her and how she had eventually recovered her waist could do much to comfort Sue. She had never been a person for press-ups and knee-bends, she had always taken her exercise in the form of something she enjoyed – walking, playing tennis, joining a netball club, playing squash – yet now even walking was denied her because of the cold. Timmy could not glow, wrapped up as he was in the pram, but had to lie there becoming chillier and chillier and that she could not permit, so her walks had been reduced to a hasty scramble along the beach and back in the dark with Jenny, just before the ten o'clock feed.

'Why not? Is feeding him the problem? Can't you put some milk in a bottle and let Brenda or Mrs Twigg give it to him?'

'In a bottle? My dear chap, I'm breast-feeding! I couldn't just change him to cow's milk, if that's what you mean. It would be awfully bad for him and I don't suppose he'd take to it.'

Dermott sighed and rolled his eyes ceilingwards. He was dressed for going out and Sue remembered that the company were doing a late matinée two days a week now, starting at three-fifteen so that the schoolchildren could go. She stared enviously at his huge sheepskin coat, at the fur-lined boots he had bought himself at the onset of the severe weather and at his bright-eyed and glowing face. Lucky, untrammelled Dermott! Not that she would be without Timmy for all the tea in

China, but she did miss her freedom to go out when she felt like it and stay out for as long as she wished.

'Look, I'm a male, but even I've heard of expressing. Why can't you do that, just for once?'

'Expressing? Have you gone bonkers? What on earth is that?'

'Well, it's . . . oh damn you, Sue, I can't think of a nice way to put it! You milk yourself into a jug or something and then . . .'

'Don't go on!' Sue said in her deepest, most shocked voice. 'You made that up, Dermott Hughes you filthy beast! As if a woman and a mother would stoop so low!'

'They aren't *that* low, just a bit saggy,' Dermott said, deliberately misunderstanding. 'Would you like me to do it for you?'

'Why, you . . .' Sue broke down in giggles and threw her typewriter rubber at him; it bounced off his head and disappeared into the piles of baby clothing and sundries which now took up more than their fair share of the room. Sue gave a wail. 'Oh, Dermott, now look what you've done, it'll take me *weeks* to sort through that lot and find my rubber.'

'I thought you typists used white-out these days,' Dermott said, peering cautiously behind the tottering pile of clean nappies. 'It's not there, it must have gone further.'

'White-out's expensive, but I do use it for top copies, I just use the rubber for my carbon,' Sue explained. 'When is this skiing trip, anyway?'

'Sunday. It has to be, we don't finish the show until Saturday night. The skiing trip's a last get-together before the cast splits up and the rep. people move back in. Well, not quite the last, because we're having a party in the theatre on the Sunday night. I'm inviting everyone from here. It shouldn't be a problem for you, because you can bring the baby in his pram and just tuck him up somewhere quiet and draught-free and sneak in to feed him at midnight or whatever you do.'

'Gosh, that sounds lovely, but . . . what about Posy, though? Who'll look after her if Jenny comes?'

'She and Bill have some arrangement with a neighbour, I believe,' Dermott said vaguely. 'I say, I wonder if you could share, get them to have your brat as well? If you've expressed yourself once I suppose you could do it twice, couldn't you?'

'I'll express myself very frankly, if you don't stop suggesting it,' Sue said, getting up and beginning to root through her belongings in a search for the rubber. 'Oh go away, Dermott and stop tempting me! The thought of skiing . . . well, it's too alluring altogether.'

'Shall I put your name down then, for the last seat?'

'Oh damn your eyes . . . YES!' Sue shouted, then squeaked and pounced on the rubber. 'Here it is, hooray!'

'Then you will . . .'

'Don't say that word again! Yes, I suppose I'll have to. Ugh, ugh, the things I'll do for skiing. Cheerio Dermott, let me get on or I shan't have an article for the post.'

'Right, I'll put your name down. And don't forget if you need any help . . .'

'Shut up! Go away!'

'I mean if you want to do a practice run and need a hand . . . ha ha! . . . then I'm only too . . .'

'Dermott, next time it'll be the typewriter, not the rubber!' A sleepy mutter from the pram behind the screen brought Sue abruptly back to her feet, for she had seated herself in front of the machine once more. 'Ah, my little love's woken up, so it's probably time I stopped anyway.' Her voice changed to a thrilling coo. 'Tim-tum, little Tim-tum, do you want some grub? And a lovely clean nappy?' She fussed over to the pram, flapping a hand at Dermott as he opened the door. 'Come on, then, Mummy's all ready for her best boy.'

'We're all going, Dermott had hired a mini-bus but it wasn't big enough so now they've persuaded Ron Winge to hire a big car, and that comic, the little chap who's playing the dame, has hired one too, and that will just about do it. Honestly, Bill, I do think it will be fun and if your Sian could babysit then we could both enjoy a day out.'

'But I can't ski . . . well, I've never tried . . . so won't it be a bit pointless, me going along?' Bill was lying on the floor, applying draught excluder whilst Jenny sat on the floor near him peeling potatoes. 'I could arrange for Sian to babysit, I think, she's always keen to work on a Sunday, but . . . well, they won't want me along.'

'They will! I will, as well. Anyway, I can't ski, I've never been given the chance. However, I *can* toboggan, so I'm going to borrow the mushroom's sledge and have a go at that.'

'Why do you call him the mushroom?' Bill asked, getting to his knees in order to reach for another length of strip. 'He's an odd little boy, but why mushroom?'

'Oh, reared in a basement in the dark I suppose, plus the way his hair grows and the way he looks at you. The name seemed to fit, but I should remember to call him Martin, I don't want to make a mistake in front of him, poor kid.'

'Is he going? Have they asked him?'

'No, I shouldn't think so. Originally it was just the cast, with Sue taking Solly's place because she can ski and he can't, but then, when Dermott started mentioning it here, everyone wanted to go skiing first and then to the party, so he revised his plans a bit. Mrs Twigg's going to take Timmy so we can go skiing – she would take Posy as well, only if you *can* come we might as well let Sian earn herself some money – and then Sue will take him to the party in his pram so that she can feed him herself.'

'She dotes on that child,' Bill remarked, cutting the strip to fit and holding it against the door. 'Hand me the hammer, would you?'

'Certainly; I'm not a bad carpenter's mate, though useless at doing the actual work. As for Sue's doting, she does, doesn't she, especially when you think . . .'

'That she was going to have the baby adopted?'

'Oh! But how do you know, I've never said anything to anyone? Did you hear rumours, or has Posy been talking?'

'Neither. I guessed. Sue's far more of a mystery woman than the fellow who had the ground-floor flat before Dermott and Solly. She's attractive, sophisticated, she has an enviable job writing for the glossies, don't you think? Yet she chucked it all up to come here and have the baby.'

'No she didn't chuck it all up, she still writes her pieces. That's how she keeps herself and Tim in luxury.'

'Luxury? If this is your idea of luxury, love, you must have a very low expectation of life! I know what you mean, though. And you know what I mean, too. She could have had an abortion, or she could have stayed in London and given birth to the child; people do both these days. Yet she chose to hide, here.'

'I gather that the father is married. Sue's very kind, you know, in spite of being sophisticated and all that. She wouldn't want to hurt his wife, or him, probably. People might have guessed . . . I don't know, something like that.'

'But she does plan to go back? What'll happen then? Are memories so short that people won't remember who her lover was?'

'Yes, she plans to go back, she's waiting for a letter which will give her the go-ahead, I think. Bill, it's no use asking me because I can't tell you. Sue's not offered an explanation and I wouldn't dream of asking. But possibly she thinks that by the time she goes back the man will have moved away, or left his wife, something like that.'

'Probably.' Bill began to hammer and conversation was suspended whilst he did so. When he finished, he got stiffly to his feet, opened the door and then closed it a couple of times, just to make sure that he had not in any way impeded its movement, and explained to Jenny, 'There, that's all right now. What are the kids doing?'

'They're sorting shells in Mrs Twigg's room. Sue and Timmy are up there too so I thought it was rather crowded, but Mrs Twigg wouldn't let me chase ours down again. She's in her element, showing Sue how to crochet one moment and showing the girls how to make a crinoline shell-lady the next, and telling anyone who'll listen that Timmy's just like Bernard was as a littl'un. Bill?' She put her arms round him. 'Come skiing? Bill?'

'Well, if you're sure they won't expect me to shove sticks on my feet and whizz upright down inclines,' Bill said returning her hug. 'I used to be okay on roller skates . . . wonder if that counts?'

Sunday dawned crisp and sunny, the kind of day to make skiing seem an ideal outdoor sport. Dermott had gone out prospecting the day before and had found exactly the right spot, not too far from the road with a pull-off for the vehicles, complete even to the extent of having a frozen waterfall against which the cast could have their photographs taken.

Jenny set off early to Bill's house and left Posy there, happy because she had Belle, her friends Ricky and Dawn and, of course, Sian who had planned a lovely day for them all. Bill and Jenny walked back, well wrapped, the air so cold that it made you cough to breathe too fast or deeply.

Sue was looking pensive; she had left Timmy with Mrs Twigg and a bottle of expressed milk. Dermott was telling her that she must not coddle her baby, that he must learn to manage without her, but Sue did not look convinced. Dermott sat next to her in the mini-bus trying to convince her further and by the time they had covered a couple of miles Sue was laughing again, excited by the thought of the pleasure ahead.

It was a day to look back on, because for once everything went just the way it was planned. They all had an attempt at skiing and some were better than others. Sue was marvellous; she could beat everyone else, even Dermott, at twists and speed and manoeuvring. She wore a real skiing outfit, navy-blue with a scarlet cap and gloves, and she also had goggles which gave her an extra-professional look. Most of the cast could ski after a fashion. Ron Winge was very good and Diane Scarlett, his leading lady, came a close second. The comic fell down a lot and Brenda, Anna and Mouse, skiing for the first time, proved surprisingly adept after a very short time.

A veil should perhaps be drawn over Bill's performance; he was too afraid of falling, Jenny said wisely, picking herself up for the umpteenth time and plodding uphill again. But it did not matter, because he and she took their borrowed sledge to another part of the slope and had a wonderful time, tearing down the mountain side at an incredible speed and mocking each other's efforts to steer straight.

They had lunch in the mini-bus, having brought a huge picnic including many flasks, some containing hot coffee, others something stronger. It was crowded, but no one minded sitting on laps, sharing a small seat and using a flask top one between three.

The sun shone all day and as the shadows lengthened it became colder, until everyone found themselves glad to bundle back into the bus and set off for Rhyl once more. Jenny leaned her head against Bill's shoulder, Sue leaned her head against Dermott's, and they both fell asleep, worn out by the strenuous exercise.

The bus decanted them on to the pavement outside No. 24, Dermott and Bill declaring that Sue and Jenny had snored horribly all the way home and everyone else shouting and talking, making last minute arrangements for the stage party that evening. Bill was to go home to make sure that Sian and the children were all right and to change out of his soaking clothes, so Dermott put his right arm round Jenny's shoulders and his left arm round Sue's and led them indoors.

'Said you'd enjoy it,' he told them triumphantly, as they reached the first landing. 'Go and make yourselves even more beautiful, if that's possible – Ron Winge was saying, whilst you two snored, that he's bringing some champers.'

Alone in her room Jenny felt chilly, so she turned on both fires and went across to draw the curtains. On the opposite side of the road someone had a garden unwalled but thickly hedged with huge laurel bushes. Sometimes courting couples cuddled in their shelter but tonight, as she glanced across, Jenny saw that there was only one man there, obviously waiting for someone. He was thickset with a flat cap pulled well down over his face, and it was too dark to make out anything else about him other than that he was a man and not a woman, but Jenny thought she could tell that he was looking over in her direction so she closed the curtains with extra care before removing her wet and dirty clothes. She had a hot wash and then, in pants and bra, went and peeped through the curtains; the idea of someone watching her window was something she could well do without. The man had gone, however, so presumably he had been waiting for someone who had arrived in the interim.

She had bought a new dress in the January sales for this occasion and she put it on; it was sleeveless and low-cut with a full skirt, and the material was a soft, gleaming organza in a shade dubbed cinammon. She had bought a lipstick to match it and Sue had helped her dye a pair of shoes in a similar shade. Looking critically at herself in the mirror, she decided that she would do; the colour made her hair look excitingly lighter and the dark lipstick added glamour to her small, pale face. A touch of mascara and eyeshadow completed the party look, she decided, heading for the door. Sue would be ready soon and they could leave together. It looked like being a good day all round.

'It's been unforgettable, darling, just like the season . . . where? Oh, Aberdeen, marvellous place, I wish I was . . . my sweet, I'll miss you more, much much more! And Annabel's *face*, when the curtain shot up thirty seconds before . . . then all the others came tumbling out . . . very lush, darling, did you see . . .'

'They're very friendly and charming, but so artificial I could scream,' Jenny muttered to Bill as the cast, their carrying voices enunciating every syllable, began to leave the theatre. 'Solly went off with one of the chorus early on; I begin to see why! And what on earth shall we do with Dermott? After Sue left he took to the bottle and look at him now!'

Dermott was very drunk. He had begun the evening well, dancing mostly with Sue and once or twice with Anna and Brenda, and no one had even wondered whether he was drinking too much. Indeed, when Jenny had noticed she had thought that it simply made his talk wittier and did not really matter, particularly as there was so much to drink and it was being so freely and generously dispensed. But there was very little food, though two or three girls did go out at about eleven and return with various Chinese dishes, only by then Dermott did not want to eat.

By midnight Dermott was, as the saying goes, legless. By one o'clock when he should either have been sobering up or sleeping it off, he discovered a new lease of life from somewhere, reeled out of his chair and managed to reach and drink the best part of a bottle of banana liqueur which no one else had fancied. By the time the party broke up he was impervious to outside events. He lay on his back on the hard stage floor, stoned out of his mind, snoring occasionally or giggling or sometimes vaguely amorous, but at no time fully compos mentis.

'We're going to have to get him back to No. 24 and it'll have to be a taxi,' Bill decided as they stood over Dermott's inanimate form. 'He's not fat but he's tall and quite heavy, we'd never manage to manhandle him all that way.'

'The principals all have cars,' Brenda put in. 'Wouldn't someone give us a lift with him?' It sounded reasonable but Bill vetoed the idea.

'He's in the theatre himself so he needs these people; if he threw up all over someone's Jaguar do you think they'd want to work with him again?'

'Poor Bill,' Anna said, patting his arm. She was completely sober and had behaved beautifully, Jenny considered. 'Tell you what, we'll all contribute to the taxi fare, though we won't travel with you, if you don't mind. I think Dermott will take up most of the available space.'

'That's true. Would someone ring for a cab then?'

Mouse volunteered and presently Jenny and Bill, feeling very like friends-of-the-bride, managed to lug Dermott to his feet with some help from a stage-hand and the girls. Sue had long since gone with Timmy, having decided that party or no party, her little son had been up long enough, but Anna, Brenda and Mouse had remained and did some sterling work in getting Dermott not only upright but also out to the waiting taxi.

However, helping him to the taxi was all they wanted to do; they would get home under their own steam they said, and probably a good deal faster than Jenny and Bill would, burdened with Dermott.

They were right. Dermott fulfilled all their worst fears. He was hideously sick just before they reached the stage door, he was sick again when they reached the taxi but fortunately before they had lifted him on to the battered upholstery, and he was sick a third time with his head stuck out of the taxi window.

It sobered him up a bit; at least by the time they reached No. 24 he was able, with help, to climb out of the cab and make his wavering way up to the front door, supported on either side by Bill and Jenny. Jenny pushed the door and it swung open; clearly the girls had guessed that no one would want to have to ring the doorbell to be let in, despite the fact that it was long after midnight. Brenda was hovering on the landing, and when they lurched into the hall she called softly to Anna and Mouse who both appeared, washed and dressing-gowned, and came down the stairs.

'Well, you've got him back; well done,' Brenda whispered. 'Prop him against the end of the stairs whilst I go through his pockets for his room-key.'

'Look Bill, you've been marvellous but you must take the taxi and go home now,' Jenny urged, pushing Bill out of the door. 'We'll cope.'

'Are you sure you can, Jenny? He's a helluva heavy lump to move. Perhaps I'd better give you a hand to get him into bed.'

'Oh, rubbish, I can manage him, but thanks very much for your help. Bye!'

Jenny watched Bill vanish down the path and into the taxi, then she shut the front door, suddenly aware that she felt the full weight of her thirty-six years and was dog-tired. Oh, for her nice cosy bed! But first she had a duty to perform. Brenda and Anna, giggling, were trying to search Dermott's pockets whilst Mouse did her best to keep him upright against the stairs. Just as Jenny walked over to help Brenda squeaked triumphantly and held out the key.

'Got it! We're nearly home and dry! I'll unlock the door and . . .' They all jumped as dreadful rumbling gurgles came from the unlucky Dermott's direction. 'Oh, don't let him be . . .'

'Too late,' Mouse remarked placidly as Dermott whooshed up, for the fourth time that evening, all over the hall. 'What a vile smell, whatever was he drinking? I'll get the mop and bucket from the kitchen, shall I?'

She did not wait for a reply but departed, whilst Brenda unlocked Dermott's door and Jenny and Anna unceremoniously seized any part of him they could grab and towed him towards his own room.

It was a nuisance that Dermott then woke up and became increasingly chatty, giggly and really rather rude, though, as Anna said, the more he fancied he could do it, the less he'd be able to. Even so it was a nuisance to have his hands pawing at you when you were trying to remove his vomit-covered clothing, and lesser mortals would probably have given up and bundled him into his bed, leaving him to repent at leisure in the morning. But Jenny, Anna, Brenda and Mouse were made of sterner stuff; Dermott had invited them to the party, after all, and it was up to them to see that he was put to bed clean, decent and on his side.

'Pretend we're hospital nurses,' Mouse gasped at one point, holding down Dermott's flailing arm with both hands whilst her fellow-sufferers tried to force his loopy, spaghetti-like legs into pyjama trousers. 'I expect they often have to change drunks from day clothes into pyjamas.'

'Not drunks like this,' Jenny said, furiously ramming one of Dermott's hairy and animate feet into the trousers and catching his little toe on the elasticated waistband. 'My *God*, I could kill him!'

'She's pullin' ma l'il toe offff,' Dermott moaned, giggling. 'She's goin' to dis . . . dis . . . dis . . . disorganishe me!'

'Shut up!' the four girls chorussed, getting into their stride. They succeeded with the trousers and began to struggle with the jacket but buttoning it proved more than they could manage; every time they grabbed Dermott round his buttons, he seemed to think it was an open invitation to be grabbed back.

'Get the water,' Jenny said at last, when they had him clothed in pyjamas and slumped across the bed. 'We'll wash the horrid creature, then shove him into bed and tuck him in firmly and hope for the best.'

'Tuck him in firmly, firmly, firmly,' Dermott carrolled, as Mouse approached him with the soapy flannel. 'Tuck him . . . tuck him . . . fuck tim . . . f . . . aaargh!' The soapy flannel entered his wide open mouth and shut him up momentarily, and indeed the brisk and heartless way in which Mouse proceeded to wash him compelled feminine admiration and masculine wails.

'There!' gasped Jenny when Dermott, cleaned and sparkling – and also volubly lamenting their cruelty – , had been pinioned by sheets and blankets in the bed. 'I never want to go through *that* again! Why on earth did he get into that state? I've seen men drunk before, but never as bad as that!'

'Who cares? I'm off men,' Brenda said as they left the room as quickly as they could, ignoring Dermott's pleas to each one of them to join him in his little cot. 'I just hope the old hen doesn't hear the things he's been saying – she'd kick Dermott out tomorrow and buy us all chastity belts.'

'Who needs a chastity belt when Dermott's the one making suggestions?' Jenny said wearily. 'Oh, but I ache in every limb! Subduing him was worse than doing karate. Well, we should all sleep sound tonight!'

That was, as they crawled off to their own beds, the general verdict.

As she had predicted, Jenny fell into a deep sleep as soon as her head touched the pillow. She did not know what woke her some time later; it might have been a bump, or someone going down or up to the loo, or simply a late-night reveller shouting outside in the street. But whatever it was she was abruptly awake, with her hair prickling erect on the back of her neck and her heart thumping noisily.

She lay listening for a moment but heard nothing more. Her eyes strained through the darkness towards a lighter patch which was the window. Belle was at Bill's, of course, with Posy, but she had locked her door, mindful of Dermott's drunken state and of the fact that the front door could not be locked until the last party-goer had come in, and the last party-goer could easily forget to turn the key.

Only silence greeted her straining ears and only the faint light from the window pierced the otherwise total darkness. The landing light was out. It also looked as though the hall light were out, which probably meant that everyone was safely in bed. Yet something had woken her, and until she knew what it was, she did not think she would sleep again.

Cursing herself for an imaginative idiot, Jenny rolled out of bed and padded across to the window. She twitched back the curtain a couple of inches and peered out. The lamplit street was deserted – not even a cat moved – and the wind had obviously dropped since the trees outside were rimed with frost.

Halfway back to her bed, she decided that if she was not able to sleep she might as well read for a while, so she turned on her bedside lamp and went across to her bookshelves, which were there courtesy of Bill who had built them in for her, and chose a copy of *I Capture the Castle* by Dodie Smith – an old favourite, it would help her to drop off again.

Her fingers were actually on the book when she heard a perfectly horrible sound, a sort of gurgling gasp and then a groan, and it seemed to be coming from right outside her door. Jenny snatched back her hand and clutched her throat – what on earth was going on? She stared at her door, moving slowly over towards it, her eyes fixed. Was someone out there, trying to get in? But the door handle did not move and there had been no sound of knocking or scraping; it was just that beastly groaning, bubbling sound.

It took considerable courage to slide back the bolt and turn the key in the lock, but Jenny did both. Then, very very slowly and carefully, she pushed against the door.

It did not open. Something was jammed against it from the outside.

Panicking, Jenny shoved with all her might and forced the door open a foot or so. The landing light was on; it flooded in, cheerfully normal, and gave her courage to peep round her door to see just what it was against it.

Then she screamed.

Right outside her door lay a man. He was wearing pyjamas but they were so speckled, spotted and smeared with blood that Jenny did not think them familiar, nor did she recognize, at first, the man's face.

His mouth was open and blood oozed from both corners, more blood ran from his nostrils, his cheek was split, his eyes were puffed up closed, unrecognizable, his hair was matted with blood. However, even as her scream died away, though Jenny knew him and was on her knees beside him.

'Dermott! What on earth . . .? You poor devil, who . . . how . . .?'

Sue's door opened and Sue came out, pale-faced, with her

hair tied on top of her head in a ridiculous little tail. She saw the man's back and gasped, then turned to call up the stairs.

'Anna? Is that you? Better come down and phone the police, I don't know what's happened, but . . . Jenny, who is it?'

'It's Dermott,' Jenny said. She backed into her room, hurried across to the sink, then returned with a soaked flannel. 'Look, he's breathing all right, but he's sort of bubbling. I'm going to try to clean his mouth up a bit, see just what's happened . . . can you or Anna ring for a doctor? Oh, and the police, I suppose, because he couldn't have done that falling downstairs, could he?'

'No, not on your life,' a masculine voice said, making Jenny give a tiny muffled shriek, but it was only Bernard coming down to join the small group on the landing, looking owlish and newly awoken, as indeed he probably was. 'I say, Anna, don't you move; the feller who done that might be downstairs in the 'all. I'll go down.'

'Should we touch him?' Anna said fearfully, as Jenny began as gently as she could to mop the blood from his mouth. 'I never know if you should move people or leave them lie.'

'I don't know either,' Sue said. Her voice sounded reedy and she kept casting quick glances into shadowy corners. Jenny looked up as Brenda and Mouse, clinging to each other, came down the flight.

'Hello you two! Know anything about first aid? Poor Dermott's in an awful state.'

'I know a bit, I was a nurse for a year,' Mouse said, kneeling down beside Jenny. 'Gosh! Is it all his head, or has someone attacked his body as well?'

'We don't know,' Jenny said. Her voice was beginning to shake slightly; thank God Posy was out of it, she kept saying to herself, thank God she isn't here to see this! 'His jacket's unbuttoned though, do you think we ought to look?'

Mouse pulled Dermott's jacket back and eased the top of his trousers down; he had been kicked or hit in the stomach, a long, dark bruise was spreading almost as they watched. Mouse pulled a face.

'Hmm, not too good. Anna, fetch a pillow or two, would

you. It's not good to have his head down when he's bleeding from the nose and mouth like that. Oh, and can someone spare some blankets? He might easily come round in shock from a beating like that, we should keep him warm.'

It was a relief to be given something to do; the girls bustled round and soon Dermott looked a lot more comfortable, though it was impossible to tell if he actually felt any better since he remained unconscious. Jenny had bathed his face and chest and got quite a lot of the blood from his hair, Anna had propped his head up with two firm pillows, and Sue, at Jenny's suggestion, had covered him snugly in all the blankets off Posy's bed, for it was bitterly cold and no one fancied going back to a bed with only sheets to keep them warm.

'Who done it, though?' Bernard said presently, as he re-joined the girls with the news that an ambulance and the police would be here shortly. 'It weren't Solly? I mean, they was friends.'

'No, of course it wasn't Solly,' Brenda said indignantly, then blushed scarlet. 'Honestly, Bernard, what a thing to say! Actually, Solly wasn't home when we put Dermott to bed, he probably spent the night with that chorus girl, what was her name – Lindy something-or-other.'

'Oh. Is 'e back now, d'you think?'

'Not unless he's stone deaf.' Jenny was beginning when a querulous voice from the top of the stairs asked what was going on and Mrs Twigg came into view, took one look at Dermott's battered face, and screamed louder and longer than Jenny had.

'Mother, shut up, you'll wake . . .'

But even if Mrs Twigg's scream had not done the trick, the ambulance would have; it careered round the corner from the promenade into Beechcroft Road, sirens going full blast, and was closely followed by a police car, or possibly two, making an equal amount of noise.

Within two minutes every tenant at No. 24, as well as the landlady, her husband and son, were all assembled in the hall, on the stairs and on the first landing, whilst the ambulance men swept in and had Dermott on the stretcher within moments. The police cleared their throats, took out their notebooks and prepared to make a night of it.

'Can we get dressed?' Sue quavered, as the officers of the law stomped up to the scene of the crime. 'It's a terribly cold night and we're all pretty shocked . . . and we none of us did it.'

The police inspector was a humane man with a sense of humour; he grinned at the nightgowned and pyjama-clad company and told them to wrap up warmly and come down to the basement, where Mrs Grant was making her kitchen available to him and his men for the short while that they would need to talk to everyone. Jenny and Sue exchanged frightened looks, because after all Dermott had been found directly outside their doors, and then repaired to their rooms to get respectable. When Jenny was ready she tapped on Sue's door and they went down to the basement together.

'Why would someone do that to Dermott?' Sue enquired, as they crossed the hall. 'He was nice, everyone liked him.'

'Someone didn't. But it was probably a gang of drunken louts, you know how these things happen.'

'Yes . . . only wouldn't someone have heard? Drunken louts aren't usually very quiet.'

'Yes, I never thought . . . anyway, the police will tell us. And then perhaps we can get back to bed,' Jenny said longingly. 'This has been quite the longest night of my life.'

'And it's not over yet,' Sue said grimly. 'I've a feeling it will be several hours before we get our heads down.'

'Good morning, Mrs Grant. Sorry to disturb you, but the door was locked so we had to ring.' Bill stood on the doorstep in casual Sunday clothes with Belle on her lead and the three small girls by his side. 'Is Jenny about yet? She did say she'd come round to fetch Posy and then we'd all have lunch at my place, or that's what I thought she said, but it's half twelve . . .' He stopped. Mrs Grant's hair was like a bird's nest and she looked extremely cross. 'Is anything the matter?'

'Oh *no*, nothing's the *matter*, I like having the police here half the night and being kept out of my bed until six o'clock,' Mrs Grant said witheringly. 'As for Jenny, she was the last to leave, I think, on account of 'im being found outside her door.'

'What? The police? Outside . . .' Bill took a deep breath, pushed past Mrs Grant and took the stairs two at a time. He knocked on Jenny's door, paused, knocked again, and then tried the handle. It did not open. He turned a suddenly very pale face towards Mrs Grant, who was standing swaying in the middle of the hall.

'What the hell's happened? Is she all right? Mrs Grant, do you have a key to this . . .'

The door opened. Jenny stood swaying in the doorway. Her hair was dishevelled and she was pale and wan, but she gave Bill a quick, tired smile.

'Look, we're all absolutely knackered, we've been up all night. Some lout got in here and beat Dermott to a pulp – he was in an awful state. They've taken him off to hospital so we thought we'd try to get a few hours sleep and then go and see how he is. Sue rang; they said holding his own.' She held out her hand to Posy, started to say something, and then broke off to give a great jaw-cracking yawn. 'Oh goodness, love, I'm so sorry, but I really am terribly tired.'

'You go back to bed,' Bill said at once. 'We'll go home and have dinner, then come round at about four and you can tell us all about it.'

Jenny touched his cheek, then bent and kissed Posy, Erica and Dawn, and stumbled back to bed. Bill watched as she climbed into it, and shrugged the covers up to her ears, then he turned away and closed the door softly behind him. He glanced down into the hall as he led the children downstairs once more, but Mrs Grant had disappeared. Posy clung to his hand, throwing a quick startled glance round the hall.

'Well, Posy, Mummy's had an exciting time it seems, with the police here and everything, but she needs a bit more sleep before she can tell us all about it, so you'll come back to dinner with us, won't you? And then we'll come round at about tea-time, and you and Ricky and Dawn can make tea and toast and Mummy will tell us what happened.'

'Yes, all right. What's a lout, Uncle Bill?'

'Oh, just a stupid young man. Come on, who's going to take Belle's lead, give me a break from all the work?'

The four of them left the house, the girls quarrelling amicably over who should lead Belle, but Bill knew that it would be a long and tedious time until four o'clock.

CHAPTER ELEVEN

'And you didn't see anyone? Oh come on, Dermott, I know you were stoned but you must have seen *something*!'

Jenny and Sue were perched on the visitors' seat, both eyeing Dermott with exasperation. They had been cross-questioned by the police for hours, had spent ages making statements and trying to remember insignificant details, had been given a thundering telling-off by Mrs Grant for not having locked the front door, and now all Dermott could do when they asked a few pertinent questions was to say that he could only remember hearing someone stumbling across the darkened room, then something – he thought at the time it was the ceiling – hitting him very hard across the head, whereupon he had lost consciousness.

'When you heard someone coming across the room why didn't you shout out or put the light on?' Sue asked in an aggrieved voice. 'Why did you just lie there waiting to be beaten up?'

'Because I thought it was one of you lovely ladies, sorry for her cruelty and coming to cuddle up,' Dermott said stiffly, through bruised lips. 'I couldn't turn the light on in case it put you off . . . *no*, Sue you little bitch, not the sight of me! I mean if one of you had decided to come to bed with me, I didn't think she'd much fancy suddenly being illuminated.'

'Dermott, none of us . . .'

'Yes, all right, but I was a bit drunk; I suppose a drunk can fantasize, can't he?'

Jenny sighed and reached for Dermott's hand, giving it a consolatory squeeze.

'Yes, of course you can. It's just that you can't possibly realize how much we all hated you, having lugged you for miles, and seeing you sicking up everywhere, and having to fight you to get you into bed . . . but was the person in your room a man or a woman? Couldn't you tell?'

'I suppose it was a man,' Dermott said, touching the

bandages which swathed his chest. 'If a woman cast herself on my chest she'd do less damage, I imagine. Three ribs cracked and something nasty done to my innards seems more like jealous-husband work to me.'

'Jealous husband? Then you *had* made an enemy!' Sue said triumphantly. 'Who's the woman, Dermott?

'Don't be daft, it was only a random remark,' Dermott said. 'What I want to know is why did whoever it was lug me up a flight of stairs and drop me outside your door?'

'You were more outside my door than Sue's,' Jenny pointed out. 'And what makes you think you were brought up there? I thought you'd crawled.'

'Crawled? With my ribs bashed in? I tell you I couldn't have crawled an inch, let alone up those stairs. I tell you I was dumped there for a reason.'

'Well then, it must have been mistaken identity,' Jenny said, having given the matter some frowning thought. 'Someone blundered into your room thinking you were . . . well, how about Solly? Or say they'd got their wires crossed completely and thought you were a bloke in with one of the other girls. Who's got a possessive boyfriend?'

'Or a . . .' Sue's hand flew to her mouth. 'No, it doesn't work, Jenny, because whoever beat Dermott up and carried him or dragged him across the hall and up the stairs would have taken him to Anna's and Brenda's floor, not ours.'

'Ah, but not if he didn't know which floor they were on. Or I might have disturbed him when I woke up. But I'm inclined to agree with the inspector that our first feeling that it was drunken yobs was wrong. Admittedly my experience of drunken yobs is limited but, judging from the way Dermott carried on, they aren't capable of quiet or stealthy behaviour.'

'Thanks,' Dermott said. 'I'd smile at you if I *could* smile. As it is, I'm sick of the whole subject and I'd be obliged if you'd forget it. It's happened, it's horrible, but I don't think we'll ever find the culprit. And anyway, I'm a lot happier with mistaken identity than anything else, because it means it isn't likely to happen again.'

'Right, we'll put it out of our minds,' Jenny said, since Sue was still staring blankly down the ward. 'Is there anything you need from home, Dermott? And when will you be out?'

'Nothing I need, thanks. Solly came in with all my soap and things yesterday and I'm hoping to be out in three or four days. But do come again tomorrow evening, if you can make it.'

When the bell rang, signalling the end of visiting, they made their way back along the corridors and out into the road, where they were very nearly knocked back into the hospital again by the strength of the wind off the sea. Sue gasped, grabbed Jenny's arm and bawled into her ear.

'You go on home, love, but I'll have to go back. I left my handbag under Dermott's bed. See you in ten minutes or so.'

Before Jenny had time to protest Sue had turned and disappeared inside the hospital again. Jenny waited for a moment, shrugged and set off along the promenade. They did not usually go around after dark alone, but the prom was well-lit and there were people about, mainly hospital visitors it is true, but nevertheless they were in groups all over the place and probably some would be walking down Beechcroft Road. But on the corner, Jenny's conscience smote her. She could not possibly go home and leave Sue to make her own way back, not with someone loose who had seen fit to bash up Dermott for no apparent reason. She turned and was halfway back to the hospital when someone behind her called her name and she heard running footsteps. A quick glance over her shoulder confirmed that it was a man in a mac, not Bill, as she had half-hoped, but Dirk.

'Hold on! I rang, but you were out so I thought . . . can I have a word?'

'I'm just going back to the hospital,' Jenny said coolly. 'My friend's still visiting. I'm going to walk her home so you'll have to make it quick.'

'Tell her . . .' he stopped. Possibly, Jenny thought to herself, he realized that commands were not too well received just at present. 'Surely if she knows you're with me she'll go back to her flat or whatever by herself.'

'Probably. But that won't do. Ah, here she comes.'

Sue nearly passed them, with her head down against the wind, but Jenny grabbed her sleeve.

'Sue, hang on, we'll walk back with you. This is Dirk.'

'Gosh!' Sue turned and stared at Jenny's companion but

did not offer to shake hands or speak to him. 'Come on then, let's make a run for it. I felt rain just now.'

Jenny had felt it too; they hurried, Dirk as silent as they, until they reached No. 24 when Dirk followed them into the hallway. Here both girls stopped short, Sue staring at Jenny and Jenny at Dirk.

'What was it you wanted?' Jenny said baldly. 'Posy's with a friend whilst I was out, but it's her bedtime.'

'I want to talk; can't we . . . can't I come up to your room?'

It was the nearest to a plea she had ever heard from Dirk and, unexpectedly, it touched her. He was so proud, such a male chauvinist pig, it must have cost him to ask when he would have found ordering so much easier!

'Well . . . I don't want Posy upset.'

'I won't upset her. Does she have to come back at once, though? Couldn't she stay with her friend for a bit longer?'

Sue had been standing with one foot on the bottom stair, now she began to mount them. She said nothing as Jenny, saying she supposed Posy would be all right with Mrs Twigg for another five minutes or so, began to follow her, but when Sue went into her room she left the door slightly ajar. Jenny was amused and touched – not that she anticipated having to call for help. Still, it was good to know that Sue was obviously on the look-out.

'Come in, then.' Jenny held the door open for Dirk but did not quite close it; she wanted to keep the interview as short as possible.

He walked in and looked round. Suddenly the room seemed to shrink, to grow smaller and shabbier. Jenny bustled defensively about, switching on the standard lamp because it cast a gentler light, kicking Belle's dish and the rubber bone under the bed out of sight, straightening the cushions.

'You've got it nice,' Dirk sounded almost wistful. 'Which is your bed?'

'Well, which do you think? The big one, of course. I'm not likely to use the single when I'm twice Posy's size.'

He turned to look at her. It was a strange sort of look; she could not fathom it.

'Posy sleeps here too? But there was a little room for her, I remember the old crone charging me extra.'

'Yes, there is another room but it's damp and, anyway, Posy would be nervous sleeping there alone.' She did not mention Belle; he must know about her, but if he did not there was no reason why he should be told.

'Hasn't she ever used that little room? Not even since Christmas?'

'No, she's never used it; I told you, it's damp.'

'But what if you want a friend in, during the evening?'

'Not possible.' Jenny did not want to sit down but Dirk, it seemed, had no such inhibitions. He settled himself heavily in her chair. He was frowning. It was clear to someone who had been married to him for almost two decades that he wanted to ask her something but was searching for the right words. Dirk did not think quickly, so Jenny, with a sigh, sat down opposite him and composed herself for a wait. Finally, he spoke.

'Then you go out, do you? Down to his place? Well, hers I mean, I suppose.'

Jenny stared at him whilst the fog which had obscured his visit gradually lifted and exposed him. He thought she had a fellow, he wanted to know if she was sleeping with someone else, he dared not ask outright or at least did not choose to ask outright so he was trying to get the information out of her in apparently aimless conversation. She stood up.

'No, I don't go and sleep around at nights, but if I did it would be no concern of yours. Is that all you wanted to know?'

'I want you to come home.' He mumbled it, looking not at her but at his big square hands, one on each knee. Jenny, furious with herself, was still abruptly pierced with pain to see him looking so old and worn, like an old dog banned from the kitchen and turned out to fend for itself.

Perhaps fortunately, that made her think of Belle and hardened her heart. He had been willing to see Belle turned out, now perhaps he was tasting just a little of the bewilderment and despair she must have experienced. It did not occur to Jenny to censure him for her own bewilderment and despair, becase they were emotions which had not troubled her for weeks and weeks. Far more distresing to her now was the occasional feeling that her duty lay back at the farm, that it was her bed and she should, if asked, lie on it. But until now he had never asked her, so the question had been a rhetorical one. Now that he had spoken the words she had once longed to hear – *come home* – what should she do? Go meekly back and take up her life where he had torn it from her months ago, or stick to her guns, stay here, be herself?

'I'm sorry.'

He looked up and then, with a speed surprising in one so large, was out of his chair and lifting her off her feet before she had done more than gasp.

'Jenny, must I say I need you? I can't go on like this! I've said I want you back, isn't that enough?'

It was strange, but the moment she was in his arms some body chemistry, or perhaps it was just instinct, told Jenny that he was lying. His desire for her, which had once been a real thing, was dead. He had killed it himself in his desire for Bronwen, now he could not resurrect it even though she believed he truly wished to do so. He began to squeeze and fondle her and she pulled back, sickened by the charade and also for the first time a bit frightened of him. He might not want her but he was a strong and determined man; he was quite capable of taking her against her wishes simply to prove to her that she could not live without him. Knowing that he believed she found his love-making irresistible, you could scarcely blame him for playing what he must think was his trump card.

'Let go, Dirk, I don't . . .'

He pushed her backwards on to her bed and followed so swiftly that his weight knocked all the breath out of her body. For a few vital seconds she could only see whirling lights whilst she tried desperately to suck air into her flattened lungs. Lying there like a landed fish with her throat burning and her chest wheezing, she felt him hook his fingers in the top of her tights and pants and bring them down to a point where he apparently considered her vulnerable. Still seeing stars, Jenny promptly brought her knees up and felt them sink into something soft – stomach? Or naughty bits? From the startled grunt and the hiss of air leaving lungs she felt her knees had been well aimed. Quickly, before he could seize back the initiative, she gave a wriggle and heaved her clothing back into respectability once more, then another wriggle designed to get her out of his reach brought her foot flying up into another part of her aggressor. She found sufficient breath to make a croaky comment.

'That's enough, Dirk, if you don't . . .'

She was half sitting up when he hit her across the side of the head with sufficient force to knock her sideways on to the bed. She gasped and groaned, felt his hands on her again and kicked, fright making her foolish, for Dirk could never bear to be contradicted – she had not fought him before and he had never struck her, but now, dimly, something kept telling her not to keep struggling, to lie still for a moment or else . . . or else . . .

He was kneeling between her legs, a hand on each thigh, and he was grinning, his hair on end, his eyes sparkling. He was enjoying it because he knew he was going to win . . . he did not realize that, in winning, he would lose everything, any tiny last chance he might have had to win her back.

Jenny stopped struggling; she turned her head sideways and closed her eyes. She lay very still.

'Cooee, Jenny – want a cup of coffee?'

If Jenny was startled by Sue's voice, Dirk must have been absolutely horrified, for he leapt off his wife and off the bed with a good three feet to spare. Jenny, opening her eyes and scrambling to her knees, thought he had never looked less attractive; face flushed and mouth half open, hair on end, trousers round knees . . . and nothing gained, either, she thought triumphantly, turning to face Sue. Saved! She was trembling and sick, her head still rang from the buffet he had given her, but she was still very much her own woman. She fished for her pants and tights and then abandoned the attempt to tidy up; her tights appeared to have been converted to stockings by dear Dirk, and her pants would never be quite the same again.

'Come in, Sue, right in. I'll have a coffee, please, but this . . . this person is just leaving.'

Dirk had his back to them. Buttoning up . . . no, zipping

up, Jenny told herself with shaking scorn. How *could* he have behaved like that – like a rapist – when he was supposed to be visiting? But, having made himself respectable again, he turned to Sue and there was something almost condescending in his manner.

'Who are you? Do you always barge into rooms without knocking? You'll see worse than that if you do!'

'And do you always knock people without asking?' Sue said, her voice deadly sweet and reasonable. 'Because you'll get more than a kick in the coconuts if you do.'

'As her husband . . .' Dirk began, but was cut short.

'No, Dirk. Ex-husband. I'm getting a divorce.'

'Oh, rubbish! I don't have any say in the matter, I suppose? I've *told* you, it's all over between Bronwen and me, there's nothing to stop you coming back tomorrow. Except . . .'

'Except that I don't want to,' Jenny snapped. 'I'm getting a divorce!'

'What for? I'm not keeping another woman, I haven't been cruel to you, I'm asking you to come back; do you think any court in the land would give you a divorce in those circumstances?'

'Oh, Dirk, of course they would! You turned me out, you had a mistress or whatever you like to call her, installed in my home. The fact that you've now discovered you made a mistake doesn't undo what you did. So I'm afraid I can't come back, not even for a weekend; if I did, that really might muck up the divorce proceedings.'

She had done nothing about getting a divorce, knew very little about it in fact, but was banking on the probability that Dirk would know less. He was staring at her, his expression a mixture of incredulity and slowly gathering rage. Jenny wished he would go and was glad of Sue's presence.

'So! And what does your lover say to that? Does he want you, is that why you're suddenly so keen on a divorce? After what you've already cost him, are you *sure* he still wants you?'

'Lover? What I've cost him . . . who?' Jenny asked, force-fully if ungrammatically. 'I'm not thinking of remarrying, if that's what's on your mind. I'm not like you, Dirk, I can survive very well without all that.'

Dirk was buttoning up his mac, but when he strode purposefully towards the door Sue stepped into his path.

'Where were you last Sunday night?' she said. Jenny, uncomprehending, watched as a rich scarlet shade darkened Dirk's face. Last Sunday had been the party at the theatre. What on earth . . .?

'At about two in the morning,' Sue added. Dirk said nothing but he picked her up by the shoulders and dropped her again, two feet to the right and clear of the doorway. Sue turned and followed him to the top of the stairs; Dirk was already halfway down.

'Come on, where were you? I bloody know, you were beating up the wrong man, you pathetic little cow-turd! Your wife and a fellow who'd had too much to drink and was flat on his back, they're about right as targets for handing out beatings and bullyings to, eh? I'll stand up in any court in the land and tell them about you, old swaggering Dirk Sayer, the respected landowning, wife-beating, dog-starving tyrant who thinks he can get away with damn nearly murdering an innocent man . . .'

The slam of the front door cut off the sentence in midstream and Sue's voice, which had risen to levels of stridency previously unknown, petered out. She swung round to face Jenny. Her cheeks were flushed to a delicate shade of rose and her eyes were bright. She pulled a face and went over to put her arm round her friend.

'Jenny, I'm sorry, I shouldn't have chucked it at him with you standing there, but I daresay you'd guessed? Anyway, I shouldn't think he'll come back and pester you again, not knowing that you know what you know.'

'How many knows is that? Which considering I don't know what you think I know . . . are you saying it was Dirk who beat Dermott up? But surely . . .'

'Think about it. Look, that row must have pricked ears all over the building I should think. Do you want to go up and fetch Posy and we'll talk whilst she has her bath?'

'Yes, perhaps I'd better. See you in a moment, then.'

Jenny fetched Posy down from Mrs Twigg and got her ready for the bath, but all the time her mind was working furiously. Was it possible that Sue was right and that it had been Dirk who had beaten up Dermott? Why should he have done such a thing? She had never intimated that there was anyone else, least of all that it was a fellow tenant. But all the time she worked and chatted quietly to Posy, the conviction grew in her that Sue was right. Dirk would never let something he regarded as his own be taken by someone else without a struggle. She had not thought of him as a coward, but it had been a cowardly act to attack Dermott when he was drunk and in bed. Dirk had been in a red rage when he left; if there had been any doubt about the truth of Sue's remarks he would have come back and forced her to eat her words. By the time Posy was in the bath she was more than half convinced.

'Dermott confirmed it, but I'd suspected before. That was why I went back to fetch my handbag . . . I mean that was why I left my handbag, so that I could go back and get it and have a quiet word with Dermott. I had a feeling he was holding something back and I couldn't understand why he kept pretending that it was *my* door he was found outside when in fact he couldn't have had the foggiest idea; by the time the ambulance men arrived he was in the middle of the landing, an equal distance from both doors, and he didn't come round then anyway.'

Posy was making bubbles with vigorous arm movements in the last of Jenny's Christmas bubble-bath. It took up all her time and energy and both Jenny and Sue, who kept their voices low, had a job to hear themselves speak above the swishings and the sloshings and the shrill little voice inventing songs as she beat the water into foam.

'I see. What did Dermott say when you asked him?'

'He said he didn't know any more than we did, but as the chap crashed his fist into Dermott's face, he'd said something like, "That's for Jenny", or he thought that was what had been said. But he wouldn't tell anyone, not even the police, because it would only lead to unnecessary trouble for you.'

Jenny's hands flew to her mouth. 'Oh, my God, Dirk thought . . . and I know where he got the idea, too. After you'd gone home and Dermott had got so drunk, Bill and I brought him home in a taxi, and when I was seeing Bill off he said something about staying because I might have a job to get Dermott into bed . . . Dirk must have been hiding in the laurels, I saw someone there earlier . . . oh, how shall I face Dermott, after this? What must he think of me?'

'He'll think you had a lucky escape the day Dirk chucked you out,' Sue said matter-of-factly. 'Look, it wasn't your fault, Dermott really asked for trouble getting as tight as that. I suppose Dirk sneaked in as soon as he had a chance and heard Dermott's drunken singing or snoring coming from his room and went in. You know Dermott said he couldn't see a thing? Well, he couldn't, not because it was dark but because the hall light was shining right into his eyes, and he didn't want to tell anyone that because he wanted people to think it was simply a case of mistaken identity or even a drunken brawl. Actually, he likes you very much and was probably quite flattered to be taken for your lover by a jealous husband.'

'Flattered?' Jenny laughed bitterly. 'Flattened, you mean. And why on earth should he like me enough to keep quiet and let Dirk off? Are you *sure* he knows?'

'Jenny, what's the matter with you? You're very attractive, didn't you know?'

Jenny pulled a face. 'Dermott's keener on you than he is on me! I've often thought . . .'

'Keen on *me*?' Sue went pink. She tightened her lips for a moment and then shook her head at her friend. 'My dear Jenny, how naïve you are, haven't you guessed why Dermott got drunk? He's in love with Solly!'

Hours later, in bed but far from sleep, Jenny was still going over what Sue had said, but more and more slowly, like an old gramophone when it needs rewinding. Dermott in love with Solly? Incredible! Solly had gone off with one of the chorus – eh?, eh? – so did Sue mean that Dermott had got himself sloshed because his woman – man – was unfaithful? That was mad, because Solly was such a masculine bloke, dark and intense and not a bit limp-wristed and Dermott was charming too, always flirting with one of the girls.

Of course they did share a flat.

But how could anyone think Solly was gay? Or Dermott for

304

that matter. It was ridiculous, Sue must have said it to shock her. Bill had never intimated such a thing, though when she thought about it, the subject had never in fact come up. Well, why should it? And at the Christmas party Dermott had got very cuddly indeed with anyone who would, and that meant most. Solly had not been slow in the cuddle stakes either. Did people like that try to make each other jealous, just as though they were . . . well, what? Well, just as if they were people like me, Jenny thought. No, the whole idea's absurd, Sue's gone off her rocker.

Only they do share a flat.

Then there was the night Dermott had kissed her outside the bathroom when she had come back from the farm and had been bedraggled and distressed. Now why should he have kissed her, because it certainly was not to make anyone else jealous. It had been before Solly joined them, for a start. And think of the way Dermott was always wandering around in his pyjama trousers, with all that lovely bare chest showing . . . he didn't use perfume or grow his hair. Sue had got her wires crossed, that was it!

There's a double bed in the flat. And the single bed's too narrow for anyone but Posy or a similarly small-sized child to get a good night's sleep in.

Shut up. Absurd. Solly isn't a *huge* man, probably he's quite comfortable in that little bed.

Dermott had tried to woo the girls into bed with him, when he had been far too drunk for pretence. Yes, but Sue had said that some men were . . . what was the word? . . . well, it was like hairdressers, unisex. What it meant was that there were men who had male lovers *and* female lovers. Hermaphrodites. Only that wasn't what Sue had said, she had used a much more modern term.

But Dermott and Solly, in bed together? Aaargh! Jenny closed her eyes tightly and told her mind to stop indulging in filthy thoughts and let her get some sleep.

'Letter for you, Sukie. Foreign, again. Who's a lucky girl, then?' Brenda whizzed the letter across the room and Sue, breast-feeding Timmy, fielded it with one hand, a smile spreading across her face.

305

'Bless you Bren, I adore letters! How's things?'

Brenda came right into the room and pulled the door shut; Sue, longing to open her letter which was a fat and crinkly one, still saw the shy pleasure on Brenda's small fair face and smiled encouragingly. It was difficult to reconcile the Brenda you knew with the brassy little creature who had all the answers and could handle the most awkward customers in the Private Shop, but she had done it to the best of her ability. Brenda had simply managed to erect an excellent mask behind which, presumably, she blushed as much as ever, only nobody saw.

'Things are great; you know Simon?'

Sue chuckled. Since Christmas most of Brenda's conversation reminded one of the kiddies' game 'Simon Says' because that was the phrase with which Brenda prefaced most remarks. And Simon had been Brenda's guest at the Christmas party and at the theatre party too, only he had not been present at the end due to a previous engagement. His not being there had meant Brenda had been rather withdrawn. . . did her sudden wish to talk mean that Simon had declared himself?

'Yes, we all know Simon. What's he done?'

'Asked me home for the weekend, to meet his parents and his sister Jane and brother Gerald.'

'Gosh,' Sue said, suitably impressed. 'Are you excited? What does it mean, do you think?'

'Well, if they're there, it means he's fairly serious, I think. And if they're not . . .', she shivered, clasping her arms round herself, her face reflecting the fact that, whichever way it went, she was anticipating an exciting weekend, '. . . well, if they're not, I suppose it means he fancies me, at least!'

'That's nice, because you'll get a lift home, I suppose . . . or will you go straight to his house?'

Brenda sometimes went back to Chester for the odd weekend, though ever since her infatuation for Simon had really got into its swing she was less and less keen to return to the bosom of her own family. There was always the chance that Simon might turn up on Saturday and take her out for the evening, so she would hang around the flat, bathed and perfumed in a housecoat and her prettiest undies, hoping that he would arrive.

'Oh, we'll go straight to his place. It's a big house in Queen's Park, with a lot of land – well, Jane has a horse!'

'Well, I'm happy for you and I hope you have a lovely time,' Sue said sincerely. 'But remember, Brenda, everyone sets their own worth; don't spend all your time thinking how wonderful Simon is and how lucky you are, the boot is really on the other foot.'

'Oh yes, but Simon really is rather special, Sue.'

Sue smiled and gave up. No use reminding Brenda how Jenny had been just like that; wildly in love with an older man, never critical, never questioning his automatic assumption of authority over her. Look where that had ended – only Brenda could not look, Simon filled her vision. Sometimes Sue wondered whether it would be a kindness to tell Brenda about Jenny's reason for leaving the shop, proving that Simon had, if not feet of clay, at least some odd tastes, but of course she would never actually do it. She was fairly sure, though, that he had kept Brenda at arm's length for so long, when the girl was plainly pining to jump into bed with him, because he had a sneaking suspicion that she might be a party to his secret passion for life-sized rubber dolls!

'All right, love, you'll learn like we all do – the hard way. Off with you and thanks for the post.'

Brenda left, closing the door gently behind her, and baby Tim burped and pushed with small clenched fists into the softness of Sue's breast, indicating that it was pretty well empty as far as he was concerned. Sue put him over her shoulder, rubbed his small solid back, sung him a verse or two of a very unsuitable song – she really must remember to forget the words some time – and then stuck him, like a determined little limpet, to the other nipple.

As he drank she gazed longingly at the airmail envelope. A reply, perhaps, to her letter telling Hugo about Tim! It had been ages and ages, but then it had probably been ages and ages before he had received her letter with its ecstatic description and the photos. But of course she could not open it, not whilst she was feeding Tim.

Presently, Tim finished, was draped across her shoulder

307

again and was then offered – and enthusiastically accepted – a helping of delicious groats. After the groats a certain something in the air decided Sue to change his nappy – not a moment before time, she chided him, lovingly washing his small pointed bottom and what she described as his absolutely enormous potentials – and then she powdered him, selected a clean nappy with a soft pad inside, fitted his small legs into a voluminous pair of rubber knickers, and settled him in the crook of her arm where he lay lazily smiling every time he caught her eye.

His smile, Sue decided, was terrific, the most terrific thing about him. The first time he had smiled, at barely five weeks, she had been completely bowled over; all she had wanted from life was another of those sudden looks of ecstatically happy recognition. But now, blasé after a thousand of his smiles, she demanded more. He had a gurgling laugh, a bit like a kitten's purr, which enchanted her. She talked and sang to him, wrinkling her nose, pulling a face, until his laugh could no longer contain itself and purred out on to the air, and only then did she stand up, hold him to her face, give him his six kisses – two butterfly ones with her long lashes, one on each cheek, one on the nose and one on the chin – and pop him into his pram.

She had permission to park the pram in the small front garden, and when the weather was sufficiently clement there he would lie, with the cat-net over the front of the hood, breathing in the fresh sea air and, Sue told him, growing bigger muscles than Mr Universe.

Getting the pram down the stairs was the cause of great hilarity for them both, because sometimes she jerked it a bit and Timmy bounced, which he enjoyed, and sometimes she pretended to go faster than she wanted to, and that made him smile too. Of course it would have been very much easier to wheel the pram down empty and then to stow Timmy away in his blankets but not, Sue thought, such fun. Thus Timmy bumped down the stairs and Sue concentrated on wondering about her letter.

Back up in the flat, she looked at it, narrow-eyed, trying to guess from its feel, its weight and even the smell of it, whether it was a good letter or a medium-good one or a best one. She held it up to the light; she could see nothing, not even the traces of Hugo's much loved, elegantly curved writing.

'A cup of coffee whilst I read and digest would be nice,' Sue said aloud, and put the letter down in order to fill the kettle. As she was standing it on the gas ring, however, she made a horrible discovery. Sue Oliver, she said sternly to herself, you're afraid to open this letter. You're so proud of Hugo, you love him so much, yet you dare not open the envelope in case fear and anger and despair come tumbling out. Now how could you think Hugo would react like that to something as glorious as Timmy?

She picked up the letter and found that her heart was pounding; she slit the envelope open and pulled out the thin pages covered with the familiar writing. For a moment her heart missed a beat – no pictures? No funny, beautiful, comic little pictures to help her to see what he saw? Then, with a real effort of will, she spread out the first sheet and began to read.

Ten minutes later, with tears pouring down her cheeks, Sue realized that the kettle was leaping and bubbling and laid the sheets down to make her cup of coffee. He was not just pleased about Tim, he was as ecstatic as she! He must have been mad, he wrote, to try to prevent a generous, motherly person like his Sue giving birth and loving her offspring. Naturally, any son of theirs would be exceptional . . . he could not wait to see the baby for himself, he had boasted all round the camp about his son, had shown the photos to every single man on the expedition, had bored them all to tears by reading or quoting extracts from Sue's letter. How had she managed to keep it a secret from all their friends? He was bitterly ashamed that his attitude had almost caused her to end her pregnancy and now he thanked God for her strength of purpose which had made her carry their child full term. But he was not so selfish that he was indifferent to the difficulties of childbirth and bringing up a baby with him so far away. How was she? . . . Was she fit and well? She must write again, at once, and this time she must tell him the bad as well as the good, she must not try to keep things from him. Left to his own devices he might not have thought it wise

309

to bring children into the world, but now that it was done, a fait accompli, nothing could thrill him more. He wished she had trusted him, yet he knew what agony her pregnancy would have been; now he could enjoy to the full the thrill of knowing he had fathered a beautiful baby boy with none of the fears for her well-being which would otherwise have made the waiting hideous.

By the time she had re-read the letter half a dozen times and almost knew it by heart, Sue was so full of happiness that she could no longer sit still. She jumped up and reached for her coat, glancing at her wrist watch as she did so; good, it was nearly twelve o'clock, she would wheel Tim to the Botanical Gardens, go in and have her lunch there and then walk home with Jenny. And during the walk home, she would tell her friend about Hugo for the first time. She had never mentioned his name to a soul here in Rhyl; even when she had decided that she could never part with her baby, it had still seemed too much of a risk to admit that she was Hugo Franklyn's wife. But now, now that he had said he was thrilled, had made it plain that their child meant as much to him as it did to her, there could be no harm in admitting that she was not a single-parent family at all, that Timmy would have the most marvellous father in the world to help bring him up.

Because she was so ecstatically happy herself she wanted Jenny to be happy too. Walking along, well-muffled against the cold, she planned how she would organize Jenny's life. First, she would get her divorced, then she would find some way of improving Bill's lot so that he could afford to divorce Daphne, marry Jenny, and take on an extra child. It was quite easy really; all they had to do was to get a good detective chasing after Daphne, so that Bill could name the fellow she was living with as co-respondent, and then she could persuade him to sell the cafe and move up to London, where a man with his abilities – and a heavy-goods vehicle licence – could hardly fail to be not only appreciated but also paid accordingly. That this would also keep Jenny within shouting distance of herself was no small part of Sue's dreaming; a beautiful and intelligent young woman, she had made a great many friends in her time but none had suited her quite so well as Jenny. Thinking about it now, she decided that Jenny was brave, particularly brave because she had had so little experience of relying on herself. Yet when the chips were down she had taken her dismissal unflinchingly and had set about making a life for herself. Sue knew that hundreds of women did it everyday, but not, she thought, girls who had been teenage brides, who had spent twenty years being coddled and ordered about and had then been flung out into the harsh world, not merely alone but with a small child to bring up. When we first met, Sue mused, striding along the pavement with the pram bouncing briskly over the uneven paving stones, when we first met Jenny knew nothing; she had only recently discovered that a man could be gay without looking like Danny la Rue in drag, she had never really handled money, she had never in her life done a paid day's work. Yet look at her now! She had worked in a shop and a cafe, she managed her finances neatly and well, she had even sorted out her emotions to the point where she could steadfastly refuse to return to Dirk, despite the moral blackmail of being desperately needed which Dirk had dished out. Jenny was quite a girl.

And Bill? *He's just my Bill*, Sue hummed beneath her breath, *an ordinary guy, you'd meet him in the street and never notice him*. That was true, all right, but she could see why Jenny seemed to like him so much. He was steady, dependable, sensitive to the feelings of others, all things which Dirk was not; the complete opposite of Jenny's husband, in fact. Secretly, Sue felt that Jenny would be a little wasted on Bill; comparing him with Hugo caused Bill to shrink in stature to not just an ordinary guy but to a boring and stodgy guy, but – fortunately – no woman ever saw her own man or someone else's through quite the same eyes. Jenny would naturally think Hugo wonderful, but she would not want to marry him. It was odd, now that she thought about it, because Jenny was strong, yet she wanted someone she could lean on. And if I'm honest Hugo isn't like that, he's still pretty unsure, Sue reminded herself. Yet nevertheless I'd walk to hell and back barefoot for Hugo. I don't believe I'm nearly as strong as Jenny, yet I don't need to lean on my man. Perhaps we stand upright together, she thought rather smugly; yes, that's it, we're together because we like to be, not because we need the other one.

Five hundred yards further along the pavement she knew she had got it all wrong, because she needed Hugo like a wilting plant needs water and he needed her. Perhaps, she thought dolefully, it was Jenny and Bill who were the free-standing models, whilst she and Hugo lolled pitifully against one another, spaghetti-legged.

The thought made her smile; she was still smiling as she wheeled the pram into the cafe.

'Sweetheart, when people have really rotten colds and sore throats the best place is bed, honest. But since it's not a busy month at the cafe, Daddy's given me time off and I'll be with you all day – until he gets home, in fact. Now this is my very own lemon-barley water, this is our portable radio, and I'm going to make your favourite lunch, so don't cry because it only makes your eyes red.'

Jenny spoke coaxingly, sitting on the end of Erica's bed, patting the child's hot and sticky hand. Erica was one of those unfortunate children who run very high temperatures and become delirious as soon as their tonsils become infected. The last time it had happened, a whole year ago, Bill had been forced to close the cafe for a week until the child's illness had yielded to medication, but now he had been glad to let Jenny take over.

'I'm not hungry,' Erica whined, snatching her hand out of Jenny's and rearing up in bed. She was scarlet-faced and glassy-eyed and looked as ill as she probably felt. 'I *must* go to school, I must! I'm the little girl in the play . . . Sarah wants it, Miss'll give it to Sarah if I'm not there . . . I *must* go to school!'

'Oh, didn't you know, Sarah's away as well,' Jenny lied cheerfully. Erica was a sensible little girl, it was the delirium talking. The doctor had been in earlier and handed out a prescription for antibiotic which Louisa-next-door had taken to a chemist to be dispensed, and had advised Jenny to keep her patient cool, give her lots of drinks and try to calm her down a bit.

'Is she?' Erica fell back on her pillows but kept turning her

312

head restlessly against the linen. 'Are you *sure*? What about Sharon? Sharon reads ever so well . . . suppose Miss gives it to Sharon?' She sat up again and pushed impatiently at the covers. 'Oh, I *must* go to school, she'll give it to Sharon, I know she will, she likes Sharon, she says Sharon never wiggles.'

Jenny's lips twitched; it was impossible to deny that Erica, whether in imitation or by natural inclination, had a sexy wiggle in her walk which accorded ill with the normal hipless, bustless and waistless shape of a seven-year-old. No doubt she had got the part for her reading and acting ability, and because of the waist-length golden hair that parents, particularly fathers, found so appealing, but Jenny, who had read the play, did not think that it was type-casting. Sometimes she thought that her biggest contribution to Bill's well-being was the fact that, under the influence of Posy and Dawn, with her own example before them, she was teasing and persuading Erica to act like a child instead of a miniature chorus girl. Poor Erica, what an inheritance Daphne had given her; a premature adulthood which sat oddly on her skinny little shoulders and made her so self-aware that she could not walk past a shop window without gazing – critically – at her own reflection. She was forever tugging down her skirts, touching her hair, anxiously running her hands over her completely flat bosom. Once, after a trip to the baths when Jenny and the three children were all changing in the same small cubicle, Jenny had observed Erica to be closely examining her small, pearly armpits in the hope of finding a strand or two of hair. It made her want to laugh and to cry, because Ricky's childhood was liable to be fleeting enough without her actually wishing it away.

But now it was clear that her charge's obsession with the play was not going to aid her recovery. Jenny poured out some lemon-barley water and tried to hand the glass to Erica, who hit out at it, spilling some on the floor and a few drops on the bed.

'No, Auntie Jen, I won't take medicine. I'm not ill, I've got to get to school.'

'Right, then,' Jenny said, deciding to take the doctor's advice albeit obliquely; he had said to keep the child cool, after all. 'Straight into the bathroom, young lady, and I'll run you a nice tepid bath so that you can be all clean and tidy for school.'

Erica swayed to her feet; poor lamb, Jenny thought, she doesn't know who she is, let alone where, but she led the child along to the bathroom, wrapped her loosely in Bill's green silk dressing gown and sat her on the cork-topped stool whilst she ran the water. Presently, when the bath was full enough, she took Erica's things off and lifted her into the water.

It helped, there was no doubt about it. Erica sighed, leaned back and closed her eyes. Jenny began to wash her down with a flannel, letting the just-warm water trickle down across Erica's burning hot chest and back, her thin arms, even her flaming countenance. She continued with the quiet soothing motion until the child really did seem cooler and was definitely a good deal calmer, and then she lifted her out and sat her on her knee with a towel wrapped loosely around her.

'Well, sweetie? Feel a bit better?'

'Yes, much.' Erica opened her eyes and looked up at Jenny; her cheeks were still flushed but her eyes had a calmer look and her lids were heavy. 'I wish you were my own mummy; you are kind, Auntie Jen.'

'That's a lovely thing to say,' Jenny said, gently patting Erica's small body dry with the towel. 'But you do have a mummy of your own, though she's away at the moment. Do you remember her well, Ricky? But of course you do, it's Dawn who has difficulty.'

'I 'member; she had hair like mine. I suppose she's having a lovely time now, heavenly, always wearing beautiful dresses and one of those gold things in her hair.'

'Probably,' Jenny said doubtfully. Was a child's idea of living in sin so clear, then? Jewellery and dresses? But she knew Erica well enough to realize that they were Erica's idea of heaven and had probably been her mother's, so when Daphne had announced she was going to better herself and have more fun, jewellery and dresses would naturally spring to the child's mind – and probably to the mother's, as well.

'But I still wish you were mine, Auntie Jen. Hello, that's what I meant.'

314

Jenny picked up her burden and put her cool cheek against Erica's hot one. Poor mite, she was not going to be right for a while yet, but she was so sleepy, her lids were halfway down over her eyes and her head lolled heavily on Jenny's shoulder. If only she could settle down and go to sleep until Louisa and the antibiotic arrived, then she might forget about the play and her part in it.

Later, Jenny was placidly peeling potatoes at the kitchen sink when the back door burst open and Bill came quickly into the room. Jenny raised her brows and glanced at her wristwatch; it was not quite two o'clock.

'Hello, what's the matter? You're supposed to be coming home when school's out!'

Bill was flushed; it was clear he had been hurrying, for his chest heaved and he had taken off his overcoat despite the freezing cold wind which had seldom seemed to drop for the past few weeks.

'I was worrying all morning about Ricky; what's she been like? She can talk such twaddle when she's delirious, poor kid, and I didn't want you worried or upset.'

'You must think me a pretty poor person to be worried by a delirious child,' Jenny said, trying not to sound as hurt as she felt. It was clear he had not trusted her to look after Erica. 'She was talking rather wildly, but she's sound asleep now. Do you want to take a look at her?'

'I don't want to wake her,' Bill said. He was looking a bit shifty; clearly he realized Jenny felt he could not trust her with his sick daughter. 'Look, I'm sorry, love, I didn't mean . . .' He put his hands on her shoulders and kissed her lightly on the mouth, then drew back and smiled down at her. 'I know you'll make a much better job of nursing Ricky than I could. It was just that she can say odd things, hurtful things, when she's like that and I didn't want . . . did she mention her mother?'

'Well, yes, she did.'

'Oh? What did she say?'

'That she was like her because they had similar hair, I think it was, and then she said she wished I was her mother, which touched me rather, and then something else about

Daphne wearing beautiful dresses and jewellery all day long, now.'

'Nothing upsetting?' He looked immensely relieved. 'There, I shouldn't have worried, I'm a fool. But if she'd made you feel unwanted . . .'

'Bill, love, if she'd screamed "Go away, you're not my mother!" I would have understood, I would have known it was the fever talking and not Ricky! Look, since you're here now, would you prefer to stay with her and send me for the other two? I can take Belle, the walk won't hurt her – in fact it will do her good, she doesn't get enough exercise.'

She expected him to refuse, to say that he would stay with her and then go off to get the children, but instead he nodded, then went through to the hall to hang his coat on the hideous coat-rack which stood in one corner.

'Yes, it might be better. I'll give her the medicine when she wakes and see she's comfy. Then you and Posy can bring Dawn home and we'll all have tea together. I meant to bring something from the cafe but in my rush I forgot; I suppose you wouldn't like to nip in when you call for the kids and pop some chops in your basket?'

'There's a stew and some dumplings on the back of the stove,' Jenny said, striving to make her voice sound light and careless. It was awful to realize that, for all his loving ways, he did not trust her to take care of Ricky, not even for the half hour it would take him to fetch the children. But then he came back into the kitchen, put his arms round her and rested his chin on her hair.

'Who loves you, Jenny-wren? Is she sleeping very soundly?' His hands moved up from her waist and he cradled her breasts in his palms. Jenny's heartbeats and breathing quickened. 'Shall we have a cuddle?'

Now was her chance to show him just how much she cared for Erica; to put him in his place furthermore. She opened her mouth to give him a piece of her mind just as he began to move the palms of his hands in a circular motion across her nipples, hardening them, she told herself, against her will.

'Bill, no, don't, you shouldn't . . .'

He began to kiss the back of her neck, then the side just under her ear. He took her earlobe between his teeth, nipping

316

very gently, and then released it to kiss her again, moving his mouth across to her throat, not an easy manoeuvre from the back.

'Is she sound asleep, sweetheart?' He groaned when she did not answer and turned her to face him. 'Pretty, sweet-lips, honey-Jenny, come to bed with me?'

She did not answer but he could read her desire in her face. He put his arm round her waist and led her upstairs. They peeped in at Erica who was sleeping as deeply as anyone could wish and breathing stentoriously enough to be accused of snoring, then he led her through to his bedroom.

She had never been in there officially before, only taking a peep on her way to the bathroom. Now she registered hazily that it had a plum-coloured carpet and that the bedspread, curtains and the upholstery on the two little chairs were all made of cream damask. The walls were colour-washed cream and the paintwork was white. It was a pleasant room, not at all Daphne-ish.

Bill jerked back the bedspread, then the rest of the covers. He was looking at her with hot and hopeful eyes and once he had arranged the bed to his satisfaction he came over to her and began to undress her with a speed and dexterity which came, she feared, of long practice.

When she was bare he rolled her between the sheets and undressed himself with equal speed, then got in beside her. He began to kiss and fondle her very gently, making her feel precious and desired until she began to stir restlessly, pushing against him, wanting more, and only then did he move over on to her.

It took them twenty delicious minutes to reach the climax of their love-making by which time Jenny had forgotten his distrust, his wish to be with Erica whilst she went out and fetched the other two. What did it matter, when he loved her so much? She could not deny he loved her, nor that she loved him. It was not simply that he made love better than she had ever dreamed anyone could, nor that he led her down paths of enjoyment which she had not known a woman could tread, it was the fact that he always ensured her fulfilment before allowing himself his own special moment and indeed, out of bed he was the same. Unselfishness was a way of life with him, he could never grab for what he wanted until he had made sure that she was satisfied.

Sated and dreamy, Jenny pushed damp hair off her forehead, rolled on to her back, and contemplated the ceiling. She saw out of the corner of her eye that the bedroom door was slightly open and was glad, because if Erica did wake and call they could be with her in seconds. Then Bill pulled the covers back. She gave a murmur of protest – it felt cold with the sweat still trickling between her breasts – but he persisted, gently but firmly.

'I've never asked before, love, but I want to look at you.'

'It's too cold,' Jenny muttered. She stared down at herself. 'All you'll see is goose-bumps.'

'And other, nicer, bumps.' He ran his hand lightly down the length of her body, making her shiver. 'You've got skin like double cream. You've got brownish hair but pink nipples. You've got the most beautiful bum in the world, like a lovely white peach, and a little bitty waist I could span with my two hands. I adore your feet, most women have ugly feet but yours are clean and pink, with dear little skinny straight toes. Can I kiss your belly-button?'

'I really don't think that would be advisable, Mr Bradley,' Jenny said primly, rolling over and sitting up. 'Give you an inch and heaven alone knows what you'd take. It's time I got respectable, we can't spend all afternoon carrying on something dreadful, as Mrs Twigg would say.'

'Unfortunately you're right, I need at least thirty minutes to recover between bouts,' Bill said. He got out of bed and began to dress. 'There's nothing like a spot of bed-in-the-afternoon to set a fellow up.'

'That's one advantage of owning your own business,' Jenny began, reaching for her bra. 'When you feel like it you can close early. Chuck me my blouse and jumper, would you?'

They were both dressed and downstairs before Erica stirred again and then Bill ran up to her so that Jenny could put on her coat, her scarf, her woolly bobble hat and her thick boots. Outside snow had begun to fall and the wind had dropped. Belle, excited at the thought of a walk, began to dance around the hall, her toenails clicking and skidding on the tiles. In the kitchen the potatoes waited to be pulled over on to the heat, the stew was simmering, there was an apple crumble in the oven and the milk for a custard was in the pan. Jenny's body glowed through her clothes, comforted by love-making and looking forward now to a brisk walk with a meal to follow. Just as she was about to set out Bill came down the stairs. He was smiling.

'Took her medicine like a lamb and fell asleep again, but she asked where her Auntie Jen was!'

'There you see, I didn't neglect her!'

'As if I thought you had!' He walked across to her, both hands held out – and fell over Belle, cavorting round the floor in anticipation of her walk. Jenny laughed, Belle grunted and Bill, scrambling to his feet, laughed too. 'So much for a last cuddle before you set off into the storm – crumbs, look at it, that snow's really horizontal! Look, perhaps I'd better . . .'

But in this at least Jenny would stick to her guns. She opened the back door and then had to raise her voice above the sounds of the wind whirling the snow past them.

'No, I'm all ready, I'll go. Be back before you know it, so have our dinner ready!'

After she had gone Bill made a cup of coffee and then began to set the table for tea. She was a marvellous girl, his Jenny; not many women could have seen his stupid panic without taking offence and being stiff and nasty about it. Fool that he was, why had he worried? What could Ricky have said, when all things were considered? But he could not forget how Ricky had once given Daphne's game away with a vengeance whilst in the grip of a delirious fever. He had come home after a long journey right across the continent and had asked where Mummy had been when he had telephoned the previous night.

'Been? Nowhere,' the youthful Ricky had said pettishly, putting her hot little face against his. 'She was in bed. She and Uncle Harry.'

He could still remember the feeling in his stomach, as if he'd been kicked by an elephant. Odd how physical it had been . . . he had struggled to get his breath, unable even to move, glued in a half-crouching position beside the child's bed with his mouth open and his brain rigid with shock. No doubt a pitiable, even an amusing sight.

That had been the first and worst moment of disillusion, though God knew others had followed thick and fast. By the time she had left, her leaving had been one long sigh of relief for them all, yet even so he could not bear to think that Ricky might make some remark which could hurt Jenny. What Erica had told him had been no more than the truth, yet the pain of it was still there, faint and faded, perhaps, but not entirely forgotten.

Nevertheless, it was all over, Daphne's viciousness, the way she blamed him for all her inadequacies as a mother and inconstancies as a wife, even her come-to-bed eyes and her full pouting mouth were forgotten, another's problem now, thank God. The present was what mattered, and the present was Jenny's supple and generous body, her clear eyes and loving spirit. He had never thought it possible that he could love someone so much, far less that someone would love him in return. Incredible, unbelievable good fortune – to have found her and made her his! Six months ago the future had held only hard work and loneliness. Now he had the best of good reasons to work and, whilst he had Jenny, no possibility of being lonely.

On the stove, the potatoes came to the boil. Bill strolled over, turned down the gas and opened the oven door for a quick glance. Everything was looking good, so when the kids came in from school they could eat. And Jenny . . . he would take her in his arms, taste the chilly fresh air on her skin, hug her slender strength and marvel all over again at his good fortune.

'Dadeeeee! Can I have a drink of water?'

Bill, pouring the water into a glass and then adding the orange juice, grinned and padded across the kitchen in the direction of the stairs – the oldest trick in the world, kids must have been saying that ever since water was invented! He raised his voice to a reassuring shout:

'Coming, love!'

CHAPTER TWELVE

March had arrived in like a lion but it seemed to be leaving like a lamb, Sue thought, washing nappies in the kitchen sink. First it had been bitterly cold, then had come the rain and gales, and now there was a boisterous but mild wind, a good bit of sunshine, and down in the small yards and sooty front gardens buds were bursting with almost audible pops.

The winter of our discontent is over, Sue told herself, vigorously scrubbing a stained patch away and seeing the nappy become white once more. Not that we were discontented, on the whole; we're a happy little crowd one way and another. Brenda was going steady with Simon, Anna had a job and for the moment, had settled down with a long, thin weed of a lad with a squeaky voice and a rich father. Mouse was fancy free and saving up to go abroad in the summer. She spoke good French and hoped to get work over there during the holiday months; then she said, when Mrs Grant was looking for next year's winter lets, she might come back.

Jenny was divorcing Dirk; it might not sound a particularly happy situation but it was, because Jenny's lovely air of calm certainty had increased and her guilt over Dermott had grown less. She had explained to him what had happened and they were good friends, though sometimes Sue saw her friend looking at Dermott with the fascinated air of one who observes a man from Mars and knew that she was still wondering whether he really was gay or whether Sue had been having her on.

Dermott was alone in the flat because Solly had finished his job and gone back to London. He was just the same, only not quite so beautiful; sometimes he was sad about his scars and the new nobble on his nose but usually he protested that he looked better, attracted more women with his virile, craggy face.

The Grants were preparing for the summer; Mr Grant had been seen to don a boiler suit and go outside to tend the garden, which was all of four foot by ten. Jenny had been fascinated to see him fastidiously pruning a rose tree, stooping to pick up the soggy piles of last autumn's leaves, which had blown into the corners, with his stoutly gloved hands and finally disturbing the earth – you could not call it digging – with a miniature garden fork. Jenny was a keen gardener herself Sue gathered, and had offered to help Bill, another avid gardener. They had apparently spent a happy weekend in Bill's back garden, digging and planting a variety of vegetables which would mature and ripen during the summer.

The Twiggs did not undo their winter barricades until May was over, Mrs Twigg informed them, but they no longer shut themselves away quite so firmly. Mrs Twigg could be seen pottering along the beach collecting shells and Bernard spent every available minute with his pigeons, carting them off in small, dirty vans to unknown destinations and then standing in the yard for hours, whatever the weather, welcoming them home.

The most important member of the household was twelve weeks old now, had a quiff of toffee-coloured hair and beamed with pleasure when familiar faces swam into his vision. He sang endlessly to himself, could blow quite sizeable bubbles and pick up his toys, taking them straight to his mouth for final identification. He had dimpled knees and elbows and was deliciously ticklish around his fat little neck. He had a crow of pleasurable excitement which the entire house knew well, and he was obviously going to be an animal-lover since even a glimpse of Belle brought his wide smile and squeaks of excitement into being; you could see he thought her kisses so wonderfully sloppy, her thick black-and-white fur so delightfully tuggable.

Letters from Hugo were rare but one had arrived only the previous day, and Sue was still at the stage where she read it every hour or so. He had written it soon after the letter rejoicing in Tim's arrival and he advised her to stay where she was, not to go back to London because they might have to reconsider remaining in the flat. It was a lovely letter, all the lovelier because of his obvious delight in the new fatherly feelings he experienced towards his son; clean air and country

322

food, Hugo wrote authoritatively, will make a mountaineer of him.

Fortunately, Mrs Grant had informed all her tenants that, provided they could leave their rooms in immaculate condition when they left, they would not actually be required to vacate them until just before the Spring Bank Holiday. 'She's 'ad no luck with her adverts, poor Clara,' Mrs Twigg revealed in the wake of their landlady's stately departure. 'Every year she puts 'em out, but mostly the lets start come June and not many of them till school 'olidays.'

With Hugo advising her against a return to London, Sue was content with her lot and with Jenny's; it gave her time to arrange something about Bill. Stupid man, he continued to look at Jenny, when he thought no one was watching, as if she were . . . as if she were Timmy, yet he had not even suggested she move in with him when she had to leave Beechcroft Road. Sue had no idea whether Bill and Jenny slept together and wondered doubtfully whether there was a human being on earth so wedded to the conventions that he would not touch a woman other than his wife . . . well, not *touch* precisely, she reminded herself, thinking of some passionate embraces in the hallway which she had glimpsed from the first landing, but make love to.

Still, whatever the reason, she would find time in the next few weeks to sort that couple out. They acted married, she told herself crossly, so they really might as well be married and have done with it. Oh, perhaps not actually in a church or a registry office – she understood the difficulties there – but living together was as good until the divorces came through.

It was quiet in the cafe now in the afternoon, but come four o'clock, sometimes earlier, trade began to pick up again. The bowls players were back in force, Jenny told Sue, and schoolchildren wanted to play on the swings and slides and then come into the cafe for ices and pop. One way and another, although they could not deny that their trade was largely seasonal, the cafe was doing well enough to support the five of them. So why . . .

The door, which Sue had left ajar so she could hear Timmy out on the front if he started to cry, crashed open.

Sue gave a startled glance over her shoulder, only partially relaxing when she recognized Dermott.

'Sue, I want . . .'

'Is Timmy all right?'

They spoke in chorus and then laughed together, whilst Dermott wagged a finger at her.

'You have the punch and I'll have the wish.'

'That only applies when you say the same thing, not when you speak at the same time,' Sue pointed out. '*Is* Timmy all right? Did you just come past the pram? It's in the front garden.'

'Yes, he's okay. Well, he didn't lean out and scream "stop that man" or anything, so I suppose that means he's okay. Look, I want to see the film at the big cinema this week, but I hate going alone. Would you like to come? I'll pay for you, naturally.'

'Sorry, Dermott, it's too complicated to organize unless I want to go out very badly. What's showing?' He told her and Sue shook her head. 'No, I'm not keen enough to start the babysitting manoeuvres. Sorry.'

'Why won't you come out with me?' Dermott asked bluntly. 'You came skiing that Sunday and I hoisted you into the theatre a couple of times. Why not now? And don't say it's Timmy, because you still go out with Jen when she can get away.'

'No real reason, I just don't want to see the film.'

'Oh balls,' Dermott said rudely. 'I'm keeping count, you know. I've asked you out eight times since skiing and you've turned me down on every single one. Don't you like me any more?'

'Sure, hon', you're one helluva guy,' Sue said in a transatlantic drawl. 'But I'm not into casual affairs, not with my husband coming home in about a month.'

'*Husband*?' Dermott's incredulity was rather pleasing since it reinforced Sue's view that Jenny – the only person she had told – really was capable of keeping a secret. Not that it mattered, she was most certainly not ashamed of Hugo, quite the opposite.

'Yes, husband. I'm married to Timmy's father. It's a bit complicated, but . . .'

'He didn't want children?' Dermott's eyes were understanding. 'I felt like that once, but not lately.'

'That's right, he didn't want children, not until he discovered he had one and then he was absolutely delighted. It was rotten of me to turn you down because of not wanting casual affairs, because I know very well you're just a friend, but . . .'

'No.' He cut across her sentence ruthlessly, a faint flush of colour mounting his cheeks. 'You were right, I've always fancied you. I'd hoped . . . but it doesn't matter – if I'd known you were married I'd have put it right out of my head.'

'I didn't say anything because I thought you and Solly had a thing going,' Sue said, highly daring. Was he gay? She had never really known; when she had told Jenny so, it was for a complexity of reasons most of which now made her feel ashamed. She wished most fervently that she had never said it because, true or false, it was a mean thing to do, to destroy Jenny's simple uncomplicated liking for Dermott. She would undo it now anyway, tell Jenny it was a stupid trick, no matter what Dermott said. He was staring at her, the colour in his face gradually deepening. He looked very young.

'Me and *Solly*? But he's a bloke!'

'Oh Dermott,' Sue moaned, putting down the wet nappy she was clutching and then picking it up again. 'If you weren't wild about Solly then why did you get so drunk at the end-of-season theatre party?'

'Because I was wild about someone else,' Dermott said. He was still looking stunned. 'Do you honestly mean to tell me that you thought I made love with that hairy little bugger? Or are you getting back at me for the way I've kidded you about breast-feeding and things?'

'Well, I . . . I suppose I leapt to conclusions. You're both involved with the theatre . . .'

'We're neither of us *actors*, you fool!' Dermott was looking a little less grim. 'What's more, not all actors are gay. By God, does Jenny . . .'

'Oh hell! If she does it's my fault, I made some stupid remark . . .'

'I could kill you,' Dermott said between gritted teeth. 'Of

325

all the stupid spiteful bitches . . .' He grabbed hold of her by the shoulders and shook her hard, until she bit her tongue and squawked, then he let her go. He was frowning, but it was puzzlement now more than anger. 'Look, you've got to tell me, what made you think I was queer?' He began to grin. 'Let alone poor Solly, the most heterosexual chap I know – God, wait till I tell him! Hey, didn't you think it was odd when he went off after the party with that Cindy girl?'

'No,' said the sophisticated Sue dolefully. 'I thought there were men who liked both – boys and girls, I mean – so when you talked about pulling the girls I thought that was just one side of you.'

'I suppose there are people like that about,' Dermott said, 'but I don't happen to know any, let alone be one! I admit there are a lot of gays in the theatre . . . look, if you'll come with me to the flicks I'll forgive you.'

'We-ell . . . you won't try and *prove* you aren't? Promise?'

Dermott was smiling now, his usual cheerful equable self. 'I promise. Apart from anything else, because you've got a husband lurking away somewhere in the background. Where is he? Abroad, I realize that, but where, and why away so long?'

Sue hesitated; she had not even told Jenny who Hugo was, because it sounded too much like boasting – my husband the Marquis of Carabis as Puss in Boots was wont to say – though she had admitted that he was a part of the climbing expedition in the Caucasus. Jenny had assumed, not unaturally, that his name was Hugo Oliver, but in any case her interest in the expedition, like most people's, would not amount to much until they were welcomed home as conquering heroes.

'He's on a climbing expedition, he's a mountaineer and an artist,' she said now. 'He should be home in a matter of weeks.' She could not stop the excitement from creeping into her voice. 'I'm . . . we're . . .' She could not go on; it was not fair on Dermott to throw her love for Hugo into his face.

'It's not Hugo Franklyn?' Dermott stared. 'Crumbs, my boyhood hero! You're not seriously telling me that you're Hugo Franklyn's woman? Gosh!'

'We've been married two years,' Sue said proudly. 'So now you know why Tim's special!'

'Now I know why you keep encouraging him to pretend to climb up your boobs,' Dermott said, grinning. 'Wait till he's got little hobnailed boots, like his Dad's, then you won't be so keen! Crumbs, I'm going to the flicks with Hugo Franklyn's woman!'

'Listen to that rain!' The girls were all squeezed into the kitchen, making toffee in one saucepan and fudge in another. Bill had said that if they made the sweets they could sell them on his counter and keep the profit. Almost at once a consortium had been formed, with Jenny as chief chef and the others as dogsbodies. Recipes had been found, heavy-bottomed pans purchased, and now the sweet-makers were boiling up their second lot; the first sweets, gaily wrapped and labelled 'Jenny's home-made fudge', 'toffee', 'sugar-almonds' or 'fondant' as the case might be, had sold as quickly as Bill had put them out on his counter, and everyone had been delighted with their extra pocket-money.

Now Mouse, with her head cocked, was drawing everyone's attention to the steady pounding of rain on the tree and the yard and on the roof above their heads.

'Bad for business,' Anna said, stirring her concoction. 'Why mustn't you stir fudge, Jen? It says you can in the recipe.'

'I don't know. You beat the hell out of it once it's cooked, but if you stir it you spoil it. How's the fondant coming on?'

'All right; phew, doesn't it smell sweet?'

'It 'ud be odd if it didn't! Are we really going to glaze popcorn, later? I adore making new things.' Sue had a huge blue-and-white striped apron on and her hair was tied back with a piece of ribbon from one of Tim's bootees. She looked the most professional of the lot but in fact she was largely renowned so far for her abilities as a taster; no one appreciated chocolate fudge as much as Sue, and it was she who had made the labels for the sweets in the form of a miniature bulging bag, with the lettering done, most professionally, in alternating black and red ink.

'Who's doing lunch?' Brenda enquired presently; she had icing-sugar dabs all over her face and a faint dusting on her hair, and she was hanging over the fudge, not daring to stir in view of Jenny's prohibition but obviously longing to do so.

'I am,' Sue said. 'Apart from the jacket potatoes it's all cold. We got some lovely salad stuff, didn't we, Jen, and Bill sold us some ham and cold chicken at cost, and I've made a trifle for afters.'

'Where is it, then?' Anna said, looking round as though she expected to see a feast laid out on the floor under the table.

'In my room, you idiot. I could scarcely set it out here, with people on every available surface and sweeties cooling, boiling and being shaped. When the spuds are ready, which will be in about twenty minutes, we'll repair chez moi and eat.'

'And this evening, when we normally have salads, I suppose we ought to cook our Sunday lunch, only I shan't feel like eating,' Mouse said a little mournfully. 'Usually I like Sundays because I eat my big meal at midday but all this money-making ruins that idea.'

'We're making sweets, not money,' Brenda said, grinning. 'Where's Dermott, by the way? Usually the whiff of food brings him running on a Sunday.'

'Gone out for a paper. Don't worry, he'll be back by the time those spuds are cooked. To be fair, he paid for the trifle ingredients so he's entitled to a share.'

'You were the one who was rather down on Dermott at one time,' Anna said suspiciously. 'What's changed your mind? You went to the flicks with him last week, didn't you?'

'Yes, I did. And I wasn't down on him, I just thought he'd bring dissent in his wake, and I was wrong. He's a nice bloke. Ah, turn on the radio would you, Mouse? There's a magazine programme on and a doctor's going to advise mothers how to bring out the best in their babies, and there's a feature on slimming as well.'

The radio had been pushed to the back of the various bags and jars of ingredients and more or less forgotten, but now Mouse brought it out and turned the switch. It was Sue's own small portable, an expensive and reliable model, and very popular on a Sunday evening because of its ability to transmit Radio 1 for the 'Top Twenty'.

'Which programme?' Mouse asked as music filled the air. 'I only know how to get Radio 1 and 2.'

'Ignoramus! It's on 4, actually; Jenny knows.' Sue waved a sticky spoon in time to the galloping tune which was being played. 'It starts in five minutes, it'll be the news, now.'

Jenny twiddled the knobs and presently an announcer's voice filled the room.

'. . . shelling in Beirut, followed by a car bomb, which . . . Extremists have claimed responsibility . . .'

No one was really listening. Sue cocked her head, her attention on the fondant which Anna was just shaping into pieces. Why not fondant babies, like jelly-babies only different, she was thinking, whilst her spoon beat time to the words now for lack of a tune.

'. . . has just reached us of our climbing expedition in the Caucasus . . .' A burst of laughter from Anna and Brenda caused Sue to start forward, hand out to turn up the sound. '. . . One man is feared dead and two others are injured. The missing man is believed to be the well-known climber and . . .', more laughter, '. . . Hugo Franklyn. He leaves a wife and child.'

'I think that fudge is just about ready to take off the heat,' Jenny was advising Brenda. 'Have you dropped it into cold water, like I told you?'

'Yes, Miss, of course, Miss,' Brenda said, sweeping a curtsey. 'You said beat it with a wooden spoon, but someone's nicked it.'

'No they haven't, it's just got hidden,' Jenny fished the spoon out and handed it to Brenda. 'Now, who's greasing the tins?'

'Sue is. Sue, can you chuck us . . . Oh!' Brenda stared round the room. 'Where's she gone?'

'Guiltily off to fetch more tins, I expect,' Jenny remarked. 'Mouse, can you chuck Brenda a greased tin, ducks? She hasn't begun beating yet but she feels the need of a tin or two.'

'Sue went off awfully suddenly, didn't she?' Jenny remarked uneasily five minutes later when Sue had not reappeared. In the back of Jenny's mind she felt that she knew why Sue had left, only she could not quite remember what had sparked it off. She closed her eyes . . . the radio, there had been something on the radio.

The magazine programme had started, someone with a sticky-sweet voice was droning on about little children. Sue had wanted to listen to this. Jenny went over to the set and began to twiddle the knobs. There were other programmes, news programmes; perhaps, if she heard one, she would find out why Sue had first turned the news up and then left them so suddenly without a word.

She found another channel on which the news was still being broadcast but tuned in only as the announcer said something about a tragedy in the Caucasus, and that further information would be provided as it reached the studio. She switched off and went over to Brenda, beating fudge with a will.

'Bren, did you hear that? Something about someone being killed on that Caucasus expedition. Sue's fellow was with them . . . did you hear who had been killed?'

'Well, it wasn't Sue's fellow, or at least I doubt it. It was that famous chap, the awfully good-looking one, Hugo Franklyn. She isn't shacked up with *him*, surely?'

'Are you sure? I didn't catch the name myself. But no, it wasn't Franklyn . . .' She broke off as the door opened and turned hopefully towards it but it was not Sue, it was Posy with Mrs Twigg hovering behind her. 'Oh hello, darling, come for lunch?'

'Is it ready?' Mrs Twigg propelled Posy ahead of her into the room. 'My, those sweets smell delicious, there's nothing like 'ome-made stuff I always say, my Bernard dearly loves a nice sticky chunk of toffee.' She turned as someone came up the stairs behind her and moved to on side. 'Sorry Dermott, dear, I didn't know it was you on the stairs.'

Dermott came into the room. He had a folded paper in one hand and his face was very pale. He looked round quickly, taking in all the details of the scene, then grabbed Jenny's arm and unfolded the paper to show the black banner headlines.

'Where in God's name is Sue? Have you seen this?'

'I don't know, she's gone . . . in her room? Downstairs, getting Timmy out of his pram?' But even as she spoke she was filled with fear because Dermott's eyes were foreboding and the hand that held the paper shook slightly. 'Dermott, it's all right, I know her fellow was on that expedition but only one man's been killed – a famous mountaineer, Hugo Franklyn. She's married to a Hugo, but to Hugo Oliver, of course.'

'No she's not. She kept her maiden name because of her job; she's actually Mrs Franklyn. My God, did she hear it on the radio?'

Jenny did not stay to answer. She flew out of the room and down the stairs. Sue's door was open. There was no one inside.

Jenny tore down the second flight and out of the front door. Moments later she was back in the kitchen, sickly white. She clutched Dermott's arm.

'She's gone . . . and she's taken Timmy! Not the pram, she's just picked him out of it and gone. Dermott, what'll she do? Where will she go? We must find her!'

The rain fell cold on her cold face, cold on her cold hands, cold on her cold feet. She walked steadily on because she could not stop, she had to keep moving whilst her mind fought to assimilate what was happening to her.

It could not be true, what she had heard on the radio, seen on the front of the *Sunday Mirror* and in the right-hand column of the *Times*. She would have known, she would have felt his death like an icicle through the heart. He could not have died without her knowing, whilst she was lying in her bed, snug and warm, or typing her column, or bathing their son.

Her feet made a queer sound on the puddled pavement, a kind of slap and slither; concentrate on that funny sound, see how many times it occurs between one turning and the next. No wonder it was raining! Someone had to cry for him and she could not. Why could she not? Hot tears would comfort, would ease the terrible, rigid cold which gripped her. But of course there would be no warmth in the world now, no warmth for Sue ever, never, never. If Hugo had left the world then she wanted no part of it for she was bloodless, remote, a part of the frozen waste that had taken him from her.

How did he die? Bravely, of course. Why did he die? Because he could not face being a father, taking on another soul for which to suffer? But how can he be dead? Life is still going on, the rain still falls, the surf still thunders on the sand and a gull stands, shivering, on one leg at the edge of the promenade; it watches her with its cruel yellow eye. Is it hoping she will lie down in the puddles and become carrion? . . like . . . like . . .

She walked on. Slap slither, slap slither went her pink mules. She thought it might be sensible really to end it before the rain began, whilst she was still numb with disbelief. What was stopping her from simply turning to her left and walking into the sea until the waves closed over her head?

Slap slither, slap slither, Sue walked on, a frown etched on her brow. She could not just walk into the sea or end it all . . . why not? Because there *was* warmth, she could feel it in her arms and against her breast, penetrating the coldness of her, trying to warm her, too.

Timmy. Sleeping. A small, familiar face, the mouth working a little, dark lashes on cheeks just dusted with rose. The blanket which she had taken off the pram when she picked him up was round him still, keeping him warm. The movements of her walk and the sound of her breathing must comfort him, for he slept on despite the cold and the rain on his face.

Presently she left the promenade and took to the beach; the tide was out and the wet sand was kinder to her feet than the paving stones had been. Doggedly, soon exhausted, she continued to walk because whilst she walked she did not have to accept what she had heard. Now and then she glanced at the sea but each time she did so her eyes went next to Timmy. When he woke presently and began to grizzle she leaned against the nearest breakwater, unbuttoned her clothes and pushed him to her breast. The rain continued, pattering on her bare breast and on the baby's exposed face until she pulled a fold of the blanket up over him. No one saw her on all that long stretch of dreary and desolate sand.

After a while she noticed that her mules were no longer pink but mud-coloured and that her legs were covered in mud and sand. She turned, then, and walked back the way they had come, noticing with mild surprise that it was already dusk and lights were lit along the roads and in the houses.

Windows caught her attention; squares of orange, yellow and blue shone out. Timmy woke again but did not cry; she could see his big eyes, dark with expanded pupils, blinking towards the lights.

She walked on.

'I've rung the police; they say there's no sign of her, no . . .'

The girls and Dermott were in Jenny's room with the door open. They all heard the front door slam as someone came in, and with one accord they made for the landing.

Sue was halfway up the stairs. She looked like a gipsy. Her hair had come untied and hung in witch locks round her face, she was filthy, the hem of her dress was coming down and her slippers were disintegrating. She was so wet that Jenny wondered if she had been dragged out of the sea, except that, even as the thought entered her head, she saw Timmy wrapped in his soaked blanket, cradled in Sue's arms. She knew that Sue had not put the child down once.

'Hello,' Sue said. 'We've been for a walk. I think I'll have a hot bath and go straight to bed.'

'Er . . . perhaps you should have something to eat,' Jenny said rather helplessly. 'Er . . . what about Timmy . . . umm . . . Shall I take him for you whilst you get . . . er . . . cleaned up?'

'No thanks. I'll take his carrycot into the bathroom with me. I shan't be long.'

'It wouldn't be any trouble . . .' Jenny began, but was overridden by Dermott.

'You take Tim with you, we'll organize you a meal and leave it in your room; how about hot soup, an omelette and then some of Jenny's delicious apple pie and custard?' He did not wait for Sue to reply but went ahead of her into her room and picked up the carrycot. 'Here, pop him in . . . My goodness, he's wet, or rather the blanket is. D'you think it might be better to strip him off right now and wrap him in a dry one? Shall I do it whilst you run your bath?'

Sue did not answer, neither did she look at him. She began to undress Timmy, throwing his things down on the floor, until she had him naked. Then she headed for the bathroom.

'Don't you want the carrycot?' Dermott said, picking it up

and following her out. 'I daresay it's a good idea to take him into the bath with you, get him all warm and then dress him again, but whilst you're getting dried you'll need the cot.'

She turned and gave him a vague, worried smile, then went down the stairs, her shoulders drooping, towards the bathroom. She opened the door, clicked the light on, closed the door. Her fellow tenants stood on the landing, listening. Presently they heard water running. Dermott, who had followed Sue down the stairs, put the carrycot against the door and then tapped gently on it.

'Sue? I've left the carrycot outside. All right?'

An indistinguishable murmur from within might have meant anything but Dermott chose to take it as a rational answer.

'Fine; then I'll start cooking you a meal to be ready in twenty minutes. Mind you don't take any longer than that!'

'Poor Auntie Sue! Did the doctor come, Mum? I didn't see him.'

'Yes, he came. Dermott showed him up, I think. Auntie Sue will be better soon, the doctor's given her something to make her sleep; now you cuddle down, there's a good girl, and sweet dreams.'

'Can Belle come on my bed?' Posy clicked her fingers at Belle, who always jumped on the eiderdown the moment Jenny clicked the light off. Belle looked guiltily at Posy, at the foot of the bed, and then at Jenny. You could almost hear her saying 'But I'm not allowed.'

'She might as well, she'll be up there soon enough,' replied Jenny. Belle, sensitive to tone and expression, promptly jumped up on to the bed, curled round and licked Posy's small, caressing hand. 'Only you must go to sleep, darling.'

'I will, if I can,' Posy said. 'Poor Timmy! Is he a not-well boy?'

'He got very chilly, but I think he's all right,' Jenny said rather guardedly. Posy listened much more than one realized, that was the trouble; quiet children always did. 'He fell asleep at least an hour ago.'

'So he did. You won't go out, will you? You'll come to bed too?'

334

'Yes, in a minute. You won't mind if I go to the kitchen and make myself a hot drink?'

'No, Belle keeps me safe. But you won't be long, will you? I am quite tired.'

Jenny's heart smote her. It had been an awful day and Posy's eyes were dark-shadowed. She might not know precisely what had been going on but adult worries undoubtedly communicated themselves to the young; look at baby Tim. Such a good baby, yet ever since he had been put in his cot he had wailed and screamed and been inconsolable. The moment he was picked up and cuddled he calmed down, only to begin yelling again as soon as his head touched the pillow.

The doctor had given Sue tranquilizers and sleeping pills and had watched her taking them before coming up to the kitchen to report.

'She'll sleep and be better for it, and the tranquilizers will calm the child as well, for twelve hours or so,' he said, sitting down on the edge of the kitchen table. He was young and very tall, with curly, light-red hair, freckles and a humorous mouth which was now grave. 'Of course she'll have to face up to it tomorrow, but by then the shock, at least, will be less.'

'I think the shock saved her because it numbs and deadens your feelings,' Jenny said quietly. 'I think it'll be harder for her when it starts to hurt.'

The young doctor nodded.

'That's true, but with every hour that passes she'll be more capable of facing up to what's happened to her. And the baby will help more than anything. She'll have to take care of him; he's a sturdy little chap but he was very chilled, she'll be lucky if the worst he gets is a cold in the head.'

'He was soaked to the skin, as she was,' Dermott said. He had made Sue the promised meal, taken it to her room and brought it back to the kitchen an hour later, untouched, and it now graced Belle's supper dish. 'She's eaten nothing since her evening meal last night and the baby's only had breast-milk. Can't you give them something?'

'Food injections?' The doctor grinned. 'Well, no, going without a meal or two won't hurt either of them. I've left more tablets beside her bed, she can . . .'

335

'How many?' Jenny and Dermott spoke at once and the doctor grinned again.

'A couple, in case she wakes or wants to lie in late tomorrow morning. But . . . you're wrong, she won't do *that.*'

'How can you be sure?' That was Dermott, hard-eyed. He had changed, Jenny thought, had shed some of his youthful exuberance in the few hours since they had heard of Franklyn's death.

'No one can be sure, but she's got the child. Women don't usually desert their kids, not women like her at any rate. Look, you're both her friends, I can tell you she's going to have a bad time but she'll come out of it, with help. And now you'd better get some sleep yourselves or you won't be in much of a state to give her help.' He slid off the table and sketched a salute. 'Ring if you need me. Cheers.'

He was right, of course; Jenny and Dermott had been exhausted by the fruitless search, and then by having to watch helplessly whilst Sue moved round in what appeared to be a daze. So they had made their way to their own rooms, Jenny first bringing Posy down from Mrs Twigg's flat.

'I'm terribly sorry to keep leaving her with you,' she had said, taking Posy's hand in hers. 'It's awfully unfair, but I couldn't just desert Sue and I didn't want this one to be with me . . . we had some worrying moments.' Over Posy's head she pulled a face at Mrs Twigg to indicate that Sue and Timmy were not yet quite themselves.

'Don't you worry, dear, me an' Posy get on fine, don't we, love?' Mrs Twigg beamed at Posy's vigorously nodding head. 'There now, off to bed with you both, see you in the morning.'

Now, moving quietly round the room with only the bedside light to illuminate her movements, Jenny brushed her hair, washed, and began to undress. To her relief Posy was already sound asleep , and when she finally slid out of the door to go up to the kitchen, Belle, too, scarcely raised her head.

Brenda and Anna were waiting. They smiled tiredly at her, then Brenda, without a word, got down another cup.

'Chocolate or coffee, Jen? I wouldn't advise coffee, myself, not after the day we've had.'

'You're right, I'll have hot chocolate, please. Have you got enough milk or shall I fetch some of mine? I did have half a pint in the fridge, but . . .'

'It's still there, we're using it for ours,' Anna interrupted. 'The old hen wouldn't come snooping round on a Sunday, too many people about. How is she?'

No need to ask who 'she' was, after what had transpired that day.

'Asleep. The doctor gave her some pills. I did ask if I should move in just for the night but he said there was no need, only I'm to keep my door ajar and Sue's as well. He's coming again after morning surgery so I'll ring the cafe and tell Bill I'll not be going in. He'll understand. I think we'll have to have a rota for a bit, make sure she isn't left.'

'We'll all pull our weight,' Brenda said. Her usually rosy little face was pale. 'It's the dead season in the shop, I can easily close for the odd morning or afternoon.'

'I can probably wangle something too,' Anna said. 'And Dermott's home all day. We'll manage.'

They sat around for ten minutes or so, discussing how best to occupy Sue, and then parted for their own beds.

Sue woke at three in the morning, checked the time on the luminous dial of her alarm clock, and then snuggled down under her covers again. She was so sleepy, not nicely sleepy but with a stupid thick heaviness which made sleep not desirable so much as unresistable. She could not think why she should feel so dull and heavy, but . . .

She remembered. The events of the previous day were as clear in her mind as though someone had repeated them all in her ear. Hugo was dead, she had gone off with Timmy and had very nearly made him ill by allowing him to be rained on all afternoon, they had sent for a doctor and he had given her pills. Now she was drugged so that she could not think about Hugo, but despite their care, she was awake.

But she had been given more pills, in a small bottle. They stood by the head of the bed and with them was a glass of milk. 'Just take one more if you wake,' the doctor had instructed. 'That'll see you sleep right through until morning. You need sleep after the day you've had.'

Her hand reached out, touched the bottle and the glass, then she leaned up on her elbow. It was still dark outside; the light coming in round the edge of the curtains was grey and pale, no more than the pre-dawn lightening of the sky that occurred in the early hours. She picked up the little bottle, tipped a pill out into her palm, picked up the glass . . . then put them both down again. She lay back on her pillows.

She was copping out. Earlier, she had been dazed, stupid with shock, so there had been a good reason for taking the doctor's pills but now she was rational and knew that to take the drug would be a cop-out. Hugo had died . . . her mind writhed away from the word and she forced it back . . . he had died probably two or three days ago and she had not yet said goodbye. Perhaps, if she said goodbye properly, in her own way, she could cope better with what had happened. She remembered all the things she had said to Jenny, when Jenny had first come to the flats – how Jenny was dependent on Dirk and so was off balance without him but how she could learn independence and by so doing would become balanced, once more.

Ah, but that had been different, Dirk was a rat, whereas . . .

Banish thoughts like that. Remember, you're saying goodbye to Hugo, letting him go, reassuring him that you *can* go on alone, that you can bring up his son and perhaps even see that his wife has a good life, which is what he would have been concerned about had he been here.

She lay quiet, her eyes closed, and presently images began to form in her mind. Hugo. Let's go right back to the very beginning, to the first moment that we met, she instructed herself, and then we'll take it from there.

She lay awake for a long time, reliving the four years she had known Hugo. Tears began to press their way out from under her lids and run down her cheeks after ten minutes but she did not let that stop her thinking. She would get it all clear in her mind and then she would say her goodbyes,

Hugo would become an unforgettable bit of her past, and she could get on with her life; she was only twenty-seven, there was a lot of it left.

An awful lot.

CHAPTER THIRTEEN

It was breathless work scrambling down from the road into the thickly wooded valley but as soon as she had heard the sound of the stream she had wanted to get near to it. Now, Jenny slid the last few yards on the rich leaf-mould and came to a halt above the bank. She sank down on to a log, noticing contentedly how fast the water flowed, how it chattered and tinkled against the many rocks in its bed. It was a delicious stream, untouched, secretive, flowing along and minding its own business, just as she had imagined it to be when she had been cycling along the road above. Now she would sit here for a few moments and drink in the peace and quiet and get her breath back, too.

Spring had advanced step by delicate step until suddenly it was May and the sunshine, previously fragile and quick to give way to opalescent clouds and showers of warm rain, began to penetrate strongly into the flat, lighting up dusty corners, beating against seldom-cleaned window panes. Jenny, working hard at the cafe, obtaining her divorce from Dirk, watching over her friends and watched over by them, had suddenly felt stifled and surrounded, as though she must get right away from everyone for a bit and take a long hard look at herself. Decisions waited to be made on every side, anxieties crowded in, and she, who had been cut off from other people for so long on the farm without even knowing it, was suddenly homesick not for Dirk or her sons, not even for the farm itself, but simply for solitude and for time to take stock.

Tentatively, almost with shame, she had voiced her need to Bill and his response had been swift and cheering.

'It's not surprising when you think of the things that have happened in the past few months,' he had said. 'Take yourself off for a day – borrow Louisa's bike and just ride away from it all for a bit. Pack up some sandwiches and make a day of it; you'll probably see us clearer and love us better as a result.'

He had been right. Cycling along in the very early morning with the dew still on the grass, dismounting to examine a

340

spider's web diamonded with drops, marvelling over the uncurling oak leaves, the hundred and one shades of green in every copse and thicket, she had felt her tension drain away and her tightly strung nerves relax. Then she had heard the stream and, propping her bike – Louisa's bike – against a convenient tree, she had gone in search of the sound. Now, sitting above the stream, the dappled sunshine and shadow making the water sparkle here and show its clear brown depths there, she felt peaceful and alone and at one with nature, not as though she had been mostly indoors and constantly in company for the past four or five months.

Was it four or five months? It seemed less; she counted up on her fingers. She had arrived in early September and now it was May . . . heavens, it was eight months, two thirds of a year. It had taken that long to turn the frightened, dependent girl she had been into the woman she had become. It had not been merely time, of course, experience had come into it as well. She thought now that Sue's loss had profoundly affected them all because it was such a deep, unsharable grief. Yet they had shared it, feeling its chilly fingers touch each one of them from the oldest to the youngest, though the youngest, Tiny Tim, could not know of her loss but could only feel it in every fibre of his small being.

Jenny's own self-reliance had built up long before, though, beginning with her realization that she could attract friends like Sue and Bill and increasing as she saw that she had strengths which had not before been tested. When she had realized that, she had made up her mind not to be crushed by Dirk's desertion but to make something of her life. At first her main thought had been to get him back but even after that was no longer her prime goal, she knew, ruefully, that it had been Dirk's commendation she had wanted for a long time.

Yet now she could face a future which did not contain Dirk without a qualm, partly, of course, because she was sure that her future would be shared by Bill. They had not discussed living together, but then neither had they discussed parting. Bill simply assumed that they would continue to work together, to make love when the opportunity arose and to bring up their children. He had been badly hurt by Daphne, perhaps it was taking him longer to accept that he could be happier living with another person – me, for choice, Jenny told herself – than he could be living alone with his girls. She was, indeed, partly of the same mind herself; had it not been for the fact that she would soon have to leave No. 24 she would have remained perfectly content with the present arrangement. It demanded nothing from either of them that they were not prepared to give – still she hung back, as Bill plainly did, from the more obvious commitment.

Dirk had not accepted that her leaving him was final; he continued to telephone two or three times a week and talked about the time when she would return. It was odd that she could love and appreciate Bill and yet never entirely shut the door which led back to Dirk and the farm. She knew now that what she had felt for Dirk had been a mixture of habit and youthful infatuation but that did not mean that she had become immune to it; bad habits are notoriously hard to break. Also, Dirk had the advantage of being the devil she knew; she could not spoil the image he had of her because it was already such a poor one, but Bill . . . ah, Bill thought she was special, and Jenny was still uneasily aware of her own many failings, secret from Bill, perhaps, until they shared their lives.

Jenny unslung her borrowed knapsack and rooted around in it until she found the orange she had packed earlier. It was warm from its recent contact with her back and she held it out until it caught a ray of sun which fell through the moving, murmuring leaves, lending it an unlikely, foreign brilliance. Self-knowledge was not always a good thing, sometimes it was downright uncomfortable. Why sit here and probe into her reasons for doing things, why not just do them and let oneself flow with the stream? If Bill asked her to move in then the question of whether she ought to would arise, if he did not, then she would simply look for other lodgings. Reasons and motives should not matter, she should simply look at the facts. She dug her fingernails into the orange and its unmistakable, slightly wicked smell met her nostrils, drowning the woodland scents, the leaf-mould, the moss and the peculiar tangy smell of the stream.

She peeled the orange and put its alien skin back into the

knapsack, then divided it into segments and popped one into her mouth. It was sweet yet sharp, bringing saliva rushing to her mouth as its juice trickled out. She ate half of it with keen enjoyment, then extracted her flask and poured hot coffee into the cap. It tasted better for the orange, she thought, sipping cautiously and blinking against the steam. Why agonize over the fact that Bill had not asked her to move in with him when life was so rich? She should not have to ask herself these things since she adored him, yet she could not prevent herself from holding back, and why should this be when they both loved and trusted each other?

She finished her coffee and rooted around some more . . . crisps, sandwiches, an apple, a piece of sticky gingerbread wrapped in cling film. It was meant to be her lunch, but . . .

She began to eat.

'I'll clean down the tables then, if you'll do the floor. Do you know, I've not enjoyed myself so much for ages? Perhaps there's more than a grain of truth in your pointed remarks about keeping myself busy.'

Sue went to the sink, filled a basin with hot water and a squirt of sterilizing solution, wrung her cloth out in it and began to clean down the tables. Bill had just acquired an allotment and so he and Jenny had asked Sue to do a couple of afternoons a week in the cafe so that Bill could dig the ground over before it got too late for planting. Anna who had also been helping out regularly ever since losing her previous steady job (Found in Broom Cupboard with Clerical Assistant), had recently acquired the unlikely post of life-guard at a school swimming pool during the afternoon sessions, hence Jenny's suggestion that Sue might enjoy the work.

Indeed, after only one afternoon, Sue was already enthusiastic; people were so friendly, so warm-hearted, so interested in Timmy, and there was no time to think, let alone brood, when you were whizzing backwards and forwards between the kitchen and the customers, fetching and carrying, ordering and washing up cups, slapping sandwiches together and shooting toast under the grill. Besides, she could see that Tim was enjoying it; he sat in his

343

pram propped up with pillows and beamed at her every time she passed. He loved the bustle and the new faces, the different voices and the admiration, and anything that Timmy loved must be good. Jenny, it seemed, had been right; physical work was not a bad way to keep your mind and body occupied.

Sue has well aware that Jenny had already done a lot for her, since Hugo's death. For a start she had firmly quashed Sue's conviction that she was the most miserable and unfortunate person in the world.

'You think I can't understand how you're feeling because it hasn't happened to me,' she had said, soon after Sue's loss. 'But dear Sue, what happened to me was worse. If Dirk had died I could have mourned him truly, but when someone is unfaithful to you and then throws you out they leave you with nothing, not even your self-respect. The happy memories are cancelled out, the years you lived with him become a hollow mockery because you know he never loved you, not the way you loved him. Your Hugo has gone but he's still *yours*, what joy you had is real and you can remember the past with pleasure, and when you cry, you're crying for what you've lost, not for what you never really had. I'm being cruel, perhaps, but you must see that there are worse things than losing the man you love to death; losing him to life injures you far more.'

At first, crippled by her loss, Sue had almost hated Jenny for those words; Jenny had only lost Dirk, who was a swine, whereas she had lost Hugo, who had been the most marvellous person ever. But gradually she began to acknowledge that Jenny was right, and it helped to restore her sense of proportion and even took the worst misery out of the long grey days which followed. When her depression was at its darkest and the world seemed echoingly hollow, it cheered her to remember that Jenny had suffered through worse than this and survived it; more, she had conquered it.

Jenny was also responsible for making her talk to Mrs Twigg, though she had not wanted to do so. Mrs Twigg, perhaps a little frightened by Sue's new coldness, had crept into the kitchen when Sue was washing nappies and had told her that she should thank her stars for the way her feller had gone.

'Never mention my Jim, do I?' she had said, her little sharp eyes softening. 'That's 'cos I can't bear to remember 'im, at the end. He went 'ard, did Jim. Weeks of suffering, dear, such as they wouldn't let a dog go through, and so little I could do! I remember waking one night to 'ear him mumbling on about being born and dying, and 'e kept saying, "Some slips out easy both ways, live easy, die easy, others 'as a struggle. It's 'ard," he said, "to 'ave to struggle to do what you don't want." When you 'ear someone you love like anythink say that . . . it 'urts, it 'urts cruel.'

Sue had put her arms round Mrs Twigg's skinny shoulders and hugged her tight and Mrs Twigg had hugged her right back. And they both cried for poor Jim Twigg's suffering, and were glad that Hugo had known nothing but the snap of the rope, perhaps, and the long cold rush of air before his life was snatched from him, quickly and cleanly, with his body's impact against the ice-covered rocks.

Dermott had been a good friend too. When he was with her he did not allow her to brood, and he was with her as much as he could manage. He was always popping up to her flat with a toy for Timmy or some special chocolates for her, or an invitation to go for a walk, have a meal or see a show. Despite her early conviction that her sense of humour had died with Hugo, Dermott had always been able to make her laugh and she was grateful to him for that, though she would not go out with him unless they made up a foursome. When Jenny hinted that she should take Dermott's devotion seriously, she had told her that one did not willingly take to a tabby cat after one had been used to a tiger; Jenny did not mention the matter again.

Yet Jenny, who had been so practical and understanding over Sue's problems, still did not seem able to come to terms with her own. Bill had not yet asked her to move in with him but when he did, Jenny would be in a quandary. She was clearly very fond of Bill and was going ahead with her divorce, she said she had no grain of respect left for Dirk, yet there was still something. Was it loyalty? Pity? The small, gritty, unavoidable residue of what had once been love? Impossible to say; Sue was sure that Jenny was as puzzled as she, but whilst it remained, she would be unable to throw in her lot unhesitatingly with Bill.

And what of Bill? Why had he not thrown open house and

heart to her friend? Sue had offered to find him a job in London, a better-paid and more congenial job, so that he and Jenny and the children could live comfortably within reach of herself and – as she had then thought – Hugo, but Bill had just shrugged and laughed and said he was doing fine, thank you. He worshipped Jenny, you could see it in a thousand ways, but he was allowing the old, miserable business with Daphne to keep him from what he must know was true happiness! Men were not supposed to be as affected by broken marriages as women, but it was clear that Bill had been hard hit by his experience.

We're a poor crew, Sue thought now, as she wiped down the last table. We're all emotionally crippled and clinging on to each other, all waiting for someone else to make the first move and dreading it. She, after all, had postponed returning to London indefinitely. Only Dermott was unhurt, still whole. Yet was that really true? Her absolute refusal to allow him the intimacy of even a close friendship was hurting him. His boyish charm seemed to have disappeared and, though Sue liked the more serious Dermott, there were times when she felt guilty for having, albeit inadvertently, involved him in a situation which had caused him to cast off the carefree, easy-going attitude which had been his a few short weeks before.

'Finished? Goodee, so've I. I'll just slip on Belle's lead, you can settle Timmy, and we'll be off. Bill promised to meet the kids and take them straight home, so we can go round there, have some tea and then come back to No. 24 in time for Tim and Posy to have their baths, and whilst we walk,' Jenny continued, slipping her arms into her faded denim jacket, 'you can give me ideas for Bill's birthday present; it's always hell buying for men who need everything.'

They chattered inconsequentially as they left the cafe, calling out goodbyes to the gardeners, and got down to the nitty gritty of birthday presents as they made their way along the road towards Bill's cul-de-sac.

'Clothes? Men usually need socks and handkerchieves and shirts. Or something for the house? Don't wrinkle your nose like that, the wind might change, what's wrong with clothes or towels?'

'Sue, what a grim suggestion, it would be like buying you nappies,' Jenny pointed out. 'He *does* housework, but he doesn't love it. He reads quite a bit, so Posy's going to buy him a paperback, but I thought I might get him something for the garden, or possibly a pair of light-weight sandals for the summer. Or new swimming trunks . . . you should see his present ones, they're next-to-indecent!'

'That sounds fun,' Sue said thoughtfully. 'Don't buy him swimming trunks then, it'll have to be something for the garden; do you remember that trip to Chester Zoo? I thought Bill would faint from envy at the floral displays. Of course it's the elephant dung, they must be positively tripping over the stuff, they can afford to spread it over every single rosebud . . . that's an idea, why don't you get Bill some elephant dung? It would be a most original present and you could attach a little card to the top of the heap saying something like "You, too, can have marrows the size of barrage balloons".'

'Filthy beast! And anyway, to say a guy's got marrows the size of barrage balloons sounds like deformity, not distinction. But of course you could say I was still part-owner of a good deal of manure – if I asked nicely, do you suppose Dirk would let Bill have some?'

'He'd probably bring it over and tip it out on Bill's head himself,' Sue admitted. 'Why not buy him rose trees? Then the dung could be a little extra.' She smirked. 'The icing on the cake.'

'You've got a lovely turn of phrase, dear!' Belle, who had been slipping along quietly beside the pram, suddenly jerked up her head and pricked her ears. 'What's Belle seen? Aha!'

Posy, Dawn and Erica were approaching them in a small gaggle, each child using a skipping rope though with varying success. Erica came on with long, even swoops of her rope, Posy came on with slightly shorter and more ragged swoops and Dawn led the field because she ran ten paces and skipped one. Thus Dawn was the first to reach them, abandoning her one skip as soon as she saw them and arriving breathless but well ahead.

'Daddy's still digging but he says could you put the kettle on please, Auntie Jenny? He'll be back in a trace of crates.'

'Brace of shakes, you little silly,' Erica corrected breathlessly galloping up beside her, her rope rotating smoothly as a wheel. 'We helped after school, didn't we, Posy? We planted hundreds of potatoes, some reds and some whites. Daddy says we can have a little bit of ground each and he's given us money for seed – Posy wants to grow radishes and spring onions and peaches but I'm going to grow carnations and sweet peas.'

'I'm going to have bananas; I like them best,' Dawn said, beaming at them. 'And I'll grow a lemon, a big one, 'cos Daddy likes them so.'

'Melon, not lemon, you little silly,' Erica said automatically. 'You can't grow melons here, they're African, not English.'

'I can! Daddy said I could! Grow what you like, he said!'

'But you can't, Donny, the sun isn't hot enough, melons are African things, not English ones – why do you think they're so expensive?'

'She might grow a melon, with a bit of glass,' Jenny said diplomatically, not mentioning bananas. 'Did Daddy say to do anything else or just put the kettle on?'

'Well, he *said* just the kettle, but I expect he meant bread and butter and things, because we're awfully hungry,' Erica explained. 'Come on, kids, race you to the house . . . Donny, if you don't use your skipping rope we'll expel you!'

Dawn gave her big sister her sweetest, most forgiving smile, waited until she and Posy were well ahead, and then ran quickly after them, waving her rope vaguely up and down.

'A born charmer, that one,' Sue said as they followed the children along the pavement and in at Bill's garden gate. 'I say, how pretty the front garden looks with all that blossom!'

'Wait till you see the back,' Jenny said proudly, taking the key from under the doormat and opening the front door. 'The rockery really is a picture; Bill's got four different kinds of aubretia, lots and lots of cranesbill, blue and magenta, a gorgeous eidelweiss and wild thyme, rock roses, some miniature Potentilla, one of those Japanese trees that grow flat and not upright . . . a conifer . . . the rockery's his pride and joy.'

Sue lifted Timmy out of the pram and carried him into the kitchen behind Jenny, then sat him in the old high-chair which Bill had fetched down from the attic for very young visitors.

'There we are, precious, now you can sit and watch us work again,' Sue said, plonking a kiss on his cheek. 'Yes, that rockery really is beginning to blaze,' she added, peering through the kitchen window. 'What a good idea it was, to have it out there, so you see the flowers first and the veggies second.'

'Or not at all,' Jenny said, standing beside her. 'I planted those broad beans and they aren't more than four inches high, even now!'

'Height isn't everything, there's succulence to take into account, and . . .' The three children, bursting into the kitchen through the back door, cut Sue's sentence off short. 'Shall I take them up to wash their hands, Jenny, whilst you deal with the kettle?'

'Much obliged, but they can wash over the sink,' Jenny said, filling the kettle and standing it on the gas stove. 'Tell you what, if you can cut some nice thin slices of bread, I'll lay the table and Ricky can put the butter on when she's washed.'

When Bill came in ten minutes later the table was laid, the kettle was simmering and Jenny was ladling soft-boiled eggs into egg cups whilst Sue made finger-boys for dipping. It was a domestic scene and Bill smiled comfortably round, with an especially wide smile for Tim.

'Hello, Tim, how's the toofy-peg?' Tim had a swelling on his lower gum which was a tooth about to be born. 'Aren't we lucky, us two fellers, waited on by five women?' Bill stuck out his chest and strutted over to the sink to wash the earth off his hands. 'Come on, which of my harem will fetch my slippers?'

'Beat him to a pulp with them, girls!' Sue shouted as the children, giggling, rushed out and came in again with the slippers. 'Come on, remember that women have got the vote, down with male chauvinists, whack Dad's bottom for being cheeky!'

Whacks were administered and Bill howled with pretended pain. Sue, in the midst of it, had to turn away suddenly, whisk Timmy out of the high-chair and bury her face in his soft, sweet-smelling neck. It was the realization that Hugo would never have any part in the fun of fatherhood, that it was all done for him, the weeping and the laughter, love and desire and hate. Was his ghost hovering now, reproachful that she could still laugh when he was remote from them, further away even than the snowy crevasse which held all that remained of him? She knew he would never behave like that but it did not stop her feeling guilty because, for one moment, she had forgotten the ache of loss.

But there was Timmy: she could not let him be brought up in a perpetual shadow. She had explained that to Hugo the night she had said goodbye to him. If he had been able to do so he would have insisted that Timmy be brought up in an atmosphere of happiness and confidence. Hugo's own childhood had been ruined by fear and distress, he would want his son to have all the good things that he himself had missed.

Sue put the baby back into the high chair, pinned her smile in position, and turned to take a slipper from Posy so that she could tease Bill by pretending to drop it into the coal bucket. Bill grabbed, Posy caught his arm, Erica swung the other slipper with pretended vigour at his bottom and Bill roared at them all.

Bedlam reigned.

Somewhere, Sue was sure, Hugo was smiling.

'There he goes; the first of the few. Oh hell, how I hate waving people off.' Sue mopped fiercely at her eyes with one hand because Timmy was tucked in the crook of her other arm. She took his small fist and waved it vigorously towards the fast disappearing train and Dermott's top half, still hanging out of the window, small and growing smaller, forlorn in its loneliness.

'I suppose you'll be next,' Jenny said to Sue. 'Mrs Grant can't wait to get rid of us now, have you noticed? Actually, she did very well, she's got a young married couple with two under-school-age kids coming in on Saturday for a fortnight and Dermott's room . . . rooms . . . will just suit them. And she says the whole place is booked solid from the Bank Holiday weekend.' Jenny turned away from the empty railway track and moved across the platform and out through the barrier, handing in her ticket as she went. 'What do you think of Bren and Anna sharing that caravan? Don't tug, Belle . . . she hates stations.'

'So do I too,' Sue said, as they emerged from the comparative shelter of the station into the gentle drizzle which was falling outside. She tucked Timmy into his pram and unhooked the brake, then turned her vehicle towards the town centre. 'As for the caravan, I think they're mad. Imagine living for three months in squalor right between the main road and the railway line.'

'It won't be squalid, only cramped,' Jenny protested. 'Anyway, I may yet sink to a caravan myself; nothing else seems likely to turn up.'

'Oh, you! Everyone's expecting Bill to take you in when Mrs G. throws us out, you most of all! Have you been house-hunting? Have you hell!'

'I have been looking, honestly, but it's the wrong time of year. However, there's a flat above the post office in Rhuddlan and a cottage near Dyserth, so all is not yet lost.'

'Suppose Bill does ask you? Just suppose?'

'I'll tell you, if you'll tell me whether you intend to visit Dermott.' Dermott's last remarks, as the train chugged out, had been shrieked above the noise but had been clearly audible. 'Don't forget,' he had shouted, 'I'm dossing down with Solly for the first week . . . Flat 22a Jubilee Street . . . And in the evenings I'm behind the bar at The Frenchman's Place and then I'll be at His Majesty's . . . stage door . . . don't forget, pop in the minute you reach town!'

'I expect I'll go and see him sometime,' Sue said carelessly. 'Now, what'll you do if Bill asks you to move in?'

'I don't know. It's a bit too much of a commitment and it's no use saying that living with a bloke isn't a commitment because Bill and I are both rather old-fashioned. I can't be casual about something important . . . but it's all supposition because he hasn't breathed a word about sharing.'

'What's to stop you suggesting it? Or you could say to Bill that you just want to move in with him until Mrs G. starts advertising for winter lets again, around September. Now you couldn't call that a permanent commitment, could you?'

'Yes, because I grow fond of the people I live with. Sue, you're every bit as bad as me – when are you going back to London? You don't want the old hen to chuck you into the street, do you?'

'No, of course not. I suppose I'll go mid-week, because it's easier to get a seat on the train then and I don't fancy standing all the way to Euston. Tell you what, why don't you come up to town and stay with me for the holiday week? If I go up on the Wednesday, say, I could get the place all ready, and you and Posy and Belle could join me on the Friday. It would give you a much-needed break.'

'It's sweet of you to think of it, but that week will be peak eating-time at the cafe,' Jenny said, half-apologetically and half defiantly. 'I couldn't let Bill down like that.'

'Oh? Not even if . . .' Sue shot out her wrist and examined her watch. 'Eleven o'clock – shall we go home and make a cuppa in our own kitchen or shall we potter along to the Copper Kettle and have one there?' She bent over the pram, lowering the flap which protected Timmy from the rain and wind, and peered in at him. 'He's sleeping like a baby . . . ha! . . . so we can park the pram alongside the window of the Kettle and see if he stirs.'

'Yes, let's go along to the cafe, then,' Jenny agreed. She was restless, as if the spring had actually got into her blood, stirring it up and giving her ideas. Yet she hated the thought of leaving the flat and guessed that Sue felt the same. Odd, because she had never imagined a sad parting with No. 24, she had seen herself in her mind's eye joyfully throwing her luggage into the back of the Land Rover and returning to the farm with a loving and repentant Dirk. Now that this was a possibility, for Dirk kept begging her to return and vowed repentance and good behaviour if not undying love, she no longer regarded it as even faintly desirable. 'What do I want?' she asked herself now, as she and Sue headed for the Copper Kettle. 'I don't want Dirk or the farm but I can't bring myself to burn my boats and ask Bill to take us in. Yet he's my lover, I believe I love him, he's given me more happiness in two months than Dirk managed to hand out in two decades; so why can't I go and live with Bill with or without an invitation?'

She knew that it was not possible without an invitation, however; she was just not the type to push herself in where she was not welcome. But . . . if he asked? There were two more weeks; he would mention the matter before then, surely?

With exactly a week to go before turn-out day Jenny woke to glorious sunshine and a light-hearted feeling that all would be well. Today things would be settled and she would know what her future held; she was supposed to be seeing a flat after the cafe closed at four, so it might prove perfect. Or Bill might ask her to move in with him. She might easily refuse, but it would do her ego a lot of good to be asked!

She had a strip-down wash in the bathroom, unperturbed even when Mrs Grant hammered on the door and made horrible remarks about winter-let people using the summer visitors' facilities; she did not like women using the bathroom in the mornings, she had made that clear from the start, a man needed the basin and mirror to shave but a woman could make do with the facilities provided in each of the bedrooms.

'Shan't be long, just another couple of minutes,' Jenny called out, pretending to have missed all her landlady's nastier remarks. 'I'll give you a shout when I've finished.'

Upstairs in the flat once more she woke Posy, supervised her dressing and then made breakfast for them both, a substantial breakfast today with cereal and eggs since they were up in good time and hungry.

'An egg? Oh, brill,' Posy said, attacking it with her spoon. 'Is it a holiday, Mum? Why are you so singy?'

'Because the sun's shining and I woke up nice and early,' Jenny said, eating her egg. 'I'll whizz you up to school, darling, and then go straight to work because I expect we'll be busy on such a sunny day. One of us will call for you after school, either Bill or me, and if the weather holds we'll persuade Bill to bring the girls down to the beach with us for a high tea.'

Two or three times lately, she and Posy had taken sandwiches, cake, fruit and a flask of tea on to the beach at about six o'clock and had enjoyed an al fresco meal, whilst Belle chased seagulls or dug holes in the sand into which she would thrust her head, emerging presently with bright eyes and clogged-up nostrils.

'I'd like that,' Posy said, dipping a finger-boy into her yolk. 'Can we swim?'

'We might, if it's still warm. We'll paddle, anyway.'

She and Bill were teaching the children to swim, though Bill did most of the work. He took them into the Sun Centre nearly every day where they splashed and flapped away for an hour, gaining in confidence if not in ability, though Erica was beginning to swim quite competently for short distances. But no matter how convenient the Sun Centre might be, nothing could beat the sea, the lively feeling of the water moving against your skin, the buoyancy of it as well as the space and its distinctive smell as you splashed and shouted.

'It'll stay fine; Belle swims best of everyone but they won't let her into the Sun Centre.' It was a standing grievance but Posy had no time to expand on it this morning. She slid off her chair, wiped her mouth with the back of her hand and ran for her satchel and the latest craze, a sheet of paper coloured and then intricately folded, with which they all told each other's fortunes.

Halfway down the stairs Sue's door shot open and she shouted 'Hi!' after them, so shrilly that they both stopped dead in their tracks and Belle's ears flattened reproachfully as a reminder that she was not hard of hearing.

'What?' Jenny called back. 'We're off to school, we can't stop – though we're actually early!'

'The flat . . . can I come with you to see it? We're at a loose end, Timmy and me.'

'Yes, of course you can. It's in Clifton Park road so if you come to the gardens at about half three . . .'

'Fine, we'll do that. See you later, then.'

Sue went back into her room and Posy, Jenny and Belle continued down the stairs and out of the house. The sun still shone out of a clear blue sky and Jenny sang as they walked and swung her arms and played silly games with Posy. It was a good day.

By nine o'clock, however, although the sun still shone, the first bright gloss had gone from the day. Bill always opened up the cafe first, but today when Jenny arrived the place was still locked and the back windows shuttered. She waited a couple of minutes, then went over to Mike who was weeding the gravel path with a rake.

'Mike, have you seen Bill? The place is all locked up, I can't get in.'

Mike leaned on his rake and surveyed Jenny and Belle with a grin; he was a middle-aged, slow-thinking man but very competent at his work.

'On a morning like this he may have forgotten the time, stayed in the allotment. You know what he is for gardening.'

Jenny smiled back. Of course, the old devil had taken time off once or twice before to finish a bit of digging. Yet he didn't usually neglect the cafe in any way; despite the fine weather it was not like him.

'You're probably right; I'd better get over there right away and see if he wants me to start without him. Thanks, Mike.'

Belle was exploring a large heap of builders' sand which had been dumped on one of the paths, but she returned to Jenny's side as soon as she realized they were not staying in the gardens. The pair of them walked briskly and were in Bill's cul-de-sac in less than ten minutes. Jenny registered vaguely that there were a number of cars parked by the kerb, so it must still be early, then she pushed the gate open and walked up the garden path. There was a way into the back garden down the side of the house and she could see that someone had indeed been digging there, but she did not want to seem nosy so went straight to the front door and rang the bell. There was a short pause and then footsteps clicked across the hall; a woman's tread. Immediately all her senses sharpened with fear. Was he ill? Had Daphne returned? She felt her pulses speed up as the door opened.

A strange young woman stood there. She wore a dark skirt, a pale-blue shirt and a dark tie, black shoes and fine black stockings. Jenny stared at her, puzzled – a nurse? Was he ill?

'Bill . . . is he all right? We work together, he hasn't been in, the place is locked up, I thought . . .'

The girl continued to look straight at her, unsmiling, her light-blue eyes cool, even a little guarded.

'He's all right. But he's busy, could you . . .'

'Oh, he's here then.' Thoroughly alarmed, Jenny pushed past the girl and went towards the kitchen. She called: 'Bill? It's me, Jenny, I've come for the key, are you all . . .'

The words died on her lips. She entered the kitchen and there was Bill, standing with his back to the window, looking straight at her. His colour was ghastly but he was obviously making a big effort to act normally.

'Hello, Jen, come in time to see the destruction at its height? Take a look. It's that old bugger next door of course; the best way he could . . . well, take a look.'

She moved past him. Outside in the back garden a well-built young man in dark trousers and a blue shirt was digging up all the young vegetables which she and Bill had so lovingly planted and reared. Another was taking up the rose trees and laying them carefully, with balls of soil round their roots she was glad to see, on the little patio which ran between the back door and the rockery and roses. The rockery . . . it had disappeared! The rocks had just been chucked on to the lawn and the plants thrown amongst them. The man who had obviously destroyed the work of almost two years was mopping a red face and preparing to dig once more. What on earth had Mr Backhouse said to get these men working so furiously, destroying Bill's adored garden?

'Darling, this is wicked, Backhouse ought to be shot!' Jenny stood on tiptoe and kissed Bill's cheek, not caring what anyone thought. Bill was the best, the kindest person she had ever known, it was a dreadful thing to hurt him so. 'What on earth did he tell them? Who are they? Why . . . why . . .'

Of course, the woman was a policewoman and the diggers were policemen! They must have been told that Bill had robbed a bank or fiddled the tax and they were hunting for the buried treasure! Trust that cunning old blighter to find a way of destroying all Bill's hard work . . . that rockery! It would take months and months just to get a few of the plants to re-root . . . it was a terrible thing the old man had done and she would be the first to tell him so.

'Look, this is vandalism,' Jenny said, swinging round to face the policewoman, who was watching them with a slight but noticeable curiosity. 'You'll have to put this all back again and some of the things . . well, replacing them isn't going to make them root again, is it? I'm sure Mr Bradley will sue for any damage . . .'

The girl, for she was little more, looked embarrased and sympathetic but she was still unruffled.

'I'm sorry, but there was nothing else we could do. Someone laid information serious enough to warrant action. We did our best to trace . . . to find . . .'

Her voice petered out as Jenny stared, then laughed derisively.

'My God, I believe he told you Bill murdered Daphne and buried her body in the garden! And you *believed* it? Bill wouldn't hurt a fly – did the old swine tell you that he – Bill – is bringing up his two kids without any help from anyone? Did he tell you that, whilst he was filling you up with a load of rubbish? Do you have any *right* . . .'

She stopped short; there was something happening outside. A loud and dreadful noise, shouts, then a keening wail which stopped abruptly with a sound like a pistol shot. Jenny glanced quickly round the kitchen; it must be Belle, she must have attacked someone because she would guess that they had no right out there, mucking about with Bill's garden. She took two quick steps towards the back door just as it burst open. A very young constable came into the room so hastily that he nearly bumped into Jenny. He was sickly pale and he was still holding his gardening fork, though he seemed unaware of the fact. He stared round wildly, then his eyes focused on the policewoman.

'Mary? Fred's gone bananas, did you hear? Can you come? Get some water, we'll chuck it in his face . . . you've never seen . . .'

Jenny, uncomprehending, began to apologize for her dog.

'Did Belle bite someone? It isn't like her, she's the most . . .' The high, keening wail started again, reaching a bubbling crescendo and then dying away slowly. Jenny went towards the back door, thoroughly unnerved, but the young constable grabbed her arm with a large and earthy hand.

'No, miss! No, you don't want to go out there, you don't want to see that!' The hand that gripped her arm was shaking, the fingers digging in so hard that Jenny nearly cried out. 'My fork went right . . . oh, God!'

He flung himself, retching, at the sink. Jenny stared at Bill. Colour had flooded his face, making his green eyes look even greener. He was hurt . . . he put his hands out to her and she went to him, but the policewoman got between them. She looked frightened now, truly frightened, all her calm gone. She hardly came up to Bill's shoulder, but she knew what she had to do.

'Stay here, sir . . . go away miss, into the front room, just while we sort things out.' She left Bill and shooed Jenny before her, like a reluctant child, until they reached the front room. As she turned for one last look at Bill the back door swung open and several policemen, the sort with peaked caps this time, surged into the room. They went to Bill and he looked hunted and afraid, so afraid that she wanted to turn round and rush back to him, but the policewoman was insistent, pushing her into the front room. 'Let them sort it out, miss; it's better, you'll do more harm than good if you try to interfere. We'll sit here quietly until they call for us.'

Jenny sat down on the couch. Constable Mary something-or-other sat opposite her, looked across at her and then quickly away.

'Bill's one of the kindest and best men I've met,' Jenny said slowly. Her voice confirmed her bewilderment and despair and she thought it might have been better had she said nothing, but having started she must carry on. 'He wouldn't hurt anyone, not on purpose he wouldn't. There really has to be some mistake.'

'He seems a steady sort of chap,' the girl said. Her voice sounded small, a little lost. 'I must say, I thought it was all spite, that old fellow was so . . . but they've found something.' She moved across and sat beside Jenny on the couch, and for the first time her self-assurance faltered. 'Look, love, you may be right, it may be a mistake, but we had to follow it up, the woman did more or less disappear, and . . . did you hear the noise Fred made? He's a steady bloke, too . . .'

Jenny glanced out of the window. The sun still shone, the sky was a clear and uninterrupted blue. On a day like this, it had to be a mistake, no one who knew Bill could believe for one moment that he could harm another human being. They must make it up to him for ruining his garden, she would buy more roses. . . thank God the kids were still in school . . . presently they would discover their mistake and she would run into the kitchen, hug him, tell him she loved him and that it was just some beastly practical joke. It was all the fault of that old blighter Backhouse, making trouble as usual. Just wait until it was all over and she could give him a piece of her mind!

Side by side, on the couch, Jenny and Police Constable Mary something-or-other waited. Together, yet so separated by their thoughts as to be totally alone, they tried to make polite conversation whilst they strained every nerve to hear what was going on in the other room.

Time passed, slow as treacle. A fly buzzed at the pane, impatient to be out on such a glorious morning. People passed along the pavement glancing curiously at the cars parked by the kerb. Far away, the church clock struck noon.

Presently there was a commotion in the hall; men's feet, deep voices. Jenny sprang to the door.

Bill was leaving, with a uniformed policeman holding open the front door for him, another lightly touching his arm, two more following him up. Jenny started forward, and her companion grabbed her arm. Jenny shook her off.

'Bill? What. . . ?'

He gave her a lovely smile, then shook his head and let his face crumple into lines of sadness and disillusion. Then they hustled him out.

CHAPTER FOURTEEN

'So you're back? You poor love, you look totally exhausted; come and sit down.'

Sue had been looking after the cafe whilst Jenny saw Bill. Now, during the after-lunch calm, she was washing up. Jenny picked up a tea-towel and began to dry crockery, shaking her head at Sue's suggestion of a chair.

'No, I'm fine, thanks. Better working than just sitting. The police were very nice to me. A detective inspector, I think he was, told me what had happened and then they let me see Bill, to work out something about the children.'

Sue glanced shrewdly at her friend's face, then continued to wash up and stack crocks and cutlery on the draining board.

'Right, you get to work. Can you tell me what happened, or would you rather not?'

'Well, the policeman said Mr Backhouse had rung them up and told them that Bill's wife had disappeared and that over a year ago he had woken up in the night with an attack of indigestion and had seen Bill burying something – or someone – in the back garden. Said Bill had subsequently built a rockery over the very spot. When they asked why he'd not reported it before, he said it simply hadn't occurred to him that Daphne wasn't coming back, only he told them that Bill had taken to having a . . . a woman in, so he thought it was time to come clean.'

'Was it true? I mean was it true that he thought . . .'

'That's almost the worst part. Apparently when they'd taken Bill off he went round to the station almost in tears, expecting to be taken to court for malicious damage. He was shattered to hear that the men had found something, in fact he actually said that Bill, though a poor gardener, was a fine, good-hearted man!'

'Hmm. It *was* . . . what . . . who they thought, then?'

'Oh, yes, Bill told them at once apparently. When I saw

360

Bill he said he'd never lied to me, he'd just never told me the entire truth. I don't know whether I ever told you, but Daphne came back about six months after she first left, demanding money. Bill didn't have any, so she said very well, she would take Erica. Ricky was in bed with a temperature and a throat infection and Bill followed Daphne into the hall, telling her she wasn't to bother the child. Then Daphne made a rush for the stairs, Bill gave her a bit of a push, she fell and hit her head against the newel post. He said he couldn't believe it at first – spiteful and cursing him one moment, still and white the next. She was dead, of course. The post struck her on a vulnerable part of her temple and she died instantly.

'When he realized she was dead he panicked; he rushed outside to check that there was no one waiting for her. If there had been he would have got help, but as it was. . . well, they'd been quarrelling pretty fiercely and he was sure they'd think he'd killed her. So he went out into the garden and dug a deep hole – it took him ages, he said, and all the time he was in the most awful sweat of fear and he kept going indoors to check in the hope that she would have come round – it was in the early hours before he decided it was deep enough. Then, because she was stiffening, he carried her out and dumped her in and shovelled earth on top. Over the next few months he began to make the rockery. He said even the next day he realized what a fool he'd been to try to hide her death but by then it was too late, he simply had to hope she'd never be missed. That was why he dared not ask me to move in with him – he couldn't risk a search being started for Daphne – and he's always been afraid Ricky knew more than she let on. Not consciously, but unconsciously, because she was rambling that night and he's heard her ramble about her mother when she's delirious. He said after the first shock he was glad they'd found out because he could stop running.'

'Running? But he'd never go anywhere, wouldn't consider it when I suggested getting a job in London!'

'No, of course not, because if he'd sold the house and someone else hadn't cared for the rockery . . .'

There was a short pause whilst both girls thought about it.

'Poor old Bill,' Sue said sincerely. 'In a cleft stick, wasn't he? What will happen to him?'

'They charged him with murder, but the detective said it would probably be a manslaughter charge in the end, unless the people in the pathology lab' find evidence which contradicts his story. If they found something which definitely confirmed it, he would probably get a very short sentence, but as things stand, he might get five years.'

'Five years? That seems hard.' Sue turned away from the sink and began to clean down the working surfaces. 'Are you glad, now, that you'd not moved in with him?'

'Glad? Good God, Sue, when I saw him in that cold, horrid little room this morning, it cleared up all my shilly-shallying. I don't want the farm, or Dirk, or my freedom, I just want Bill! Isn't it odd, when the chips are down the *for better for worse* business comes into its own – I want Bill at any price, on any terms, even if it means waiting for years. Whatever he did he did innocently and in defence of those two kids and everyone who knows him will know that's true. Anyway, there's something . . .'

At this point the bell attached to the door gave a ting, and the conversation had to be suspended whilst fizzy orange, ice-creams, tea and biscuits were served to a family party, but later, in another lull, Jenny returned to her theme, though by this time Anna had wandered in and first had to be told all that had gone before.

'Well, Jen, even if they give him five years, likely he'll only serve three of 'em,' she remarked when Jenny had finished. 'Of course it's being talked about. One of the teachers said if he hadn't hidden the body he could have got as little as eighteen months – if they could prove it was the post done the damage and not Bill's fist, of course.'

'Thanks very much,' Jenny said gloomily. The three of them were sitting at the table in the corner drinking tea, with one eye on the clock. 'What I started to say to Sue earlier, though, is that I've an idea Ricky knows more than Bill thinks, or more than he's prepared to acknowledge, perhaps. He doesn't want the kids involved, of course, but I do think it might be worthwhile talking to her, if we could just get someone kind to come and listen – an impartial witness sort of thing.'

'Why? What gives you the impression that she knows

362

anything?' Sue asked, finishing her tea and giving Timmy one of the hard biscuits which aid those who are trying to produce their teeth. 'Surely she'd have said something if she did?'

'Not necessarily. Or rather, perhaps she's already said something, only no one realized quite what she meant.' Jenny turned to Sue. 'Do you remember that day I looked after Ricky when she had tonsillitis and she started talking about her mother, and about the lovely jewels and pretty dresses she'd be wearing?'

'Yes, I remember. You were hurt because you thought Bill didn't trust you to look after Ricky.'

'That's it. Well, when I thought of her exact words, I remembered she'd said something about Mum being in heaven . . . which I took not at all literally . . . and then, later, there was something else. She'd said that Mum would have a gold thing in her hair and then went muttering off the way delirious kids do, and then suddenly came out with a clear sentence. She said, *Hello, that's what I meant*.'

'Hello . . . halo! The gold thing in Daphne's hair was a halo!' Sue sat bolt upright, the colour rushing to her cheeks. 'She saw! She's known all along! And Bill suspected it, so he tried to keep you away when he realized Ricky was ill and might easily blurt something out.'

'Well, that's what I think,' Jenny admitted. 'So I'd like to see if I can get something out of Ricky, but in front of an impartial witness, not one of us.'

'I know a girl in the police,' Anna volunteered after a thoughtful silence. 'She's not been in all that long, but she's stationed in Rhyl. Would she do? Only she'd have to come round in ordinary clothes, I'm not taking a copper to No. 24.'

'She'd be ideal,' Jenny said gratefully. 'Only . . . I wonder if it might be better to take her, and the kids of course, round to Bill's place? We could ask her to come to tea . . . could you do that, Anna?'

'I'll give her a buzz if you like,' Anna said, getting to her feet. 'I'll phone the station and ask 'em if she's about and if she is I'll have a word.'

'Now? Right this moment? You're a dear.'

When Anna had taken their proffered ten pence pieces and

gone off to use the public telephone outside the garden, Sue turned to her friend.

'I thought the old hen had agreed to you having the kids at your flat for a few days? I thought you didn't want them at Bill's just yet.'

'Nor I did, but she might remember better in her own house – Erica, I mean. And we've got to face facts, whether they find Bill guilty or innocent they won't do it for a good few weeks yet – the inspector said probably another ten or twelve. We can't stay at No. 24 after the Bank Holiday so, now that the garden's more or less straight, we can start spending the odd afternoon there, just until we move back in properly.'

'Then you will, you really will? Move into Bill's place?'

'I really will. I wish Bill could be there, but he can't, so I'll move in without him. That way, I'll be waiting.'

Whoever Jenny had expected Anna to arrive with, it had not been the young policewoman who had sat with her in the front room that fateful morning, waiting to see what had been discovered under Bill's rockery. But it was her, this time with her hair loose and dressed in jeans and a sloppy sweater. At first glance she looked very different.

But her eyes had the remembered expression; calm, a little guarded, not friendly or unfriendly but neutral. Anna brought her in chummily, telling the children that this was Mary Lucas, a friend of hers from school, who had come to tea.

They were in the kitchen with everyone acting normally, the children sitting round the table whilst the adults saw to their wants and propped themselves against the draining board or dresser with cups of tea to hand. The only change was that, instead of Bill's large, casually dressed figure, Mary Lucas stood with them.

Jenny, looking at her sideways, thought that she still looked like a policewoman when you examined her closely. Her dark hair had a parting so white it might have been chalked on, her hands were without rings and her nails were short and spotless. Her jeans were dark blue and obviously new, and her sweater was completely smooth and fresh. She made Jenny's heart sink a bit and Jenny wished Sue had been able to come, but Sue had had to stay and manage the cafe, leaving Timmy with them for the afternoon. She looked at Mary Lucas again; she was so impregnable somehow, so neat and unstained. She was like a Kleenex tissue poking out of the box – what sympathy could she have with a normal, sweaty, vulnerable human being?

She was not unintelligent however, for without anyone quite knowing how she did it, she was chatting to the children in her low voice, leading the conversation round to how hard it must have been for Ricky's and Dawn's daddy to look after them all by himself.

'. . . especially when you aren't well,' Mary was saying, as if she had known them all her life. 'I remember how useless my father was when I was ill, he couldn't even sit on my bed without tipping over my medicine! You were ill during the winter, weren't you, Erica? Daddy said you nearly missed being in the school play!'

'Yes, I had one of my throats,' Ricky said complacently. 'I get awful throats, don't I, Jenny? I'm delir . . . del-something; that means I talk awful wild and I don't know people, that word. I'm delicate, aren't I, Jenny?'

'Yes, you are rather,' Jenny said, smiling. Her heart had suddenly started to hammer with fear that they might lead Ricky on to speak and he might say quite the wrong thing. Suppose Ricky said she'd seen Bill hitting Daphne over the head with a hammer? Kids were odd little creatures sometimes, they liked to dramatize the simplest incidents. But she could not draw back now, she must trust Ricky as she trusted Bill. 'Daddy once told me you were ill the night Mummy came back and wanted to take you away to live with her.'

Erica had been eating an egg and cress sandwich; she went very still, the sandwich frozen halfway to her mouth. She put it back on her plate in slow motion. The other children were dedicatedly eating, even Timmy was cramming a rusk and most of his fingers into his hopefully open mouth.

'Oh . . . then. Yes, I was poorly. I heard Daddy say that Mummy couldn't take me away because I was so poorly.'

They waited. Was the silence as crackling with tension as

she felt it was, Jenny wondered, or was it just a natural pause in the conversation? She helped things along a bit.

'Would you have liked to go with Mummy, if you'd been well enough? It might have been fun . . . only you're such a help here, we'd never have managed things!'

Erica picked up her sandwich again, bit, chewed, and then spoke with her mouth still half full.

'I was ill, Jenny, far too ill to be dragged out into the cold air . . . Daddy told her so. She tried to come up the stairs and get me but he wouldn't let her. He gave her a push and told her to leave me alone, because I wasn't well.'

This time the silence stretched on far too long but Jenny dared not break it. Was it enough? Need they involve Ricky further? After all, Bill had never said she should be asked to remember something better forgotten. But Mary Lucas had no such inhibitions.

'Daddy was right,' she said decidedly. 'Night air isn't good for delicate chests. Then what happened? Did Mummy go away after that or did she try to persuade you to go with her?'

'She went. She fell over and bumped her head on that post thing at the bottom of the stairs. She lay there . . . Daddy knelt down beside her and tried to wake her up . . . then I went back to bed. In the morning she'd gone.'

This time the tension was not just Jenny's imagination. No one ate, the three children, Timmy included, just stared round-eyed at Erica, who had finished her sandwich and was idly pushing her crusts round and round the plate.

'Did you see her leave, love?' It was Anna this time, her voice deliberately slow and soft. 'Or did you hear her go?'

'See her? No, not really. I was ill, you see. When Daddy knelt down and kept talking to her and she didn't answer I thought she was being very silly – she did things like that sometimes – so I just climbed back into bed.' Erica turned to look at the three adults, her eyes flickering from face to face. 'I asked Daddy where she'd gone though, and he said away and not to worry. I was very hot . . . I said had she gone to heaven and he said . . .' She stopped short, a hand flying to her mouth.

Jenny forestalled any more prompting by speaking herself. She felt that they must clear the matter up once and for all and then forget about it.

'Daddy told you the truth, didn't he Ricky? He said that Mummy had gone to heaven but that it was a secret and you mustn't talk about it.'

'Oh, I'm glad he told you, Jenny, because I'm not too good at secrets. He came upstairs you see, and I was crying and all hot, and he cuddled me better and got me a lovely cool drink and then he told me where Mummy had gone. In the morning when I woke I was well again, quite better.'

'I expect your temperature had dropped,' Jenny said, striving for normality, but Erica shook her head.

'Oh, no, it wasn't that. It was because I knew that if Mummy was dead she couldn't make me go away with her,' Erica said sunnily. 'Can I have a honey sandwich this time, please?'

The board nearest the door which led out on to the communal landing creaked. We've been here nearly nine months, Jenny thought, as she and Posy carried their suitcases out through the open doorway, and we've done nothing about that noise, yet it was one of the first things I noticed when we moved in. What a lot had happened since then! How could she possibly have guessed that when she left No. 24 at the end of her allotted winter let she would not return to the farm nor to Dirk, but would be going to a semi-detached suburban house to look after another fellow's two children whilst he was in prison?

'Is the taxi here, Mum? Are we taking Auntie Sue to the station first or are we taking our things first? Why can't we all come in the taxi with you to the station? I'd rather see Auntie Sue off than go to school and so would Dawn, wouldn't you, Donny?'

Posy, dancing up and down on the landing wearing school uniform but with her winter coat slung round her shoulders – it was too big for the case – glanced hopefully up at her mother. It did seem a shame to make her miss the move, but on the other hand, moving with three small children and a dog would be pretty exhausting and she needed all her energy the way things were.

'You know very well, love, that we're taking these things first, then we'll come back and take you three to school, and then I'll fetch Auntie Sue and the taxi will drive us to the station for her train. So come along . . . who's going to stay here and help with Timmy?'

Posy and Erica glanced longingly from Belle to Sue's closed door, then, unanimously, chose Timmy. Jostling and giggling, they rushed to the door, beat a brief tattoo on it, and disappeared whilst Dawn picked up Posy's abandoned suitcase and stoutly lugged it downstairs, beaming at Jenny's thanks.

'I'll come with you, I love car rides,' she said as they reached the hall. 'Are we really going to live in our house? All of us? Posy and you and Belle too?'

'That's right.'

'And Daddy? When he comes out of prison?'

'Donny, darling, who said. . . ? Oh well . . . yes. Daddy too,' Jenny said, admitting defeat. Useless to suppose that other children would keep their mouths shut; Bill's trial would be the talk of the town, so his children might as well get used to it. She and Dawn carried down the last case and some bulging carrier bags and then the taxi driver was at the door, helping to lug their baggage into the cab, and they were off on the first stage of today's many journeyings.

'Oh hell, why am I never ready? Hang on, love, I had to change His Lordship's nappy, it was gooey as hell too, so I had to wash him, and that meant some unpacking . . . heavens, is that the time? Oh, oh, *how* Hugo hated unpunctuality!'

Sue stood in her doorway, her coat half on, the baby hampering her movements as she struggled to get her arm into the armhole without putting him down.

'Let me take Tim,' Jenny said practically. 'Is this all that's left of your luggage? I saw piles and piles go off in the big yellow van yesterday.'

'Yes, just a little suitcase,' Sue said with masterful understatement as Jenny tried to heave the case off the floor and had to take both hands to it. 'Oh, and I've a couple of bags here and my haversack . . . how I hope Dermott heeds my frantic telegram and meets me at the other end. If he fails I don't know how we'll ever reach the flat.'

Timmy gave his familiar excited squeak and Jenny, looking over her shoulder, was horrified to see Belle mounting the stairs confidently and wagging her plumed tail at the baby.

'Belle! Oh damn the dog, I thought I locked her in the kitchen, but of course Louisa was there, bless her, helping me to get sorted out, so I suppose she left the door open and Belle decided to come and find us. Oh dear, the taxi driver wasn't exactly ecstatic when he found she was coming on two of our previous three journeys!'

'Curse him for a spoilsport,' Sue panted, gathering together an assortment of bulging dustbin liners which did not, it appeared, qualify as luggage. 'Can you screech down the stairs and get him to come up for this case? It's heavier than I thought.'

'I noticed. And screeching isn't quite . . here he comes,' Jenny said as the taxi driver, sighing, began heavily mounting the stairs. 'Come on, let's start moving.'

They clattered down the stairs, Sue taking Timmy and Jenny with a hand on Belle's collar. Somewhere up above someone else was clattering down too, and a second or so after they reached the hall the Twiggs arrived; Mrs Twigg was still a bit sniffy after her tearful parting with Posy – come back often, lovey . . . I will, I promise I will! – and she hugged Sue and kissed Timmy with moist enthusiasm.

'We've 'ad some funny winter lets before, but I can't bring to mind any as I've missed like I'll miss you,' she told the two girls. 'We shan't forget you . . . don't forget us! Come back and visit, mind, or drop us a line, Bernie and me. We'll think about you, and wonder about you. We allus does . . . but this time it'll be different, we've been like a family . . .'

Did she say it every year? Had there ever been, before, such a rich and unlikely conglomeration of people and events? Surely not, though Mrs Twigg had from time to time mentioned others: Mr Simons who set fire to his bed and nearly roasted; the Delfont twins, a high-wire act, who had fought over little Miss Ellie, a conjuror's assistant, and had both spent the night in casualty being stitched up; the woman who played her radio all night to hide illicit activities, never more than darkly hinted at; the child who sleep-walked and consequently fell downstairs, frightening everyone out of their wits. They were legends which Mrs Twigg talked about from time to time – shall we become legends, Jenny wondered, as they milled about the hall saying their goodbyes. Will it be Sue, the beautiful young girl with a secret sorrow, and Jenny who went to bed with a wife-slayer, and Dermott, the fellow beaten up by a jealous husband?

Mrs Grant came up from the basement, very officious but carried away by the emotions of farewell into reminding Jenny, for the fifth time in a week, that they would be welcome to return come September, that she always enjoyed the winter lets and hated the coming of the summer visitors, only the money, you see . . . it's a big house, takes a lot of money to keep it nice . . .

Everyone trooped out to the taxi. It was a lovely morning, all soft summer sunshine and flower scents. Mr Grant's solitary standard rose was covered in large pink blooms. Belle was the first to hop into the taxi, then Sue climbed in, took Timmy on her lap, and Jenny got in as well.

'Goodbye, goodbye,' Sue shrieked out of the open window as the taxi trundled down Beechcroft Road. They waved until they turned the corner, then settled back for the short drive to the station. 'God, I'm tired out by all that emotion! It's odd how I shall miss them, though.'

'I'll miss you,' Jenny said ruefully, gazing out at the sunny streets. 'Will you come back, Sue? For a week or so? What will you do about Dermott? Asking him to meet you at the station will raise his hopes, poor boy.'

'I hope you'll come to London as soon as Bill's . . . problems . . . are over,' Sue said. 'As for coming back, who knows? Rhyl's a great place to be in winter – and probably not bad in summer, either, though I'd avoid August, I think.'

'Tell me about Dermott, you didn't mention him. Do you intend to see a lot of him?' Jenny would not ask the obvious, because she knew from her own experience that you don't just slide out of love with one man and into love with another; it takes more than wishing.

'I might. I can hardly remember what he looks like,' Sue said cruelly. 'You know how it is, Jen. I want to be me for a bit. With Timmy, of course.'

'Yes, I . . . oh, we've arrived. Look lively, Timmo, let me take you from Mummy first and then you can squeak at Belle.'

They tumbled out of the taxi, Sue shedding a feeding cup, two teaspoons and a bag of Jenny's fudge as she went. Exclamations, sighs from the driver, more squeaks from Timmy and a bit of grovelling, and they were ready to make for the platform.

'I hate goodbyes,' Sue said, suddenly forlorn, as they queued for the barrier. 'Does Belle need a platform ticket?' She giggled suddenly. 'No, I see she doesn't.' Belle had squiggled her way past the queue and was patiently waiting for them on the platform, her tail waving gently from side to side as they neared her.

But when it came to the actual moment of parting, time was so short that emotional farewells were impossible. The train came in, crowded, Belle caused a good deal of confusion by hopping aboard before anyone had thought to lay hand to collar, by the time Jenny had abstracted her and apologized to all and sundry the guard was slamming doors, and the last she saw of Sue was one slender hand, trying to wave through a tiny little ventilation window in the carriage itself, whilst her beautiful, mobile face pulled itself into various odd shapes.

Jenny waved and waved and the tears ran down her face, and long after the train had gone she stood on the platform, with Belle pressed against her knees, trying to pull herself together. There had been so much happening at the same time that she had never really let herself believe that Sue would go, it had been like a bad dream from which she would wake sooner if she refused to let it worry her.

Presently she wiped her eyes with the backs of both hands, blew her nose on a tissue, and glanced around her. The platform was deserted save for a porter trundling a trolley full of huge sacks from one side to the other and a man coming slowly down the steps from the incoming platform. He looked across at her, hesitated, then lifted his hat. It was Mr Croft.

'Good morning, Mrs Sayer; I trust you're well? It seems a very long time since we last met.'

371

He was still tall, thin and oily but she bore him no grudge. After all, she had escaped despite him, she could afford to be generous. She smiled.

'Good morning, Mr Croft. I'm . . . quite well, all things considered.'

'Yes, yes.' He looked a little shifty. 'I could have sworn that all Mr Dirk wanted was to get you back, but it seems . . . you know, of course, that he's changed his solicitor? After all these years?'

'I'm sorry,' Jenny said sincerely; he would feel the loss worse than an ordinary man, she felt. He would probably find it easier to lose his wife than a valued client. 'Actually, I think you may have got it wrong, though. I'm divorcing Mr Dirk . . . he would still like me to go back, I believe.'

'*You're* divorcing Mr Dirk?' Some people, Jenny thought crossly, might have found his incredulity rather insulting. 'But . . . wouldn't it be worth holding on, is it . . . he *doesn't* want you to leave him?'

Plainly, it was all too much, so far as Mr Croft was concerned; a penniless woman divorcing a rich and eager farmer was a clear case of man bites dog.

'No, he doesn't want me to leave him.'

His brow cleared and the mental wheels behind it, which had been whizzing furiously, seized on a solution and slowed once more.

'You've met someone else – another farmer?' He gave her a narrow smile. 'Are congratulations in order?'

'They are indeed, though unfortunately we shan't be able to marry for a while.' Some imp of mischief made her continue. 'He's on remand at present and I've been warned he may be sentenced to several years, but in the meantime I'm looking after his little girls and waiting for him.'

He boggled; there was no other word for it.

'*That* man? The one who did away with his wife? My dear Mrs Sayer . . .'

'Yes, it's that man, but he didn't do away with his wife, it was an accident. The only really bad thing he did was to hide her body after her death, which was silly more than bad, actually. My solicitor thinks he'll get a minimum sentence when all the facts are gathered together.'

'And you're divorcing Mr Dirk in order to . . .' Words obviously failed him. He shook his head, looking at her with mournful respect. 'Well, Mrs Sayer, you've surprised me today, and there aren't many who can do that!'

'Life's pretty surprising, but people are totally unpredictable, never forget that,' Jenny said reprovingly. 'Not all women want money and security and nothing else, Mr Croft, there are a surprising number of us who find out by chance what a con marriage can be, if you're tied to someone really selfish.'

'Now come, come, Mrs Sayer, you don't mean that or you wouldn't be considering remarriage,' Mr Croft said. 'You'll be talking about burning your bra next!'

He looked pleased with himself; plainly he thought the remark very daring. Jenny smiled.

'How can I burn my bra when I don't wear one?' she asked sweetly if untruthfully, and had the satisfaction of seeing Mr Croft's eyes fly incredulously to her neatly encased breasts as she turned away. Now he'll wonder for years whether he somehow missed his chance with a loose woman in more senses than one, she thought with satisfaction as she crossed the station yard and made for the main road.

She hugged her amusement to herself like a lover all the way to the cafe, but as she was unlocking the door she felt it begin to ooze away, to be replaced by the beginnings of a miserable depression. Oh Bill, how can I go on without you? Oh Sue, what shall I do without your scatter-brained ways and your never-failing support?

Answerless questions, they buzzed in her brain as she entered the quiet dim room and began to throw back the shutters and prepare for the day ahead.

'Heard from Sue again?'

It was a week since she had left and Anna was now a permanent worker in the cafe for, try though she might, Jenny had been unable to manage by herself in the long stretch between one o'clock and four-thirty, when they closed. Now she was trying to make sandwiches and barm cakes for the tea-time rush, because she would be fetching the girls from school soon since Louisa was taking her two to the dentist and would be unable to cope with all five.

'Not since she rang to say they were settling in and finding it easier to adapt than she'd expected. Dirk came round last night though; I might have guessed that, client or not, old Croft would dash back to the office and give him a buzz the moment he found out what I was doing.'

'Oh? What happened?'

'He was rather sweet, I suppose. He blustered a bit, said he wouldn't have Posy brought up with a murderer's kids, and then when I told him to get out and Belle growled, he backed down and apologized and actually offered us asylum!'

'Asylum? What on earth do you mean?'

'Well, not a mental institution! He offered to have me, Posy and the Bradley children until Bill came out. Of course the inference was that I'd stay with him . . . but it doesn't matter, I said no.'

'What did he say about Bill? I mean I guess he didn't know about you and Bill, did he? I always thought it was him who beat Dermott up, though I never said nothing.'

'Not much. Anna . . .'

'What?'

'Oh, nothing. It doesn't matter. How many tuna and coleslaw rolls do we sell on a sunny afternoon?'

It was as good a way as any of not having to ask the question which had been on the tip of her tongue; is Bill so unattractive, she had wanted to ask, because Dirk's whole attitude had been one of incredulity that a woman like her could find Bill bearable, even as a boss. That she had already taken him as a lover and intended to marry him just as soon as she could was, suddenly, not something she felt she could tell Dirk. If she did so and he was rude about Bill, then they would have a real rip-roaring slanging match and that wouldn't do anyone any good. As it was, she had agreed to take Posy to the farm every other Sunday, provided she could take Dawn and Erica too, and he had agreed.

'You go off, I'll cope with the rest,' Anna said now, cutting across Jenny's thoughts. 'The rush doesn't start till after school finishes and you'll be back by then.'

Jenny thanked her, grabbed her shoulder bag and fled,

hurrying along to such good effect that she arrived outside the school gates at least ten minutes before the bell was due to go. Since it was fine and sunny she walked up the cinder path, admiring the back gardens over the various hedges, some thick and well nurtured, others thin with gaping holes. Belle, slinking along ahead, preferred the ones with gaps; a skinny border collie could squiggle into quite a few gardens when the hedges were thin and investigate a tortoise taking the air or a rabbit hutch with a terrified inhabitant crouched at the back, as well as a variety of fascinating smells and other people's dustbins.

Pondering over Bill's good looks or otherwise, she realized that she could not possibly judge because for her he was as handsome as any film star. She knew he had clumpy red hair, millions – possibly trillions, if you counted them – of freckles, a pair of greenish-grey eyes with light lashes and a sturdy body, and that some people might think him plain, but she was not – could never be – one of them. He was well-covered and cuddly but never overweight, his hair was goldy-red and trying to curl, his broken nose suited him – a straight nose would have been dull and boring.

I'm a lost cause as a bra-burner, she thought, wandering along in the warm sunshine. I am hopelessly and possibly even foolishly in love with a perfectly ordinary man and independence, if it means forsaking Bill, doesn't appeal one bit.

Belle emerged from a garden licking her lips and Jenny realized that she had been raiding strawberry beds again. She shook her head and wagged a finger at Belle, calling her a naughty girl, but did not go to the lengths of putting her on her lead. I'll watch her more carefully, she thought guiltily as she came level with the thickest part of the school hedge, she mustn't think she can steal strawberries with impunity.

It was the same bit of hedge that she had stopped by last year, she realized, only then it had been bright with the colours of autumn and now it was a clear ringing green and starred with tiny yellow flowers. Behind it, a class of children were assembled to play a game.

With a sense of *déjà vu*, Jenny stopped and listened.

'We'll play "Poor Jenny" now, we've got time before the bell goes, so get into a circle, children. Now Fay, don't be silly, you're a big girl now . . . would you like to be Poor Jenny? Right, then you go into the middle and the rest join hands. Off we go!'

The voices were every bit as shrill now as they had been last autumn, the tune just as wistful. Jenny stood still and listened.

> Jenny's alone in the ring,
> Who will come dance with her?
> Who will come dance with her?
> Jenny's alone in the ring.

As the sweet, mournful melody died away Jenny thought about that other Jenny, the one who had stood here listening to that same tune ten months ago, and who had identified with it so painfully; was I ever so foolish, she thought disdainfully, and so naïve? She had felt so alone and unwanted, at the end of a period of happiness with only misery ahead, but she had been completely wrong. Real life, the type where there was suffering and joy, hard work and laughter, had sprung into being almost from the moment she had heard that song, because soon afterwards she had met Bill, then Sue, then the others, all the rich mixture of people who had made up Mrs Grant's winter let.

Behind the hedge a bell clanged, its harshness softened by distance. The children who had been playing so near were running back to the school building and she could hear the teacher's voice fading as she followed them, admonishing, encouraging.

Jenny whistled to Belle and they began to walk towards the school gate. Posy, Erica and Dawn would be out in a moment, perhaps with tears, to tell her what had happened to them in school today. Jenny was alone, but she was strong. Whatever they needed she would provide; if they were hurt she would comfort, if they were happy she would share their pleasure. Day after day, for years if necessary, she would go on, running the cafe, bringing up the children, managing the money, coping with life.

Jenny alone, but waiting for Bill. It was not an ending now, any more than it had been last autumn, even if the prison gates were to clang shut behind him for a number of years. It was simply another beginning.